41 AND A HALF KISSES FROM MR LEROI

© Hara Nikola, 2016

Author: Hara Nikola
Translator: Irene Angelidou
Text editor: Anatoli Fitopoulou
Cover designer: Vassilis Ioannou
Production supervisor: Platon Malliagkas - www.mediterrabooks.com

Title: 41 and a half kisses from Mr Leroi
ISBN 978-960-93-7895-6

Hara Nikola

41 AND A HALF KISSES
FROM MR LEROI

a novel

Dedicated to Johnny, for the most part.

Table of Contents

PART ONE

Chapter 1

Early Morning in Shadow Street

Dawn was slowly breaking in the street with the locked houses. The horizon had turned crimson in the east. A breeze was roaming the neighbourhood and making the curtains flutter. It was strange; all windows and all doors were tightly shut at that bewitching hour when darkness fights daylight. But the breeze sneaked in. And made the curtains flutter.

The girl had been standing for a long time right in the middle of the neighbourhood with the locked houses. She was looking towards the far end of the seemingly unending street. Her tawny hair fell to her waist. Her naked feet seemed fastened to the asphalt. From where she was looking at the back of her [dream] self, it was impossible to make out how old she was at that point. Five, fifteen, twenty-five? Besides, a dream ignores such rationalities.

The only thing she knew with certainty was that happy people didn't live in that quiet street, behind those silent windows, as one may easily have been led to believe. Shadows lived there, empty ghosts, images with no consciousness.

Vera must have been around five years old when she first heard the spooky tale about the shadows. Odysseus[1], sailing with the north wind, reaches the country covered by clouds and fog beyond the ocean. A frigid night hangs over the wretched people of this land and no sunlight reaches them. He descends alive to the Kingdom of Hades. From the depths of the deepest darkness, the souls of the dead gather around him creating an unimaginable roar. This had greatly puzzled her when she was a child. How can a living man descend into the underworld?

Even now, when she is no longer a child, she sometimes catches herself wondering what Odysseus is doing in her dream with "his eyes red from the waves' salt[2]."

But she didn't have the chance to think carefully about it because the dream instantly changed pace; it definitely became more interesting.

Paper planes started falling like rain from the depths of the sky. One of them brought Mr Leroi to her. He was perched on the paper plane and he was smiling in a very cinematic way. Whatever comes let it come; it will eventually find an open door to slip in through.

Then a large part of the dream was censored and burst like a bubble in the jar of forgetfulness. Somewhere near dawn, there, in the same street, at number zero, where Vera has been living for years, something delightful was finally happening.

She dreamt that she was lying in bed with Mr Leroi. God knows what had happened earlier but now she was lying in a state of complete relaxation, and he was kissing her back.

One by one, his kisses peppered her body. His caresses were not exactly tender, nor would you call them passionate, just playful... From the base of her neck, he travelled down her shoulders and, from there, down her spine, until he reached her waist. But she was very ticklish there. She doubled up with laughter not only because of her shudders, but also because he had the habit – the funny habit! – of counting his kisses ... thirty-nine ... forty ... forty-one, perhaps even forty-two. She had trouble remembering.

Then he dissolved in the morning light like a mischievous, empty ghost of the night. He climbed onto a paper plane and flew out the window.

Who was Mr Leroi? Officially, he was the hero of a recent blockbuster. He was a good-for-nothing, ruthless adventurer. A very handsome man, nonetheless.

After he filched a rare figurine from the Museum of African Art, he realised that he was in over his head, and then everything went to hell in a handbasket. The said artefact was carrying a curse; an obsessed collector who wanted it for himself appeared; a few femmes fatales got in the way; hired killers beat him up two or three times. In the end, he even came face to face with the Devil himself.

Now, Heaven knows how he escaped safe and sound from this story, and how he ended up in her bed. But how could the poor guy get to the bottom of things with so many ruffians lurking about nowadays?

That was the dream that sent the spinning wheel whirring. That began weaving the fairy tale. How could I forget about it? It glows like a firefly in the rainy weather of those days.

****

This technique is of course called a flashback, thanks to which I am able to watch the old Vera in her previous life.

The book she started reading the night before is lying next to her bed. Antonis, her boyfriend of a few months, is currently sleeping on the same bed. He's a nice guy; she has no complaints.

Vera is awake but still groggy. The coffee pot is gurgling and the computer is warming up as it runs Windows 2000.

She paces nervously back and forth. She sort of knows what she wants, but she's unable to carry it out. First of all, there is her burning need to interpret the dream but she worries that it isn't going to be an easy feat.

What was Mr Leroi looking for in her sleep? What did he want from her? Could anyone just barge into her dreams? And why forty-two kisses, which might not have been exactly forty-two, but forty-one?

Secondly, she's in a tizzy because she wants to write a novel. An enduring story. One which will allow her to truly get to know her characters, walk beside them and — why not? — mature in their company.

She is eager to start writing but something is holding her back. Her hands are tied with invisible membranes. She is flooded by feelings of worthlessness.

Antonis woke up at some point and is now dragging his slippered feet towards the kitchen.

'You can't just have coffee,' he says tenderly, 'it'll give you an upset stomach.'

She listens to the familiar sounds of their breakfast being prepared: the toaster shuddering with a resounding snap, the coffeepot gurgling. Then the smell of freshly toasted bread, a glass of fresh juice, a piece of toast slathered in butter and honey.

Antonis has blue eyes and an open countenance that only a disturbed person wouldn't like. He dumps his clothes all over the place, even though he knows she finds it infuriating. His smile is that of a man on good terms with himself. His sense of fulfilment is obvious on the nights he returns from an exhausting news report. It's a good idea to have him keep his hands hidden in his pockets; otherwise, the jerky movements he makes result in the annihilation of knick-knacks.

Their relationship, in a nutshell, is like the music playing during a cinema intermission. It is merely pleasant to listen to while waiting for the film to continue.

'So, are you writing new TV scripts?' he asks when he sees her sitting in front of the computer.

Vera gets irritated just hearing this question.

What new stories could a scriptwriter come up with for a beast of a TV series with the pretentious title *The Footsteps of Fate*? A TV series that is well past its 2500th episode and is heading towards its 3000th. Nothing new; it's entirely impossible.

'No. I'm thinking of writing a book.'

'Ah, really? That's very interesting! And when did you get the idea?'

He tries to straighten his dishevelled hair. His look is professional, just like the hound that discovers the hare.

'Just recently...'

'And what's it about?'

'Forget it, I'll tell you when I get there!'

He makes no comment. He walks to the window and takes a look outside.

Vera goes near him and presses her nose against the glass. There, that tiny flake that breezes past and sticks on the windowpane doesn't promise anything good.

She is left speechless by the spectacle, as if she has been bewitched. Thousands, maybe millions of flakes pop up out of nowhere. The milky sky produces them incessantly and abandons them at the mercy of the north wind that swirls them wildly about. The howling of the wind has an eerie melody, a malicious music that is unlike any other.

Antonis looks excitedly at the sight; nothing is capable of sapping his morale. According to the Meteorological Office, a severe winter with extreme weather phenomena is coming, and he is rolling up his sleeves, overjoyed to be diving into the battle of informing the public.

****

I watch the old Vera. She is drinking raspberry leaf tea. She hates it but she is forced to drink it every time she visits her friend.

Vicky has a large supply of this brew and an unerring instinct of getting involved with outrageously unsuitable men. Such was the one who walked out on her and their child after three years of marriage because the house was never as clean and his boxers were never as well ironed as he would have liked.

Vera had thought back then that this was a funny reason for getting a divorce but, all things considered, there are no funny reasons for people separating. All reasons seem pretty serious to her.

Heavy snow keeps falling out on the street. The snowflakes are giving a dance recital with graceful pirouettes. The night is silver, filled with small crystals. And unusually silent. Vera watches her breath take shape and form frozen plumes. Her eyelids flicker as her eyes tear from the cold. She slipped a few times as she walked on the downhill roads that led from her house to the peripheral road of Lykavittos Hill and then up to Neapolis.

But she needs to confide in someone about her artistic pursuits and knows that her friend can help her. She just has to open her magical deck of cards, that of applied logic.

Vicky's method is simple but effective. You sort out the important from the unimportant. You keep the former, discard the latter and stop worrying about them. Now, from the important things, there are those that are amenable to a solution and you spend your grey matter on them, and there are those that are impossible to solve so we don't let them concern us.

That's Vicky, a mathematical genius in the science of everyday life.

But at that moment, she doesn't appear to be in the mood for empathizing with Vera's problem.

'Grab a seat. Have I got news for you!' Vicky catches her by surprise the moment she steps into the untidy three-bed flat. The cigarette smoke mingles with the scent of the aromatic candle. The house is a mess; cigarette butts everywhere and unwashed dishes heaped in the kitchen sink.

Her face is illuminated as she lights up a cigarette. Her blonde curls are tied back. Her brow is furrowed but her gait reveals a person who doesn't give herself a hard time about anything. She walks lightly and gestures expansively with movements directed at a theatre audience. Vicky is a woman who has deep faith in herself and woe to anyone who doesn't share this view. There is an ease in the way she lazily stretches out on the old velvet couch, with her endless repertoire of grimaces.

'Don't pull those faces so often. You'll get wrinkles,' Vera would warn her on other occasions, only to get the familiar line in response:

'I don't care about the established standards of commercialized beauty.'

Today, though, something unexpected is happening. This is not the friend she has known since her school years, but an infatuated woman who is raving about her new fling: her married co-worker, who has been courting her with a rain of flowers, presents, innuendos, passionate sighs, and so on.

She is talking nonsense and Vera can see it, but she lets

her friend finish her story... and then... and then...? Then, she will wake her friend up.

He gave her a lift home from work in his car the day before yesterday with the excuse that it was raining... She felt the need to heighten the suspense with giggles and suggestive glances. And then... and then?

Vera can't believe her ears! What is all this that she is hearing? A serious and perfectly respectable 32-year-old woman fooling around like a schoolgirl for the sake of an idiot.

'I imagine he kissed you!'

Vicky bursts into naughty titters.

'Yes! How did you know?'

'Honestly, have you completely lost your mind? What else could he have done? Propose to you?'

She immediately regretted the sharpness behind her words, but it was too late.

'Look,' she tells Vicky coldly, 'you know that I'm against having affairs with married men. Just think, what are the alternative outcomes in such a story?'

She adopts her prosecutor's look. She herself is not sure if she is criticizing Vicky so severely because of her friend's amorous blunders or because of the indifference her friend showed towards her own problem.

Vicky's frown deepens even more. That's how she reacts when she is taken by surprise. A deep wrinkle appears between her eyebrows.

'First scenario: You form a passionate relationship and

you stay locked up in your house just to see him for a few hours and always under stressful circumstances.

'Second scenario: He keeps telling you that he will leave his wife, until you wake up one morning and bang your head against the wall for the years you wasted on a sorry-excuse-of-a-man.

'Third and worst-case scenario: If, by miracle, he does divorce his wife, you will be with someone who will do the same to you somewhere along the way... because someone who has cheated once will probably do it again.'

Vicky is left with her mouth hanging open. Her cigarette is completely spent but she holds on to it as if she is afraid of the definitive process of stubbing it out.

'Life, you know, is not math. Putting two and two together and coming up with solutions to a difficult equation.'

'Life certainly isn't a math equation, but it doesn't hurt to have a bit of sense from time to time.'

'You're being very cruel, Vera. Life, you know, also involves the unpredictable, and sometimes it includes a touch of magic...'

'Yes, and by chasing after the unpredictable, you are constantly stumbling upon unbearably predictable boyfriends who dump you into the wastebasket when you stop catering to their needs.'

'What's left then?' Vicky explodes.

She shoots up in anger and draws the curtains open. The snow is still falling heavily and beautifully, framing the unkempt block of flats across the street. She forcefully pulls them closed as if she wants to release her anger on the inanimate pieces of fabric.

'Do you think that there are many worthy men out there? And that they are all waiting for me? You act as if you don't know how things are, Vera. All the nice guys are taken. Then, what's left? Would you believe that I'm excited with the idea of getting involved with someone who'll have no time in his life for me?'

She collapses back onto the sofa and lights up another cigarette.

'I'm sorry, darling. I just wanted to warn you. These games are really dangerous.'

'I love you, Vera. But sometimes I really wonder if you have any grams left of what is called a 'heart'.'

Her eyes turn into twin pools, greyish and merciless.

This was the epitome of ingratitude. She hadn't expected to hear this. She feels as if she has been stung by a scorpion. *After all, we've known each other for 22 years and you met him just yesterday! Do you know what 22 whole years mean?* she felt like screaming.

****

The old Vera goes back out on the street. It's freezing cold. The snow has stopped falling. Deadly silence. Up there, the universe is expanding, cold and inexplicable. Down here, just her. Small, alone and confused.

The street lamps emit silver gleams of light in the frozen

night. She is walking as fast as circumstances allow her, trampling on the pristine snow.

So, she is hard-hearted, is she? Or even worse, completely heartless! Well! When does a human heart turn to stone? How can anyone realise that they've shut themselves off from the world?

There are moments when time appears to have stopped. Everything sinks into a frozen stillness. Nothing seems to change in your life, while you persistently seem to be wandering around in a nightmarish labyrinth. No matter how much you struggle to move forward, you discover that your feet are stuck in the muddy snow its paths are covered with and you can't take a single step further ahead. Such feelings last for years; even a lifetime. Finally, you begin to suspect that the fairy tale of Sleeping Beauty is a frightening allusion taken right out of the heart of human experience.

****

I watch the old Vera.

Before the River of Inspiration overwhelmed her with its liberating waters, she had to face the Terror of the White Page. I wonder if the Creator felt the same panic in front of an empty universe.

She takes the decision to use her last card. Despite the lateness of the hour, something tells her that she can count on the opinion of her old manager.

'How are you, love? It's been a while since I last heard

from you!' Pelia's voice with its lovely timbre sounded reassuring as it reached her ears.

Pelia was one of those rare people who aged gracefully. She has the charm of maturity; the wisdom and sweetness of a person who loves life and knows how to enjoy it.

Also, she is a wonderful writer, one of this gifted woman's additional talents.

Vera more or less explains her concerns.

'I have planned its architectural structure with precision. I have divided it into chapters and have a structured plan of the story.'

The other woman nearly burst into laughter.

'I see... but don't stick to it. Kundera said that the mathematical structure in his novels isn't deliberate, it naturally imposes itself as a necessity of the form and doesn't need any calculations[3].'

'Pelia, I'm very far away from being Kundera. I need firm structural materials for the base of my story.'

'Excuse me but are you planning on building a house?' Pelia seemed to be laughing at her. 'I don't mean to offend you, but what seems to be your problem?'

'I can't write a single word. Nothing comes out,' she complained in disappointment.

'That doesn't seem very strange to me,' Pelia chuckled in amusement. 'You have the method but you lack the spark. Intellectual capacity and an analytical process are only half of the qualifications of a good writer. The others are intuition and mental momentum. In other words, emotive strength.'

'I'm afraid that this is exactly the point where I'm stuck for good.'

'Look, honey. Writing is not a strictly cerebral affair. The road that leads from your head to your hand must pass through your heart too. Otherwise, I'm afraid that you've lost the game.'

Great! And how do I do that?

'I can't give you a foolproof method,' Pelia said. 'You must find out for yourself. Try to let yourself go,' she said with an affectionate laugh. 'Make sure you have fun, first and foremost,' Pelia advised her before hanging up. 'Fun never precludes seriousness[4].'

****

That's it, as far as the old Vera is concerned. My life will be in the first person from now on.

Because now I know that people, happenings and our dreams often 'speak' their own secret language of symbols and connotations. They try to warn us. To protect us. To mobilize us. But, we don't listen to them. We ignore them. Because we are locked away. I was unaware of this back then. That's why I had so many questions. That's why I was angry and confused.

Antonis returned unexpectedly at around eleven, bone tired and bad-tempered. He threw his coat and gloves in a corner and they dropped onto the floor. He rubbed his hands together to warm them up and sneezed two or three times. He started cussing about the chaos that reigned. He had frozen his toes off sending news reports from every news 'hotspot', their jeep had got stuck in the snow and a farmer had had to give them a lift in his tractor.

Why doesn't he go to sleep in his own house once in a while? I sulked, but then felt sorry for him. So I lay on the couch, longing for my lost peace and quiet. Antonis grabbed the first magazine he found and shut himself in the bathroom.

That night, I went to bed tired, disappointed and more worried than ever.

I was utterly clueless about what was to follow. How could I ever imagine that miracles do happen? That for one and only special occasion, the sky brightens, and it happens just for you?

So, I had another unexpected visit around dawn. There was a heavy door; it was locked. I was sitting behind a desk and using a typewriter. Suddenly, the door shook from loud knocks. I didn't dare to stand up and open it. But the door was broken down and Mr Leroi appeared on the doorstep. He was wearing a long trench coat, a hat and glasses.

'What do you want?' I stuttered bemused.

'What rude behaviour! Is that how you treat guests?' His gaze betrayed irony and discontent.

'What are you looking for?' I foolishly asked him again.

'Just ... for you to treat me to something sweet,' the familiar stranger laughed. 'Do you have any melomakarona?'

I shot up breathless from my sleep. I felt as if someone had crashed into my dream and had invaded my sleep through the resulting cracks. The intensity of this crash had frightened me more than the dream itself. I must have shouted when I woke up because Antonis was also startled awake.

'It broke down!' It was the only phrase I kept repeating as if I were hypnotized.

'What broke down? Who?' he stammered.

'The door!'

'What door? Is someone at the door?'

He turned on the light and jumped up agitated. With one clumsy move, he sent the lamp on the bedside table crashing to the floor.

'Not that door, you foolish man!'

'But, what door? The balcony door perhaps?'

'No... no... nothing... It was just a dream, it's gone now... go back to sleep!'

'What did you see, Vera?'

'I don't know. I don't remember. But it frightened me.'

He gave me a quick kiss, tucked himself under the duvet and instantly went back to sleeping like a baby. But I couldn't go back to sleep. I was beginning to feel frustrated. I couldn't possibly allow a Star System creation to invade my dreams in such a way and upset me.

What's more...I didn't know how to make *melomakarona.** I knew how to write. Just that! I felt that this was exactly what he was asking of me. To write something beautiful for him, something to sweeten him.

I lightly slipped out of bed. An invisible thread was

---

* Pastry made of flour, olive oil, honey and walnuts

tugging me towards my home office. I turned on my sea-shell-shaped desk lamp and grabbed a pen.

I started writing like a maniac, obeying a blind urge. I wrote without pause, without tearing out any pages, with an increasingly higher fever, until my hand started cramping and I had to stop.

Only then did I realise what I had refused to accept for so long, and the fear returned. It was as if I hadn't been the one writing! As if someone else had been guiding my hand!

This sudden 'visitor', reassuring and tantalizing, pestered me incessantly in my mind, and in my blood, and showed strange moods.

Stranger still!! I knew who he was with complete certainty. Someone who had grown bored of sauntering alone in the vastness of the universe, who had met me somewhere, perhaps by accident, and grabbed me. A kindred spirit. An ally.

Chapter 2

The Man who Made Fairy Tales

Constantinos! He's the co-traveller of my dreams. The undeniable protagonist. What do I know about him? A few things that had occasionally caught my eye in newspapers and magazines.

'The young actor that comes from Thessaloniki.'

Twenty years must have passed since the moment he appeared in show business. I was in secondary school then. All the girls were infatuated with him; they religiously collected the teen magazine posters featuring him.

'A charismatic creature who nobody fails to notice.'

He was one of those artists that the media loved to envy.

'A brilliant but self-destructive man.'

'A life filled with films and exciting romances.'

'The famous actor who spread his wings for an international career in France.'

His relationship with the actress Nadia Karatza had just come to an inglorious end.

These were the few details that I managed to retrieve from my memory about this particular person. Oh! And that he was married to a French journalist. Or was it a photographer? I wasn't entirely sure.

'I smoke a lot, I like to drink ...ehm... a little too much, and I fall in love with dangerous frequency. I learned to do everything in excess. I don't know what 'moderation' means. I dislike mediocrity. Even the golden type.'

Such statements, and naturally his tumultuous lifestyle, had made him the target of journalistic indiscretion.

I suddenly recall another one of his statements, when an interviewer had asked him how he felt when he shaped a new role.

'Just like when I was a child and moulded human figures out of plasticine,' he had answered with earnestness. 'It's just that my part is a little more complicated now. I also have to breathe life into them. That's why I love my job. Because it allows me to play. In every possible meaning of the word.'

Great! This is the man I have to deal with. One who imagines himself to be a minor god. That's all I know about Constantinos Aravantinos, and it suits me just fine. It's *enough* that I 'see' him so often.

Because Constantinos certainly was the permanent protagonist in all these remarkable events. He was there waiting for me, in the depth of my dreams; he gave me oysters with pearls, and sometimes some kind of strange seashells.

So one night, before he disappeared from my dream, I mustered the courage to 'ask him' about a few things that concerned me.

'Who are you?' I made a timid start.

'Don't ask silly questions. The whole world knows me!'

He seemed to be amused with my awkwardness.

'And what are you doing here?'

'I came to wake you up. You called for me.'

'Ah!'

Was I sleeping so deeply that I needed forty-one and a half kisses to wake up?

'Are you afraid?'

'...No...'

'Don't lie to me! Fear is good; it keeps you alive.'

'And... how are you going to do that? How are you going to wake me up?'

'You'll see.'

'And what must I do?'

'Follow me. Investigate my life. And don't be so crabby.'

'I... is there something I can do for you?'

'You? I want you to catch me because I have fallen and feel broken to pieces these days.'

The following nights, when he was on hand, I asked him a few questions that had been torturing me for years.

'Where do film characters go when their screen role is over? Do they still exist somewhere?'

'They do,' Constantinos said. 'They live, of course, in Never and Always Land. They live only for the present and, like children, they think that they will stay ageless forever. It's a little boring, there's no denying it, but that's heaven for you!'

So, that's what happens. The old film characters go to heaven!

'Have you really met the Devil?' I dared to ask him when we had finally become 'best friends'.

'Of course,' he swelled with pride.

I looked at him speechlessly and with my eyes wide open, eagerly waiting for him to continue.

'It's not as terrible as you imagine,' he laughed, noting my shock. 'It's simply very rare. As rare as meeting your true love. That's why most people shouldn't be afraid. It's not very likely to happen.'

****

Then I started re-watching his films. If he has something to tell me, I thought, this is where it would be hidden. For the first time, I notice that most of them are supernatural thrillers, loaded with mysterious symbols. One evening, I got back home carrying three DVDs with me. The first film I watched was *The Legend of the Sleeping Mountains*.

I could finally examine him undisturbed. He was there in the small TV screen, 'in the flesh' and a dreamer. He is wandering around an eerie mountainous region of Greece in the 50s; a romantic but determined detective who is investigating seemingly unrelated murders. The locals claim that the civil conflicts are the cause of the killings, but he has a different opinion. In the end, he defeats the ghostly murderer and finds the love of his life in the face of a beautiful countrywoman.

The second film *Don't Awaken the Unknown* was a Greek-French co-production that he filmed when he moved to

France. This is where he wore his most charming guise, that of the ruthless adventurer Leroi. He was exactly the same as when he had 'visited' me in my sleep a few nights ago and had 'inspired' me – compelled me would have been a more apt description – to begin writing my book.

At that particular moment, Antonis opened the front door, dragging a string of hot gossip and news behind him. He was talking about scandals and corruption in view of the elections.

As if all this weren't enough, he happily informed me that he had made plans for us to go out. Once more, I had to disappoint him.

'You'd better go on your own,' I told him. 'Anyway, I want to stay in and write.'

'Again? What's got into you and you're constantly writing? I don't think it's a matter of life and death!' He gave me a concerned look, his hands stuffed in his pockets as I booted the computer.

'I don't know. It might be!'

****

My dreams are crystal-clear, like a freshly washed window-pane. They are the magic mirror I look into in order to gaze back at myself. As my story begins to gain shape and form, I allow myself to feel happy.

The greatest difficulty I faced those days was when I had

to wake up, to leave the Gates of Dreamland behind me and cross the threshold of Waking Life.

One morning I was woken up by the sadistic ringing of the telephone. I didn't even have the time to be naturally reborn into reality. And, unfortunately, I knew very well who was on the other end of the line when the phone rang so irritatingly.

'Vera, are you still sleeping?'

Instead of a 'good morning', I get criticism. Oh well... I'm used to such things.

'Wake up, dear. I'm talking to you!'

I don't even have the courage to answer her.

'Why are you calling me so early in the morning, Mum?'

'It's not even morning! It's already eleven o' clock! I called you to see how you are. Because if I waited for you to call...'

A thorny silence. The truth is that I hadn't called her for four days. An unforgivable transgression. I pretend to listen to her for a while longer as I stretch and yawn. In the meanwhile, I give Theophano free scope to launch her attack with sharp mutterings.

'Honestly, what are we going to do with your life? When are you going to come to your senses? When are you going to lead a normal life? Like every other woman?'

Probably never, I yawned.

'Honestly, what do you want from me?'

'Don't raise your voice at your mother! I feel severely agitated about the unstable life you are pursuing,' she instantly grew angry, making her strange mixture of simple and more sophisticated words sound even funnier.

Theophano didn't lack education; she tragically lacked determination. But that's what happens to people who constantly wigwag between two opposing sides and a lifetime is not long enough for them to pick a side. They torture themselves above and beyond and end up being absurd and annoying.

But I was in no mood to laugh at that moment. It was as if I had my mother in front of me. She is sitting on the velvet couch with the purple pillows. Next to her there is a side table made of ivory that she brought over from Egypt, along with most of the house's other pieces of furniture, which she looks after as if they were her crown jewels. Her legs are demurely crossed at the ankles. She is wearing a shirt stiffly buttoned up to her neck and a long skirt. Her hair is gathered into a bun. She might still be wearing the tortoiseshell glasses that she needs when reading a book, invariably of Christian content.

Prim and proper to a ridiculous degree, Mrs Theophano, née Fokas, had many pleats in her skirt and even more hair. And all of it had to be constantly under control; not something to be taken lightly.

'I have called you to remind you that this coming Saturday I look forward to receiving you for lunch. Of course, your dearest Aunt Argyro and Uncle Nikiforos will also be attending. Oh, by the way, that little ... journalist is not at all welcome. It is strictly a family gathering,' she pointed out, just to remind me once again that she had not forgiven me my divorce.

'Alright, mum, I will come alone,' I acquiesced. There was nothing in the world I wanted less than to start quarrelling with her. That would ruin my day. 'Yes, I will be there on time...'

'And, please, take care,' Theophano insisted. 'I require that you appear dressed respectably, and not how you usually would, in those undignified jean trousers. Pick out an elegant dress or a modest skirt suit. If necessary, if you do not have anything appropriate, I will gift it to you.'

What is tragic in this life is that you are unable to choose your parents. They are imposed on you from a higher place. And no matter how much you learn to handle them little by little, they have spent more years than you in this world and know more tricks. So, I had discovered with disappointment that it was no use getting angry with my mother. No matter what I told her, she would always have the last word.

I try to think of something pleasant in order to recover and my eyes fall on the small seashell lamp on my desk. I love it because it gives me its light and keeps me company during the countless hours of my writing. Sooner or later, everybody finds the object that truly personifies them, that encapsulates many meanings and expresses a few of their unspeakable secrets.

****

My mother, for example, always carries a fan with her and uses it to cool herself whenever she has hot flushes, which happen very often from when she was a young girl.

My mother's fan has soothing properties. It somewhat calms her hysteria. It also has 'travelling' properties. It carries the winds of the desert thus far, the khamsins that whip the city with a veil of sand when they blow savagely.

Then, the echoes of a mother country – idealised to the extreme – forever lost, inevitably reach her ears. The drawling, doleful voice of the muezzin, the Corniche with the dark-hued buildings, the cars, and the tall, slim palm trees. The minarets that melt in the light of the sunset.

Such a light, which blurs the outline of things and makes the Bedouins and the camels look like mirages, can only dissolve all certainties and make them appear hazy.

Her father's vast cotton fields, a mythical fortune that was quickly lost after his death. Their house, a three-storied neoclassical building in the Quartier Grec with the silk-swathed salons and the gilded mirrors, ended up a boarding house for upstart lodgers when Nasser's domestic policy measures were imposed.

Theophano travels back forty-four years to the past, to when she left Alexandria forever. To the glamorous socialite who was born there, who felt the first thrills of love, and who lost her home, her innocence and her childhood at the mere age of sixteen.

There were palm trees, pharaoh fig and caoutchouc trees, cactuses and ficus trees in the garden of their house. And a large banana tree. Petros is standing underneath that very plant. Watery shadows circle them in the gloomy night and bring bad tidings. Fear and insecurity about the future of the Greek community pervade the stifling atmosphere.

Petros smiles timidly. His almost girlish face is downcast. He came to say goodbye to her with a basket filled with mangoes and a small gift he slips into her hand. An ornate fan made of ivory and ostrich feathers. Theophano will never be able to separate these two in her disturbed mind. Was it the elegance of the disgraced princess-city or that timid smile underneath the thin moustache that she never got over?

That's why she married Apostolis Kalogeras in Athens. Because he looked nothing like Petros. He wasn't a doctor, he didn't wear linen suits, nor did he smile shyly like a girl. Kalogeras wasn't slim-built and gallant. He was a working class man; sturdily built and self-made, who, strangely enough, had the gift of telling beautiful stories. Because deep down, he was sensitive and affectionate.

But my mother never discovered that. I had the pleasure of discovering it, being his favourite. She spent her whole life by his side without ever taking any notice of him. She didn't know that you had to first unlock a person if you wished him to tell you his own fairy tale.

But she married him because she couldn't bear the polished memories – she didn't want to remember – even though she knew she would never forgive him his humble origins. And this became the noose that strangled their marriage.

Theophano was very young back then. She didn't have the experience and courage to face the storm that had struck her life. Raised in the lap of luxury with governesses and tutors, she was completely defenceless and out of her depth when she came to Greece. How could she endure the nostalgia of the sweet life she had left behind her and fit in with the dull reality that awaited her?

It was sometime during those years, I believe, when the first signs of her disorder appeared. It was this insecurity that pushed her to anchor herself in a compulsive way to the only value that she discerned would be everlasting and would possess limitless power. Religion. It was a blind faith that slowly became an obsession and turned into a neurosis that bedevilled all of us not a little.

****

When I listen to my mother talk, immense anger pours out of my cells. The roots of my anger run very deep. I have felt the intolerable burden of this woman's presence since I was very young.

When the lights dimmed and the stories wore their nightly clothes, it was an agonizing time for me. My mother's shadow lengthened on the wall; it became enormous as she leaned over me to say goodnight.

'Have you said your prayers, Vera?' she would ask with a voice as sharp as a blade.

I would hear the hands of the clock counting the seconds of panic. I knew I couldn't hide from her; she knew everything, she was all-knowing in an inexplicable way. No secret stayed sealed in her presence. I would burrow under the covers.

'Get to it!' She would grab me, upsetting my covers. She would drag me to the holy icons – the house was filled with them – and force me to kneel.

'Say your prayers!' she would demand in a clipped voice. 'Dear Lord, look after my mummy and my daddy... Say it, Vera! Or else you will stay there all night long.' She was capable of doing that, I was sure of it.

'My baby brother, my aunt, my uncle...' I would unwillingly mutter while I felt myself sweating despite the cold. My knees ached from kneeling on the wooden floor and I was afraid that any minute my stomach would betray me and THAT would start! '...The tomatoes, the flies, the bugs,' I would add with glee. I always found a sneaky way to take revenge for myself.

'You are a filthy girl!' she would scream. 'A monstrous creature! You are mocking your own mother! I am the one who gave birth to you. I am going to die, Vera,' she would start crying hysterically. 'The Lord will soon call me to his side and you will weep with bitter tears!'

At the sound of these words, my younger brother, who was partial to her, would jump out of bed and start bawling. At that time, I had begun to be tormented by THAT, as I would call it. At unsuspecting moments, even when everything seemed quiet, which rarely happened in our house, I broke out in cold sweat, my knees felt weak, and a disgusting taste filled my mouth. Then I had to immediately run to the bathroom and throw up or else I would die.

I would be in bad shape for days, humiliated, I refused to put anything in my mouth. She naturally rushed me to the best doctors. She made me undergo all kinds of tests to placate her guilt. In vain. They found nothing wrong with me. But I kept getting even thinner, wasting away.

'They have used witchcraft against us, Vera. That's it!' She would find the most 'convincing' explanation then.

Then the parade of priests with their blessings and their holy water started. The house would reek for days from the heavy scent of incense and the Dark Ages.

But I kept throwing up all the time; day by day, the knot in my belly, that kept me from swallowing any food, turned into stone.

'Everything will be alright, baby girl!' my father would tell me. 'Everything will be alright, you'll see!' And he would absent-mindedly stroke my hair.

But nothing was alright. No matter how many doctors my mother visited, or how many sedatives she took, her condition remained unchanged, slowly worsening.

And my father had already started to shut everyone out, to dissolve into thin air, and escape through the cracks like his cigarette smoke. It was then he stopped telling me bedtime stories. If there's something I never could forgive my mother for, it is this: For making my father disappear and the fairy tales stop.

In puberty, I found more effective ways of getting back at her. I dressed provocatively and struggled to keep my balance on platform shoes. This made her furious. She looked at me and crossed herself with disgust.

But I already felt a new form of power fluttering within me. I knew I was beautiful; I could see it in the eyes of the boys who flirted with me since I was thirteen and followed me on the street. When she found out that I was dating someone, she turned deathly pale.

'You are a whore,' she burst out. 'You will die in the middle of an abortion or from a venereal disease. Keep that in mind!'

She pierced me with the most paranoid glare I had ever seen. For the first time, the terrifying thought that my own mother would gladly kill me occurred to me. She broke a chair in her path and almost wrecked the door of her bedroom with the force she used to slam it shut. All night long, she growled behind the locked door like a wild she-wolf. From that moment, locked doors, lost souls and empty streets haunt my sleep. The next day, she threw me out of the house.

'Show your mother some compassion, dear,' said Aunt Argyro, who took me in, trying to reconcile things. 'She is a wounded animal that is licking her wounds.' But a bitter feeling of abandonment was telling me that I was the wounded animal.

Then I would find refuge in the only place where I was welcome and loved. In my stories. There, I became a small fairy or a beautiful princess of a bygone era. Sometimes an ill-treated orphan who found justice and love in the end – why not? I could do anything I wanted in my stories. I found relief and comfort there. And since there was no one to tell them to me – my father had already abandoned us to live with a pretty seamstress – I told them to myself.

'Calm down, Vera,' I would tell myself in the semi-darkness with my eyes trained on the ceiling. 'You're living in a fairy tale! That's all! And there is an evil witch in every respectable fairy tale, isn't there?' But there ought to be a handsome prince wandering around there somewhere... One who takes the girl by the hand and leads her to his palace and happiness. Isn't that how fairy tales go? That was exactly what I needed to believe in. Because I was waiting for him. The hero of my story.

When I met Christopher, I believed that I had found him. That's what I thought with the naivety that many centuries of womanly folly had bequeathed to my genes.

Christopher had the air of a man of the world. He initially worked in the PR department of his MP uncle's office and, when the uncle stopped being an MP, he took over the corresponding department in a big marketing company.

From the first moment I met him, it was love at first sight. He gave off the sense of a healthy, well-built male, with a very comforting self-assurance.

I made many mistakes with Christopher. I mistook the lust-at-first-sight that brought us together and I rashly christened it 'love'. I mistook his coolness for authenticity and I thought that he was genuine. But, he wasn't.

Strangely enough, he was well received by my mother. It might have been because the she-wolf would temporarily turn into a kitten in front of people from wealthy families who flattered her vanity. Or even worse – and I don't even want to think about it – because she sensed that Christopher was the right man to 'tell' me her truth in his own way: That all men are dirty bastards unworthy of your trust.

****

I have pointed this out before. The more you surrender yourself to bad thoughts, the more they will circle you to attack. So, you soon find yourself starring in something that has a nightmarish similarity to Hitchcock's *The Birds*. But, fortunately, some doors still open in this house and twists occur.

'Vera, we won,' Antonis exclaimed with enthusiasm. He shut the front door with a bang and instantly stumbled over a stool placed in his path. He nearly sent it directly to the TV screen. I managed to come to its rescue at the very last minute by making a heroic effort. Lost in his rapture, he grabbed me in his arms and started twirling me around.

'Oh, really? What happened?'

The truth is that the aftermath of the political campaign fever with the exit polls, the debates and the fanfares of the electoral victory has reached me, but I refuse to pay any attention to it.

'It was a triumph! Didn't you watch the news?'

My discontent disappears and I catch myself smiling in gratitude. The bad thoughts had fled thanks to his arrival.

'No! Tell me... who won?' I said. I really felt very foolish;

my boyfriend works himself to death from morning till dusk in the front lines of politics and I'm completely in the dark.

'Honestly, sweetheart, where have you been?'

He opened his arms in a gesture full of magnanimity, as if he were forgiving the whole world. Fortunately, he didn't seem to be in the mood to get angry with me. These were historic moments; he wasn't going to give my ignorance the time of day.

'Tell me, who won the elections?' I chased after him to the bedroom where he was undressing.

'We did, darling!'

Who's 'we'? I had no idea which political party he supported and in such a zealous way. He didn't pay any attention to my words. He threw me on the bed and started kissing me with fervour. He overpowered me and I let myself get swept away by his excitement. Like a raft that had been parked for years on the sandy beach and the first wave to come swept it away. When the northern wind abated, Antonis left, a winner in every way, to join the sea of people celebrating in streets and squares.

****

As for me, the joyful hour of bedtime has arrived at last. And perhaps I will meet him then. How strange all these things are. And how wonderful! A man who was unknown and indifferent to me till yesterday has become a most intimate and beloved figure.

It wouldn't take me long, though, to discover another

unexpected and painful aspect of the issue. A few days later, I was home alone, as usual, watching one of his films. *One Night in the Middle of Dinner* was the title. It was a thriller set in Paris during the interwar years. An eccentric chef takes it upon himself to solve the murders that occur in his establishment, as a result of which his business is very close to going bust.

You constantly like to travel to the past, Mr Aravantinos, I thought. *We have never seen you fight the present. You just know how to deal with some ghosts and demons that jump out of the past. As though you're not a creature of this world.*

At that moment, the answer to the question that had been haunting me for so long struck me like lightning. Why do I see *him* in particular? Why him?

Because he was the only one capable of breaking the spell. Because he was the only one with the strength to exorcise evil. *Because we were both plagued by the same demons*, I concluded my reasoning and was left speechless.

****

When the second DVD started playing and I was still numb from the discovery, Antonis appeared. He looked tired but satisfied. His career appeared to be taking off at that time and he was often away from home. He put his hands in his pockets and leaned against the doorframe. He looked at me absent-mindedly, as if he wasn't really looking at me, with a quiet acceptance of the fact.

'Are you watching him again?' he wondered. 'What's

with you and this sudden obsession? Do you like this spooky guy that much?' he said with a hint of jealousy.

'Why? He's a very good actor.'

'Yes, I don't doubt he is...'

Then he forgot about it as he discovered the spinach pie that I had brought from my mother's house a few days before. He sat at the kitchen table and started chewing with relish.

I turned the TV off and sat opposite him.

'I would just say that he inspires me.'

'He inspires you ... how, exactly?'

'With the book I'm writing.'

'Oh!'

And then he added, as if suddenly enlightened, chewing all the while: 'It's a shame, then, that such an awful thing happened to him. I forgot to tell you in the turmoil of recent events.'

'What awful thing?'

'He had a very serious accident with his car, somewhere on the outskirts of Paris, and he's in hospital.'

'When?'

'It must have been two or three months ago. I don't remember exactly. But, don't you read any newspapers?' he said, exasperated.

No, I hadn't read any newspapers nor had I watched TV since I started writing. My bridges of communication with the outside world had suffered dangerous gaps.

'Where are the newspapers? I want to find them. Will you bring them to me?'

'Have you lost your mind? The newspaper archives are closed at this hour!'

'Then, you tell me! How exactly did it happen?'

He looked at me apprehensively. His gaze betrayed that he didn't think of me as the sanest of creatures in the world.

'In a spectacular way! I would even call it cinematic. His car careened off the road, while he was attempting to make a turn, on a day with torrential rain, and it ended up in the river that runs next to the road. It was swept away by the current, but it stopped when it crashed into a tree trunk. He's in a coma and the doctors aren't very hopeful,' he summarized the tragic event.

My heart beat louder and louder as he spoke until it completely stopped.

'Honestly, is this really that serious for you?'

It must have worried him very much to see me turn such a ghastly white.

'Don't you think it's serious that a man is in danger of dying?'

'Do you know how many people all over the world are in a sorry state? I haven't seen you give a fig about them!'

'But he's the hero of my story!'

I must have shouted out in despair because he gestured to me to keep my voice down. The plate slipped from his hands. The kitchen floor became full of crumbs and broken porcelain pieces.

'If he dies, what am I going to do?'

'Look, Vera,' he said with calm resignation, 'if some gentlemen come and stuff you in a jacket with very, very long sleeves, don't worry. It'll be for your own good!'

Chapter 3

The Jellyfish on the Ocean Floor

I hope to remain unbowed in the light of these new discoveries. Things have turned serious. Until now, I had seen it as a game, a bit bothersome perhaps, but still a game. But not anymore.

I am now swimming at the bottom of the sea where the jellyfish, compared to the monsters that lazily swim around, are the most harmless creatures, the most innocent.

'Where are you? Where are you?' I anxiously ask him at night, but Constantinos refuses to answer.

'I feel so alone,' he tells me sadly. 'I need to hear a story. I want you to tell me this story.'

I melt when I hear him speak like that. I begin to unravel the fairy tale; it's the only thing I can do for him, who hadn't entered my dreams for his own amusement, as I had thought in the beginning.

The story I write for him flows through the tips of my fingers without any conscious thought. The title also decided itself...

Many kisses from Mr Strasse

Great disorder reigned on the first floor of the old block of flats in Psyrri. The room with the battered desks crammed next to each other was small; stuffy cigarette smoke floated in the air like balls of cotton. Decay marked the ceiling and the walls with the yellowed engravings.

Jenny continues to press the keys of the typewriter unfazed, but her eyes fly back and forth in curiosity. First, they rest on the shoulder of her boss – Mr Delatolas was the good-for-nothing director of an imports-exports company with many connections abroad, but she had gotten wind of the fact that all of this was just a smokescreen in order to cover up for his illegal activities a long time ago – and then on the expertly tied necktie of Delatolas' assistant.

This young man called Diamantopoulos baffled her; he seemed to be ignorant of their work's dirty background, but, on the other hand, that would be unlikely, since he had wormed his way into everything.

Anyhow, both of them were in Delatolas' office at that moment, opening and shutting drawers in a panic, leafing through invoices and sloppily stuffing various documents in a file folder.

'Jenny, remember what I told you,' Delatolas told her as he hastily put on his jacket and hat, 'if anyone asks you, I left this morning for England, for a serious business matter.'

Unfortunately, Jenny knew very well who was going to ask her.

Just then, loud knocks made the locked front door of the office shudder.

'Oh, not again,' she clutched her head in despair.

The boss and his assistant froze for a moment; they instantly grabbed the file folder in question and hurried to flee through the back door.

In fact, Diamantopoulos, in a fit of panic, almost jumped out of the open window onto the shingled roof of the neighbouring house, but the other man grabbed him by the collar at the last minute and dragged him to the back door.

Jenny almost split her sides laughing but she managed to get a hold of herself as the front door was forced open from outside. Three police officers burst into the office.

'Where's your boss?' one of them, a pasty man with red blotches on his forehead, menacingly growled, brandishing his gun.

'Don't hassle the girl about it, Vangelis,' their chief pushed his hand aside. 'Delatolas is most certainly abroad on business. Isn't that so, Jenny?' he said with the appropriate dosage of sweetness and slyness in his voice.

'Since you know where he is, why do you ask?'

She kept typing with intense concentration in order to make her acting more believable.

The chief removed his hat and trench coat with slow movements, hung them on the metal coatrack, and half sat on her desk, staring at her intently.

The other two police officers had wandered into the other rooms and were going through everything that fell into their hands with a fine-tooth comb.

'I'll get him one of these days,' he mumbled and lit a cigarette after stroking his beard.

Then he started painstakingly folding pieces of paper into small paper planes.

'What are you after, Jimmy?' she dared to ask after a while.

'You know what I'm after. Do you happen to have one of those boxes with the amazing melomakarona you bake lying around in the kitchen?'

'You made such a fuss just to come here and eat melomakarona?' she was struggling to keep herself from giggling.

'Not just for that.'

He gave her a meaningful look as he eyed her from top to bottom. His piercing eyes seemed to be able to see through her thin dress.

'Would you also like some coffee with them?' she said with obvious sarcasm.

'I'd most gladly drink a cup of Greek black coffee,' he ignored her mocking tone.

'The next time you make a mess, make sure they clean up afterwards, because I'm going to be the one – again! – who's going to spend the whole night cleaning up this...' she wanted to say 'pigsty', but she didn't, after all.

The search of the premises was completed about an hour later, with the usual meagre results. The cursing police officers were preparing to leave.

'Jenny ... you'd better not get married!'

'Why?'

'Because one day you'll become my wife,' were the chief's

parting words. He slammed shut the dilapidated door behind him and vanished from sight.

'He's such a bastard,' she sighed in despair as she took in the chaos that surrounded her. The countless pieces of paperwork scattered everywhere. A swarm of mismatched objects seemed to have been hurled from within the open drawers onto the tiles, chairs and desks by a sudden squall.

Dimitris – Mimis, or Jimmy to his friends – Strasse was the son of a Greek-German adventurer and a Greek immigrant; he was a Greek citizen and an Orthodox Christian, but nobody could vouch for the goodness of his methods, let alone swear to the integrity of his character.

He was a dirty cop who was up to his eyes in various suspicious dealings. It was well known in the streets that he held great influence; he could save a criminal from the executioner's block – figuratively speaking – for the right fee, of course!

'It's such a shame. He's such a handsome man,' Jenny caught herself daydreaming.

Then, she rolled up her sleeves and started putting order to the chaos.

****

The story takes place in the 1970s. It has a passport and travels through space, time, and depth. Strangely enough, it also has a bit of humour; I had no idea I was capable of something like that.

Jimmy and Jenny will become really close, despite her reluctance. He will be fired from the police force and will set up a private detective agency. Then, they will be forcibly taken to Germany by a Jewish client of Jimmy.

Hunted by German spies and Jewish kidnappers, they will start searching for a treasure hidden by the Nazis in a medieval castle thirty years earlier. And as if all that weren't enough, they will have to face many strange phenomena in the dark corridors and the full-of-trap corners of the castle.

They will take part in a strange dance, the Dance of the Immovable Roses, during which a moment of hesitation on the line separating knowledge and ignorance might be fatal. It's a reference to the endless flow of *karma*, the ceaseless reincarnation dance, whose curse they will not be able to escape unless they quickly grasp its meaning. They will understand many things there; they will learn to manoeuvre and evolve.

But they will lose Alexander, Jimmy's idealistic assistant who secretly followed them. Alexander and his partner will eternally stay frozen in that fateful Dance because they didn't understand its meaning.

With Alexander, I sketch one of the story's key characters because he symbolizes the extreme sensibility one has to let go of, since he is in danger of becoming fossilized because of it.

At some point, the heroes will find themselves facing a she-wolf that sprung out of the darkness, just like the nightmares of the past that emerge from the depths of childhood. The beast will be killed by the bullets of their kidnapper, the Jewish David Ezra, but after he injures Jimmy first.

Their Jewish rescuer is an ambiguous figure. He doesn't represent the paternal archetype that exterminates the wolf.

I had been unable to clarify to whom this form corresponded because it didn't come from my past – it came from the future, but of course, I didn't know that yet. Only when everything became clear and all the pieces slipped nicely into place would I understand, but that would only happen much later.

The dense forest surrounding the castle, a fairy-tale-like place with all the tension of the symbols it encapsulates, will be where the final scene takes place. There, the heroes will encounter a caravan of wandering gypsies and a witch who will show them the way.

Eventually, Jimmy will heal his wounds while Jenny will discover how rough and arduous the road that leads to the spring from where the pure water of life gushes is.

****

Constantinos is laughing in my dreams.

'What a story!' he says.

I'm happy to see him laugh.

'You made me write it! I don't need your sarcasm,' I answer and I hastily wake up in order to go back to writing.

A river of inspiration gushes from within me. I have to hurry before it changes its mind and dries up; I have to hurry because... because it's a matter of life and death.

A devilish wind was threatening to tear all the shingles off the roofs when I stepped out into the street. It was strange weather. The sky looked like a white shawl that had been dragged through the mud. The creaking shop signs; the small trees lining the pavement, struggling to stay upright against the wind; the laundry hanged to dry lashing about wildly; I was surrounded by these disconcerting sounds. Carrying my umbrella, I took the road to Neapoli. I knew I was going to hear a repeat performance, but how could I abandon my friend in such a situation?

Vicky opened the door with a frown on her face and unwashed hair. Her face was even cloudier than the sky. She sat back in an armchair and lit up a cigarette. Every available space around was occupied by overflowing ashtrays, mugs of dried coffee and discarded chocolate wrappings.

What a fine example you provide for your daughter, I would have told her on another occasion, but, at that moment, we had another burning issue at hand.

'The problem isn't that you can't find a respectable man to spend your life with,' she got directly to the point with unfocused eyes. 'The worst part is,' she continues, 'finding someone that isn't worth your while, and yet you insist on giving them a piece of your heart. You want to give, not to take, and he throws it back in your face. "I don't want it, woman, I don't need it, you can stick it where the sun doesn't shine for all I care!"'

'Do you know what I imagine sometimes?' I whispered dreamily. 'That I'll meet a man who will tell me: "I'm here for you," and I will ask him: "Here? Where?" "In this world," he will answer.'

But I stopped daydreaming because I was close to tears. Once more, I patiently focused on listening to the same tear-jerking story. The married man who wants to have fun and creates a cheap, fabricated romance with whoever is naïve enough and has a need to believe him, and this flimsy romance crumbles after a single night of passion. The finale: Wrecked hearts. Tons of used tissue paper. No happy ending!

'Do you get it?' she exploded. 'He doesn't give me the time of day! Two or three times were enough to satiate his "passionate feelings" for me! He says that he doesn't want to ruin his marriage. He feels guilty for having cheated on his wife. He is such a coward and a fool! And what was I stupid enough to do? I ended up pursuing him, sending him desperate texts and begging him to meet me even just once.'

'I always believed that love makes a fool of you,' I said, lost in thought.

'You have no reasons to complain,' she sniffed. 'You have Antonis; he's a nice guy, Vera.'

'He is nice. But I don't think we have much in common.'

She pressed her lips together with an obstinacy that only Vicky can demonstrate so vividly. She went on smoking silently for several minutes, lost in her thoughts.

My eyes fell on the carpet, which was covered in cigarette ashes.

'And you also have a child. It's not something insignificant,' I tried to comfort her. 'Where's Marina?' I said in an attempt to change the subject.

'Her godmother stopped by and picked her up. They've gone shopping for Marina's birthday present.'

'Get up,' I told her with sudden inspiration. 'Go and wash your hair, we're going out to lunch. We can go to that excellent taverna in Theseio that Antonis has mentioned to me.'

The truth is that I hadn't left the house for so long that I thought it would be good for both of us.

'It's out of the question,' she abruptly cut me off. 'I have to cook lunch for my kid. I'm making some pasta. Do you want to join us?'

I turned her offer down politely and left in a hurry.

I wasn't worried about my friend. I gave her just a couple of days of feeling down in the dumps. Vicky would wade for a while in the shallow waters of the drama that played out, without her being in any actual danger, and then she would crack open the deck of cards of applied logic. She would see that the solitaire game she was playing couldn't be solved and she would take the right decisions. She would lazily stretch out on the couch, smoke three or four cigarettes one after the other and would demolish a couple of chocolate bars. Finally, she would end up repeating her favourite motto: 'As long as I'm fine, I don't even care if ten sheep fall down a mine.'

At that moment, though, I didn't want to burden her with my problems; namely, that Antonis barely showed his face anymore. He was completely preoccupied with his career. I was lost in a world of my own. I guess I can't give him what he needs. I don't even have the time to think if that makes me sad or relieved.

****

The hours lazily rolled by that night. The hands of the clock wound round and round in circles noiselessly and without any purpose. Strangely, I was not in the mood to write. My story was not going anywhere. I felt the need to go out and get some fresh air. The walls had created a stranglehold around me and I felt I was suffocating.

I got into the car and started driving purposely around the streets. I slipped into narrow roads that I had never been in before. I drove down roads with unfamiliar names. And there I was. Without realising it, I found myself on the street with the locked houses. Everything was quiet. The houses were two-storied, with big verandas and lit windows. No one was out walking in the streets, not even a cat. Everything held its breath. I was all by myself on the other side of the locked doors and I knew with spine-chilling certainty that shadows lived within. But – it was strange – instead of being gripped by fear, I breathed more easily.

I urgently needed a drink. So I started looking for a bar. I left the car and I tried to walk as lightly as possible so that my heels wouldn't make any noise. I was paranoid that my mother would appear from behind a door and start criticizing me.

'What are you doing wandering about by yourself so late at night, Vera?'

When I spotted the pink lights of the bar called Magic, I knew I had reached my destination. At that moment, a pack of stray dogs disturbed the silence of the street. They were barking as they chased a motorcycle. They disappeared round the corner of the street and then everything was quiet once more. The wind – a troubled wind – dragged a few bedraggled pieces of carton around in an empty alley.

I should have thought that this place looked quite suspicious. But I didn't. All I wanted was a drink. I felt light, free and desirable. I hadn't even noticed that I was wearing tight leggings and a shirt that I usually wear indoors because it's somewhat daring. I had accessorized this 'homely' outfit with a pair of clashing high-heeled shoes. My appearance was a bit provocative and cheap.

But the man sitting at the bar – the bar's only customer till that moment – noticed all that. The place smelled of neglect and decadence.

I thought the same about the rough-looking man with the jean jacket and the curly hair. He sharply exhaled his cigarette smoke and then suggestively dragged a finger over his lips.

I ordered orange vodka. The barmaid couldn't hide the surprise in her eyes as she served my drink. I guess it was because I looked incompatible with the place, entirely foreign to that environment.

I was looking for something without knowing what that was; I was waiting for something – what was it? – perched on the shabby barstool while my mind screamed at me: 'Get up and leave, what are you doing in this place?' But something inside me had an entirely different opinion and kept me nailed to my seat.

I wasn't sure, but I thought I caught that man's eyes stuck on me like a dried piece of snot. I feared that I would throw up. But, instead of getting up and walking out of there, I ordered a second drink. Now that I think about it, I firmly believe that it wasn't me acting like this. Someone else was directing my moves on my behalf: he was the one who was playing me like a violin, who had turned me into his puppet once again. And this person had tremendous power over me; I knew that then. But why would he do something like this to me?

Everything around me wobbled dangerously as I got up to go to the toilet so that I could splash some water on my face. I was convinced of the cocktail's dubious quality but it was too late to do anything about it. There was a sensual smile on my face when I looked at myself in the dirty mirror. I refreshed my lipstick and turned toward the door. But I didn't make it out.

'What good wind brought you to our place ... baby?' The man with the jean jacket and the lecherous lips blocked the exit with his body. His voice sounded like the snorting of a wild animal as it reached my ears. He stank of alcohol, stale sweat and cigarette smoke.

Normally, I would have told him to shove off and let me through; I would then have run away from this place. But, I didn't. On the contrary, I found myself back in my seat, giggling drunkenly and sipping from a drink that he had bought for me. Five or six other bar clients of the same species as my 'friend' took up every available barstool near us.

I don't remember how much time passed by – parts of my memory went missing from that point on – until the moment I found myself with him at the back of the bar, in something that looked like a storage room, and in an uncomfortable position. I vaguely remember that something was pressing insistently against my back and that he was snuffling near my face, reeking of alcohol. I don't know what sudden flash in my clouded mind was the trigger that pushed me to get away running, leaving him gobsmacked.

Then, I found myself in my bed; I don't know exactly how that happened. It was as if an invisible hand had lifted me up and placed me on the soft pillows, on my feather mattress, away from stale cigarette smoke, dirty toilets and sour breaths. The only thing that betrayed my night of debauchery was my hair that stank and the unpleasant roiling in my stomach.

'Forget it,' Constantinos said early in the morning with false regret. 'I guess it was very stupid of me.' But his gaze showed nothing that looked like remorse for the dirty game he had played at my expense, and that angered me above anything else.

'What the hell did I get myself into?' I managed to wonder before I fell into a leaden sleep.

****

This incident was very upsetting, probably because it forced me to think about the dual nature of things. Hidden behind his magical presence in my dreams was another self, which now appeared before me. Disgusting, unpredictable and horrifying. Or was it his true self? I was in no position to tell these things apart. We had completed each other from the beginning...

After that, my life took another unexpected turn. It took me days to realise that the senseless incident of that night was not etched on my forehead. After I managed to bury my shame for the crummy way in which I had endangered myself, a new side effect started tormenting me.

I always had a sensitive sense of smell, but at that time, it had started to intensify. I would greedily sniff the air for any kind of scent. My nostrils would flare as they took in tingling smells. I would buy bottles of benzene and stick them under my nose and sniff them with pleasure.

I didn't understand what this new madness was. I had never used addictive substances, so how could this be explained? The bad thing was that I knew someone who was used to these vices of famous people and who seemed to be playing a new cruel game. But even though I kept asking him insistently on many of the following nights, Constantinos kept his lips sealed.

'To Rome,' he said one night. 'I want us to go to Rome together. To look down on the Eternal City from the top of its highest hill.' And I figured that we would be eternally united if I offered him what he was asking for.

Then, the other menacing spectre of my life, Theophano, took it upon herself to give me her own outrageous explanations.

'Did you think that he wouldn't ask for anything in return? This man, Vera, has sold his soul to Satan. Who knows which dark forces he's in league with. I don't know what's going on with you, my daughter, but don't distance yourself from the Church. I will repeat it and I beg of you: Return to the Lord's side, or else this possessed man will take your

[64]

soul. He will give it to Satan in return for his own soul, which he gave up long ago.'

I woke up drenched in sweat and panic-stricken. For the first time ever, the mad ramblings of my mother appeared to be really convincing. If you think about it, why would he do something so nice for my sake? Why would he become my inspiration and my guide through the dream world without getting anything in return? And what else could he ask of me? What would be more precious than my soul? And my stupid and infatuated self was prepared to offer it to him without even negotiating on the matter.

A vague premonition whispered to me that the two dominant personalities I was carrying within me, my mother and Constantinos, would clash with each other in the end, but I hurriedly rid myself of these thoughts.

But I knew that I had to do something, and urgently. The following day I paced back and forth in the house biting my nails. My stomach could only take water; sunlight was a nuisance so I closed all the blinds; the slightest noise caused me great distress. I lay on the bed and wrapped myself up in the duvet. The May heat barely touched me; I was terribly cold. I felt my body was numb but my bones hurt. A paranoid idea started to cast a faint light in my mind; it started taking a distinctive shape as the time went by.

The man who flowed relentlessly through my blood, the man who haunted my dreams was persistently asking something of me and I had to give it to him. No matter the cost.

****

When night fell and the shadows in the streets and in my mind grew larger, I climbed into the car and started driving aimlessly around as though I was lost. I was desperately looking for something. I tried numerous ways, driving in and out of the most remote of streets, many times, ending up in a dead end. I was desperate in the end, certain that I wasn't going to find it. A sense of loss and disappointment consumed me.

Suddenly, a pack of stray dogs barking like mad surrounded my car. They were chasing a scruffy cat that was desperately trying to escape them. Without knowing the reason why, I followed behind them in my car. And I finally got there. Stray dogs always know the way.

The gaudy letters on the sign of the Magic Bar shone like scrumptious lollipops. I went on shaking legs, nervously clutching my bag. The Man With No Name was there. Huge relief washed over me as if I had met the dearest person in this world to me. He's wearing the same dirty pair of jeans and the same lecherous smile. He slowly raises his eyes and gives me a calm look. A glint of triumph can be faintly seen deep in his gaze.

'I knew you'd be back,' he gruffly muttered. 'What brings you here again, baby?'

'I need a favour,' I hurriedly swallow a mouthful of whisky, choke on it, and start coughing. 'I want some white,' I blurt out with whatever courage I had remaining. 'Cocaine,' I rush to make myself clear. I only had the barest idea of what they call these things in the streets.

'Is that so? And how did you come by the idea that I have anything to do with that shit?'

'Please,' I grab him by the hand. 'I'll pay you! I'll give you as much as you want!'

He seems to find my despair amusing.

'Will you look at that,' he said in a muffled voice. 'Who would have thought? And I thought you were a good girl. But, good girls are the ones you should expect to turn out this rotten!'

I didn't even hear the insult. It barely reached my ears.

'Please,' I repeat, not knowing what else to do.

I try to give him an attractive smile that ends up looking like a disappointed frown. He bursts out into hoarse laughter.

'Fine,' he says after a minute of endless waiting. '...Uncle will do something for you. But, you better watch out, if you rat me out, you'll find yourself six feet under!'

He gets up and disappears at the back of the bar. I let out a sigh of relief. When he finally comes back, he casts wary glances around him like a hunted beast. He puts a small newspaper wrapped parcel in my hand. I feel the urge to kiss his hands for joy. I take out a wad of bills and stuff it in his pocket.

I never found out if I paid the real worth of this madness. I will never find out the true cost of a person's humiliation. I'm not even going to ever learn his name, but I couldn't care less!

He continues sipping his whisky unperturbed, without sparing me a single glance. It's as if I'm invisible to him.

'Now beat it,' he says through his teeth with contempt. 'Get outta here. I hate junkies.'

He didn't even bother to come on to me again. What a joke!

Back at the house, I throw my bag in a corner, unwrap the tiny package with trembling hands; my heart is thumping with excitement and my throat is dry. I'm a bad girl and I'm insanely enjoying it for the first time in my life. I'm ready to commit the biggest sin of my life and my veins are pulsating forcefully in my temples. But what exactly am I supposed to do? I have no idea.

I try to remember everything that I have seen in films; I snort the white powder lined in front of me without being sure that I'm doing it correctly.

An amazing feeling comes to reward me. I feel incredible, I feel on top of the world, and I celebrate with all of my senses. My head feels different, as though it has expanded. Or is it just that my mind expanded and cleared? It has truly become sparkling. I burst out into happy laughter. My head found the place it deserves, I giggle.

At last, I'm united with him in life and death. In good and evil. I feel happy. Whole. I'm no longer half a person. He and I are one for eternity.

Later – how much later? – I burst into tears. A bottomless grief gushes over me from within and tears me apart.

'I want to see you,' I say, 'I want to touch you. I want to rest my head on your lap and hear you tell me a fairy tale. Stop hiding at the bottom of my dreams, Constantinos. Stop being lazy. Do something for your own sake, dammit!'

PART TWO

Chapter 4

If You Have the Devil in You...

'Vangelis is an aesthete,' Venetis said to his company with a meaningful look as he pointed at the pale man next to him. 'Tarkovsky's filmography is the highest point of reference for him.'

In the meeting room, about a dozen Philippe Starck armchairs are arrayed around a long and narrow oak table. At present, most of them are occupied by the people who will take part in the PPM (Pre-production meeting). My life's principal characters in the months to follow are drinking coffee and munching on biscuits.

'Tarkovsky's films, and quality film-making, in general, are the substantiation of the seventh art,' the man called Vangelis answered with a philosophical air.

'And of course, Bergman's and Alain Resnais' films. You must have seen, I imagine, the film *Last Year at Marienbad*,' he added with a faint touch of irony. 'The stylized photography, the apotheosis of form, the fragmentation of the narrative. Generally, I would say that commercial cinema doesn't express me.'

When I entered the room, Avramoglou's intense presence dominated the larger part of the 'frame'. He towered over everyone, and a cigar dangled from his mouth as he wandered around the room with feline grace, despite the extra weight he carried on his bulky frame. Every now and then, he would take noisy breaths. At the same time, he appeared not only to be in tune with his surroundings, but their absolute master as well. From the first moment I saw him, I felt a sense of overwhelming security, something that hadn't been part of my intentions. Then, I was surprised to realise that I didn't know his first name. I had never heard anyone mention it.

He was just Avramoglou to everybody, the successful television and film producer. He came from a working class background, the child of Greek refugees from Kokkinia, and had grappled with various professional activities throughout his eventful life.

At the beginning of his career, he had been a broadcaster for the National Greek Radio and a journalist in various, mostly sport, newspapers. After that, he founded a record label and networked in the publishing industry. He even did a stint in jail for tax evasion. He got involved in the theatre circuit, then he bought a small television station, and this production company was his latest accomplishment.

I observed him for several seconds – he was unapologetically foul-mouthed, from what I had heard, and thunderous in all of his outbursts. Mercurial was a fitting description for all of the above.

When I saw him from up close, it no longer surprised me that this man was only known by his surname.

Knowledge of someone's first name always involves a greater sense of intimacy with the person; then, there's the assumption that they also have moments of weakness and family memories: from birthdays, cakes, candles, kisses, and all the rest. This man, who was rumoured to be as tough as nails and ruthless, who hand-picked his associates under the strictest of rules, and who was more tight-fisted with money than the meanest banker, didn't give you the impression of having experienced any of these things.

One by one, the rest of the people in the meeting escape the shadow of anonymity and proceed to identify themselves.

Stamatis Kalogeropoulos is the production manager. Tall, with an immature look and an oily face. You are tempted to consider him naïve by the way he looks at you with a smile – but something in the back of his eyes warns you that you would be the naïve one if you believed that. I quickly discover that Stamatis has the annoying habit of approaching everyone just to whisper something conspiratorially in their ear and instantly burst into boisterous laughter, accompanied by 'friendly' nudges in the ribs.

The next person they introduce me to is Vangelis Sideris. 'Don't worry about him being such a runt,' Avramoglou laughs as he introduces me to the man who is the assistant director, 'he works like a dog.' The 35-year-old man extends his hand in polite greeting. He is slim and very pale. His physical characteristics are flawless when examined independently one from the other; they are mediocre as a whole. He is a dandy with old-fashioned charm. His gaze is enlivened by hints of compassion and understanding, but his cold smile suggests that he wouldn't hesitate to push you against the wall the first chance he got.

'You've heard of Pantelis Venetis, of course,' Avramoglou continues the introductions.

Finally, a truly warm handshake. Up until recently he had been involved in short films, and then he directed his first full-length feature film and won a sweeping victory at the Festival of Thessaloniki. The director charmed me at once with his impressive figure and the kind-hearted smile he sent me from under his blond moustache.

'I hope and desire we will get on well, Ms Kalogera.'

'I don't see why we shouldn't.'

'You must know that when an author is tasked with writing a script, especially if it's based on one of their own books – which rarely ever happens – then they will without a doubt clash with the director.'

'But I'm also a script writer, so I will strive to see things in a strictly professional way, I assure you.'

I was glad to see Yiannis Avgoustakos' laughing face among the others. Yiannis was the director of photography and he was a very well-liked old hand in the film-making business. An open-hearted character, spontaneous and a jester (always with a joke at the tip of his tongue).

The woman who languidly offers her hand to me in greeting reminds me of a mature Greta Garbo. She is wearing a thin cashmere sweater, a satin skirt and velvet pumps. A few, but expensive, pieces of jewellery complete her somewhat sombre – in hues of purple and black – outfit. She is using a long mother-of-pearl cigarette holder with half-closed eyelids. Even the cigarette smoke seems entranced by her presence, the way it enfolds her like an enchanting innuendo.

'Mrs Katia Avgerinou will be the set and costume designer.'

She was a Lady, with a capital L; she just lacked a veiled hat to complete the image of an old-era heart-breaker.

'And Manolis, the casting director,' the producer ends the circle of introductions. He most certainly is the good guy of the story, the dogsbody. He is young, with a handsome face, and the ability to overcome all difficulties. He is one of those people who know when to be informal and when to be professional.

****

Two and a half years ago, when I locked the pack of printed pages in a drawer, I didn't have the slightest idea about the events that were in store for me. I was just possessed by an inexplicable eagerness to get rid of a work that I no longer recognized as my own creation. The emotion that flooded me back then wasn't complete satisfaction, as I initially thought, but an unexplainable discomfiture.

Did I write all this? I asked myself. *And how did I come up with all of this?* This befuddlement lasted for a long time and I didn't even dare touch those papers. So, I locked them in a drawer in order to punish them for gaining their independence from me so soon, and I let time go by. That's when I saw Constantinos in my dreams for the last time. 'My hands are tied because of you, Vera,' he complained and showed me his hands. They were trapped in a paper web. 'You are keeping me a prisoner.' The very next day, I started looking for a publisher.

A few months after the book's publication, I got a call from the company ZX Production Movies. I didn't meet Avramoglou in person back then, just Alcibiades, his personal assistant. He had conveyed his employer's opinion word for word: 'It has a well-thought-out plot and lots of suspense.' I understood then that things had escaped my control. The die was cast.

****

Far away, where the cement sea of urban housing ended, another sea began, the real one, but I was unable to make it out from where I was. Behind the giant glass windows, Athens lazily spread out in the urban haze. I could see long lines of cars stretching as far as the eye could see along Kifisias Avenue. The light of the setting sun was already reflected on the windows of the tall glass buildings.

The smoke from Venetis' pipe, the cigars and the cigarettes had created a stuffy atmosphere in the room. The ashtrays were overflowing and the coffee had run out hours ago. The leftover crumbs from the cake and the biscuits showcased that the meeting had to come to an end. But, I was mistaken, since there were still important issues to discuss.'

'Interior shots will be filmed here, in Studio Lamda, in Paeania,' Venetis said. 'As for the castle's exterior shots, we'll have to go to Germany, of course.'

The discussion was extended in order to include the castles of Germany, the location scouting that Avgoustakos and Venetis would need to do on the fly, the internal shots, Takis' worries about proper lighting, and ended with the scenes with the wolf and their post-production editing.

'When do you expect us to start, Pantelis?' Avramoglou stepped in.

'It's reasonable to say that we can start in three to four months,' Venetis replied. 'We have to hurry; I don't want us to get caught in the German winter.'

It was Katia's turn. She would give us an idea on how she imagined the sets and the costumes through a collage she had created with a combination of magazine cut-outs and her own designs. She smoothed her eyebrows with unrivalled gracefulness and stood up.

'The atmosphere should give off an old-fashioned feeling,' she explained with certainty. 'At the same time, we must be careful to avoid the kitsch element that rightly or wrongly characterized the 1970s. I'd prefer vintage furniture – I already had a look in the appropriate stores – and props reminiscent of that decade's design. I believe that I have a few very interesting proposals ready. We will certainly have to closely collaborate with Mr Avgoustakos. Lighting plays a very crucial role in the way objects and fabrics are recorded on film.'

At some point, the discussion turned inevitably to the

burning issue of casting the leads. Venetis had already made a written proposal for the role of Jenny, but he wished to further support it. 'I have already proposed Evelina Agriotis for this part,' he declared in a voice that didn't leave much room for argument. But I noticed a slight hint of anxiety behind his self-assuredness, though I was unable to discern the reason.

'She is very similar to the type we are looking for. A feminine woman with a strong personality, seemingly fragile, but determined when needed.'

'I have no doubt that she is very suitable for the part,' I felt the need to agree and the rest of the team didn't appear to have any serious objections.

'The part of the shrew will fit her like a glove,' I heard Stamatis mutter beside me.

'As for Jimmy's part,' Venetis continued, 'the suggestion of George Alexakis is just a first possibility... But I would like us to give it some further thought.'

'This is where I'll disagree with you,' I objected. 'He isn't the right age, Pantelis. I want a lead actor aged between 38 to 40 years old. He isn't even 30, and it shows. So... I have a more ...distinct preference and I would like us to discuss it!'

I mustered all of my determination and I took a deep breath.

'I suggest that we seriously consider the possibility of casting Constantinos Aravantinos.'

An uncomfortable silence fell over the meeting room. Venetis cleaned out his pipe with profundity, Stamatis, his ear, while Vangelis doodled on a piece of paper, with his head hunched over the table. For a few seconds, I was worried that no one would ever speak to me again; they would think I was crazy or a freak. Even I was surprised at the extent of my audacity.

'Do you have any idea how high Aravantinos' net worth is?' Avramoglou broke the chill over the meeting room. 'It will take us way over budget.'

He was looking at me mockingly through his glasses, with his beady eyes narrowed. From the way he was looking at me, I could swear that he had the burning desire to spit on me.

'And, anyway, he has disappeared from the film industry these last few years, after the accident he had. It's as if the earth opened and swallowed him whole,' Stamatis remarked.

'That's why it may not cost us as much as we would imagine,' I grabbed the chance to say.

'A star, Vera, isn't always the best option for a film,' Venetis patiently explained. 'Our job gets easier when we use lesser known actors, with fewer demands. Rumour has it that he's a cantankerous character, eccentric, and he always causes scenes...'

'Wonderful! That's how I imagined the lead actor...'

'He sounds like a complete fool to me,' Avramoglou made his comeback. 'Don't you know what kind of parts he always picks? He always plays the outcast!' He lit up his cigar for the tenth or so time.

'Sometimes, you don't pick the parts, they pick you,' Venetis said with a serious look.

'Even worse!' Avramoglou answered wearily and sank deeper into his seat. The chair groaned under his immense weight.

'That's not necessarily bad for an actor,' I made a last attempt. 'In any case, I would like us to have a serious discussion on this subject. Only and if we completely reject the idea, can we move forward.'

'Personally, I believe that casting Mr Aravantinos is a marvellous idea,' Katia's voice sounded calm and completely self-possessed amidst the silence that had fallen over the meeting room.

'A star of his calibre will add a certain gravitas to our film. A simple discussion with him won't cost us a thing.'

I finally found myself on a small piece of land after that sudden flight I had flung myself into. I felt a sense of gratitude towards the woman who became my unexpected ally at such a difficult moment.

'Anyway, we'll have another discussion on the matter at some point,' the producer hastily wrapped things up.

'I don't imagine that you want me to bring you Jack Nicholson as a guest star,' Stamatis goaded me with a foolish snigger.

'No, I won't request anything too excessive from now on.'

***

It was nearly dark when the meeting ended. I got out into the street with a feeling of wonderful anticipation. Spring had started unfurling its first signs of arrival. The bittersweet scents of honeysuckle, sour orange and jasmine floated in the air. It was quite cool, still being April and all. The trees next to the sidewalk shivered in delight. I took another deep breath, smelling the air around me. *When spring arrives, it really means it, leaving no room for doubt,* I thought. I could say that I was almost happy.

When I got back home, I decided to relax by having a bath. I filled the bathtub with bubble bath and sank into the foam. I wanted to give myself a special treat for the courage I had shown that afternoon, but mostly to prepare for the Next Day's Trial.

On the following day, it was my mother's birthday and the whole family had been invited over for a celebratory meal. And, unfortunately, I knew very well from bitter experience what these family gatherings – which luckily for me didn't happen very often – meant. She only took the trouble to invite us twice a year, one time at Christmas and the other on her birthday. I never understood why she kept celebrating the latter with such religious reverence.

Theophano would welcome me in the same way she always did: impeccably dressed and with perfectly coiffed hair.

'My little girl, how much I've missed you.' She would hug me tenderly but with great care in order to avoid wrinkling her ancient, though well-preserved, cashmere skirt suit.

But this was just the skin of the 'orange'. The 'orange juice' had a tarter taste. She would inspect me from head to toe with haughtiness and something that looked like suspicion, and she wouldn't rest until she discovered some fault in my appearance. She always found something derogatory to say about the way I dress, which wasn't respectable enough; about my hair, which wasn't exactly sleek; then she would go on about my romantic relationships, which were never serious enough; and then she would end up criticizing my moral character, which had never been spotless, according to her. Even if she didn't utter some caustic remark about one of these areas of my life, she could retrieve some arrows from the quiver of the past with horrifying ease. As happened the last time we had a family meal.

'Have I told you what my parish priest – an excellent, educated man – advised me when Vera was 12 years old and I had taken her to church for confession? "This child is possessed by seven demons, Mrs Fokas. You have to show the utmost care, for if you do not rein her in, she will undoubtedly fall into the road to perdition".'

And she uttered this monstrosity with the utmost seriousness at a table set for dinner, in front of uncles, aunts, and sisters-in-laws, who all hung on her lips, with eyes as round as saucers. Because, among her many talents, Theophano also possessed an unsurpassable flair for the dramatic. Only the heavy chandelier, the Bohemian crystals and the tablecloth remained unmoved by all that rubbish.

This story with the seven demons, which I now remember and laugh about, definitely had a great impact on me when I was a child. I wouldn't exactly say that it frightened me, but it had deeply troubled me.

If I truly have those little devils in me, then where exactly are they? I would wonder. The idea of asking the 'esteemed Father' flitted through my mind, but I restrained myself. My mother would wither me with a glance, as usual, and call me ill-mannered and insolent. *Could they suddenly spring from my ears, my nose, or even worse, my mouth, and make me look like a fool? Because it can't be, they might feel suffocated in there and come out at some point!*

That's how I learned to protect myself when they tickled my ears, or when I sneezed, but mostly when I had the urge to sing or laugh, because you are more open then and all those forbidden things that you hide inside you might rush out. I wasted several years of my life without laughing – I had no serious reason to do so – without singing, and without sneezing.

A few years later, when I started to feel the first thrills of love, I had a sneaking suspicion about what the words of that ... excellent Father might mean. But, by then, it was too late for me to give in and for Theophano to assert her authority over me.

'I'm no saint, mum,' I murmured. 'Neither do I foresee becoming one in my current life. I don't have the strength to hate you anymore. But, I can't love you either. I'm sorry, but it's the best I can do for you.'

Not that my mother had lost her legendary ability to make me hopping mad. The important thing was that I didn't hate her. I didn't have the right to hate anyone anymore because I had had a great epiphany: I had learned that miracles do happen. It was as if I had been offered a wonderful new gift-wrapped reality, the most precious gift I had ever received in my life.

****

'Small' wasn't the most fitting description for The Beast. This trendy bar in Psyrri was in fact Lilliputian. Built with stone and decorated with candelabras, candlesticks and rustic wooden benches, it emitted a medieval feeling. I liked the place, I felt comforted by the warmth projected by the stone walls and the peace that reigned over the place, despite the chatter of the customers and the loud jazz music. But, soon enough, I found myself fiddling with my ring or my earrings, since spirits in my group were running low.

Ares and Rea were smoking one cigarette after the other without uttering a word in-between – I guess they had had a falling-out. George seemed to be indifferent towards everyone and everything and had wholeheartedly given himself over to repeated yawning, with one of his arms loosely draped over my shoulders. It was a typical gesture, neither romantic nor affectionate, one might say.

I couldn't understand George. It hadn't been that long since we had become a couple, but I had caught onto the fact that this introverted creature with the countless insecurities would be difficult to approach. The stress caused by his position as the art director of a big advertising company appeared to put a stopper in our relationship.

For as long as we had been together – nearly four months – he insisted on travelling every weekend, every single weekend, to the island of Andros to see his family. It was the only place – with his mother – where he claimed to be able to really relax. Once more, I asked myself what part I really played in his life – he was always dead tired during the weekdays, and away during the weekends – but the answer that I would give myself was disheartening. But, he was particularly gentle and sensual the few times we spent the night together and that was something.

That night, he bid me goodbye at the entrance of my house. He started muttering with an apologetic look that he had to leave, that he had to prepare for his trip on the following day. I almost told him to go to hell. I went up to my flat boiling with anger. 'Serves me right,' I thought. 'I didn't appreciate Antonis as much as I should have. Now, let's see what I'm going to do with this momma's boy.'

****

Saturday morning dawned with the greatest potential. Slim slices of light trembled on the floor and on the walls. The previous night's bad mood disappeared as if by magic. A secret voice whispered to me that yes, life could be truly beautiful, even though my boyfriend probably took me for granted and my mother was crazy – there was no doubt about the latter.

At around eleven o'clock, the phone rang with quite a cheerful sound.

'Good morning, Vera. I was told you were looking for me. I just returned from Paris last night and I just received your messages.' Nikos Papanikolaou's voice sounded like a wonderful omen to my ears.

Papanikolaou was a world-famous journalist. He was one of the few remaining bon viveurs, an avowed bachelor with countless successes with the fairer sex, despite his mature years. He was a true citizen of the world with one leg permanently in Paris, where he had constant collaborations with the French television, and the other in Athens. In his nonexistent spare time, though, he frequently found the opportunity to pop over to London for the occasional assignment.

'I need you to do me a huge favour.' I tried to make my voice as sweet as possible, without sounding as though I was begging. 'I'm sure that you're in the position to find a person that I'm urgently looking for in Paris.'

'Who?' he calmly asked as if finding missing persons was one of his daily habits.

'I want you to find Aravantinos for me. In fact, I want you to make sure that I get to meet him. Am I asking for too much?'

'Ah, no, it's no big deal. I'll find him for you,' he told me.

How simple life becomes when you know the right people. Papanikolaou was Theophano's old family friend. His family also came from Egypt.

'Even though lately he hasn't been frequenting his known haunts,' he added after a while. 'What do you want him for?' His journalistic curiosity reared its head.

I explained the situation.

'I see,' he said, coughing drily, 'I'm sensing something newsworthy here. Of course you know what I want from you in return,' he reminded me of my obligation.

'Anything you want,' I laughed.

'I want the first interview with him and the exclusive if there is an agreement in the end.'

****

A week later I was in the extremely pleasant position of bursting into Avramoglou's office like a hurricane. While I was waiting for what seemed like hours in the huge waiting room with the Arne Jacobsen Egg chairs, I was biting my nails from anxiety. But, I couldn't help but admire the producer's excellent taste in picking office assistants. The young man sitting behind the desk was a sheer work of art; he could easily become a model... if he wasn't one already.

'Mr Avramoglou, I'm heading for Paris,' I dramatically announced to him when he condescended to receive me in his office.

'And why should I be jumping for joy?' He spared me an indifferent look as he sat behind his heavy mahogany desk, smoking his ever-present cigar.

'I meant that I'm going there to meet Aravantinos, to discuss the script, and our film, with him...' I finally sat myself down on the leather couch, though a more apt description would be that I sat at the edge of the couch because I was twitching with excitement.

Something like a fever had come over me in the last couple of days, ever since I received Papanikolaou's call. 'Look, you have a good chance of meeting him next Sunday evening. His wife is having an exhibition of her current work and he will be wandering around there somewhere.'

'So long and may the Lord be with you,' the producer said sarcastically as he continued to smoke incessantly. 'And if you manage to do anything, give me a call! But, keep something in mind, Ms Kalogera. I haven't given the final 'ok'. We haven't even talked about this. That man will work with us only if his financial expectations are grounded and realistic. Otherwise, forget it!'

'Good, just let me talk to him,' I gathered the remnants of my courage. 'I find it hard to believe that a man of your perceptiveness and ... education ... (this was quite sycophantic...) would fail to see what a great asset this would be for our film. Anyway, if you don't help me, I'll try on my own,' I made a last attempt.

'Do you need anything else, Ms Kalogera?'

'Yes, Stamatis.'

'What do you need him for?'

'To come with me. I don't speak a word of French and we might have to talk to the people managing him there and ... I won't be able to deal with it on my own, I'm afraid.'

I flopped back on the green sofa and I felt that I was seconds away from bursting into tears from the stress. I must have presented a very funny sight because Avramoglou burst out into raucous laughter.

'I see,' he finally said, quite pleased. 'You have the devil in you, Vera, don't you?'

'I do,' I said, my eyes welling up. 'That's what my mother used to say!'

Chapter 5

A Ridiculous Déjà Vu

Paris is the ideal place if someone is in the mood to ponder over fate and people's destination. An imposing city, with an incomparable charm. And with a clear intention of imposing itself on you, no matter what.

The clouds travel hurriedly in the sky. Half of the city's population is walking within the labyrinthine network of foul-smelling underground passages. The other half endures the temperament of a schizophrenic and erratic climate that changes every five minutes.

Everything in the City of Light is designed to make you feel insignificant before the ruthless flow of history. Before the range (the 400,000 exhibits of the Louvre are enough to make your knees feel wobbly) and perfection of the works of art.

Impressive granite buildings, arches, statues of kings and saints, Gothic masterpieces and sculptural compositions, elaborate gardens and churches, everything screams of the human race's need to surpass itself. To rise up to heights that are elusive to its stature.

I wandered the streets aimlessly for several hours. Evening found me walking around Le Marais. Hidden between brick buildings, which used to be the residences of the 17th century's aristocracy, I discovered small shops that hid many treasures.

While I was waiting for Stamatis and Papanikolaou to arrive at our rendezvous, my eyes browsed through the antique toys in a window shop. I was feeling cold but trying to ignore it. The *17 Minuten Gallery* was right next door. A large sign was proclaiming the opening of the exhibition *African Nights*.

'*I photographed these teenage African girls wearing primitive masks, almost looking like statues. The women seem to be performing a mystic ritual in the streets of Paris. I feel like a reporter who is recording the multifaceted ways of human existence*', the photographer, Virginie Lysenne, explained in the exhibition's leaflet that Stamatis reluctantly translated for me.

'*Virginie Lysenne attempts to approach the many faces of women and black culture from different perspectives. Ms Lysenne's work involves meticulous research and a perceptive mind in order for her to be able to enter an entirely different world,*' the critic continued.

The gallery gave off the feeling of having been used as a brandy distillery in the past. A heavy distiller was at the centre of the hall. Dozens of miniature bottles with elaborate labels lined a shelf. The wooden table in front of this shelf, filled with glasses and trays, served as the bar. A video that was being projected at the other end of the hall was explaining the mystical properties of the mask and its importance in African ceremonies.

When we entered the gallery, the place was teeming with people. They – the entire intelligentsia of the city who had gathered there – were trying to exchange their views under the decadent beats of the Afro-dance music playing. Papanikolaou started greeting people right and left. Luckily, that gave me the time I needed to compose myself. I leaned against a wall and let my eyes wander around.

When I finally spotted him, my mind shut down and stopped receiving any information. He was standing with his right hand stuffed in his pocket. He was holding a glass in his left. He was having a conversation with a dark-haired woman who was flaunting her mature beauty in an off-shoulder gown. He was trying to appear confident but his right hand, which would occasionally stray to nervously ruffle his hair or rub his chin, gave him away. For a split second, I had the urge to turn back, open the door and run away. No one would notice my departure, either way. I was suddenly overcome by a sense of futility about everything I was doing. What was I doing there, trying to meet a man that was practically a stranger to me?

All this time, I could 'use' him any way that I liked in my dreams. But now that I was seeing him up close, so real and independent, with something that I took for audacity that he continued to breathe regardless of my wishes, as if the mysterious 'relationship' that had brought us together had never existed, as if I had never known the feel of his skin or heard the beating of his heart. I had felt him so close to my heart back then. But all of these things only had a place in my dreams. That aloof creature with the don't-talk-to-me-I-bite demeanour was a stranger to me. I couldn't predict what his reaction would be when I shared with him everything I had carefully prepared to tell him. To tell him? Tell him what? I was horrified to discover that I had completely forgotten my words. I was suffering from the notorious accursed blackout and – what was worse – it was too late to turn back.

Papanikolaou had returned, had grabbed me by the arm and was pushing me towards him. Stamatis had stayed behind, gaping at a black beauty; she was apparently one of the models the photographer had used.

'Constantinos, I want to introduce you to a very good friend of mine! Vera Kalogera is an author and a scriptwriter, and she's eager to meet you!'

I shook his hand, only to discover to my great surprise that he wasn't made from the material dreams are made of, but that he was alive, a bit sweaty, and somewhat nervous. I found myself unprepared to meet his eyes that were looking at me searchingly and that were honestly as expressive as in his films.

He was handsome. With a forbidden beauty. With that infuriating favour that nature freely confers on some of her chosen creatures. A hint of lasciviousness played on his lips, but it was overshadowed by the innocence reflected on the rest of his face. He's a child who likes to play, but also a charming man, I instantly thought.

I felt uncomfortable, naked and defenceless in front of him. I was afraid that he would think I was mental, this man I had been staring at for so long without uttering a word.

'Remind me, please, what do I know about you?'

He narrowed his eyes as if he was trying to remember something. He was wearing a dark-hued turtleneck and kept touching his throat nervously.

'Nothing... but, I'm afraid that you will soon find out,' I had somewhat regained my composure.

Papanikolaou had already abandoned us in order to turn his attention to his numerous acquaintances.

'Why?'

'Because I intend to kidnap you!'

'Excuse me?' Visibly uneasy, he clutched at his trousers so hard that they became wrinkled.

Jesus, where did I get the idea to say something like that? I thought and felt embarrassed.

'Perhaps I've already kidnapped you and you haven't realised it yet!' *This is the first time I spout such nonsense,* I was once again embarrassed because of what was coming out of my mouth.

He left his trousers alone and started messing with his hair.

But after the small initial shock, he started playing my game, and even seemed to be enjoying it!

'Huh, interesting! And, are you going to demand ransom?'

'Yes... no... I don't know. Anyway, that's not the issue at hand.'

'Then... You intend to kill me!'

'Ah, no! I can't do that! I may... mistreat you a bit, but these things happen in stories.' I was suddenly afraid that he would think I was crazy and take flight. He actually took a step back, but that was just so he could get me a drink. He didn't even ask me what I would like to drink, he made the choice on my behalf.

I desperately scanned my surroundings for Stamatis and I spotted him a bit further away. He was hanging about next to a plain French woman, trying to flirt with her.

Constantinos returned holding the biggest glass of brandy I had ever seen. As for myself, I really needed that drink he brought me, that ruby alcoholic drink called Calvados.

'So, you were saying?' He pressed his lips together to keep himself from laughing. 'Ah, yes, that you would kidnap me. Does that mean I will be your slave?'

'Not at all! You will be the main character of my story!'

I took a gulp from my drink and felt it burn my insides. I started gaining shreds of courage right away.

'You will put me in a story, if I got it right!'

He was pleased about finally making sense of things.

'Exactly!'

'And what kind of story is this?'

'What kind of story would you like to hear?'

'Any kind of story. I don't mind, as long as it's good.'

'I think it is.'

'And what will I be doing in it?'

'You will laugh, cry, eat melomakarona... You will even dance.'

'One more question. In the end, will you set me free?'

'No, you will!'

'Now I'm confused...'

He had that confused look that made him look absolutely adorable. Seeing the way he pursed his lips, I decided that his eyes weren't the only interesting feature on his face.

'You don't have to. Also, I can't reveal the entire plot to you right away.'

'When then?'

'Tomorrow, perhaps? Do you have any free time?'

While I was explaining the cryptic words I had shared with him, Stamatis came over and introduced himself.

'So, you just arrived today from Athens?' Constantinos absent-mindedly asked him.

'Yes, we came to speak to you, Mr Aravantinos, about the project that I imagine Ms Kalogera talked to you about.'

'By the way, did you have a good flight?' Constantinos said, as if he hadn't heard Stamatis' comment.

'Yes, a very good flight,' Stamatis easily answered.

'Without any turbulence?'

'With nothing of the sort...'

'Without any disturbing dreams?'

We were both puzzled by his persistence.

'And why do I have the feeling that I know you from somewhere?' he asked, suddenly changing the subject and looking at me directly in the eyes as he said these last words.

'Huh? Oh, no, I'm sure you're mistaken.'

'I'm sure I'm not mistaken!'

I soon after bid him goodnight and, after exchanging a

few common pleasantries, I made a hasty exit. I needed some fresh air.

'I'm staying. From what I can see, this is a very interesting exhibition,' Stamatis said meaningfully.

As I made my way through the crowd, I spotted Papanikolaou. He was having a conversation with a beautiful woman in her mid-thirties, who was dressed in a masculine-style suit and was wearing wonderful white-gold earrings. Her hair was gathered at the back of her neck in an elegant chignon. *That must be his wife, Virginie.* I recognized her from the photos I had seen of the two of them in magazines.

I felt great relief when I stepped into the crystal-clear night. I took a deep breath. The pale glow of the lights reflected off the sheen of the freshly scrubbed streets. The illuminated Eiffel Tower dominated the skyline in the background. The air carried bursts of humidity combined with frost. The bistros and restaurants had their doors wide open, ready to welcome the public. I spread open the city map and looked for the nearest tube station. I started walking really fast trying to clear my head.

****

I thought that I had lived one of the most difficult days of my life, but the next day wasn't much better. At around half past eight, I went downstairs to get some breakfast.

Stamatis was already there; he didn't seem to notice my bad mood. He was noisily sipping his coffee and – yes, I wasn't imagining it – some indiscreet gazes had turned towards our table. He was buttering his bread and then adding honey while he chattered on and on about the boobs and drool-worthy bums he had ogled at the exhibition. He was starting to become tedious.

I shook him off and went for a short walk around the city. A sickly sun peered through the clouds, only to go back in hiding behind them a few minutes later. Who could be in the mood for a walk in such lousy weather? A heavy storm broke out soon afterwards. The hail furiously battered the pavements and the marble-lined streets. But when I exited the underground, the sun had reappeared; this time, more vibrant. I lazily strolled towards the shores of the Seine.

The *Bateaux Mouches*, packed with people, gently sliced the river waters. Lovey-dovey couples enjoyed the spring sunshine as they walked on the path holding hands. A pleasant breeze made the tree branches sway. The cafés were full.

Only when I came to stand outside the Gothic masterpiece that had assumed legendary proportions, did I come to realise that everything that had been written about Notre-Dame had been more than deserved. A fabulous demon world that cast ironic glances towards the little people beneath them, birds and grotesque monsters perched on the gables and the obelisks, figures standing unmoving throughout the centuries. In the impressively vast interior of the church, silence and reverence reign. The huge crowd of people, which is buzzing like a beehive outside, is speaking in whispers.

A sudden weariness led me to take the first seat I found available. I stayed there for a while, deep in thought, marvelling at the chapels harmoniously lined one next to the other, the skylights with the wonderful blue stained glass, a sculpture of Pietà, and a 14th century statue of the Virgin which stood on the left. I walked up and down the cross-shaped aisles, I felt wonder at my insignificance, and, finally, I bought a replica gold coin – a souvenir – and left after putting it in my pocket. I felt a bit better. A bit calmer and more settled down.

****

Mr Lamartinie, Constantinos' French agent, lived in an old block of flats in a side road of Champs-Élysées. I rang the ornate brass doorbell, where Mr Lamartinie's name and occupation were listed, and climbed the stairs to the fourth floor, lightly dragging my fingers over the wonderful bannister. I hesitated a long time before knocking on the door.

I couldn't admit even to myself that I lacked the courage to see him again. A pigeon that was perched on the window ledge started pooping quite shamelessly; it seemed to me like an ill omen.

I finally rang the doorbell. Mr Lamartinie himself greeted me at the door. He was a grey-haired fifty-year-old with an athletic figure, dressed in a tartan jacket with a dark-coloured foulard wrapped around his neck; he was also wearing a strained smile.

'Oh, *geia sas*, Greek, ah, Greek,' he sighed with what seemed to me like uncontained joy. 'Good mohning, evening, 'allo, this is *malakas* – Constantinos taught me this,' he explained as he demonstrated his entire knowledge of Greek in a flawless accent, with a heavily pronounced 'L' standing out. Then, he told me, in very bad English, how he had visited two Greek islands, Crete and Rhodes, during the holidays.

'You shouldn't skip on visiting Corfu next time,' was my indifferent quip.

Constantinos was already there. He was talking on his mobile while drinking tea. He had a politely detached – almost distant – attitude, and his gaze gave nothing away. I couldn't read him at all. He was wearing his ordinary daily attire (which I regularly saw him wear in paparazzi shots) of a baggy shirt worn over equally baggy trousers, and trainers, all the while fiddling with his hair.

Soon enough, Mr Lamartinie's assistant, an attractive young French woman with a light gait, brought us coffee. Her skirt rustled cutely as she handed out the folders with all the necessary notes.

'It's not him!' was the first thought I had when I saw him. He wasn't the same man I had met the night before. Who was he? My imagination was in overdrive. Perhaps he has a lookalike. With immense relief, I saw Stamatis appear at that moment.

Finally, a man with unruly hair, eccentric glasses and a rainbow-coloured scarf turned up. He worked for a French production company, from what I could tell.

I gave everyone a copy of the story's summary in French, and also the step outline, where the story's details were briefly described. To Constantinos, I also gave a copy of my book.

'I see,' Constantinos said thoughtfully when he finished reading the paragraph.

'He's just like me,' he remarked. 'The main male character, I mean. He has almost everything that represents me. But he's also something different at the same time, and that's interesting.'

'The truth is that I've seen many of your films and I kept all the elements I liked from them.'

The agent started a detailed discussion with Stamatis; I couldn't understand a thing they were saying and that made me feel very uncomfortable.

'He's asking if they could buy the rights so that they can film it here in France,' Stamatis finally informed me, 'and I told him that it was out of the question, since pre-production has already begun in Greece.'

The French man appeared to scowl at this point.

'The script is really interesting. There are many plot twists, there's humour and, of course, plenty of fairy-tale-like elements, which makes filming incredibly fun. You must already be aware of that, since you know what kind of films I make,' Constantinos cut in. 'The problem is...' he continued with a frown, 'that I'm booked for the next six months. I've signed on with a procedural series that's going to be produced by a French channel. There's nothing I can do about that, I'm sorry...'

After he dropped his bomb, he calmly continued to drink his tea.

'Yes, Mr Lamartine told me the same thing,' Stamatis affirmed, 'but unfortunately, we can't wait that long. We plan to start filming in two to three months at the latest.'

So, the discussion halted at the first dead end, which didn't seem to be the only one.

'Also, there are a few parts in this story that are a cause of concern for me,' he said, somewhat thoughtfully. 'For example, Ms Kalogera, there are many scenes where I'm supposed to be smoking, and I'm trying to quit. I also have doubts about the ending you have planned. I would like a more unexpected turn of events, an extra twist in the plot would make it more interesting, I believe,' he continued as if he was talking to himself.

'We could have a more thorough discussion about all of this if and when you decide to accept our offer,' I said stiffly, my hopes a step away from collapsing.

'May I ask you one more question, Ms Kalogera?' His look was completely different, suggestive and full of licentious innuendos. He obviously was the same man I had met the night before and he was ready to utter something outrageous. 'Do you enjoy having sex?'

He said it so softly, so indifferently, that the word in question was barely audible.

'Excuse me?'

If once upon a time the heavens had opened up for me, couldn't the earth do the same at that moment and swallow me whole?

'I'm not asking you a difficult question. I simply asked you if you like making love; is there another way to say it?'

He continued to look at me with a teasing smile, a challenge in his eyes and his forehead creased in his attempt to appear clever. I felt the urge to slap him.

I took a look around, feeling incredibly awkward. The French people, who didn't understand many of the things we were saying anyway, were whispering something among themselves. Stamatis had turned red in an attempt not to burst out into guffaws.

'I don't see what that has to do with anything...'

'If you do me the favour and answer, I'll explain it to you right away!'

'Well... Yes... I guess so...' I finally said hastily, as though I was eager to get rid of the words.

'Great,' Constantinos said, quite pleased, and got up from his chair. He strolled around the room and then came to stand over my shoulders. He bent over me and leaned close to my ear. 'Because I don't like working with repressed people,' he finished explaining his way of thinking and made me reach even higher levels of nervousness. 'They are ill-tempered and crabby; they always create problems in their line of work, in their love lives, everywhere.'

I had never heard of a weirder way of choosing colleagues. I instantly disliked him at that moment. What was the reason for this provocative, aggressive and rude behaviour towards me? I could find no explanation. But, of course! Politeness, modesty, and speaking softly weren't the ingredients this gentleman had used to build his legend. Everybody knew that.

I continued to feel an intense dislike for him for a few

more minutes until he grabbed me by the arm. 'Can I talk to you in private?' He held me back in the large hall with the colonial furniture while the others headed towards the entrance hall.

'Vera, you don't mind if I call you by your first name, do you?'

'Go ahead...' I mumbled with a frown.

He paced around the room a few times, without saying a word, and then he stood next to the window. A light drizzle had started falling outside. Small droplets of rain peppered the windowpanes. I heard the wind blowing furiously over the roofs of the Parisian houses.

'You said that you've seen my films, right?'

'Yes, many times. The most recent ones, I mean.'

'And did you write this story with me in mind?'

'Exactly!'

'Which of my parts do you think is the most interesting?'

'I don't know... All of them have elements that I like... Which one would you say particularly represents you?' I shot back at him.

I sensed that I had to watch out, I could smell danger. From where exactly? You could never tell with this man. He abruptly turned towards me and I saw a playful – bordering on sarcastic – smile under a pair of darker than dark, sombre eyes. It wasn't the first time I had sensed that captivating ambiguity which surrounded him like a gift or a curse.

'I'd say that I find Mr Leroi quite charming. He has all that strange charm that somebody meets in dark characters.'

'I agree with you.'

'I'm glad!'

I was relieved. I couldn't wait to get up and leave. His questions were leading to some kind of trap, I felt invisible nets wrapping around me, snares and claws lurked in the air.

'I'm glad we both agree!'

There was a strange echo in his words, like the spider's triumph, when it has skilfully weaved its web and sees its unsuspecting victim approaching.

'Because I have a message for you from this guy.'

My whole body froze. My mouth felt dry. I wondered how this scene would end though I didn't have the courage to watch it till the end. Would it be too rude of me to get up and leave in the middle?

'He sends... Well... He sends his regards! And kisses... And I'm not sure... Not really... but I think there's something I've forgotten.' He seemed to be worried that he would be scolded for forgetting. His evil look had evaporated.

'What?' I managed to utter. 'What did you say?'

I honestly thought that I had misheard. For a few moments, I really believed that I was having another one of those dreams, those unexplainable and mystical dreams I had welcomed in the past. Dizziness, something like vertigo, closed in around me and I was afraid that I would faint.

Constantinos let out a fake laugh as he witnessed my distress. It was as though he wanted me to understand how false this laugh was, to have no doubts left. He came and stood beside me, laying a gentle hand on my shoulder. I flinched as if I had been stung by a jellyfish.

'I don't see why you reacted like that. It was just a joke,' he clumsily tried to explain himself. He couldn't possibly be such a bad actor. I was so ticked off that I finally snapped out of feeling flustered.

'To tell you the truth, I didn't find it very funny,' I frostily told him as I walked to the door.

'And by the way...' (This will show him! I would never again let him make fun of me so blatantly.) 'Make sure to have a better memory next time!'

He was staring at me blankly, with a cold-blooded murderer's certainty of his victim's inescapable demise.

I slammed the door behind me and grabbed Stamatis by the sleeve.

'We're leaving this place!' I was very near hysterics.

'What's got into you?' he asked, quite miffed. I had interrupted his drooling over Lamartinie's pretty secretary.

****

What does he know? How could he possibly know? What are all these strange things he's telling me? It took me a long time to get over the shock. Dozens of tiny dreams beat their wings within my chest like canaries that see a cat's claws. It was my duty to protect them.

I won't let him fool me with his tricks. I decided to react. *If he knows so much about me, I certainly know as much about him. He is the hero of my story.* How could anyone imagine a book character keeping things from the author of said book? It's unthinkable! *But perhaps all of this is nothing more than a ploy of my imagination, a completely random event,* I thought to myself a bit more calmly. 'I'll find your secrets, you bastard, I will. I just need to remember!' I said to myself as I shivered from the cold and the anxiety I felt. My feet had started hurting from walking too much.

'*What does he know?*' I asked myself the same question for the hundredth time as I went to bed. '*How could he possibly know about the things I see in my dreams? I guess it's a case of a guilty conscience not needing any accusers,*' I concluded so that I could finally get some sleep. Apparently, none of this meant anything; the guy just loved playing games.

Dawn was breaking in rosy ribbons over the dark roofs of Paris and I was still 'inspecting' his body in my dreams. Did he have a scar or something that meant he was a wizard? But he kept evading me and dissolving like a ghost. In the end, I thought that I noticed Harry Potter's scar on his forehead.

****

On my third day in Paris, the surprises kept coming. A bouquet of red roses was waiting for me at the reception desk in the morning. 'I'm sorry if I offended you. I really didn't mean to,' the note that came with it said. 'Let's have dinner tonight and continue our conversation from where we left off.' He had added an address and detailed information on how to find the restaurant. '8.30pm, I'll be waiting. Au revoir. C.A.'

Another curious incident seemed strange to me that morning, but I didn't give it much thought at first. A lady (dark-haired, wearing a long colourful skirt and a beret on her head) was having breakfast by herself at the table next to mine.

She got up to leave – she had her luggage with her – but forgot a book on her seat. Deep in thought, I let a few minutes trickle by before I reacted. My eyes were drawn to the book. I didn't know why I was staring at it so intently: it had a shabby white cover and a title that said everything and nothing: *Thought Power* by Annie Besant.

'There was a lady here... she just left,' I said to the receptionist. 'A Greek woman,' but I didn't go on... Without even thinking it through, I decided with blind impulsiveness to keep the book for myself.

'There are no other Greek guests in the hotel apart from you,' the young man informed me after checking the hotel guest list. 'Is there something you wanted?'

I didn't mention anything about the forgotten book. I returned to my room and packed it in my suitcase. Soon, I forgot all about it.

****

In the end, it was as I had feared: I spent the whole morning doing something that I normally detested. Shopping for clothes and shoes. 'You should go to *Printemps*,' the receptionist advised me, 'it's a big department store. You will find whatever you need there.' After leaving behind a bunch of sales persons frustrated by my indecisiveness, I returned to the hotel in the afternoon carrying a lot of shopping bags, with my credit card maxed out, and having regretted buying all these things. The black uneven dress with the embroidered flowers turned out to be too sexy. I was hoping that the pink mohair cardigan that came with the dress would cover up this fact. As for the boots, they had higher heels than I was used too.

But when I got off at the *Place d' Italie* metro station, wearing the leather coat that I had had the foresight to bring with me, I began to feel wonderful. I didn't remember ever having been the recipient of so many appreciative male looks before.

'You look very beautiful,' Constantinos absent-mindedly noticed when he saw me. It didn't sound at all like a compliment but rather like a polite remark.

The bistro was warm and quiet with a minimalist aesthetic. Discreet chandeliers hung low from the ceiling; they almost touched the tables with the linen tablecloths. The red leather lining of the armchairs and the sofas was the only sign of luxury. 'This place specialises in Alsatian cuisine, but it also has dishes for more everyday tastes available,' he explained to me. 'It was founded a century ago. I like it here; the food is amazing, and it's the hangout for many of my colleagues,' he added.

He was having a Kirsch cocktail while he was waiting for me, and he ordered the same for me without asking.

He was quite nervous and awkward. It was as though he didn't know what to do with his hands. 'Since I quit smoking, I don't know what to do with my hands,' he told me as an excuse and started perusing the menu.

'Do all stars act like that in their private moments?' I was looking at him with a tender expression that I rushed to hide. In the half-light of the restaurant, he seemed rather pale and appeared to have lost weight; nothing reminded me of the bright creature I knew. I glanced at the menu. A thousand questions that had nothing to do with ordering dinner were making my tongue tingle.

'Do you always live in my dreams, Constantinos? Do you know what I dreamt of last night?' I was burning to ask him. Instead, the only thing I could utter was this:

'What is cassoulet? ... And sauerkraut?'

'Don't order any of those, you won't like them,' he abruptly replied.

I preferred to keep myself otherwise occupied instead of starting a clumsy interrogation that I had a feeling would have no substantial results. It was obvious that he was still unwilling to confide in me. Despite everything I felt, I kept myself – with great difficulty – from blurting out: *'Do you know what an important part you have played in my life? Do you know how precious you are to me?'* Instead, I said: 'I'll take a rabbit and hazelnut terrine,' relieved that I had managed to control my impulses. He ordered sea bass in a cumin butter sauce.

'I'd like to order the sauerkraut too,' I stubbornly insisted. 'Isn't it a local delicacy? I want to try it!'

'Fine, but I warned you.'

A while ago, I had noticed that the bright-eyed young

woman with the cute bob sitting at the table next to ours kept stealing glances at Constantinos. At that moment, she got up and approached him with a shy smile. She asked him for something, probably an autograph. With an uncomfortable air and with annoyance evident in his face, he shook his head 'no', and the girl returned to her table with her head lowered. She looked so crestfallen that I sympathised with her sadness.

'I get incredibly annoyed with things like that,' he said in an unapologetic tone.

'You can't do everything possible to gain publicity and then act offended when people recognise you. There's a price for everything,' I thought to myself, but I decided not to make any comments. I wasn't the ideal person to give lessons in proper conduct; I wasn't fit for it at all.

We started a neutral conversation on creative cuisine, which had already been quite popular in France for many years. I assured him that Athens wasn't lacking in that respect; dozens of restaurants with excellent food were springing up everywhere. When our order finally arrived, I discovered that the French cuisine was at least worthy of its reputation. Though not divine, it was mildly exquisite. With the sauerkraut being the exception. He was looking at me with a smile as we chatted; I was half-heartedly picking at the sour cabbage until he couldn't stand it any longer and started laughing.

'If you don't like it, just don't eat it. I'm not going to scold you. I'm not even going to say "I told you so".'

'No, I'll eat it! Since I insisted on ordering it, I'll eat it,'

I pompously declared, despite feeling that one more bite would make me throw up.

He observed me for a while, without saying anything. 'Who taught you to do that?' he calmly asked. 'Who taught you to punish yourself, Vera?'

It was tragically funny, but true. It had taken 35 years of my life, a failed marriage to a serial cheater, writing a book, travelling to Paris and ordering a random dish in order to realise the nature of the worm that had been slowly devouring me for so many years. I had obsessively continued to torture myself with the naivety of a martyr. Because of the wrong choices I had made, my foolish determination to see them through, and the egoism I liked to call dignity. And why did I do all that? Because I had been unable to live up to the expectations that had been imposed upon me. Because I hadn't satisfied the irrational demands of an insatiable and merciless superego. Because I had never been the proper daughter my mother wanted!

'Nobody...' I said in surprise, '... nobody. Let's forget about it!'

Only after we opened the third bottle of wine did he seem to relax. And when the atmosphere between us shifted to something 'warmer', I decided that it was the proper moment to launch ... an attack...

'I would like you to know something ... as far as the discussion we had yesterday is concerned,' I adopted my serious look. 'If you don't accept this part, no one else is going to play it. The film won't be produced, no matter how devastated this would make me feel. It's simply the truth.'

I watched him for a few minutes as he silently stirred his crème brûlée.

'Look, Vera, if we are to work together at some point, there's something you need to know about me. I'm the one driving. You may have the keys, but I'm the one behind the steering wheel.' (Just a figure of speech, he explained, because he hadn't touched a steering wheel since his accident).

'I don't like being pressured into anything, and even less to be blackmailed in this way.' He had a very sweet smile, but you could easily discern the prickly nature hidden underneath all this sweetness.

'I know!'

'I'm glad, that's a good start. But, since I don't like keeping you in suspense – here's the reason why I invited you here – I'm going to tell you a secret. I want this part! You're right, no one else should play it; I'm going to be the one to do it. That's my decision.'

'I know,' I almost squealed with joy. I sent him a beaming smile.

'You know many things... In your book, you describe me pretty vividly in various scenes.'

'When did you find the time to read it?'

'Last night. I must admit that I really liked it.'

'Thank you.'

'So, will you tell me where you learned all these things about me? Are you stalking me, Vera?'

'Yes... no... I mean...'

The caramelized apple felt stuck in my throat. This wasn't the tarte Tatin's lucky day.

'...I just let my imagination run free.' This wasn't entirely a lie.

We left the bistro at around 10 o' clock, and, as usual, it was raining and a hellish wind was blowing. The street was empty and dark. Droplets of rain lashed at my face, but it was good for me as it pulled me out of my daze. I didn't think of opening my umbrella, so I walked in the rain by his side for a while, till the taxi arrived to pick us up.

'Shall we go for another coffee or even a drink?' he whispered to me in the taxi.

'Where to exactly?'

'Some place where you won't be able to escape when it's convenient for you.'

Now *that* was a doubled-edged comment. Was he or wasn't he flirting with me?

'Alright, lead the way.'

I closed my eyes for a few moments. I felt light-headed; I was unsure if it was due to the wine, or his aftershave, or even worse, to the fact that he was so close to me, so unbearably close. If I made the slightest movement, I would be able to touch him, and then I would be unable to resist, to stop myself from kissing him. But then I would make a complete fool of myself; I could sense it.

****

The taxi drove through illuminated damp streets, the Boulevard Vincent Auriol, crossed to the east side of the river and dropped us off at the Cité, Quai des Orfèvres.

A five-storied building with wrought-iron balconies rose before us. The elevator with the metal gate began its slow ascent to the top floor after he pressed the button. The crystal-covered lamp emitted a mesmerizing light. After we exited the elevator, we found ourselves in a half-lit corridor with a nostalgic scent. The sound of our footsteps was drowned in the green carpet.

The door to the flat opened with a slight creak, which was followed by my muffled exclamation. I had seen this place before! Everything was just like I remembered! The rust-coloured sofa, the thick carpet, the vintage armchairs. The Klimt painting with the two eternal lovers lost in a passionate kiss that was hanging from the wall left me no room for doubt.

I had been in this house before, but it was on a different night, in a dream.

'Oh my God!'

'What's wrong?'

'Nothing,' I hesitated. 'I just have the impression that this house seems familiar... that I've been here before.'

'It must be the so-called déjà vu,' he smiled and headed for the kitchen.

'Yes... I guess so...'

'Do you want coffee or would you like a drink?'

'Some white wine, if you have some.'

I took my boots off and made myself comfortable on the couch.

'Can I ask you a nosy question?' I put on a mischievous

smile when he returned with our drinks. 'Is this where you bring all of your ... lady friends?'

He didn't seem at all discomfited by the question.

'Once in a while. Does that bother you?'

'Not at all. In fact, it's the exact opposite. It's a very warm and erotic place. I really like it.'

I inched much, much closer to him while I stifled a playful giggle.

'I wouldn't want you to think that you are such a case...'

'Don't spoil it... I would like you to make me believe that I actually am such a case. I would really appreciate it.' I was struggling to make my voice sound deeper and sexier, uncertain about my success.

I embraced him tightly; he was warm, so real and human that I was near tears. I started unbuttoning his shirt. I had already discarded all of my reluctance concerning mixing business with pleasure at the front door. A sudden and completely unexplained tenderness came over me. I wanted to hold him in my arms and whisper sweet nothings to him, but instead of that, I whispered something naughty in his ear and then I realised that things weren't going so well. He seemed apathetic, showing no interest at all. He looked wooden, completely out of his depth, and made no attempt to hide it.

'Have I done something wrong?' I pulled back and looked at him questioningly.

He got up from the sofa and walked to the window. He nervously stroked his hair without saying anything.

'Look, Vera. It's not that I don't like you, but ... let's say that I'm not used to all of this any longer. I mean...'

'There's no need to apologise. You don't have to...'

And after I counted my fingers many times and found I had exactly ten, and after finding every word I wished to utter unnecessary and foolish...

'I have to go,' I stuttered, 'I have to pack, I have a flight to catch tomorrow morning.'

'I lied to you earlier,' he continued absent-mindedly, as if he was already in another dimension where I couldn't intrude. 'I never bring women here... not anymore... not since then... I only come here when I want to relax or study a script. I'm sorry if I gave you the wrong impression.'

'I understand. It was my mistake. I hope that all of this won't have a negative effect on our collaboration.' I extended my hand towards him but he pointedly ignored it.

'Anyway, I don't want you for ... that.'

The insinuation was more than clear. He could have said: 'I don't want you just for **that** and given me a small hint of happiness. But, he didn't say that.

'Then why did you bring me here? What do you want from me, Constantinos?' I leaned back in my seat, deeply weary.

'To show you my place. So that you could tell me if you like it.' His playful look convinced me that he was messing with me. 'What do I want? That's a good question. I'd really like to know ... who are you really, Vera?'

Who was I? This was a serious question. My brain short-circuited once again and refused to work properly.

Thankfully, the pretty phrases that I had been preparing for days came to my rescue.

'I'm... I'm a reflection,' I said with difficulty, 'a reflection of your own image. I'm what you imagine I could be. No matter what that is; it's me.' And I truly felt that I could play any part for his sake. 'You lead the way, I just follow. I'm something like an extension of you...'

I was glad that I had finally managed to utter even a tenth of everything I had to say to him. I also wanted to talk to him about the dreams, about all the nights I wrote about him, and open my heart to him in a way I had never done with anyone else before. But he interrupted me with a frown on his face.

'You use pretty words! But they sound too much like something out of a book.'

'That's the only way I know how to talk!'

'Don't get upset. I didn't mean to offend you. What you're telling me brings me even closer to the answer I've been looking for. So, your stories are what I want from you.'

'My stories? What stories?'

'Didn't you tell me I'm your inspiration? That you wrote this book for me?'

'Yes, I did say that!'

'Great! Then, your head will be able to come up with more beautiful stories for me, isn't that so?'

'Yes... I guess so...' In reality, I was capable of writing anything for his sake, but I decided not to share this with him.

'That's what I want from you... to tell me a few beautiful

stories. And, of course, I'll be the main hero in all of them. I have to be the lead. Do we have a deal?'

'You will have to continue being my inspiration for this to happen.'

He gave me a wide smile and the sky seemed to become clearer over this city that had yet to see the slightest sign of spring.

'And what do I have to do?'

'Nothing in particular. Just be yourself. That'll be enough for me.'

'I knew we would get to the difficult part. There's a slight problem here. If I tell you that I honestly don't know my true self, will you believe me? If they asked me to play this part, I'd find myself in a very awkward position.' He burst into laughter, obviously pleased with himself for managing to say something so witty.

'Good. Then, let me tell you!' I blurted out spontaneously without realising the gravity of everything I was promising. 'Let me study you and describe you, and then you can tell me if it's accurate.'

'You're very kind,' he said after a while, thoughtfully.

Kind? Damn it! So, my efforts to come across as a bold woman and a femme fatale had been in vain. I finally had to set this incongruous role aside and accept that you can't turn yourself into a bad girl. You either are one or you aren't!

'The best part of me is what lives inside you,' he continued, engrossed in his thoughts. 'I believed that I had lost this part of me for good, and now someone unexpectedly has given it back to me.'

'I like the things you say,' I told him with a wide grin, 'and they're quite romantic. I never expected this side of you, to be honest.'

'I have others too. Just wait and see.' He sent me a look that made the room feel warmer; it even escaped the confines of the room, and probably affected the entire city. I was capable of going to the ends of the world, and even further, just to see that look again.

I kissed him on the cheek and got up to leave, bidding him a hasty goodnight before I closed the door behind me. I ran down the stairs almost in complete darkness. It was the only way to avoid making the most passionate romantic declaration I was ever to make in my entire life. Or to indefinitely postpone it. The words I wanted to tell him hadn't ripened yet. Nor was he ready to hear them.

A small amateur band of three musicians was standing next to a nearby fountain. One of them was playing the accordion while the other two were still tuning their guitars. As if by an invisible sign, they started playing a melancholic song as soon as I exited the building. It was from Bizet's Carmen:

> '...L' amour est un oiseau rebelle
> Que nul ne peut apprivoiser,
> Et c'est bien en vain qu'on l'appelle,
> S'il lui convient de refuser...'

The melody haunted my steps for quite a while. The Seine flowed silently down its everlasting routes; wise and icily indifferent.

> *Love is a rebellious bird*
> *that no one can tame,*
> *and if you call for it, it'll be quite in vain*
> *for it's in its nature to say no.*

My blurred gaze (at that very moment, I realised that I was crying without being able to explain why) kept me from noticing that Paris was looking at me through a thousand eyes; it wasn't my imagination. Posters announcing his participation in that popular mystery series had filled the streets.

> *Love is a gipsy child*
> *It knows no rules.*

I left Paris the very next day with mixed feelings and with the sense that I had been crushed by a steamroller. At least one, perhaps even more. I wasn't sure. But, there was also the same painful resignation that he had left his mark on me. Or that I was carrying him within me, just like I used to. Since when, I wonder. Since always?

> *If you don't love me, I love you,*
> *But, if I love you, then beware!*

****

When the plane took off, I discovered the forgotten book; it was the first thing I touched when I opened my handbag. It was supposed to be in my suitcase. I began to absent-mindedly leaf through it. It wasn't a scientific treatise, as I had originally thought.

It was about the transferability of thought through vibrations first in the physical body and then in the astral body, which generates waves in the brain's dense molecules. These vibrations affect the physical plane and the waves spread out until they reach another brain and affect it too, the book said. Essential prerequisite: the people who 'communicate' in this way must be kindred spirits and there has to be a genuine longing for communication without the interference of any selfish considerations.

It went on to explain that consciousness is not subject to the physical limitations of space but is wherever a person is able to respond to its call. And a special chapter was devoted to cases of communication in the astral world during sleep, dream scenes that are turned into a memory after waking.

'The dream is the recording of an out-of-body meeting and should be treated as such[5].'

What had I done while I was in the dark? And how could so much knowledge reside in ignorance? The answers to my questions, the affirmations to all of my anxieties were in this book that an unknown woman had randomly left behind.

And this wonderful feeling of completeness that I 'knew' all this, that I had sensed it long ago. The only thing missing had been its theoretical verification. Now, I had that too.

Chapter 6

The World of Dreaming and of the Universe

'People travel to another world when they are asleep. A lighter, more delicate world. That's why they often feel as if they are flying. When you are asleep, a part of yourself, your etheric body, wanders into the etheric plane. It meets other souls there and shares information and experiences with them.'

Melina was speaking calmly and appeared completely sure of everything she was talking about. She had the exact same look when she told me about her brother's marriage and her relationship with her sister-in-law and their adorable children. This woman has an Indian beauty. Her eyes, the only part in a plump body that demonstrated intense intellectual activity, exuded warmth and energy.

I never thought that I would meet such a self-aware and completely happy person in this corrupted world we live in. Melina gave off a sense of kindness and generosity; she was so understanding that I felt comforted just looking at her. She talked with childlike enthusiasm and always had a wide smile on her face, as if she wanted to enfold every poor creature into her arms and gift them with a precious drop of love.

'So, do you believe that we are able to get in touch with this world through dreams by using the power of thought? That it's possible to 'meet' a person who's far away from us?'

'I don't simply believe it. I'm sure of it. I have even made a successful attempt. The power of thought is immense. We are connected to the Universal Network. Distance is inconsequential. You can be hundreds of miles away from the other person. Every time we think, a type of energy, which could generally be compared to electricity, is produced. The nature of this energy is positive when it comes from balanced and creative persons. You must have noticed that work performed under the guidance of inspiration is the source of joy, peace and trust. This feeling is softer and sweeter in the upper levels. There, we can sense Love and life's abundance that leads to the state of Cosmic Harmony.'

I didn't know what to say.

'Melina, what do you really think is wrong with me?'

I spent so much time chatting with this strange woman, as if I had known her for years. I opened my heart and revealed my burning secrets to her. As long as I believed that it was all in my mind, I didn't feel the urge to go deeper in search of answers. But, I had reached ground zero. The questions I had demanded answers. It was a matter of life and death to find them. That book in the airplane was just the beginning, the thing that set everything in motion.

'You were ill,' she said with a warm smile, 'and now you are starting to get better. Your illness was caused by pent-up bitterness, disappointment and anger. By established guilt and remorse. You were weighed down by toxic layers that have just begun to retreat. Isn't that so? No illness can resist this treatment – the best time is when the patient is asleep – except if it's caused by karma.'

'And who did this? Because I had no idea of any of this!'

'Your Guide. You have a guardian angel up there. He sent Constantinos to you, be sure of that! We all have a guardian angel, but most of us can't hear him. There's so much noise around us. You have to submerge yourself in the silence of your mind in order to be able to hear him.'

How simple and believable everything unexplained that had happened to me sounded when Melina explained it. It wasn't just that she had opened a door for me to a new world full of wonders. The most important thing was that all of these things involved a different set of moral principles and I was wholly unprepared.

'Then... There... Let's call it the dreamscape, I felt that there were very strong bonds between me and this person... I don't know if you understand me. A stranger, someone who held no significance for me up to that very moment.'

'Something like this only happens to kindred spirits. Human beings gain this endless devotion, deep love, and this kind of higher spiritual communication only at the end of their evolutionary process. It's so wonderful, what you're experiencing, isn't it?'

In the end, life is full of strange things that don't have to seem real to be real. Just like Truth.

****

It hadn't been my idea to go to Melina. Vicky had come up with the idea a few days earlier when we were at my house – Panagiotis, Vicky's new boyfriend, was also there.

We were sitting comfortably on big throw pillows on the floor and talking about many things while munching on nuts when I decided to share the questions I had about the inexplicable mysteries of my past dreams with them. It was the first time I had talked to anyone about this subject. As it turned out, it was obviously a bad idea.

'I know it sounds unexplainable, even bizarre, but that's the truth,' I finished my recount straight off the reel.

'Jesus Christ,' Vicky said in amazement, her eyes wide as saucers.

'Strange, very strange,' Panagiotis commented. He let me finish my story, but he was looking at me as though an alien being was standing in front of him. 'It can't be; there must be some sort of explanation!' he muttered uneasily. 'There must be a logical explanation, it can't be!'

His rational mind couldn't accept the unexplained so easily.

'It sure is strange,' Vicky said. 'How could you possibly keep seeing the same man and him asking you... I mean... being your inspiration when writing stories? Could the guy be a psychic?' she timidly suggested.

I threw her a withering look.

'What does that have to do with anything?'

'It doesn't, but it might,' she insisted. 'Don't many

wealthy and famous people get involved in such dark situations?'

'Nonsense, I believe that it's simply an uncanny coincidence,' Panagiotis concluded with relief. 'He happened to say something accurate by chance and you clung to it because you know what they say about grasping at straws...'

'Yes, that's what I've come to believe, too...' I unwillingly mumbled. I didn't want to believe something like this at all, but I didn't have a more credible explanation.

'Let me get this straight, you see him in your sleep, he says and does many weird things, then you meet him in real life, and he lets you believe that he also knows you. How do you explain all of this?' Vicky calmly asked me, seeing the despair in my eyes.

'I don't know... I can't explain it, and that's what has caught me unprepared. And you remember from school how I hated being caught unprepared by the teachers. So, I haven't done my homework this time, as well ...At least, not yet.' I fell about laughing, finally letting myself relax.

'So...is Mr Aravantinos handsome?' Vicky gave me a look flooded in innuendos as they were preparing to leave.

'Handsome, yes... and very peculiar.'

'I hope he doesn't turn out to be handsomely disappointing,' Vicky said in an obviously sarcastic tone. Apparently, since "once bitten, twice shy", she checked every potential romantic prospect for sharp teeth, even mine. 'Listen,' she said with sudden inspiration just as the front door was ready to close behind her, 'perhaps Melina can help you with all of this!'

'Melina who?'

'Yiannis Argyriou's sister, do you remember him?'

Yiannis had been the most popular boy in our high school. Tall, dark-haired, brown-eyed and with an athletic build. All of us girls were crazy about him; we would all bend over backwards to reach any wayward balls first and return them when he played basketball. But, unapproachable and arrogant as he was, he didn't notice any of us. And then rumours started circulating that he wasn't the warmest ... admirer of the fairer sex; we all got a slap in the face and calmed down.

'So,' Vicky continued with profundity, 'Melina used to dabble in eastern philosophies, such as Zen, yoga, karma and all the rest since back then. Why don't you give her a call? She delved deeply into these matters!'

'Maybe... I don't know... We'll see.'

How could I call an old acquaintance after so many years and start bothering her? I had never been particularly friendly with her.

I was left all alone once more to ruminate on the mysteries of Paris. I was on the edge of torturous indecision, with a horrible tension dogging my steps and leaving me unable to relax for a single moment.

I was anxious for a message from him, a phone call, anything that would confirm his presence to me, his thoughts. He didn't even visit me in my sleep anymore, even though I desperately called for him, so that he could give me one of those dreamy hugs that made me feel as though someone were giving me the world.

It would be better if he didn't accept the part. It will save us a lot of trouble. I had no idea what kind of premonition was talking from within me in such a degrading voice. I couldn't even bear to imagine how many and how big these troubles would be. I didn't even know the new lines that would be added to the script; nobody let me read it so I had the illusion that I was the one writing it and that I could very well pull the strings of fate and of the characters in this tale.

****

I did meet Melina. Completely by chance. A blind urge pushed me to enter an occult bookshop during a day of torrential rain. I spent quite a while in there, turning the pages of sometimes naïve, sometimes incomprehensible, books until I decided that none of them lived up to my expectations. I thought of giving up.

Then I heard a woman's voice behind me, a voice that could only be made of velvet, judging by the warmth and empathy it exuded.

'Are you looking for something in particular, Vera? May I assist you in any way?'

I turned around.

'Yes, it's really you! You haven't changed at all,' she said excitedly. 'It might seem strange, but I've been thinking about you these last couple of days,' Melina explained to me a little later. 'Yiannis mentioned something about you at

some point. You've written a book that was recently published, isn't that so?'

The sister of my old classmate was one of the bookshop's
three owners, though I struggled to recognize her because of
her weight gain.

Somehow like this, I confirmed – with what certainty
balancing on a tight rope can offer – that nothing in my life
happened by chance. Not even in this story. Someone had
to give me answers about all of this, and this someone had
been found... as if an unknown force had sent her to me in
a magical way.

****

In the afternoon of the following day, Venetis and I had
planned to meet at Avramoglou's office. May was well on its
way and, as everybody knows, it's the season when it's completely normal for the birdies to sing, the bees to buzz, the
flowers to bloom, and the fish ... to do nothing in particular.
Of course, all the above belonged in some idyllic countryside
because a tribe of humans from another planet, which was
desert-like, grey and without any countryside, had come to
live in Athens. These people built this city in their own image: with concrete, bricks, iron and hot asphalt.

'How did it go, Vera? Did you work things out with
Aravantinos?' Avramoglou sarcastically asked me after he
finished adding sugar to his coffee, signing a few papers and,
naturally, lighting up his ever-present cigar.

'"Our guy" doesn't have any free time; he's very busy,' Stamatis butted in.

'I believe that he'll accept the part in the end,' I said with certainty.

'What makes you believe that?' They both seemed surprised.

'Just ... a hunch,' I said with a cryptic smile, only to earn an irritated look from the producer. 'He told me so himself,' I finally explained.

'Look, in any case, we need to have some alternative options on the bench. For example...' Venetis didn't have time to finish his sentence.

At that moment, Evelina Agriotis stormed into the office swaying her hips; dazzling, and incredibly sexy. Her hair was a fiery red; her neckline plunged almost to her navel; her black trousers were skintight and her heels were ten inches high. She started giving kisses, hugs and sugary sweet words to everyone in sight while you could swear that fragrant flowery bouquets flooded the place. She had given birth to her daughter a few months ago but nothing on her flawless silhouette gave away her recent pregnancy.

'What does this rabid sex kitten have to do with my heroine?' I was dumbfounded.

'Don't worry, we will smarten her up,' Stamatis whispered, noticing my panic.

'Baby, what do I hear?' she playfully asked Venetis as she sat on the arm of his chair and leaned on him. 'Are we in discussions with Aravantinos?'

'We are not! Ms Kalogera is insisting on it and is making our lives very difficult,' Avramoglou interjected with ill temper.

'Pantelis! I want him! I want him! I want him!' She stamped her stiletto heel three times on the floor and pouted with babyish coyness.

'Who?' Venetis asked. He had been stupidly staring at her all this time, and not just staring, he was practically devouring her with his eyes.

'Aravantinos! We'll make an amazing couple, don't you think so too, sweetheart?' she asked me.

'Yes, certainly,' I gulped and threw Avramoglou a look.

He was glaring at Evelina with the obvious intent of throttling her... and then throwing her off the third floor, perhaps.

'Yes, I also believe that he is the best choice for the part,' Venetis said.

Avramoglou banged his hand on the table.

'Stop all this talk about Aravantinos right now. We have other issues to deal with. As if everything else weren't enough, we also have to deal with Aravantinos' playing at being a diva! And why doesn't he give us a straight answer about his intentions? So that we could know how to proceed?'

'He first has to tie up a few loose threads with a French TV network,' I patiently explained.

'I will wait for twenty days! Not a minute longer,' Avramoglou threatened. 'Then, we will take another route. I already have many distinguished actors begging me for this part!'

We then discussed the permits we would need to get from embassies and consulates in order to be allowed to film in

Germany and reached the major issue of casting the part of the Jewish Man. After many slanging matches, we agreed, to my great joy, on Minas Hatzipetridis. A great figure of the old Greek cinema, he had received many awards in local and international festivals; the character actor was a safe option for a supporting, but very demanding, role.

'So... how did you finally convince him to accept?' Stamatis with his eternally silly smile tried to pump me for information. 'Don't tell me you slept with him so quickly!'

I almost choked with laughter.

'Yeah, right... as if Aravantinos would be dying to have me in his bed!'

'Don't say that. I saw the way he was looking at you...'

'Can I ask you something? Is sex the only thing on your mind?'

'Of course not! There's also fucking!'

'Is there any difference between the two?'

'Yeah! Fucking is a one-time thing; after a couple of times, you get closer to the other person, so you have sex, and after the third time, it's a relationship. I can show you what I mean some time, if you want!' He was very pleased with himself for being able to blurt so much bullshit.

'Go to hell!' I shot at him between bursts of laughter as I left the office. But I instantly remembered something and rushed back in.

'Pantelis, I'm sending a young man to see you for the part of Alexander. He's a very good guy, a new talent. I've worked with him in a soap opera.'

'Send him to me,' Venetis absent-mindedly said, his eyes fixedly trained on Evelina's bust. 'What's his name?'

'Alexander Papazisis. I'd like to ask you to look after him. This boy has a bright future!'

'Ok!' he said while his gaze went on feasting on the delicious body of the female protagonist, his eyes gradually slipping downwards.

****

The twenty days of the deadline passed and May had also come to an end. Filming was to start at the end of July and still no news from Paris. I literally felt that I was drowning; on one hand, there was the heat and smog; on the other, there was my endless anxiety and Avramoglou frothing at the mouth, which made my life pure hell.

The worst part was that I didn't have any dreams worth mentioning to warn me about what would happen or give me some inspiration. After what occurred in Paris, I got scared and without making a conscious decision, I went and locked my dreams up.

On the last day of May, I sat down, penned a telegraphic note and faxed it to Mr Lamartinie, FAO Mr Aravantinos. *'Constantinos, I'm sorry, but we don't have any more time at our disposal. You have to give us an answer ASAP. I hope and wish that it will be a positive one. Anxiously awaiting your news. Take care. Vera.'*

Three days later, I got a call from Stamatis.

'Good news,' he told me happily. '"Our guy" is due to come to Athens next week. He just announced it to us.'

'Great,' I said with unnatural calmness. I could finally breathe easily.

On the same night, a deep voice, like an old beloved song that lulls you to sleep, caressed my tired nerves. It put them back together, piece by piece, at the spots that had begun to fray until it completely calmed them down. Later, when I thought about it once more, I couldn't decide whether it was his eyes or his voice that I had fallen in love with.

'What's going on, Vera? Why the panic?'

'What took you so long, Constantinos?'

'I think I explained that I needed a little time.'

'I thought you weren't interested anymore.' I was ready to burst into tears.

'If you had slightly more trust in me, you wouldn't think anything like that. I keep my promises. Or I make none at all. I take my acting very seriously.'

'Fine, I'll be waiting for you. See you when you get here.'

A cool breeze permeated the room as if someone had switched on an invisible air conditioner to battle the summer heat.

****

'He said that he didn't want any reporters around. His arrival is incognito!' Stamatis stressed.

Avramoglou seemed unfazed by this news.

'He has kept us waiting for so long, and now he makes more demands,' he huffed in annoyance.

'Are you coming to the airport or will I have to do everything by myself again?' Stamatis asked me.

'No, I'll wait for you here.'

I insisted on holding up a last line of defence. I wouldn't rush like a silly schoolgirl to welcome this conceited actor who had ignored me for so long and had ditched me in Paris – I didn't even want to remember this last part. I wish I could delete my memories and throw that ... unfortunate incident into the recycle bin.

But until they showed up, I was biting my nails with nervous anticipation. Only when they entered the company offices, at around four in the afternoon, did the pieces of my heart finally settle into their former place.

He had let his beard grow. And his hair had gotten longer. He was wearing a loose shirt buttoned up to the neck and he seemed to be tired. His eyes searched for me when he entered the room. He gifted me with a faint smile and a peck on the cheek.

My book was a small boat that had crossed seas and washed me up on his shore. It was a paper plane that had flown over many countries and landed at his feet. My book was the bridge.

Stamatis was a whirlwind of activity: ordering coffee for us and requesting that no one bother us.

Venetis was eyeing him from head to toe as if he was trying to decide the best way to frame the actor.

I was looking at his fingers. Long, thin and beautiful, as

if they had been playing the piano from the moment he had been born, as if they were meant to tune a woman's heart. He was wearing two chunky rings on the same finger of his right hand. Perhaps it was some kind of new fashion. Once again, I was annoyed by the unfairness of nature. Why did it perfectly shape some people down to the tips of their fingers while others were left to their own fate?

'Welcome to Greece, Mr Aravantinos,' Avramoglou said, frostily at first. 'We've been waiting quite some time for you to honour us with your presence!'

Constantinos didn't seem to stumble on the rocks of his sarcasm. He politely asked for some tea and requested that we immediately get to the point.

Avramoglou monopolised the discussion. I quickly learned – I guess I was the last to know because the others appeared to have been informed – that filming had been postponed for two months. Then what had all the fuss been about? Was it just to get on my nerves, put pressure on me, and ultimately humiliate me? I could find no other explanation.

Second and most important of all was the ace that the producer pulled out of his sleeve. He was almost certain of collaboration with a big German TV network and, in this way, some troublesome financial problems seemed to have been happily resolved.

That's why he never mentioned Constantinos' high fee ever again, or his inability to meet these demands. That sly fox! I was left speechless. I was unsure if I had to begin admiring him or start being slightly afraid of him. Who knew what other hidden aces he kept up his sleeves and when he was going to reveal them?

When the meeting ended, everybody seemed quite satisfied. Constantinos received a copy of the final version of the script so that he could read it at his leisure and asked for the contract to be sent to his agent first before he signed it. With a calm look, he announced that his stylist, and his acupuncturist, would be arriving on the following day and that he required they be present on set at all times. With the same indifferent look, he asked to be provided with an expensive two-seater sports car for his transportation needs while he was in Greece: a perfectly reasonable demand, according to him. I was dumbstruck when Avramoglou nodded his head affirmatively. I couldn't believe my eyes or my ears.

****

But the surprises didn't end there. What awaited us when we entered the Margo Hotel in Vouliagmenis Avenue, where we had reserved a room for our guest, was deeply unpleasant. I had picked it out myself: it was quiet and isolated, had a wonderful view of the sea and was decorated with elegant pieces of famous designers.

As soon as we stepped into the hotel lobby, the flashes started. A pack of hounds had been lying in wait for us. They rushed towards us with deafening shouts and pushing one another as paparazzi are prone to do. We were besieged by blinding flashes that were thirsty for pictures, and microphones starving for news.

'What can you tell us about your new film, Mr Aravantinos?'

'What made you take the decision to accept this part?'

'How does it feel to be back in Greece?'

'Will you tell us a few words about your co-star and your new associates?'

For a few seconds, I couldn't see anything else apart from the colourful bugs dancing before my eyes. When everything got a bit clearer, I saw him clutch his head with a look of desperation in his eyes, as if he was lost. His eyes darkened.

For the first time ever, a thought flashed through my mind, and only later did I have the time to process it: this image of the 'film star' that everybody had of Constantinos couldn't have been further from the truth. He was nothing like the man you would expect; one who was conceited and had the ease and eloquence to deal with such demonstrations in his daily life. At that moment, he looked like a child who had lost his mother in all this chaos. A wave of tenderness swept over me; I instantly felt the need to protect him.

'Wait a moment, please. Mr Aravantinos isn't prepared to give any interviews,' I said stiffly but, of course, no one paid any attention to me.

'Alright, guys, give us some space!' I heard Stamatis' booming voice. 'We'll hold a press conference in a few days and then you will find out whatever you want to know.'

In the meanwhile, Constantinos had regained his composure, 'It's alright. I'll talk to them.

'I'm very happy that my new project will be filmed in Greece. I've been wanting this to happen for a very long time. I believe it will be an amazing and well-made production. All of my new associates are extraordinary. That's all I can say for now. Thank you.'

He didn't even spare them a smile. But he did satisfy their curiosity and stopped them from asking more questions. The signs of irritation were evident on his face as he retreated to his room. He had been staring intently at the ceiling of the lift and was nervously fiddling with his shirt buttons on our way there.

'I'm really sorry about what happened. I honestly had no idea. You have to believe me.'

'I know it's not your fault. I just had a terrible headache, and all this chaos was nerve-wracking, and it just made it worse.'

He seemed intent on not saying another word. I bid him goodnight, deeply distressed. I dared to kiss him on the cheek, which he accepted with indifference, and I let him get some rest.

'Who did that? Who called the press?'

I was extremely pissed off. Stamatis was driving along the congested Poseidonos Avenue.

'I don't know,' he said with uncharacteristic seriousness. He was preoccupied with the endless line of cars in front of us.

'Do you want me to tell you what I suspect?' He didn't bother inquiring about the suspicions I had.

'Did Avramoglou do it?'

This suspicion had been bothering me for a while. The longer I thought about it, the more probable I found it.

'I told you I don't know. I have no idea if he did it. I'm not his mother. But I do know a thing or two about him and you should seriously keep it in mind. If you go against him, or he doesn't like you, you're screwed! And he can't stomach Aravantinos, you must have realised that by now. As for you... I'm not completely sure what his impression of you is.'

It seemed to me that an invisible threat was floating in the air as we drove up Alimou Avenue.

Chapter 7

The Cursed House

I spent that summer with only myself as company, touring the Greek islands – numerous Greek islands tempting you to explore them – like a lost soul. The cicadas gave me headaches with their chirping in Sifnos. For no reason at all, the happy voices of the carefree tourists in Rhodes seemed to pierce my eardrums. You can't really say you have experienced the Greek summertime if you don't walk up a countless number of whitewashed stone steps under the hot sun, but in Serifos they were far more than I could handle. Everything was perfect in Athens. The silence was so thick at midnight that you could cut it with a knife.

30th August. 'Only a cigarette and one more day remains. Sifnos, Chrysopigi.' I wrote on a pack of cigarettes. One cigarette, one day. I was counting the days like a convict who longs for freedom. I wandered around as if I was moonstruck, and in my absent-mindedness, I lost a pair of sunglasses, two hats and several lighters. I scribbled random lines on the back of cigarette packs and watched idly as the wind lifted up waves. I returned to Athens with a bag full of empty boxes and several ticket stubs.

****

I convinced myself that I wasn't dreaming when I saw the lorry with my own eyes. First the lorry, then the wires. So many wires and all of them so tangled up.

Take baby steps, I said to myself. It was at this moment that I realised that I had spent a profoundly lonely summer. I had to get used to other people's presence again. And there were so many of them gathered in the studio – shouting, gesturing and making incredible noise.

So, let's see. A huge lorry was parked outside the entrance of the studio in Paeania. It was from the *Design Centre* stores and workers were unloading sofas, armchairs and bedroom furniture from out the back.

In the vast space of the studio reigned the chaos of preparation. Machinery, chairs, boxes thrown right and left, scattered everywhere. No one noticed me when I came in.

Avgoustakos was behind his console, setting it up by pushing its countless buttons; the gaffers were setting up the lighting and the electricians were untangling the wires and the plugs with admirable skilfulness; the assistant camera operator was setting the camera on the tripod and cleaning its lens; the dolly grip was bolting the rails for the camera dolly in place.

Vangelis was leaning against a pillar as he chatted with Stamatis. His eyes were scanning the space around him. Venetis was testing the monitors with Marianna, the script girl, constantly by his side. I was the only one who felt like a fish on dry land.

Vangelis was the first to come and greet me; he even complimented me on my tan. *At last*, I thought, *someone's finally noticed*. But he had ulterior motives. He always started by saying something nice and then proceeded to ruin your day, as I would soon find out.

'Anyway, I want you to know that I don't agree with Pantelis' vision, the way he sees things. Personally, I would prefer another approach. Slow motion shots, a not faithfully realistic representation with poetic allusions that take shape through the characters, the frames and the pace of the film. Do you get what I mean?'

His right eyebrow was forever climbing higher than the left, giving his face a permanent sarcastic look. A tight smile always played on his lips; it never turned into a full smile. He was trying to gain a foothold, to see whether it would be possible to count on me to take his side. To which purpose, I had no clue. Apparently, there was rivalry between Venetis and him.

'And, as for the continuity script, I don't understand his need to be so strict in everything. A bit of improvisation during filming never hurt anyone. But, it's more than obvious that he isn't some sort of genius that thrives in chaos.'

I began to suspect that he was one of those guys who were dying for intrigue and would stick their nose into everything, wasting an incredible amount of grey matter on things like that. This suspicion alone was enough to cause me displeasure. I hastily excused myself.

'You didn't really expect to work with Fellini, did you?'

I found Avramoglou – a gigantic "gorilla" who growled in my fairy tale – in the corner where the props were being prepared. I didn't remember having included such a creature in my story. He had his back turned to me, but his posture alone betrayed his irritation. To be more precise, he had picked a fight with Katia.

'What is this, woman? Is it possible for a Greek cop in the 70s to have decorated his house with obscenely expensive furniture from... *Design Centre*, with *Le Corbusier* armchairs and *Noguchi* – or whatever that Japanese man is called – coffee tables? Are you out of your freakin' mind?'

Katia had her arms crossed over her chest. It was as if she was telling him that there was a wall standing between them. Her long, elegant fingers could only belong to a pianist, and her stare, icy and deadly, could only belong to Katia. She was looking at the producer straight in the eye as if she would gladly shoot him. Her outfit – she was dressed in her favourite icy black clothes and stiletto shoes – were helping her in this respect.

'Mr Avramoglou, listen, I have learned to be very demanding in my line of work.' Her voice sounded like a delicate rope that never moved up and down; you could have complete trust in it because it had a core of steel even if it seemed to be thin and flimsy at first glance. 'You didn't expect me to just faithfully recreate a police officer's flat, because then I would be reproducing a poor image. And if you wish to have things done so poorly, you can manage by yourselves; I wonder why you hired me. You have to understand that the atmosphere I am trying to create aims at leaving the viewers with a sense of elegance and good taste, because it is the details that count in the end.'

I felt the need to lend her a helping hand, though she didn't seem to need it.

'Ms Avgerinou is right,' I said tentatively. 'This furniture is very interesting.'

The *Le Corbusier* armchairs were perhaps a bit ostentatious, but the rest of the set was amazing.

'I really like them!'

He turned and looked at me as if I was the last person he expected to see in front of him. I was afraid that he would take it all out on me.

'You have a screw loose, we already know that,' he growled.

'We're trying our best, Mr Avramoglou. We're all trying to get the best results, and all we hear from the powers that be is ... baseless remarks.'

He turned his back to us, fuming, as if he couldn't deal with both of us at the same time. He left growling to himself, something about 'stuck-up' and 'crazy women', crowned with his anger like Saturn with its rings.

'Don't mind him, he always acts like that, like a baboon,' Katia said serenely and sat in one of her armchairs. She lit up her pipe and trained her eyes on the other side of the room. *She must be around 55*, I noted. The same age as my mother.

'I know him very well,' she continued after a while. 'I've worked with him in the past. His favourite hobby is making people feel like garbage. He has an inferiority complex about his working-class background. No matter how successful he has been in life, he carries it with him as though it has been stamped on his forehead.'

'Anyway, you will allow me to congratulate you, won't you? You've made very good choices.'

She gladly gave me a tour through the irregular piles of furniture and framed pictures. Desks and chairs from the antique market in Monastiraki, rare furniture from an antique dealer she had been working with for years; the engravings had been ordered from Kolonaki. I was starting to get swept away by all the enthusiasm. I had suddenly entered a magical wonderland, a benighted Alice that found one thing more wonderful than the next.

At that moment, I caught a glimpse of a boy's lanky figure in the background. I excused myself from Katia's company and approached him.

'Vera, you're here! I'd like to thank you for your help, I mean ... for giving me the chance to take part in his film.'

I kissed him on the cheek.

'It was my pleasure, Alexander. You're too good an actor to stay buried in small parts.'

A faint blush appeared on his cheeks.

'Thank you,' he said, shyly.

From our first meeting, I had been impressed by his good manners and the innocence reflected on his face. An enchanting innocence that kept you grounded. He was one of those people who treat even the air they breathe with delicacy. Fragile and low-key. He had every eye turned on him when he walked, but he kept gazing forward. He must have been around twenty-two – and still a drama student at the National Theatre Drama School – when he was scouted and started landing acting jobs in TV series and theatre productions. But, his talent was still being wasted on supporting roles, disproportionately small to his talent.

Even though appearance-wise he fit the description of a spoiled rich brat to a T, you could see him as nothing less than a genuine romantic figure. He came from an old and quite wealthy family. They had massive vineyards at Mesogeia and they had been in the wine industry for generations. His parents lived in Ekali but he lived by himself in a spacious loft in the neighbourhood of Psyrri. He said that he wanted to live downtown, in the heart of the city, near the small theatre companies that staged innovative productions.

His parents had intended him for a lawyer and had financed his studies in the top universities, but he ruined their plans and followed his natural inclination. They were cold towards him for a while but that didn't last very long as they didn't have the heart to disappoint their only son and, eventually, they supported his choices.

'We're playing Shakespeare this year,' Alexander said with barely concealed excitement. 'The premiere is in October, so, you know, I'm going to be very busy.'

'I imagine it will be an ... imaginative production,' I teased him.

'Yes... something like that. The play is *Much Ado About Nothing* and I have been offered the part of Claudio. Thalassinos has some ... avant-garde views about the sets and costumes.'

'I'm so happy for you.'

I left him to himself and approached Venetis.

'Is everything going smoothly with the script, Vera?' he asked me, lost in his world.

'What do you mean? The actors got the script long ago!'

'Yes, I know,' he said, still engrossed in his own thoughts, 'I mean the changes that have to be made.'

'What changes?'

'Constantinos asked for them... Find him and talk about it. We start shooting in two to three hours at most.'

At the back of the building, a part of the unused space had been turned into a series of small dressing rooms for the actors. Venetis had announced that they would follow a daily twelve-hour shooting schedule. I found Constantinos discussing it with Evelina and I noticed that they had found the time to become quite friendly with each other.

'Look,' Evelina twittered as she spoke, as lively as a gold-finch, 'I'm lit-er-al-ly swamped with work this year! On one hand, there's the film, on the other, the TV series that has been renewed for a second season. In November, we're play-ing Marivaux at the Theatre of the South ... I don't even have the time to pee, excuse the graphic example!'

She moved gracefully amidst piles of discarded clothes and bathrobes and overturned shoes before stopping in front of the large mirror to check her hair. Holding a cup of coffee, he silently listened to her with a smile of something between condescension and compassion on his lips.

'How are you, sweetie?' Evelina hugged me and air-kissed me. 'You have become soooooooo preeetty!' She obviously found it cute to stretch the vowels in a word. 'What's with that look on your face? I'm going to have to scold you!'

I had no idea what look she meant; terribly anxious, I guess.

They had indeed given her a 'makeover', just like Stamatis had promised. Her hair had been dyed a modest brownish colour and she had a fringe à la Veronica Lake covering her right eye. She was wearing a simple floral dress and high-heeled shoes. *Why doesn't she look at all like a secretary to me?*

'Ms Agrioti, will you come to the makeup chair?'

Eleana entered the room wearing a tight cotton shirt and a heart-attack-provoking miniskirt that showcased her perfect, slim legs. Countless cheap bracelets jingled on her wrists. She was Avramoglou's distant niece, an impressive girl from the suburbs with blonde wavy hair that fell down her back and an endearing slight lisp.

She is sexy, but in a vulgar way, I found myself adopting Katia's way of thinking.

'What kind of changes did you have in mind for the script, Constantinos?'

'I want you to add a line at this point,' he told me, pointing to the script. 'I want to say: "Human cells can even absorb the most intense of passions. The body can grow used to anything." It came to me in my sleep and I liked it.'

'But, it doesn't fit the script!'

'I don't care. I want to say it! Do what you have to do to make it happen!'

My anger suddenly evaporated and I felt the urge to laugh. He was so funny, acting like a petulant child. It was obvious that he was used to people satisfying his every whim. *I shouldn't be giving him so much encouragement; I'll definitely regret it,* I thought, but, in the end, I decided to indulge him. However, in order to do this, many things needed to be done; a whole dialogue needed to be reworked from the beginning.

'Have you any idea what a difficult position you've placed me in?' I protested.

'I assume you'll be present whenever filming is taking place,' he said moodily when Venetis' secretary left in order to update the script with the new lines.

'I'll visit pretty often, but...'

'You have to be here all the time!' he abruptly interrupted me.

'Whatever for?'

'Because I need you! There might be some other changes to be made in the script, you never know!'

'But the script has been approved; we can't keep making last-minute changes!'

'Of course we can! If one of my lines doesn't seem to fit my character, what am I supposed to do?' He wrinkled his forehead and tightened his lips in a display of childish stubbornness.

And what about the soap opera that was starting – for the tenth consecutive season – next month? As my bad luck would have it, a new cycle of episodes had been approved for the longest running series on Greek television *The Footsteps of Fate. Will I ever rid myself of this silly soap opera where quotes like "I will love you until the earth stops turning" and*

"Only heaven knows the limits of my love" can be found in almost every single episode? I pondered in despair.

'Please, Vera, do it for me! I feel different when you're here with me; I'm much calmer,' he explained, tenderly.

With a sudden epiphany, I sensed that if I started agreeing to everything he asked of me from the very beginning, then I would be unable to refuse him anything in the future, and that frightened me.

'Okay,' I finally said, 'I'll be by your side.'

And the series can go to hell! Anyway, it had been such a great source of irritation for so many years that in the end I would end up trying to chew on the same bland crap – just like a goat – ad nauseam.

When we finally got rid of Avramoglou at around noon, it seemed that the entire crew sighed with relief. Once rid of a presence that had loomed over them like a heavy and cumbersome shadow, everyone began to move differently. Their movements stopped being tense and their faces relaxed. I sat quietly in a corner and greedily took in everything around me, trying to capture every tiny detail.

Venetis read through the lines of the first scene with the actors. Avgoustakos consulted him about the best position for the camera. They went through several rehearsals until everything was finally ready for the shooting. From that moment on, Venetis was given free scope to demonstrate his effusive personality. Calm but decisive, he gave succinct instructions to the actors and crew; and with full knowledge of the manipulations required, he perfectly coordinated this motley crowd.

During all these preparations, Evelina never left his side. She whispered things in his ear, sent him lascivious smiles and acted all coy around him. He treated her every move as if it was completely normal and predictable; sometimes, he even turned and looked directly into her eyes as if he was trying to guess her hidden desires.

'Can I ask you something?' I let my nosiness take over as I went and stood next to Stamatis.

'Those two ...were they ever involved?'

'Where have you been?' he said as he munched on roasted pumpkin seeds. 'Haven't you heard? They've been involved for many years. Even before Evelina got married. They were crazily in love!'

'And why did she marry Evangelinos in the end?'

'Because Venetis is also married, and has been for a long time. She wanted to get even! Got it?'

I see! A lesson on the ethics of sexual relationships is always useful.

****

Everything was ready at around two in the afternoon. *Scene 1, Take 1*, read the clapperboard that Vangelis clapped in front of the camera lens.

'I want you to start with a tracking shot,' Venetis explained to the cameraman. 'Then, focus on the typewriter and finish with a close-up of her face.'

Evelina sat behind the desk and started pounding the keys of the typewriter; the actors playing Delatolas and Diamantopoulos were ready to start violently riffling through the drawers; Constantinos put on the trench coat, hat and glasses his part required.

'Roll sound. Roll camera. Action!' Venetis gave the signal for filming to start.

I watched in wonderment as all those details, words, looks I had imagined were filmed frame by frame. The characters that I had given life to through my written words took shape. Real people were giving them life, motion and thoughts.

The cinema. The dream.

The eyes close when we go to sleep and there's darkness behind the closed eyelids; the same darkness falls in the cinema halls. The dream comes in a rebellious mood, ready to cancel the coordinates of time and space, to pull thin threads from the tangle of the subconscious. Everything teeters at the edge of reason, and this is something accepted and understood. The film will do the same. It will remove space and time and will make us accept, without any hesitation, this wonderful lie that contains the truth: art.

ι|ιι|ιι|ιι|ι

'How was I?' Constantinos asked with barely concealed anxiety when we took a break at lunchtime.

'Very good,' *though a little tense*. I didn't share that last bit with him.

'Very good? That's not enough! I want to be more than just 'very good'!'

'You are, Constantinos. Try to stay relaxed and everything will be perfect.'

'I want to be perfect,' he insisted, 'for your sake.'

You are perfect to me, no matter what you do, I almost told him, but I held my tongue. I had already given him all the encouragement he needed.

I went home that night with the feeling that the day contained the seeds of all that was going to happen. 'Human cells can even absorb the most intense of passions.'

'Be careful what you write,' Melina would have said. 'Words have tremendous power.' I wondered whether this phrase contained the end of this story. It sounded so prophetic.

The joining, the end of love. I already knew the beginning. The disease of love that strikes at you relentlessly; I could already feel it invading my blood, the struggle of this element to dominate me. And, what would happen next? Would I find completeness? Peace? Would I even care? What else?

In the meanwhile, a sweetly poisonous time intervenes when you get burned and like it, when you get tortured like one of the damned souls of hell and enjoy it, a time that you are condemned to live through. But what is the point of falling in love? What is the purpose, since everything will end and the desire will be absorbed by your cells?

****

'Constantinos is suffering from internal verbal diarrhoea. His technique may be flawless, but look at his acting. He can project an unfathomable range of emotions, something which other actors would take years to perfect. You'd say that he has made it to the top. But then he grows bored. He lets himself go and then he has to start all over again. Boredom is a price he has to pay,' Katia said.

Whenever Katia and I had a little free time on the set, I was more than pleased to sit with her and comment on the things happening around us. This woman had intellectual brilliance and sharp intuition. She was able to look beneath the surface and get straight to the heart of things at a single glance.

'People like him constantly change jobs, loves, roles, places of residence,' Katia continued. 'Each script is a one-day fling. Narcissism is the disease of the talented. The whole world depends on their personal worldview. People are worth his time only if and when they rotate around his axis. He feels very unprotected and exposed when he's around people and so he finds it necessary to have excessive control over any information and circumstances that involve him. I don't think he trusts anyone or anything.'

Despite my objections, I couldn't help but admit she had a point.

'Strangely enough, Norman Mailer writes that no love is as intense as the love shared between two narcissists. They deeply need each other.'

****

'Want to hear a story?' Katia said one day quite unexpectedly while the two of us were drinking coffee during our break. 'You may find it interesting.'

She told me the story of a house that was cursed — her words — and this surprised me. I didn't expect Katia to indulge in stories about haunted creatures knocked down by fate. She started by telling me that her neoclassical two-storey family home in Patras was still standing at the time of her birth. It was an old mansion that had been built according to the tastes of a raisin merchant from Patras at the beginning of the century. A renowned German architect and great craftsmen had been hired for its construction. She could recall every detail, as if she was seeing it right in front of her: From the attics and the high-ceilinged halls to the cellar in the basement, and the wooden staircases with the ornate banisters. The rococo mirrors, the downy duvets, the sanitary fixtures imported from England, the Viennese dinnerware, the three-door walnut wardrobes; they were all a testament to the mansion's nobility and wealth. There was also a garden where hyacinths, camellias and jasmines blossomed.

She made a short pause and took a deep breath.

'Yet, this beautiful mansion brought misfortune to

everyone who ever lived there,' she said almost to herself with noble sorrow. Her eyes focused on the dreamy scene she had created before me. I imagined it coming to life in my mind's eye.

The first owner lost everything in the Great Raisin Crisis, which devastated many merchant households and brought the families to the brink of poverty. Katia's grandfather, a shrewd Ionian man, bought it for a pittance and started hosting extravagant dinners and balls. It became the meeting place of Patras' high society.

But it also brought him misfortune. His wife, a beauty of an impressionable temperament, left him and their three children; she eloped with an Irish adventurer and followed him to the misty landscapes of the north. The evening dinners and balls stopped. Katia's grandfather was left behind to wander around in his beautiful neoclassical home like a ghost. They both sank into grief and decline.

In the early 70s, the house had aged beyond repair and huge sums of money were needed for its restoration. Her father, a practical banker, gave it to contractors through a quid pro quo system and a five-storey building was erected in its place. He was compensated with three luxurious flats in lieu of payment, flats he intended to leave to his children. But Katia's two brothers died; one from meningitis and the other from acute peritonitis. Somewhat like this, her suspicions were confirmed that getting rid of the house was not enough for the curse to disappear.

I had become uncommonly fascinated by the story. I felt

a cold shiver running down my spine and the back of my head going numb. I thought I saw that cursed house, and even the unhappy ghosts of the previous inhabitants, right before my very eyes. Katia's melancholic look that made me shiver was surely to blame. And then what happened? I wanted to ask, but held my tongue.

'I still wonder what might have been the source of all this suffering. What was to blame for my family's misfortunes,' she concluded. A deep sadness trickled from her eyes, *just like the mastic tears from the tree's wounded bark*, I thought with sudden inspiration.

'Have you ever wondered why life seems to put so much pressure on some people, inflicting irreparable wounds and leaving slashes on their skin?' I tried to comfort her, though it turned out to be a poor attempt at doing so. 'Maybe it's because the best hidden elements of our selves will gush out of these slashes,' I continued, fascinated by my own reasoning. I liked the metaphor with the mastic tears and thought to put it to good use.

Katia gave me a kind but condescending look, her wry smile betraying that she wasn't taking me more seriously than she would a 12-year-old child. I felt as naïve as a newborn rabbit.

'We are all defeated by life in the end,' was the only answer she gave me, 'even when it seems that we are victors.'

Luckily, she soon recovered and continued with less tragic events. She told me about her own path in life. She had studied History of Art in Florence and Costume Design in England. Then, she moved to Athens, got married and had a daughter. She designed costumes for more than forty – Shakespearean and other – productions and for more than ten films. Her most recent collaboration was with the Greek National Opera for an operetta. Our chat was abruptly interrupted by Constantinos, who had made a habit of butting in on my conversations.

As I had suspected from the start, it didn't take him long to become bold enough to start giving me a rough time. He demanded last-minute script changes countless of times, even if it only involved a tiny detail, and then, as if he was trying to frazzle my nerves, he even added his own lines.

He was constantly trailing after me, waving a bunch of papers around: 'How did you imagine this scene playing out, Vera?' He would even call my landline almost every night. 'I'm going through the script, what would you say if we added a few things?' or 'What did you think of that scene I filmed today? And I want you to be honest with me!'

At first, I was flattered. I loved how he would ask my opinion about everything, anxiously waiting to hear my praise and receive my applause. But, after a while, I began to find it tiresome. He seemed to be attached to me with an almost childlike vulnerability and in constant need of winning my approval and favour.

'Honestly, when did I adopt him without noticing?' I wondered.

'Tell me the truth, Pantelis,' I went and asked Venetis one day. 'Is the script well-written?'

'Yes, why do you ask?'

'I mean ... am I clear in my descriptions of what the actors have to do?'

'Clear as day,' he said in a flat voice.

'I leave no room for misunderstandings and ambiguities, right?'

'What's with the insecurity all of a sudden, Vera? If there was a problem, wouldn't I have asked you to fix it?'

****

'What would you say if we had dinner together some time?' I had finally found the courage to ask him out.

'I thought you'd never ask!' Constantinos exclaimed. 'You had promised me when we were still in Paris, Vera!'

He showered me with many complaints about my negligence. I listened to him complaining and tried not to laugh, but then I got stressed out. Once again, I had to go shopping; none of my clothes fit the occasion.

We went to The Anchor for seafood, just like I had promised.

The restaurant, tucked in one of the alleys of Kastella, didn't look impressive, but it had an amazing, creative menu. Just like every other night, it was full of people: politicians, journalists and artists had turned it into their hangout; you had to get on a waiting list in order to find a table. The illuminated port of Piraeus shone brightly through the huge glass windows.

When the head chef realised who Constantinos was, he rushed to kindly greet us and even picked out the table where we would be seated.

The chef, who was jolly-faced, good-natured and chubby, – just like any self-respecting chef ought to be – took our order himself. He also sent us the sommelier right away to help us choose the right wine. Although the evening had started with a lot of promise, it didn't turn out too well. From the moment we entered, Constantinos started sulking.

'There are too many people in here,' he remarked.

He sat tensely in his chair and began looking around him horrified, as if he were waiting for some journalists to suddenly pop out of some corner and start bombarding him with questions. The wonderful food didn't help in changing his mood; he barely touched the lobster with wild rice. The monkfish liver, the highlight of the head chef's creative inspiration, didn't fare any better.

The only thing that made him relax was downing one glass of wine after the other. Even though he ate the chocolate and amaretto tart with relish, he drank his espresso without uttering a single word.

Throughout our dinner together, I was on pins and needles. I wasn't suited to the role of entertainer and couldn't find anything to say to lighten the mood.

'I don't know what to do with my hands,' he grumbled. 'I think I'll take up smoking again.'

I'll get him a string of worry beads as soon as possible, I decided.

Then he sank into melancholic reflection, commenting on how he found Athens so changed, and how nowadays he felt like a stranger not only in Greece but also in Paris, as well.

'I can't find anywhere to belong,' he said melodramatically as if he were reciting lines from an ancient Greek tragedy.

I had no idea if giving him a hug and comforting him would help at all with the state he was in. The thought flitted through my mind, but I didn't think it would be appropriate.

Towards the end of our evening together, he made the announcement that was the final blow to me.

'Virginie arrives tomorrow,' he said. 'I called her and asked her to come no matter what. I feel very lonely here. I know I haven't been the most pleasant company.'

He bid me goodnight at the entrance of his hotel without any trace of guilt in his voice as he said: 'I have to admit I get a little maudlin, sometimes.'

But you have to take me as I am, he didn't say it, but it was implied.

He caught me by surprise when he hugged me tightly and held me to him for several seconds. I hadn't been expecting it. He took my breath away. He kissed me gently in the middle of my forehead, just over my eyes. I was unsure how to interpret it. Was it a brotherly kiss or that of a tender lover? Or perhaps of a child asking for help?

'Come up to my room.'

It was a demand, not a request. I followed him, feeling awkward. His room – a small suite in earthy tones with a huge bed and understated furniture – was on the third floor. I regretted my decision the moment I stepped in. *His wife is coming tomorrow and I ... tonight ... what am I doing?*

'Constantinos, are you up for a game of *Biriba*?' I don't

even know why I blurted this out. The truth was that I didn't dare touch him, I was afraid, and I said the first thing off the top of my head.

'What? Are you kidding me?' he said, annoyed. He took off his jacket and clutched at his head. He doesn't look well. He wearily falls back onto the bed with his shoes still on. 'And whoever loses will have to take something off?' He smiled slyly. 'Well, we can keep that up till dawn!'

'Don't look for innuendoes where there aren't any...'

Surprisingly, he agreed to the game, but not without grumbling.

'Look how the mighty have fallen. I don't believe it. A woman wanting me only for a game of cards! Just one round,' he made it clear.

He poured himself a glass of whiskey on the rocks; I had already had enough for one night. My head is spinning and my mouth is dry.

Near the end of our game, he can barely keep his eyes open. He lets out a mighty yawn and falls back onto the pillows.

'Stay with me,' he says in a voice bare of any pretence. 'I'm afraid of the whirlpool returning and taking me away.'

'And where will it take you?' I enter the game of delirium and drowsiness in the hope that I will fish some information out of him about the things I'm burning to find out.

'To sea. To the bottom of the sea. But you'll be there too, won't you?' He starts laughing. His voice slowly becomes fainter – as does his laughter – and they become an echo in a bottomless deep.

'Yes, I'll be there too.' My heart is pounding like crazy. 'What are you doing on the seafloor?'

'I'm gathering sea shells.' He speaks slowly, spelling his words out as if he wants to make me understand a lesson I have heard many times but that has yet to sink in.

'And ...what do you hear?'

'I hear the words of the people above the sea. So many words, I can't make them all out. They're all talking at the same time, I can't stand it.'

He seems annoyed that I ask him things that are obvious to him. He clutches at his head once again and tries to yawn, but he doesn't have the strength.

'What colour are the shells?'

'They are pink and have their own shine.'

'After that... what are you going to do?'

'After that? Hunt bats!'

His voice has become an imperceptible whisper, his eyes grow heavy. I need to know more before he falls asleep on me. And what happens next?

'What are the bats doing at the sea?'

'Do you know that you ask too many questions? The bats aren't there. They're in your mind.'

I become frightened; he has started telling me strange things again...

'What are you doing in my mind, Constantinos?'

'Don't you want me there? I came to tell you that I know...'

'Know what?'

'What you did to bring me back to life.'

I find it impossible to ask any more questions; my lips are unable to utter a single word.

'I want to tell you about that demon. The demon of lust; isn't that what they call him? Don't worry, I'll tell you what you have to do. In the past, I thought that if you kept getting shagged, it would be enough to keep him away. I was wrong. You need to abstain from sex. For three whole days.'

His words are drunk; the vowels hop around and the consonants are soaked in wine. He burst into laughter once again. I am sure what he's saying is gibberish; I no longer pay attention to it. Then, he falls asleep with his clothes still on; he sleeps like a log. I take his shoes off and cover him with the duvet. I lie down near him and listen to his quiet breathing.

This creature, sleeping with his lips half-open next to me, looks like it belongs to infinity and to no country. He is dark like love and beautiful like an angel. No matter what he says, no matter what he does, I always have the feeling that he came from elsewhere, that this isn't his homeland.

I look at him absent-mindedly and ponder on the nature of beauty. I have come to the conclusion that we find someone beautiful when they inspire us. Not with lifeless visuals, but with images that rouse you and make the sheets crackle. I feel a small pinprick of nostalgia every time I come face to face with such beauty that faintly reminds me of who I really am. A foggy memory, fleeting like a second, but as sharp and as strong as the flash of a camera. That's why beauty is precious, and sometimes, completely subjective.

I have a rare, precious opportunity to stroke his cheek,

and his hair as it falls on the pillow. I feel so lucky for this wonderful stroke of fortune that delivered him helpless to my touch. I gently touch his lips and he smiles in his sleep. I would have liked to stay awake and gaze at him, but, before I know it, I too fall asleep. I feel like a wreck.

I leave at dawn, walking on tiptoes in order not to wake him up. I exit the hotel with the receptionist's suggestive look following me.

****

His wife did arrive the following day and stayed for five more. Virginie is beautiful and gets excited at the drop of a hat. She has soft eyes that change colour depending on her mood, and purple eyelashes. Her smile is very bright. She loves to dress in a boho style and her excellent fashion sense allows her to mix and match the most clashing pieces, but more elegant pieces are also a part of her wardrobe. I couldn't help but take notice of what a well-matched couple they are.

Virginie rarely set foot on set; she was incredibly bored. She loved wandering around Athens and taking pictures in secluded neighbourhoods. It was her wish to hold an exhibition with the portraits of ordinary and working-class people, toil; this was her new project. Their toil seems very picturesque to the eyes of the upper class. In the end, his wife left in high spirits since she had gathered so much material. I can't say that I wasn't glad when she left. I would be lying. My joy was so obvious that everyone noticed.

****

That same night, however, I didn't dream of Constantinos. I saw the haunted house in my sleep. I was lying on a bed with a wooden headboard and a canopy from which white gauze bed curtains hung like shrouds. The blankets smelled of mothballs. The whole house reeked of mould and jasmine. I didn't know if I was awake or dreaming when I heard children's voices and laughter coming from the top floor.

'Who left the children on their own?'

I got out of bed; the worm-eaten planks creaked under my feet. I started to climb the marble staircase leading upstairs. The children's voices could be heard louder than before; incoherent cries and angry shouts, as if someone were scolding them or as though they were hitting each other.

'I have to see what happened to the children.'

I opened one door, then another. They were nowhere to be seen. But the voices became more and more piercing to my ears. I found myself in a room with rose-patterned wallpaper when I suddenly encountered the girl. She had her back turned to me and she was staring out the window. The burgundy-coloured velvet curtains submerged the room in a nightmarish dusk. The shadows danced on the decrepit floor. The girl turned abruptly towards me. She looked a bit like Eleana, but with long brown hair and a more aristocratic look: her upturned nose and grey eyes looked just like Katia's. She was laughing happily; something very pleasant had happened to her and she was trying to share it with me. Then I noticed that she was wearing a long lacy wedding dress. I couldn't understand, no matter how much I tried. Where were the children? Who was this girl and what was she trying to tell me?

Suddenly the girl's face assumed an expression of anguish, as if she was drowning. She was now desperately trying to speak to me. Muffled sounds were coming out of her mouth. In a final effort, the 'bride' lifted up her hands. And then I saw it. Horror gripped my heart with black talons. The girl's hands were almost completely severed from the wrists and were dangling by a strip of skin like useless earrings. The blood that dripped down, staining her snowy white wedding dress, had created two thick puddles on the floor. And the girl was still struggling to tell me something.

I woke up with a scream so loud it could have roused the entire building. My head felt numb. My eyes were darting right and left. My heart was beating at a furious rate. I was afraid that I would fall dead. I turned on the light with shaking hands and sat sobbing for a long time. I cried for that girl, whoever she might have been, who had died so young, who had been so beautiful and so unhappy, and who had fought to warn me about something, and I had been unable to understand.

****

The next day, I was burning with curiosity to ask Katia, but I lacked the courage to do so. I kept orbiting her for hours, caught in two minds.

'You know, I was leafing through some old magazines about interior decoration,' I told her in the end. 'I want to buy a new bed and I'm really fond of those romantic canopy beds. You must have had one of those in your house.' It wasn't the cleverest conversation starter, but I could think of nothing better to say.

'We did have them, if I remember well,' she answered me absent-mindedly. 'Every respectable household had such beds.'

'Actually, I saw one that I liked: with a carved headboard and a canopy with white gauze bed curtains.'

Katia gave me a wary look. 'I guess it must cost a pretty penny,' she simply remarked.

I couldn't get anything out of her in this way so I made the big decision to tell her the truth: 'Katia, I saw the house you described to me in my sleep last night.'

'I see you were really affected by my story,' she said with a smile. 'You may write about it if you wish to do so. I won't demand a fee for "using my intellectual property".'

'That's not a bad idea. But, if I am to use it, I need a bit more information. A beautiful girl lived there.' I barely understood how I found the courage to blurt it out: 'A girl with brown hair and grey eyes that...' I wasn't imagining things; Katia literally froze. Her eyes turned into two grey bruises, the colour of metal a modern designer would use to create a minimalist table.

'Take this pillow and mend it; it has become frayed,' she told the dresser in irritation. 'I don't understand how this happened; did someone have a pillow fight yesterday?' She lit up a cigarette, without a holder this time. 'That girl you just described was me,' she finally said with great effort. 'But I was barely grown up when...'

Her face instantly shuttered. It was obvious that she wasn't going to give me any further details.

****

More than a month had passed, October had already settled in. Shooting at the Paeania studio was almost done.

That Saturday was the last day. I walked up the road towards the set with a strange sense of foreboding. Something was coming to an irrevocable end. I didn't like it all; it filled me with sadness and an undefinable fear. As I walked in, I crashed into Alexander, who wasn't paying attention to where he was going since he was absorbed in his reading.

'What are you reading? Hasn't your part ended?'

'No, today. I still have a few scenes to film. But that isn't the problem! Would you do me a favour, Vera? Can you help me rehearse my lines? Can you read Hero's part, while I act Claudius?' He gave me a copy of the Shakespearean comedy. 'The opening night is in a few weeks and I'm completely unprepared,' he said in a panic-stricken voice.

We entered his dressing room. An old sofa, a mirror and two fabric armchairs packed with clothes were the only things in the room.

HERO

O, God defend me! how am I beset!
What kind of catechising call you this?

I tried to keep a straight face. This part was completely foreign to me.

CLAUDIO

To make you answer truly to your name.

HERO

Is it not Hero? Who can blot that name
With any just reproach?

CLAUDIO

Marry, that can Hero;
Hero itself can blot out Hero's virtue.
What man was he talk'd with you yesternight
Out at your window betwixt twelve and one?
Now, if you are a maid, answer to this.[6]

We were interrupted by a loud knock on the door.
    'Alex?' Eleana barged in with a huge smile on her face
that suddenly faded away when she spotted me. Alexander

grew visibly uneasy. He hastily pulled her out of the room with him. They kept whispering to each other for some time – I think I heard some muffled screams – and then Alexander returned to the dressing room by himself with his head lowered, as if he had been slapped.

'Is there something wrong, Alexander?'

His look had completely changed; his youthful carefree spirit had dissolved like a drop of oil in a glass of water. He was clutching the theatre script in one hand and was making vague gestures with the other.

'No... Everything's good...' He started tying his shoelaces nervously.

It had been several days that I had noticed the make-up artist persistently pursuing him, but I never imagined something would happen between the two of them. Anyway, Eleana had flirting with every male down to a fine art; anyone could see that. The young woman was a great 'temptress', as Stamatis would say, and he would be absolutely right. Alexander grabbed his jacket, ready to put it on and make a dash for it.

'Well, not everything ... Alex!' I was astounded. The black lace knickers – a thong, of course – that appeared when he lifted his jacket left no room for doubt. I saw him stumble as if he was ready to die of embarrassment.

'Look,' I told him placatingly, 'you're a grown man, but I hope you know what you're doing. And ... you see ... there's also the part where I think you aren't the only one she's involved with.'

'I'm going to get some fresh air,' he mumbled and rushed out of his dressing room.

He couldn't have made a worse choice. I felt sorry for him, but, at the end of the day, it wasn't my business.

I went to the set and found Venetis having a conversation with Avgoustakos. The chaos that surrounded us gave off a sense of finality. I informed them of my intention not to accompany them to Germany for the time being. A health problem of my mother would delay me for a while. Yiannis let me know that Constantinos 'must have fallen asleep somewhere in the studio. Again. He wasn't feeling very well.' I left to find him.

****

I knocked lightly on the door. I thought I heard a faint 'yes?'. I pushed it open and entered. In the faint light of the room, I saw Constantinos lying on the floor on a thin mattress. Shadows flickered fleetingly; they played on the floor for an instant and then faded away behind the window blinds.

'Come in, Vera,' he said without opening his eyes. The stillness and serenity of the room embraced me. The noise of the set could be heard in the distance.

'Aren't you feeling well?'

'I have a terrible headache,' he sighed, 'and I'm trying to relax for a while.'

'Is there anything I can do for you?'

'Stroke my hair for a bit, please, like this.' he said guiding

[174]

my fingers through his hair. I held his head in my hands, gently massaging his temples, his forehead and his whole scalp until his tension seemed to evaporate. I thought that he had fallen asleep, judging by the sound of his calm and regular breathing.

He looked so delicate and unreal – almost ethereal – that I was afraid he would slip through my fingers and fade away. I tried to get up without waking him, but he didn't let me. He placed a hand at the back of my head and brought me back down to meet his lips. An avalanche of pictures rushed before my eyes in a frantic montage as he kissed me: his face was a dark mirror. The black waters of the well ... the witless women who look for their reflection on them. The women who seek to find the name of their beloved. The deadly whirlpools that drag you to the bottom ... Then, it is far too late to turn back ... they keep whirling and dragging you ... down ... down. The oyster without its pearl ... the shell slowly erodes, what purpose did it have now that it was empty, a mere shell?

The asphalt melts under the heat of the summer sun... the hot aura... a shaking column of steam. Something evaporated from my body and was absorbed by his. The whirlpools that snatch you back into the sea ... Even though it is compassionate, the sea dumps you half-drowned on the sand. So many images in so little time. His kiss lasted as long as a dream. No more, no less.

'I think you worked some magic on me,' he whispered. 'The pain's just gone. What did you do, Vera?'

'Nothing... I'm glad you feel better.' I stood up with

difficulty and hastily walked to the door. My head felt almost ready to burst from the pain. As for my heart, I was unsure where I should look for it.

'Stay for a little longer,' he said in a very soft voice. My legs moved on their own. I turned back, as though I had been hypnotised, and came to kneel by his side. I stayed there, looking at him, as he breathed quietly with his eyes shut.

'Will you do something for me, Vera?' he whispered sweetly with a naughty smile. His hand disappeared under my skirt. 'A kiss is not enough to help me relax.'

I barely hesitated. I knew very well what I had to do then. An all-powerful director was giving me directions and I could do nothing but obey.

'Be quiet, they'll hear us,' he told me unfazed and put a hand over my lips.

I wasn't that bothered by the naughty smile that was proof he was immensely enjoying this game. I was more surprised by myself. How did I end up having sex without even realising how the hell it had happened? Just like that, without any feeling...without any protection or foreplay? I felt as if I had been the star of a soft-core porn film, and the worst of all, I had found everything completely natural. He was as important to me as the air I breathed; without him, I would suffocate. I mean, it goes without saying.

I soon discovered that his oh-so-annoying smile was contagious because I found myself smiling just as widely, for no reason at all. Where the funny part was, I couldn't tell.

Chapter 8

Signs of a Storm

A May beetle is buzzing under a hat. Somebody trapped it while it was blithely gazing at the sunlight reflected on the parquet. Now it is kept imprisoned, but it slams its body against the dark walls and is constantly struggling to escape.

I am the beetle and you're the hat, I imagine saying to my mother. *Someone has to let me escape from you. Otherwise, I will always walk in darkness.*

I look at her hands: two wrinkly stains on the white bed sheets. That's what mine will look like one day too. It's unavoidable, no matter what I might try to do. Her nightdress is impeccably ironed and crisp. On the bedside table, there's a bottle of water, rubbing alcohol, disinfectant wipes and an old religious Christian text that has become tattered from too much use. Her hair is gathered at the back in a bun held in place by lots of hairspray. I wonder if my mother has had this hairdo since birth.

Afterwards, I'm thinking that perhaps someone has already pulled that hat off of me — off of the trapped beetle

— and I simply haven't realised it. I insist on keeping my eyes closed because I'm scared of being in the light.

'You have abandoned me, Vera! Both you and your brother! Why did I have children if they aren't here to support me in my old age? Where is he now, can you tell me? He isn't even answering his mobile phone!'

The truth is that I have a younger brother who is obsessively dedicated to his year-long studies in England. Even I have almost forgotten what he looks like since I haven't seen him for so long. Fanis was an introverted child, whimsical and melancholic, and with many insecurities. He spent his childhood clutching his mother's skirt and Theophano had clung to him in despair, seeing her son as her only lifeline. She had smothered him, slowly but effectively, and had created the ideal mummy's boy.

Then, unexpectedly, my brother suddenly rebelled against this tyranny when he was around twenty-two. It appears he had exhausted every bit of patience he had while living with such a despotic mother, and travelled to the other end of Europe to study mechanical engineering. Since then, we have lost almost all contact with him. He only visits for fifteen to twenty days every summer, only to disappear once again on some Greek island or other, dragging his boring English girlfriend along with him, a different one every time.

'Do you call this a family? Are we anything more than acquaintances? Who cursed us?' Theophano whispered with bitterness.

She seems weary and very angry, but I'm used to seeing her in this state so it doesn't strike me as unusual.

'You strayed from the path of God, Vera; that's why He abandoned us. I will carry this burden to my deathbed...'

Unfortunately, I knew the answer befitting those who look to accuse others for their misery and never themselves. But because she looked so ghastly pale and weak, I preferred to hold my tongue.

Out the window, you could make out the long stretch of Kifisias Avenue, bustling with traffic.

'I bet that one of those blonde tarts is leading him by the nose. As soon as I get better, I'll go and find him. Perhaps I'll manage to bring him to his senses,' she said melodramatically as she leaned her head on the pillow.

'He has a duty towards his mother! I gave up my life for both of you! You cannot remember I exist only when you need my financial support.'

It was the third day she was bedridden in hospital after a sudden bout of acute gastroenteritis.

'How can my stomach remain intact with so much poison and bitterness that you serve me every day,' she continued her morbid game.

I knew this game well; it always ended in a fight if you dared to move one of your pawns. My mother had to move and control everything; the others were not allowed to play, they could just be simple spectators – just like spineless schoolchildren.

'Calm down, mum, everything will be fine.'

I struggled to keep my temper but I felt my courage deserting me. I felt the great need to escape to the hospital's courtyard to smoke a cigarette.

'And you, my little girl, why don't you take better care of yourself?'

Great, we're moving on to more local problems now, after we've finished solving the international ones, I thought, horrified.

'I've told you so many times. You have such a nice figure: wear a pretty dress to show it off. And why do you dye your hair? Your natural hair colour suits you better. You're no beauty, Vera, so you should accentuate your best features. Time flies by, when are you going to rebuild your life? Do you want to remain a divorcee for the rest of your life? When are you going to have a child?'

'I'll take care of it tomorrow, Mum!'

'And now you mock me?' she grew angry.

Neither the illness nor the stomach pains were able to stem her anger. I felt the atmosphere become dangerously oppressive, the entire room was filling with poisonous gases. For a while, we didn't talk to each other. In the meanwhile, a nurse entered, picked up the tray with leftovers and left.

'I'm very happy with my life,' I said as calmly as possible and tried to escape into the hallway.

'Happy? With no husband, no child; what kind of happiness is that? Wandering around aimlessly like a stray dog!'

When would I finally find the courage to face my mother without anger and hysterics, without running away?

The hallway smelled of antiseptic; there was quietness and cleanliness. The nurses came and went at a leisurely pace. The hollow clacking of their white clogs resounded along the corridor. At that moment, a stretcher came an inch away from hitting me, a nurse yelled at me to get out of the way, and two doctors rushed over to the spot. Startled, I took two steps back and came face-to-face with the man I had been hoping never to see again, dead or alive.

'It's good to see you, Vera.' Christopher's greenish eyes narrowed into slits. He eyed me predatorily from top to bottom. His hair was closely cropped, as always. His whole physique exuded the air of a healthy and well-built beast – definitely a beast. *How had I not seen all this back then?* I blamed myself. *What was it about him that had won me over? The hell if I understand!* Even his cologne had deceitful undertones.

'The feeling isn't mutual!'

'Why are you being so aggressive? I've wanted to find you and congratulate you on your success for a very long time,' he continued with a bland smile. 'I always thought you would do great things one day!'

I was close to an angry outburst. He was really going too far.

'You used to think otherwise, and my memory works perfectly. You would tell me that I was an immature little girl who lived in her pink dreamworld. Well, I might not have told you this before, Christopher, but, fortunately, it's never too late. I prefer living in a dreamworld to living in a cesspit. Because when you swim in shit, you'll have shitty dreams!'

'That's how man was created, sweetheart: from shit and dreams. I've been struggling to teach you that for years. But you insist on only seeing the ideal side of things.'

'And you deal with the shit.' I hated myself for getting carried away and playing his game.

'I wonder why we couldn't be happy together. We would have provided each other with a complete worldview.'

Christopher would die if he didn't always have the final word. It literally sickened him. I turned my back to his mocking smile and went outside to smoke that much-needed cigarette.

And how could I explain that strange affection my mother still held for her former son-in-law? They had never completely lost contact with each other, always keeping up the appearances and formalities required by the hypocrisy of their effete class. It was the same hypocrisy that had pushed her to give me this amazing piece of advice:

'You don't give up on your marriage so easily, Vera. These things happen in the best of families. Do you think you're the first woman to go through something like this? Do you think that not many women have been in a similar position? What should we do then? Ruin our families because of a misstep? That's how men are; I always told you that, but you never believed me.'

She stressed that she wasn't defending my husband but the institution of marriage. It didn't take her long, of course, to launch a counterattack, accusing me of being unable to keep my husband, to give him a child in order to put him on the straight path. And this was unfair, so unfair. Only God knows how much I had longed for that child. How many costly and painful tests I had agreed to undergo but which had borne no results. All of my efforts had proved futile; my body had refused to obey. Perhaps our bodies – at that moment I had this nagging suspicion – sense more things than we know, more than what we wish to admit.

I don't remember what my answer to her accusations was, or if I said anything at all. The only thing I remember is that I got up like an automaton, feeling incredibly confused, and left her high and dry in that patisserie café, sitting in a chair, clutching a teaspoon in her hand. I left so that I wouldn't start screaming hysterically in front of all the other customers, so that I wouldn't scream out everything I had suppressed for years in her face. I basically left because matricide is considered a heinous crime in our country and I had to avoid such an aberration at all costs.

But that wasn't the only reason for wanting to get rid of my mother. At times, a bunch of wonderful excuses had presented themselves. The most obvious one had been five years ago, three days before my wedding.

That afternoon – it was Wednesday – I was having the last fitting for my wedding dress and, as is common on such occasions, many people were coming and going in the house: friends, relatives, my future sister-in-law, my mother-in-law and even my brother, who had decided to honour us with his presence.

I was admiring myself in the mirror, feeling very beautiful. The simple gown made of shantung silk was the best thing I had found in bridal magazines and that's why I had decided to have it custom-made for my wedding. Everyone said I looked great in it; I would combine it with a long organza stole and elbow gloves. The seamstress, who was kneeling on the floor, was putting in the last pins when Theofano burst in to check if everything was going according to her instructions.

'What's this, Vera?' She turned as white as a sheet when she saw my wedding gown.

'What do you mean?' I tried to stay calm. 'Don't tell me you don't like it. It's been through a dozen fittings.'

'Your breast!' my mother stammered. 'People will be able see your breast! You will not enter the church wearing that! It is ... it is obscene! Didn't I tell you...'

'Mother, please, this is my wedding. All wedding gowns look like this. It's too late for any alterations now so let's stop having this conversation.' I was glad that it was already done and my mother could do nothing about it – that had indeed been my plan – but I was sadly mistaken.

'Listen here! If you think that I will let you make us a laughingstock for everyone ... Have them say that my daughter flaunts her body in church, you are mistaken.' She was sputtering and had begun to sweat.

'Vera's mother is a bit upset,' my mother-in-law intervened. 'If you'll excuse us...' she said as she tried to push Theophano out of the room with her. But who would be able to stop a rampaging she-wolf?

'Guess again,' she screamed, beside herself, 'if you think I will let you humiliate me in front of everybody, you shameless female. You never respect anything.'

The seamstress was staring at her with fearful eyes; my mother-in-law was about to collapse; my brother watched everything with a cold indifference, so many years spent abroad were enough for him to acquire the English stoicism. *Getting the hell away from the lot of you was the best thing I've ever done:* his eyes seemed to be saying, betraying his thoughts.

I was left frozen, and terribly disappointed, mourning the wonderful bridal gown I never got to wear. This turn of events turned out to be so unlucky, and so humiliating, that I never got over it.

In the end, I got married in a wedding dress I hadn't picked for myself and whose style didn't suit me at all – Theophano moved fast and bought me a very pricy high-collared wedding dress made of silk – to a man I might have picked out myself, but who didn't suit me either, as was later proved.

Christopher didn't seem to be particularly concerned about the incident.

'You know that your mother's nerves are shot. So many doctors have said so. Why do you always find ways to upset her?' That was the only comment he made.

But I was sure I was facing an uncertain future. The seeds of misfortune had already been planted, and my mother had tended to them with her own hands.

Two years later, I caught my husband in bed with Christina. I had returned home earlier that morning, after a business meeting had been cancelled, and as usually happens in these cases, I had been completely clueless. The first thing that surprised me was the strange but familiar perfume that lingered in the air. Straight after that, I heard soft voices and low laughter coming from the bedroom. And while my legs seemed to be nailed to the floor and weigh a hundred pounds, my heart felt as if it was receiving multiple electric shocks and was fluttering madly, beating against my ribcage like a bat trapped between dark walls, shrieking mutely. I don't know how long I stood as still as a statue clutching my bag in my hand. My mouth had gone dry and I was awkwardly scratching my nose. When the laughter turned into loud moans, I turned towards the door with the intention of leaving. I thought I had entered the wrong house and was disturbing the people living there. That's how stupid I felt. But, at the last moment, I stopped, grew irked, and dug my feet in.

'This is my house, damn it! I'm not going anywhere. This ... sick pair should be the one to get lost.'

I was more consumed with curiosity to find out the identity of the other woman than distraught by the thought that this man, whom I had realised a long time ago wasn't worthy of me, had betrayed our love.

It didn't bother me so much that he was shagging his mistress in our bed. Nor did it bother me that my 'friend' was shamelessly rolling around in my brand new Benetton sheets with her high heels still on. What really hurt me was the suspicion that perhaps I was partly to blame for what had been going on right under my nose for who knows how long. Because I didn't like wearing high heels in bed or outside the bedroom – I couldn't stand them at all – and, even worse, because I didn't scream so lustfully when we made love. As it turned out at a later date, Christina wasn't the only one of my so-called 'friends' to have succumbed to my husband's charms. Only Vicky had slapped him when he came on to her – there was no escaping this man's sleaziness – and, since then, she has remained my only friend.

What a cheesy story! And how banal! I furiously exhaled the smoke from my cigarette. Looking back, I shouldn't have taken it so hard. But this incident was essentially the culmination of all the things that had previously happened to me, and it sent me to the street with the locked houses for good; the street where you don't feel anything because feelings are frightening, where food, drink and sex are simply biological needs and nothing more, where the empty souls permanently live.

Afterwards, someone took pity on me and sent Constantinos to me; a man who knows how to break spells. 'Just listen to my words and let me buy you a drink. Then, all this bad luck will disappear,' or so he said in one of his films. That's another thing he did with my life: he uttered many magical words and used a lot of tricks in order to revive me, in order to succeed in waking up the fairy tale that had been slumbering for years in my inner frost.

How crazy life can be sometimes. Crazy and wonderful and unpredictable. You just need to embark on the first miracle that passes before you and cross the sky of your expectations with it. I took a deep breath and smiled to myself. My mood had already completely changed.

'I don't need you here anymore. The private nurse will be here any minute now. You may go,' Theophano said when I went back to her room.

I straightened her bed linens, went and bought her a

bottle of water and made sure that the nurse was really about to arrive. Then, I left, feeling a huge surge of relief.

****

'When are you planning to come and join us?' Stamatis anxiously asked two days later. It was almost nightfall; a beautiful sunset unfurled its orange ribbons over the Acropolis. Even though we were at the beginning of October, the heat hadn't really retreated.

Vicky and I were sitting on the terrace of an ouzo bar in Theseio, lazily admiring the view as we waited for the appetizers and beers to arrive. A persistent breeze was disturbing tablecloths, tents and women's hair, but no one seemed willing to abandon the wonderful view and move indoors.

'In two or three days. So, tell me, how are you getting on over there?'

'Like shit,' Stamatis spat out. His slightly husky, nasal voice reached me loud and clear through the phone.

'Why? Is there a problem?'

'The problem is that everyone has a problem with everyone else.'

'Meaning?'

'Where to start? Well, of course, with your ... boyfriend. He's gotten on everyone's nerves: he's irritated with everybody and blames everybody. A word of advice: Get your ass over here and do something to keep him in check.'

Sometimes, I bristled with indignation over Stamatis' crude language and I very much wanted to tell him that no one was 'my boyfriend', that I wouldn't get my anything over there, and that no one could control Constantinos. But, I was thirsty for the information he had and that's why I didn't start using my French on him.

'Evelina had a fight with Venetis during shooting,' he continued, 'and now there's an ongoing 'cold war' between them. She says that the local environment frightens her and gives her awful premonitions. She keeps crossing herself like a nun.'

I forgot all about my irritation and burst out laughing.

'Hatzipetridis had a minor accident; he sprained his wrist and we had to rush him to the emergency room. Do you want to hear more? Ah, yes...' he said, as if he had forgotten the most important thing, 'That lad, Alexander – is he gay or something?'

'No, he isn't,' I interrupted him. 'Is something wrong with him?'

'He's down in the dumps and walks around with a permanent scowl. It looks like he doesn't get along with Constantinos.'

'Oh, dear,' I sighed, 'but, tell me about the castle. Is it beautiful?'

'It's good,' Stamatis, who was chewing something, said in a bored voice. 'Like any other castle.'

Thanks for nothing, I thought.

'Is Alexander somewhere nearby? I want to talk to him.'

The sky was starting to lower its dark blinds. Night was falling with ominous forebodings. Several clouds may have gathered in the horizon but I was more concerned about other things and not particularly about the weather forecast.

'Hey, Vera,' Alexander's voice sounded a bit weak.

'What's going on, Alex?'

'Nothing, what should be happening?'

'You don't sound too happy.'

'Well, you see, here is ... different.'

'What do you mean?'

'It's strange. At night, the wind whistles threateningly, and in the mornings, the fog makes your heart feel heavy. Venetis is very pleased, since he has captured some amazing shots, but I don't like this place at all.'

Oh, he has let his romantic imagination run wild, I smiled.

'Now, about something else: how are you and Constantinos doing?'

'It's awful, Vera,' the young man took the opportunity to vent. 'He makes me feel like trash! You can't imagine how he treats me!'

Jesus, a grown man is jealous of a boy, I thought.

'Look, don't mind him. Do your job as best as you can and don't pay attention to anything else.' What else could I tell him, seeing he was ready to start crying?

'What's up? Has all hell broken loose?' Vicky was overflowing with curiosity.

The appetizers and the delightfully cold beers arrived at just the right time. A melancholic and mystical dusk was falling.

'That's what happens when you put a lot of roosters in the same henhouse. They are at each other's throats!'

'That's a good metaphor!' Vicky burst out laughing. 'And ... are you going to play the referee?'

'What else can I do? I'm leaving the day after tomorrow!'

While Vicky and I nibbled on our food (Vicky thought a variety of six dishes was a light snack. It would have to be seven different dishes and more for her to consider it a proper meal), she shared details of her relationship with Panagiotis with me, and said that the two of them made quite the couple, and that everything seemed to be going well, and how much little Marina liked him. I listened to her without saying a word. I could barely put a single forkful in my mouth; everything seemed bland and taste-less. So, I contented myself with downing beer, one mug after the other. I had had a strange taste in my mouth for days, a bittersweet taste that his kiss had left on my lips. I barely allowed myself to eat, avoiding anything that might alter it.

'What's bothering you?' Vicki said when she saw my absent-minded gaze.

'Nothing, I'm just a little afraid ...' I finally put my fork down and leaned back in the chair.

'Afraid of what?'

'You see ... he's so spoiled, so strange – and also married – but I ...'

Vicki stared at me with her blue eyes wide open, her fork dangling in the air and with baited breath. Even her blonde curls seemed to be on the lookout so that no one overheard us.

'... that I will fall in love with him in the end!'

'Oh,' she said with relief, 'the only thing I don't under-stand is why you use the future tense. The present tense fits you better. Or rather the present perfect,' she corrected herself. And then went back to stuffing her face with vegetarian and regular meatballs. Nothing was able to put a curb on her legendary appetite; I wondered how she didn't weigh a ton with the huge quantities she ate.

'Of course, you've said some interesting things about having an affair with a married man in the past – don't think that I have forgotten them – but let us let bygones be bygones,' she added, with her mouth full.

'Yes, I did, and I admit it: it's stupid and hopeless to have an affair with a married man, but in this case, things are slightly different. He's the protagonist of my story. Do you understand what this means to me?'

'Look, honey, any man we fall in love with becomes the protagonist of our very own personal story,' she stated as she took a drag from her cigarette.

'I like what you said, just let me write it down.'

I took out my notepad and started writing. I had the good fortune to carry one of the famous Moleskine notepads, which was a constant companion to quite a few famous people, in my purse; it was the leather-bound, pocket-sized version, to be exact. While I was writing, Vicky was staring vacantly at me, enjoying her cigarette. This girl had the unique ability to find enjoyment in the simplest things: a good, solid meal, a cigarette, and a cup of coffee made her feel complete. I felt a little jealous of her because of it.

Why couldn't I be content with material things and with set views? Why did I always look for elusive things, dreams and difficult romances? We were so alike in appearance that they often mistook us for sisters, but character-wise, Vicky was the more down-to-earth alter ego that I was missing.

'Why do you say that?' she said in puzzlement. 'You're a very sensible and positive person, and not someone deluded. Sometimes, you're even more rational than you should be. But if you have indeed fallen for this guy ... we'll live through some difficult times.'

'Is that what you think?'

'What am I supposed to say? The bad news is that this gentleman is not only married, but also an actor.'

'And is that important?'

'It is! What is an actor? A man who pretends to feel something in front of a crowd. Why wouldn't he also do it in his private life?'

What is an actor? That's a good question. In the past, I often pondered on this matter. I would say that actors are a beam of light in a dark universe of oblivion. An actor must remind us of something – something very old – in order to become our favourite. Someone kissed us once with a kiss that has been forgotten, but a faint memory of it persists – without knowing if he was an angel or demon – and this kiss innocently slumbers in our subconscious. That's the image an actor comes to occupy: your guide through the paths of your dreams and your subconscious, your perfect self, what you could be, but will probably never become, and that's why you admire it. The actor changes many faces, and has experienced so many things that others would need to live again and again in order to live them.

****

When I got home, I heard the phone ringing off the hook from the front door. It was as if I was seeing myself starring in a nightmare. Where were my keys? Naturally, they were lost in the least expected corner of my bag. Then, my shaking and clumsy hands completed the disaster; the keys kept falling to the floor, jamming in the lock, not opening the door.

'Vera, where have you been? I've been looking everywhere for you!'

'Why, Constantinos? Did something happen?'

I was slightly worried; the tone of his voice promised nothing good. He sounded very angry and he kept huffing and puffing in order to get rid of some of the tension he felt.

'How could you do that?'

'What did I do this time?'

'How could you write such things in the script?'

'I don't understand.'

'I'm reading that scene in the castle, at the Room with the Gowns, where Jimmy and Jenny are in that giant bed, under the silken covers etc. etc... And they're making love and she undresses him etc. etc... Are you out of your mind? Did you imagine I would take my clothes off in front of the camera?'

'But that's how you shoot a romantic scene,' I wearily mumbled.

'I don't care! I won't do it! You should have known I wouldn't!'

'How could I? You're an actor, you must have dealt with similar situations ... scenes, I mean. I assumed you had...'

'And because I'm an actor, do you think that I'll be willing to play anything you come up with? Have you seen me do this in any of my films?'

That was – partly – true.

'Yes, I have.' I was referring to the *Dream of the Butterfly*, one of his oldest films.

'I was very young at the time, and I also had a special relationship with my co-star,' he shot at me with a vengeance, 'so I felt more comfortable.'

'All right, do the scene with your clothes on. I don't care.'

'Are you kidding me? It'll be too bland. I won't do it at all!'

'You can't do that. The film has two, three erotic scenes in total. If we cut them, the film will only be fit for Sunday School and not the cinema.'

'I wish,' he sneered. 'Then, at least, God might intervene, because things here have gone from bad to worse. Everything's a mess: there's neither a plan nor a specific timetable. Do you know that we have yet to get permission to shoot in the castle and we're just sitting around wasting our time? We can only shoot the exterior scenes, and even those with difficulty because it keeps raining. I'm not used to working under such conditions!'

His arrogance was getting on my nerves.

'Alright, I'll discuss this matter with you when I arrive, but for that particular scene, there's nothing I can do. You had the script from the very first moment, we kept nothing secret from you, you read it, and accepted it. You can even wear your coat in bed, if you want, but the scene will be shot.'

He ended the call with an abrupt click; that was his reply. Why did it seem to me that the handset was boiling mad and an invisible hand was ready to hurl it at my head?

Chapter 9

Checkmate in a Dangerous Game

The small town was dozing under the sickly afternoon light. In these places, the sky looks like a huge church dome that only lets small amounts of light in. The two-storied houses with the attics and the smoking chimneys on their pointed rooftops looked very picturesque. The streets were soaked by the persistent drizzle. There was just mist, cold and humidity. And the night that was quietly creeping closer like a cat. An inexplicable melancholy weighed heavily on my heart. Indeed, this place was ... different. Alexander was right.

The taxi I took from the train station dropped me off in front of the Lydiaheim Inn, where the rest of the film crew was staying. No one was out walking on the street. The nearest building was a factory about half a kilometre away. Fields stretched all around the hotel as far as the eye could see.

The inn was an old – at least a century old – four-storied building with small balconies on the upper floors. The windows of five lofts dominated the top floor of the well-preserved building.

I climbed the stone steps and rang the doorbell. Its ring echoed eerily in the deathly stillness.

'Oh, willkommen, Frau...' An old nun with a friendly face gave me a warm welcome.

As soon as I crossed the threshold, I felt as if I had stepped into a hot oven. I was instantly greeted by a pleasantly warm atmosphere that smelled of freshly baked bread.

'Kalogera,' I introduced myself and explained in German that I belonged to the film crew that had booked the entire inn. Frau Matilde looked incredibly happy when she greeted me, as if she was welcoming back her own daughter who had been living abroad for years.

She was a plump woman in her sixties, of medium height and stocky. Her face was white and plump like a loaf of bread that had just come out of the oven. She was wearing a blue uniform with a white apron and a matching cap. She picked up my bags as if they weighed nothing more than a feather, placed them in a small – coffin-like, I thought with a shudder – luggage lift, and sent them to the third floor.

To my great chagrin, I discovered that the building had no lift, my room was on the third floor and, worst of all, it didn't have its own bathroom. Some of the rooms shared a communal one.

That's what you get when you're the last one to arrive, I thought as I climbed the stairs panting. Next to me, the lovely nun practically hopped up the stairs like a young girl.

The room had a great view and a small balcony; that was at least something good. But, there were no shutters on the windows and the curtains were completely sheer; this had me a bit concerned. I barely had time to hang my clothes in the wardrobe when there was a knock on the door.

It was Katia; she was wearing a stunning kaftan where all the colours of the rainbow were intertwined in an expressionist ensemble. She kissed me on the cheek. She had the room next to mine and we shared the balcony. Everybody else was filming in the castle, which was about fifteen kilometres outside the village. The previous day, they had finally been given permission to film the interiors of the castle and they had left quite early in order to make up for lost time.

She invited me to her room, which was exactly like mine. It had a duvet-covered bed with a metal frame, an antique wooden desk, a double wardrobe and a washbasin. She offered me some chocolate and told me about things I already knew. That the tension between the members of the crew was ready to ignite at any given moment, that everyone's frustration grew bigger with each new setback. In general, everyone's nerves were as taut as bowstrings.

After leaving Katia's room, I decided to take a shower to relax. I came out of my room wrapped in my bathrobe and headed towards the shared bathroom down the hall. That's when I saw the Scarecrow for the first time. I felt guilty for giving her that nickname, but the poor woman who wandered around with a mop and a bucket in her hands had been the recipient of nature's entire ill will. Very tall and awkward, she dragged her left leg as she walked, as if it was rickety. Her face was deformed, with her lower teeth noticeably protruding from under her lip. Some sparse hair hung from her scalp and her thick glasses made her appearance even more deformed and ugly. A shudder went through me as the cleaner slipped past me, grunting something unintelligible, and went into the bathroom to tidy up. I waited patiently for her to finish cleaning it so that I could use it.

At around 8 o'clock, the others returned from filming, worn out and dejected. They all settled in the large dining room for dinner – about twenty people in total. Venetis, who had a thoughtful look on his face, was having a whispered conversation with Avgoustakos. Evelina frostily announced that she wasn't hungry and flounced off to her room. Hatzipetridis was the only one who was somewhat calm and cheerful, while at the other end of the table, Stamatis continued his chattering unfazed, trying to inject some cheer into the tense atmosphere. Eleana was sitting very close to Alexander and was whispering something in his ear with a naughty smile. He listened to her without saying a word.

Constantinos barely said 'hi' to me before sitting in another corner, sulking. *What a moody person*, I thought, frowning. *How on earth can I have a ... weak spot for such a man?*

And while we were having dinner, with Frau Matilde cheerily running to and from the kitchen, serving us schnitzel with potato salad, I decided to put an end to this story once and for all. And what was the story, anyway? A kiss and an ...unfortunate incident that hadn't even been enough to be the start of a new chapter between us? And it seems that for actors, having flings is as common as taking a walk in the park. Not to mention that rumour has it they have no heart. This suspicion became a certainty on the very next day.

****

We started filming very early in the morning. The sky looked like boiled milk with a little cocoa. The wind was pulling leaves off the trees and twirling them around.

I was consumed by curiosity for that famous castle. From the way it was described, I had imagined it to be something extraordinary. At the last turn of the road, and after we left the dense forest of beeches and birches behind us, I finally saw it; crowning the top of a hill. An imposing presence, it overlooked the plain that stretched before it, sown fields, and tiny villages. A genuine descendant of the Middle Ages.

Four very tall towers defined its dimensions. The thick walls that connected them, built of solid stone, flanked a courtyard paved with gravel. Countless pointed turrets rose towards the sky. The guard of the castle-turned-museum opened the heavy gate with the baroque embellishments and let us through, politely greeting us.

The interior was quite well preserved. The fact that it was a folklore museum was a major bonus for us, since many authentic 18th and 19th century furniture pieces, antiques, and other valuable materials were available to our production.

I walked silently into the anteroom; Corinthian columns supported the upper floor. The start of a wide staircase with a granite bannister was on the left. The ticket office was on the right.

The enormous wooden door with the sign 'Eingang' – Entrance – opened, powered by an invisible mechanism. I noticed a faint sadness in the carved wooden faces of the saints, the icons and the medieval statues that filled the first rooms.

Soon the place was crowded with voices and commands. Blasts of light dispelled its dark mystery. Hurried people invaded even the most isolated corners, disturbing the silence.

'Jimmy' was passionately kissing 'Jenny' on the long spiral staircase, and this kiss lasted for what seemed like hours. It was about ten seconds, that is. She had completely surrendered herself to his arms, her fingers tangled in his hair, and he held her tightly around the waist.

'Okay, we have the shot,' Venetis abruptly stopped the shooting of the scene.

'No, I'm not happy with it. Let's have one more go,' Constantinos insisted, and Evelina passionately agreed.

And time started flowing excruciatingly slow once again. I kept looking at them and thought that I was going to faint. I crumpled every piece of paper I was holding in my hands. I even broke a pen that I had with me in order to curb my nervousness. *The bastard! He did it on purpose to get back at me!* I promised myself that I would get even at the first chance I got. His gaze confirmed all my suspicions when he approached me. It looked too angelic to be true.

Somehow like this, I was shocked to realise that it was too painful for me to continue going against him. Refusing to do him any favours was just a wrong move in a game I had already lost. He had carefully prepared his next steps and I had already become a pawn in his hands; I saw it clearly. But, neither he nor I could have imagined back then who was holding the checkmate move for themselves in this painful tournament.

****

That same night, my sleep wasn't very restful. I was nestled underneath the fluffy duvet that smelled of lavender and I was sweetly drifting off when a raven started cawing outside my window. I shot up in alarm and it was ages before I could go back to sleep.

At around dawn, I dreamt that I was in my family home and Constantinos was my guest. The door to his room suddenly opened and I saw him in a passionate embrace with an unknown woman. *In my own house? Does he have no shame?* I thought. The scene I witnessed seemed so vulgar that I turned my eyes elsewhere.

'Why so shy, Vera?'

He had a sarcastic smile on his lips when he said that.

'You're a manwhore,' I said with deep bitterness.

'I'm the manwhore when you're the one who uses me in such a way in your dreams?' His laughter had become the growl of a wild animal. 'Get used to it, sweetheart,' he continued defiantly, 'you can't escape me because ... I am you!'

I woke up feeling numb. For a long time, I didn't even dare blink. A bunch of questions were cluttered in my head, demanding answers. And what did his words – 'I am you' – mean? I shivered like a leaf.

In the morning, I had the opportunity to meet Matilde's other half: Frau Hilda, who was on her way to the laundry room and was carrying a basket filled with clothes that needed washing. Tall and skinny – she was around sixty – with a slightly humped back but the same friendly look as Matilde, and a heavenly smile.

The washing machines were located in the basement, along with the dryers, the drying racks and a huge table that was used as an ironing board. This was also where the storerooms and the linen wardrobe could be found. The ground floor was occupied by the kitchen, the reception desk and a sitting area with comfortable sofas, low tables and a stone fireplace.

The other floors consisted of double and single rooms. It didn't take me long to discover that Venetis and Constantinos were staying in the best rooms; each of them had an en-suite bathroom and fireplace. So that we don't forget who the most important people are.

****

Three days passed and we had settled into a normal shooting schedule. Things were going pretty well, if you excluded the weather that always ruined our plans, Evelina's whims, and Constantinos' perfectionism that reached an alarming degree of paranoia.

We also had to deal with unexpected delays due to last-minute script changes, a situation that didn't let me relax for a single moment. One such change was suddenly needed one night at around midnight. I was exhausted and was getting ready to go to bed – I had already put my nightgown on – when I heard sharp, impatient knocks on the door.

'Good evening, Vera, I need your help,' Constantinos rushed into the room like a tornado, waving – as usual – a bunch of papers, pages of the script, around.

He began blurting out his worries, not for a single moment showing that he was aware of how late it was. 'You write that the two of them are *"dancing passionately, practically glued to each other, swaying sensually"*... etc... etc... Can you make it slightly clearer? How exactly do you mean all this?'

He looked really confused. If I didn't know the kind of games he played, I would have easily believed him. His forehead was wrinkled in puzzlement and his eyes were wide open.

'I don't think I've written anything strange. I'm quite clear ...'

'Oh, really? Why don't you show me then?'

He pulled me into his arms before I could react and he began to twirl me around to the beat of a Brazilian mambo, whistling the tune through his teeth, and then he turned it into a tango, all the while spinning me around. 'Is it like this?' he asked jokingly, as he dragged me around like a ragdoll. He had found a new game and he was enjoying himself immensely. Then, he swept me away to the rhythm of a waltz, and said, 'Or perhaps like this? Will you tell me now, Vera?'

I couldn't hold back my giggles when I saw him so excited.

But then my laughter dried out. He pulled me flush against him and I felt his quick breaths caressing my ear. His heart was beating strongly beneath his shirt. I was just wearing a nightdress, a slip of clothing too thin to protect me; I felt almost naked in his arms. He knew it and was having fun with my embarrassment. He began whispering the words of an old Leonard Cohen song to me – the one called *I'm your man*, a favourite of mine. It's an incredibly romantic one, the singer promising to do anything the woman he loves wanted, even if that meant hiding his face behind a mask.

'You do know that this is the director's responsibility,' I pulled back from him, quite troubled. I didn't want him to realise that I was trembling.

'I don't care about the director! I want only you to tell me about myself. Am I good?' He pretended to be anxious so smoothly, and he looked at me with that childlike curiosity that must have earned him many extra points when dealing with women.

'You're perfect,' I applauded him. 'You're amazing!'

'I know!' He puffed up with pride and burst out laughing.

'You do, huh? Do you also know that you're a jerk, a liar and a big scoundrel?'

I started laughing again as I playfully punched him on the chest a few times. He grabbed my hands and pulled me into his arms.

'Oh, I also have another question! Afterwards, you write that he kisses her so passionately that he gives her a taste of heaven; now this is where I don't understand a thing,' he whispered near my ear, his mouth too close to let me escape him, his breath tickling my neck all the way down to my shoulder. 'How can a poor man make a woman get a taste of heaven? You write whatever you like and then I end up with a bunch of questions.'

I took a short breath – so as to clear my throat – I swallowed and gave him a strained smile. It was impossible to stop my voice from trembling.

'I haven't written anything like that.'

He looked at me silently for a few seconds, with half-lidded eyes. His lips formed a grimace that almost looked like a smile. I didn't know if he was trying to keep himself from laughing, or whether it was the prelude to an in-depth confession. But, triumph glimmered deep within his eyes for what he was obviously about to get and we both knew all too well what that was.

'Yes, you're right. You didn't, but ... it's implied! I also know how to read between the lines,' he insisted confidently.

In a flash of courage, I picked up all the scattered pieces of the femme fatale hiding inside me – they must have been pitifully scant – and looked at him straight in the eye.

'And ... what is written between the lines?'

No childlike curiosity lingered in his eyes any longer. It had vanished, as if it had never existed, and in its place, darkness and brutal determination circled around his pupils, and this is where I found myself sinking. He took my lips in a deep endless kiss that found me completely defenceless, that didn't give me any room to protect myself behind the locked door of my heart, and so the feeling of his kiss crept deep inside me, and I just let it rob me blind. It left me completely breathless; I could hear my blood pounding at a frantic rate.

'Nice try, Mr Aravantinos! You're very close to your goal!' Where did I find the courage to be funny at this hour?

'My pleasure, ma'am!' He looked delighted, as if he had finally been given the remote-controlled toy car he had been dying to get.

'It's just that I will have to make changes in this script. I don't like what I've written. I don't like you giving such kisses to other women.'

'Very well! We can rewrite it together!'

He dragged me to the desk and sat me on his lap. He began to crumple his papers into little balls, which he then shot into the bin; in the meantime, I began reworking the script on the computer. That night, we spent many hours in each other's arms, deleting and typing, making new suggestions for the story, weaving new threads around the plot, creating the perfect scenario with the Delete and Enter commands.

'Did you miss me at all?' he asked me at around dawn.

'Very much...'

'How much?'

'A lot!'

'So, you did think about me...'

'All the time!'

'All the time?'

'And a bit more than that!'

Then, he carried me to the bed.

'Why did you let me wait so long for you, baby?' he asked me, but words were redundant at this point. Everything was once again crystal clear between us. We had already made countless rehearsals for this irrevocable act for millions and millions of years – since the human race was still a dark seed in the bowels of the sea – and we were very familiar with the rhythm, movements and sighs.

I was sinking deeper and deeper into a velvety and silky hug, and I had the luxury of slipping my fingers through his hair, touching his skin with my fingertips, breathing in his gentle scent that still held a faint hint of his cologne, his breath burning me. *How could his lips be in so many different places at the same time?* I wondered. *Is he working his magic on me again?* I let myself fall completely under his spell until I discovered with horror that no matter how much I struggled to say something, I couldn't form a complete word, only fragments of syllables and vowels.

A magical creature, an elf, had slipped into my bed and had stolen my voice. Who to trust with such a confession and who would believe you?

'Yes,' I finally said, and it was the only thing I could utter, perhaps because it's a short word and comes out easily in such circumstances.

So, that was enough for me, and I heard myself repeating it a dozen times, each time with a different echo, until the first light of dawn appeared. As if that was the only word I could mumble, just like a young baby that was taking its first tentative steps and was learning how to read the world from the start, at the dawn of a new day.

I woke up as happy as never before. I stretched out lazily and decided to stay in bed for as long as I could. He was gone, having left early to go to the shoot.

****

This small happiness didn't last for long. That very night, a strong wind suddenly started blowing and scattered the clouds in the sky; the dead leaves that had formed a thick carpet on the ground were swept away. The yellowed leaves danced in a neat swirling pandemonium. They even circled around the taxi that was dropping the woman with the silky hair and the expensive earrings off in front of the inn's door.

I closed my window with great difficulty and rushed to get dressed before heading for the dining room.

'We aren't eating in tonight,' Vangelis announced, right after I spotted him coming out of his room. 'Yiannis discovered a Greek taverna near the Austrian border, about fifteen minutes from here.' After a moment of hesitation, he continued: 'We do need to meet and have a talk, the two of us.' He grasped my arm with a gesture of intimacy in order to stop me from leaving. His eyes shone like a snake's in the fading light. 'You must have noticed, of course,' he began, as if I had given him permission to do so, 'that Pantelis has the tendency of keeping everyone under his thumb. I don't think that he implements your script in the best possible way. The angle he has chosen to showcase it with is unsuitable. Pantelis is a loyal follower of commercial cinema. He's just Avramoglou's employee and nothing more. You know how 'much' Avramoglou understands of culture and aesthetics. For example, I'd give the film an oneiric, more surreal, tinge. I would see it moving between dream and reality, without the viewer ever being sure of which they are faced with. You see what I mean?'

He spoke very seriously and mournfully as if he was announcing a fact of the greatest importance. He was looking for accomplices in his ambitious aspirations – it was obvious – and I wouldn't spare a gram of my grey matter for intrigues and plots.

'You're right,' I replied, 'now that you mention it, I agree. And I have a brilliant idea! I've been inspired by the eerie atmosphere of this inn. Hasn't it touched you too?'

He gave me a careful look, with one eyebrow firmly higher than the other, to determine whether I was serious or not.

'We may as well murder Venetis, and then the two of us can take the reins. You're smart enough to find someone to frame for the murder. Then, with my support, you can take his place. What do you think?'

'I was right when I said that you watch the worst crap in cinema,' he burst out laughing, supposedly taking part in the joke.

****

'It's a good opportunity to eat something other than sausages and schnitzel,' Avgoustakos approved of that night's outing. 'The ... chef swore that they make the best ribs. They also have live music playing tonight.'

An incorrigible foodie with a generally exuberant personality, Yiannis had once again worked his magic.

'Where is Constantinos?' I asked.

'In the sitting room with his wife. She arrived unexpectedly just a while ago to surprise him.'

Suddenly, I feel as if I've been punched in the stomach. Pain erupts within me and slithers like dozens of tiny 'snakes' through my veins. I clutch my belly and breathing becomes very difficult.

When Frau Hilda says 'Good evening' to me in German, her jolly face and serene expression get on my nerves.

Where the hell do they find so much happiness to smile about all the time? Could they let me in on the secret?

I believed that I wouldn't have the courage to face the Frenchwoman, but I actually discovered that I wasn't so overcome with guilt.

'I missed him very much,' Virginie explained in broken Greek.

I held her hand in a friendly kind of gesture and I felt it – small and bony – fluttering like a baby bird that had just hatched from its egg and was struggling to survive. I could trace even its smallest bone. *This woman is afraid*, I sensed, and all my guilt was let loose at once.

'I hope you don't make him work too hard here,' she said and let out a flighty laugh.

'No more than necessary.'

She added that she would only stay for a couple of days

and that was the only good news I heard. I fixed my gaze on Constantinos, trying to read any signs of anxiety in his face. Despite my hard efforts, the book of his thoughts remained locked tight, its pages sealed. *He knows this part really well, he must have played it quite successfully before,* and for the first time I wondered how many different faces this man had. Because, since he was an actor, I knew he had many.

In the large living room, the fire crackled in the fireplace, the flames licking the logs. Evelina, gorgeous as always, was sitting at Venetis' feet – apparently the two of them had made up – and she was flirting with him. Even his moustache was smiling.

Stamatis was standing up, snacking on peanuts and drinking whiskey; Hatzipetridis, who was into healthy eating, was holding a glass of apple juice. 'I will have a bit of salad,' he said to Stamatis. Eleana rushed to hang from Vangelis' arm as soon as he appeared. She stuck her mouth next to his ear and her perfect leg against his. She was wearing a mini skirt, as usual, and towering stiletto boots that reached above the knee. *Sexiness needs sacrifices,* I thought absent-mindedly and didn't pay them any more attention. I couldn't care less who Eleana's next target was. When Katia made her appearance – she was the last one to arrive – Avgoustakos said it was time to go.

'I'm not coming,' I said, pretending to have an annoying headache.

I wished them a fun evening out and went upstairs. I paced up and down my room in a bad mood for half an hour.

Shortly afterwards, Frau Matilde knocked on my door and kindly asked me if I wanted to have dinner with them. The dining room was covered in a strange silence. To my surprise, I saw that Alexander was there too. He was sitting at one corner of the table and was half-heartedly munching on a breadstick. He was trying to appear absorbed in the book he was holding in his hands, but it was clear that his mind was elsewhere.

'I've had enough of them,' he began to explain the source of his frustration. 'All this noise they make gets on my nerves. And their stupid little jokes, God! I'm really sick of the whole lot of them.' He threw the book aside with a nervous gesture and grabbed his forehead.

'What's the matter with you, Alexander? It's something to do with Eleana, isn't it?'

I sat opposite him and got straight to the point. I saw his desperate need to discuss the matter.

'Eleana who?' He reluctantly turned his eyes elsewhere and stared blankly ahead. 'My Eleana? Everyman's Eleana?' He paraphrased the Shakespearean quote and continued reciting lines from the play in a melodramatic way:

'Do not live, Hero, do not ope thine eyes,
For, did I think thou wouldst not quickly die,
Thought I thy spirits were stronger than thy shames,
Myself would, on the rearward of reproaches,
Strike at thy life.[7]'

'Look, don't take it too hard. You're still too young to worry about such things. You have your whole life ahead of you, Alex, you should loosen up a bit.'

I had the urge to laugh as I gave him this threadbare piece of advice. His words hid both boasting and despair, something that I didn't expect to come from a young man of his age.

'What would you do in my place?' He picked up the book again and began to fiddle with it as he held it between his hands. He gazed almost pleadingly at me, as if he was expecting me to find the solution to his romantic troubles.

'I ... It's different with me,' I finally said awkwardly. 'I'm in a different phase.'

I didn't feel like I had my whole life ahead of me. I had reached that strange point in life where the threat of finality hangs over everything. You can't go back and make corrections; mistakes count double and triple as much, and if you didn't have the chance to love someone or something unconditionally – a man, a child, an idea – your heart turns forever into stone. And you have lost the game, for sure.

Chapter 10

A Very Brief Death and a ... Final One

We were at the entrance of the castle since morning, taking additional external shots of its surroundings. Venetis' voice reached my ears from a distance. He was instructing the cameraman on how to position the hand-held camera so as to capture the panoramic shot the director wanted. An icy breeze swept through the branches and slipped its cold fingers through our clothes. The dull sky didn't seem to be in a bad mood at the moment, but that was no guarantee that the weather would stay on our side.

In a corner, Eleana had spread her make-up equipment on a bench and was applying foundation on Alexander's pale face. She leaned over him and gave a little giggle.

I guess they're back together again, I thought.

Katia's assistant had set up an ironing board and was pressing the lead actors' costumes one last time.

Eleana, after finishing with Alexander, started removing the rollers from Evelina's hair and used a comb to loosen the curls.

'Oh, I can't do all this by myself,' she coyly complained

every so often. 'Do you know how many make-up artists they had in the production of *Rainbow*?' She randomly
mentioned a recent big American – what else? – production. 'Fifty! I don't know where to start! I feel like I'm
drowning!'

'Don't be afraid! I'll rescue you!' Stamatis volunteered.
'Just make sure you're wearing the same shirt you have on
now when I do. You'll look very sexy with a wet shirt cling-
ing to your body!' He came closer to her with an exaggerated
lustful look.

'No, no! I want Constantinos to save me!' she squealed
and turned to Constantinos for help, pretending to be panic-
stricken. 'Be honest with me, would you save me if I was
drowning, Mr Aravantinos?' she chirped as she fluttered her
eyelashes. It was something that only Eleana could do so
gracefully.

'Of course, sweetheart, without question.' He put his arm
around her shoulder with 'fatherly' fondness.

At around three in the afternoon, the weather decided that
it had been kind enough to us in the past few days. A sudden downpour appeared on the horizon, accompanied by
lightning and thunder.

How nice, I hope it rains, I thought with glee.

The outburst of the storm feels liberating. It washes away
the world's contaminated energy and releases a refreshingly
new one. That's why I love the rain, especially in the form
of sudden showers.

The crew technicians didn't seem to agree with me. They

ran around swearing, rushing to cover up the filming equipment and load it in the van. Within a few seconds, the storm broke out.

****

Back at the hotel, I took a quick shower, put on dry clothes and ran down the stairs to his room. I felt an intense longing to see him face to face, to have him to myself, to tell him how much I liked his acting today, to touch him, even for a little while. Time had gone by excruciatingly slow during shooting and it had been torture staying away from him; I didn't want to give myself away.

I knocked on his door twice but got no answer. Passing in front of Evelina's room, I heard his voice.

'Remind me to marry you when we get out of here.'

'You'd better, because I'm already thirty-one and at thirty-two I'll feel as if I've lost the game, Jimmy!' Evelina shrieked at him.

'Never reveal your true age to a man, sweetheart.'

'Then, you should never promise a woman that you'll marry her if you don't mean it!'

The truth was that they were having a very convincing 'fight'. *They're rehearsing*, I thought with a smile. I started to leave when I heard Evelina's voice.

'Baby, would you get my bathrobe for me? It's behind you.'

And this line wasn't in the script. At least not in the one

I had written. Who would have said ...Baby? I was flabbergasted.

And what was that part about him getting her bathrobe? Did it mean she was standing naked in front of him? I left, holding my breath, hoping no one would find me out... that I wouldn't become a laughing stock.

I began to pace around my room, very upset. I must have walked back and forth between the basin and the bed three hundred times, waving my hands around as if I was surrounded by myriads of bees. That word buzzed in my ears like a poisonous wasp. An out-of-control swarm of 'insects' droned around me, humming the names of Eleana, Evelina, Virginie, and of who knows how many more women. I had to exterminate these bugs before they poisoned me! But how could I fight against them when I was so vulnerable and miserable?

I turned on the laptop and started making a few minor changes to the script. By around eight, darkness had completely enfolded the inn.

'Good evening, what're you doing, are you writing?'

Constantinos' head peaked through the open door.

I hadn't heard him knock... or hadn't he knocked at all?

'Yes, I am,' I snapped at him and continued to type furiously.

He came up behind me, hugged me and kissed my neck.

'Can you let go? Can't you see I have to work?'

The computer was emitting desperate whining sounds from the violent treatment it was receiving.

'What's wrong, Vera?' His face darkened.

'It's nothing!'

'How can you say it's nothing? I heard that there's a very good restaurant nearby and I came to ask you out to dinner. And now you're treating me this way?'

'I'm not hungry!'

'But I'm starving! I haven't eaten anything since morning and I feel exhausted.'

'You can go downstairs and have dinner with the others.'

'I don't want to have dinner with them! I want to go out!'

'Then you can take Evelina out to dinner. You two make a wonderful couple,' I said as I remembered what the actress had said about the two of them the first time I met her.

'Evelina? Why her in particular?'

'Why, because you'll have many interesting things to say to each other ... baby!'

I knew that I was being ridiculous with my jealousy, but I couldn't help it. The poison had seeped deep within my bones. He made several grimaces, trying to stifle his laughter.

'So, were you eavesdropping?'

'Of course not! I just happened to be passing by her room...'

'I won't say she's not cute...'

He looked at me with his familiar irritating smile that lit the fuse of my anger. *I'll deal with you*, I thought, *but later. After the film is finished. A lead actor in hospital would be completely useless at this point.*

'Look here, Vera,' he suddenly grew serious. 'I need to make something clear if you want us to get on well with each other! I can't stand jealousy and similar antics. I find them awfully bothersome. Not to mention I find them totally unjustified. I'm not going to start apologising for the things other women tell me.'

I was ready to spit out something biting about his arrogance but he opened the door and I realised that he wasn't joking, he was ready to leave. All my resistance was swept away and scattered by the wind; it was utterly torn apart.

'Don't leave ...' I was sure that I didn't say it out loud, that this thought simply came to me with tremendous intensity, but he heard it. And, fortunately, he didn't turn his back on me. I was in his arms before I could prepare myself. I heard a strong sigh of relief escape my body, as though it had finally found the last piece of the puzzle it had been looking for over the years, and it fitted so beautifully with the rest of the pieces. We shed our clothes in mere seconds, perhaps it was thanks to another one of the magical skills he had. My suspicions melted away. His hands seemed to be everywhere at once. I kissed him like I never had before, biting his lips as if I wanted to devour him.

'Talk dirty to me?' I whispered.

In response, he started listing, without hesitation, everything he intended to do to me in every ... explicit detail. Of course, I couldn't form a single word. Even though I had suggested this bright idea, I was biting my lips with embarrassment until I burst out laughing.

This didn't seem to make him pause; he continued saying and doing whatever came to mind. Once again, I was lost in the middle of an uncontrollable whirlpool while I let him – without any complaints on my part – break through the doors of my body, one after the other. My connection to the world got fainter and fainter until it completely faded away.

'Didn't you say you were hungry?' I asked him a little later while we were still in bed. He smiled at me as he stretched out and lay on his side, completely satiated. He was soon fast asleep.

I didn't sleep for many hours that night. I stayed awake and gazed at him, gently stroking his hair and his ear. I thought it was the most lovable ear I had ever seen.

The few noises of the night came from the street outside – a cat meowing mournfully, a car driving by – disturbing the quietness. The full moon's light entered through the window and bathed the room in amber. A wonderful serenity made my heart clench.

I was trying to listen. In the silence of the night, the slightest noise sounds like a fingernail tapping against a crystal wineglass. Yes, the noises were crystal clear that night, but I was struggling to hear what was hiding behind them.

In the distance, in the heart of the night, I'm looking to find the voice that calls to me in my dreams, but I can't, despite my dogged efforts. My mind is an empty speaker that reproduces echoing voices, nerves and hysteria; the unrest of the people surrounding me in the last few days.

On the other hand, I know very well that sexual passion is the most potent drug and, depending on how it will affect you, you will either get drugged out of your senses or it will sharpen them to an incredible degree. The second case applied to me. Perhaps that's why I felt, rather than heard, a slight noise outside the window. Was someone out on the balcony? And what were they doing in this bitter cold?

My fear subsides when I think that it may be Katia, who probably can't sleep and went out to smoke a cigarette, since smoking isn't allowed indoors. I get up like a cat that has sensed danger and go to the window. I hold my breath. There's no one there, just the absolute silence. Even the wind has completely died down.

****

I spent the entire following day in a cloud of stupor and sluggishness. Fortunately, everyone was too busy to pay attention to my state. Almost everyone... As if my tiredness wasn't enough, I also had to deal with Vangelis' constant moaning. I never understood why I attract these nutcases. Though I tried to see him as a colourful man with high artistic pursuits, I couldn't keep my temper.

'Now do you see?' he approached me, looking terribly disappointed.

His right eyebrow had lost its usual arrogance and was now crawling on the same level as the left. His ears seemed to have been experiencing the same lows. He looked like a stray dog searching for a new master.

'I told you; Pantelis is not a man who's going to take risks by experimenting during shooting. I suggested that we shoot this scene from many strange angles, which would showcase the surreal side of the matter. He didn't even bother discussing it with me. He has also shown that he's unable to make proper use of the depth of field in the frame.'

'I happen to believe that Venetis is a very talented and experienced director,' I stopped him in his tracks. 'But even if what you say is true, he must have his reasons for choosing this approach.'

'I didn't say he isn't talented, you misunderstood me,' he pretended to be offended and slithered away, leaving me in my haze.

I had to find the time to talk to Pantelis about the snake he was nursing in his bosom, but I kept postponing it.

The only moment my mind felt clear was when I hugged Alexander and kissed him on the cheek in order to congratulate him on his performance. In the scene that had just been completed, the young man had given everyone a real lesson in acting; I hadn't been wrong to believe in him. The sharp glare that Constantinos threw my way didn't foretell anything good.

I froze as he pinned me with his narrowed eyes, which gave him a menacing air. I had suspected for a very long time that he must be a little short-sighted, but he refused to wear glasses. So, he was looking at me with an expression that I could only call hateful. But, I couldn't find any good reason why he would hate me. When I understood the message hidden behind the glare, I let go of Alexander and sat next to Venetis. I started taking small sips of my coffee in order to stave off the cold that had wrapped itself around me.

****

That same evening, Avgoustakos convinced us once again to go have lunch at the famous taverna The Acropolis, which was close to becoming our hang-out.

'That's what all tavernas are named here,' Yiannis said with a laugh, 'Alexander or Acropolis or Athens. You should definitely join us, Vera, 'he insisted. 'You missed out when you didn't come with us last time; we had a smashing time. Their moussaka is finger-licking good!'

He had already begun salivating at the thought of moussaka.

I promised to join them, but a bit later. I had to make a few adjustments to the script since Constantinos had created his usual mess.

At ten o' clock, I was the last one to arrive at the taverna in the small Corsa I had rented. I got out of the car without wearing my coat, locked the car shivering, and walked hurriedly towards the building. The others seemed to be having a good time because I heard drunken laughter, toasts being made and lively music. Everything got mixed together in sweet confusion after a very stressful day.

I didn't have time to see where the shadow that grabbed me by the arm and slammed me against the wall had sprung from.

'What are you doing?' I screeched. His hand shut my mouth.

A pair of Germans exited the taverna and stumbled towards their car.

'Oh, darling,' the German man lisped to his lady friend in their native language, 'these Greeks are so noisy.'

'I want you to say you're sorry,' he whispered menacingly,

his palm still holding my mouth shut. His voice was sharp and metallic, and even icier than the wind. 'I'm sorry I tried to act like a femme fatale today, I'm sorry I tried to make you jealous. Will you say it?'

I nodded breathlessly in agreement. 'Sorry,' I murmured in a numb voice when he finally pulled his hand away from my mouth.

At last, I was able to look at him straight in the eye. Once again, I could have sworn that I had never seen or known this man with the wild hair, the roughened eyes and the pursed lips.

'I will never do it again.'

'I will never do it again,' I repeated, like an echo.

He then let me go and just walked away. I was shivering from fright.

'Only, you could have said it in a better way, don't you think?' I said in an outburst. 'You scared the hell out of me! And if you want to know, I wasn't trying to act like a "femme fatale". And it wasn't my intention to make you jealous. I like Alexander, that's all. He's a very talented young man. I was the one who introduced him to Venetis, and I feel responsible for him. Do you understand? It never occurred to me that a ... big star like you could be jealous of a mere boy.'

After my anger deflated a little, I saw that he was clutching at his head and that he looked a complete mess.

'Aren't you feeling well?' I went to his side, feeling worried.

'It's nothing serious, just a freaking headache, but it'll

pass.' He closed his eyes for a while, and stood still, at the mercy of the night and the frozen wind.

A gentle breeze of tenderness caressed my ear and whispered that this great star was nothing but a deeply insecure and frightened child. I hurried to make that light breeze that was spouting nonsense die out before any damage could be done.

'Forgive me, Vera, sometimes I say and do things I don't mean.'

Constantinos seemed torn apart; he was staring at me with a weak smile and an unfocused pleading look. I hadn't seen that expression on his face before, and I have to admit, I didn't like it. If women fall in love with men because of their strength, but love them for their weaknesses, I stubbornly refused to move to the second stage. I had breezed through the first at breakneck speed and the terror I felt for my recklessness had left me paralysed.

'I didn't mean to scare you; I hope you won't hold it against me.' He gave me that look of his that made me unable to deny him anything.

'Why do you hate Alexander? Can you explain it to me, since we're having this conversation?' I asked him as gently as possible.

'Who said that I hate him?'

'That's the impression you gave me.'

'How do you come up with these things?'

He had fully reclaimed his self-assuredness. He had regrouped himself within seconds and was ready to launch a counterattack.

'I just wanted to teach him a few things, but I might not have done it in the most elegant way.'

'Like what?'

'That he can't be dreaming of a career in acting if he continues doing everything this way! I know it's hard, but it's the truth! And he has to face it.'

'Could you make it a bit clearer? What's wrong with Alexander that he can't have an acting career?'

'You act as if you don't know him. How far do you think he'll go with the shyness and modesty routine that makes him stick out from the others? How many of our profession's hardships can such a sensitive person take? I'll tell you: very few. He'll fall apart somewhere along the way.'

'Aren't you being too extreme? Things aren't exactly as you describe them... '

He smiled, but it would have been better if he hadn't. His face was a mask of sarcasm and disgust. I turned my back to him, fuming, and walked into the taverna. The first thing I did was make a pit stop at the restroom to reapply my lipstick and fix my hair. I also splashed some water on my face to calm myself down.

I entered the hall and sat next to Katia. She was very elegant, though her outfit – a velvet dress in royal blue – was too formal for the occasion. A sparkling sample of almost ascetic minimalism.

'What do you think of the food? Is it any good?'

'The grilled trout isn't bad at all, and their wine isn't awful. However, I would recommend you get bottled wine.'

The taverna called Acropolis was one of those exotic

eateries that prosper mostly abroad. They are considered the best investment a Greek immigrant could make. Folk decor with Caryatids, white embroidered curtains, byzantine oil lamps and engravings with heroes of the Greek Revolution of 1821.

The owner was a charming man. He suggested I try the taverna's specialty, which I ordered, along with a bottle of wine.

The group was in high spirits. Venetis and Stamatis, who were leaning against each other, were singing between bouts of drunken guffaws.

'Why couldn't there be a diet wine?' Evelina grumbled. 'I have to be careful because even the tiniest sip could make me gain weight. I hate this.'

'Of course there is,' Vangelis rushed to tell her, 'didn't you know?'

'Oh, really? Where?'

'In France, where else? It's a very recent invention from what I've heard.'

'Panteliiiis, I want it, I want it, I want!'

I expected that she would start stomping her high heels on the floor in a display of coyness, and I wasn't wrong.

'You must give me a little kiss first,' Venetis sang in high spirits.

And she did, with a smacking sound.

I was sure that, within the next few days, a dozen bottles of this wine would arrive at the inn. Venetis always catered to her whims.

Eleana, after dancing sensually to an oriental song, went

back to practically sitting in Alexander's lap; the young actor was obviously feeling on top of the world. Avgoustakos was busy devouring his steak. Vangelis was smoking, seemingly lost in thought, but his eyes kept scanning everyone. His blasé look showed quite clearly that he found this place too kitschy for his refined tastes. I felt odd amid this cheerful scene.

Constantinos was sitting silently on the other side of the table. *What is he doing over there?* I was surprised to see him bum a cigarette off Evelina and light it up. *But, he said he quit smoking.*

'This ouzo is divine,' Venetis said, bringing the glass up to his nose with the look of an ouzo connoisseur. 'It has the correct proportion of anise and fennel; you can barely taste the ginger and cardamom,' he concluded.

Vangelis listened in silence with a condescending smile on his thin lips.

Stamatis must have drunk himself blind because he was singing out of tune, making clumsy gestures, and trying to force Marianna to sit on his lap, though the girl resisted. Marianna was a very good girl, sweet and very reliable in her work. Venetis couldn't make a single step without the script girl by his side. I had noticed the full-of-longing glances she cast at Alexander. But, unfortunately, he only had eyes for Eleana.

'I see you don't have much of an appetite,' Katia said. She had been watching me playing with my food.

The roasted meat with orzo in the Dutch oven had claimed all of my attention, as if the meaning of the world was hidden under the pieces of veal and pasta and if I stubbornly dug through it, I might find it.

'Katia, I feel I'm suffocating,' I said and left the orzo in peace.

'If you feel the need, and, of course, if you trust me, you can come and talk to me,' she said, almost fondly.

Towards the end of our dinner, Mr Aristides served us walnut cake with chocolate and I was glad that I would have a bite to eat. It was past midnight when we noisily left for the hotel.

****

The next day, the set was a great hustle and bustle. The twenty extras that had been sent by the German agency for the Dance of the Immovable Roses arrived in the morning, creating additional disruption. The sound of a foreign language spoken around us and their German-type smiles threw us off.

Accustomed to century-long silence and melancholy, the dark passages of the castle experienced hours of glory and grandeur.

Katia and her assistants were lost in a sea of taffeta and muslin that made up the costumes and hats, the corsets and slippers of the era. The Dance of the Immovable Roses was to be shot as if it had started at an earlier time, at around the 1750s.

It was a crucial point, one of the film's climactic scenes, where Jimmy and Jenny would discover that in order to unfreeze from the stillness of the magic dance and move forward, they would have to muster all their imagination and intuition in order to discover what was required of them to understand and exorcise. It was the moment when they would lose Alexander's character who, along with his beautiful partner, would stay forever petrified because they hadn't realised what they had to do.

Eleana was looking worn out.

'Luckily, they'll be wearing wigs and we won't have to style their hair,' she muttered in a daze as she set about doing the actors' makeup one after the other.

On top of all this, Evelina suddenly appeared, looking frantic, with panic in her eyes; she was holding a tissue over her forehead. 'Ah, please, sweetie, do something about this pimple. Oh, my God, it's that walnut-chocolate cake's fault. Oh, why do I have such a big sweet tooth?' she wailed as if it was the end of the world.

At that moment, I really admired Eleana for keeping her cool. I would have slapped Evelina if I had been in her place.

On that day and the next, I didn't see Constantinos up close at all. His behaviour had become strange, if not downright rude. When we were shooting, he was cold and very formal towards me. In vain did I try to find out what was wrong. In the evenings, when we returned to the inn dead tired, he would disappear to his room. I didn't know what to do. I constantly changed my mind and fretted.

On the night of the third day, I decided to swallow my pride and go find him. My strength had run out and I was missing him terribly. After all, the kiss on the cheek I had given Alexander was no excuse for such behaviour.

I had to find out what was going on. Even though a secret voice insisted that I shouldn't go, I ignored it and headed to his room. All the possible and impossible conversations we might have played out in my mind and I learned all the answers by heart. But, I wasn't prepared for what he did tell me. That's what always happens; you're never prepared for the worst. So, I went to the second floor and knocked on his door. I got no answer.

'Do you need something?'

I almost jumped right out of my skin when I suddenly found him behind me. He was wearing a thick jacket and a knitted cap; they were soaked from the humidity.

'I went out for a short walk,' he explained as he unlocked his door.

'What happened, Constantinos? Did I do something wrong? Why are you avoiding me?'

I desperately tried to keep things light-hearted. A little longer and I would burst into tears.

'I'm not avoiding you. I just needed some time to think about a few things.'

'Like what ... things?' I said with bated breath at the mournful tone of his words.

A few minutes went by before he gave me the answer I needed. It was as if he had been carefully choosing his words so that they were clear and effective. Either that or he was coldly calculating which weapon would more effectively take me out of my misery.

'Well ...' he began in a cool voice, 'I don't want to give you any false hope. Something might have happened between us ...'

'You just call what we have "something"?' I really wanted to scream.

'... but I'm afraid that this can't go on much longer. I admit that there's some kind of attraction between us — he cleared his throat – but...'

'But?' I was worried that this would be the last word I ever said. "She died with a BUT stuck in her throat", I could almost see the headlines.

'... but we belong in different worlds. We lead independent lives... And moreover, this situation is risky for my mental well-being and professional performance. I can't jeopardize this, it's very important to me. I hope you know what I mean ...' he trailed off, exhausted.

I saw that he had made enormous effort to say all that.

He was looking out the window, distracted by the stormy night that brought thousands of ghosts and vampires flush against the windowpanes. I could clearly see those nightmarish forms beckoning to me with sad expressions, but they didn't frighten me at all. The cause of my panic was right there before me, and it was a man. What harm can the undead do to you when the living prove to be incomparably more frightening?

And while I was standing in front of him, totally lost, 'I heard' strange voices talking to me inside my head: *Don't listen to what they say about us*, the first vampire, who seemed to be the most experienced, said. *We aren't bad people. Nor*

did we suddenly decide to start sucking other people's blood.
We're simply unlucky beings. We failed to find true love and look
at what torment we now have to face.

The second one nodded in agreement, and then, many
others gathered round to tell me their sad stories. I vigor-
ously shook my head, after clutching it between my hands,
convinced that I was going crackers.

So, that's it, then! Whoever fails to find love becomes a
vampire! It was a shocking revelation.

'Yes, I understand ... but you started this, Constantinos. I
tried to keep myself away from you. You know that, right?'

I timidly took a step closer to him and tried to touch his
shoulder, or his hair, but I instantly pulled back.

'You're right. It may be my fault, but it doesn't make
this story any less of a mistake. It's better to end things now
and keep ... a beautiful memory in our minds of our time
together.'

'What you did was ... not at all...' I struggled to clear
my throat from the waves of despair, '... not at all ... honest!' I finally said with great effort. 'Not toward me, and not
toward your wife, do you know that?'

His eyes darkened to a dangerous dark purple shade;
how did they become so drastically altered in colour?

'Don't talk to me about honesty,' he hissed. 'Honest people may go to heaven, but on this earth, they go to hell!'

I looked at him with my mouth hanging open. This
couldn't be the man I knew. He wasn't the child with the
insecurities and the 'innocent' questions. 'How can a poor

man give a woman a taste of heaven?' I didn't know how to answer his question back then.

How can a man — not poor, by any means — give a woman a taste of death? I would gladly answer that question!

I felt the need to burst out into loud laughter, to make fun of my own stupidity, my dangerous naivety, to abandon myself to my fate, and become a sad vampire, since it was absolutely certain that I would never find love. Not on this cursed planet. I grabbed my stomach; I felt it twist itself into knots.

'What bullshit are you trying to feed me? We aren't little kids who don't know what they're doing!'

I needed to tell him everything that was on my mind because I felt that at any moment, I would die, and the dead don't get a second chance to deal with their unfinished business.

'What I understand is that you're a coward, a liar, nothing but ...trash! That's what you are!'

'I never promised you anything, Vera,' he murmured.

'You're a coward!' I screamed in his face. 'And that's what I hate most in a man. And I hate you!'

I slammed the door shut and stormed down the hallway. I didn't want for anything in the world for him to see me fall apart, or give him the pleasure of making me cry.

'Dear Lord,' stammered Frau Matilde in German as I bumped into her. She was carrying a pile of linen. She was so shaken that she even gulped back her angelic smile.

In the next few days, of course, she would have more

opportunities to get upset, but the old woman didn't know it yet. She didn't even suspect what trouble she had got herself into when she rented her peaceful inn to these 'insane Greeks'.

Rain started to fall furiously, lashing against the windows. I collapsed on the bed, clutching at my stomach. I felt the approaching disaster. A knife kept carving my heart out; it was unending torment, repeated over and over again, with burning pain gushing out. I was shaking and sweating. My body ached. Uncontrollable spasms wrung my insides.

I could only compare this pain to the horror of drug withdrawal and, although I had never been in a similar situation, I could fully understand these miserable people.

I will leave, I decided, after bawling my eyes out for some time. *I have to get away from here, I can't stand to see him again.*

Still feeling distracted, I got up and feverishly began to pack my suitcase; I just shoved all my clothes inside without any care. Then, a horrible suspicion struck me like lightning. It was coming back! The panic attacks – the thing I used to call THAT – had returned! After so many years, they had found me once again. I barely had the time to run to the bathroom and spew all the anger and disgust that nauseated me. After that, I felt a little better. I splashed some cold water on my face and I crawled back to my room.

After I calmed down a bit, my feet led me next door. I timidly knocked on the door and entered looking like a drowned cat. Katia gave me a look of sympathy and a touch of pity.

I was desperate for a few kind words that would act as painkillers and leave me with a small glimmer of hope. But I wasn't meant to get even this.

'I don't want to cause you more pain, Vera, but I feel obliged to tell you my opinion,' she said in a drawling voice. We had stepped outside, onto our common balcony, and were smoking in the cold. The night was pitch-black: the moon had pulled its cap down to the ears, not in the mood to show its face tonight. At the far end of the road, only the poplars with their naked branches could be seen.

She listened to me with a calm, unmoved expression. None of the things I told her with a broken heart seemed to surprise her.

'He's just an actor and nothing more. I never thought much of Aravantinos. I believe that his career and his professional success are the only things that matter to him. Such people have sold their soul to get where they are.' She made a pause but, on seeing my blank expression, she went on.

'I'm afraid he had planned everything he has done with you from the start. Sex is an excellent way of keeping someone under your thumb.'

'What are you trying to say?'

'He used you, sweetheart, to make everything go his way, and now he discarded you, because you're of no use to him.'

Was it just me, or did I sense a touch of sadism in her words? Or perhaps some slight feelings of anger that smouldered behind her icy composure? *A lady never loses her self-respect for any man, even if he is called Constantinos Aravantinos.* That's what her whole attitude cried out, and it helped me pull myself together. But I didn't even have a drop of courage left to follow her advice.

'Is that what you really think?' I must have looked like a 12-year-old that has her first innocent – but mortifying – questions.

She put her arm around my shoulders and pushed me into her room.

'You're in love with him, aren't you?' A smidgen of compassion could finally be seen in her eyes.

'No, I'm not!' I stubbornly said, and this gave me a pleasant surprise. 'It's only sexual attraction. I'll get over it! I'll make myself get over it!'

'Where will you go? Stay for a while, you're in no state to go out on your own,' she tried to make me stay when I tried to leave.

'Let me go. I want to cry in peace.'

'As you wish,' she said in a resigned, but collected, manner, as she crossed her arms. 'But don't forget about Hecuba.'

'Hecuba?'

'From the Iliad, Hector's mother. And Niobe, and Andromache, and so many others.'

'What are you trying to say?' I murmured in confusion. This was no time for mythological references.

'That your problem isn't the greatest tragedy the world has ever known. That's what I mean, sweetheart.'

****

It was after ten o'clock when I went out into the dark city streets to get some fresh air. I desperately needed to get out of my room. Tiny droplets of rain kept falling on my face, but the frosty October air felt refreshing. I hoped that some of my bitterness would be washed away.

I wandered around like a lost traveller and I couldn't decide on the main cause of my suffering. Was it because the door to my promised Eden had been slammed shut in my face and I found myself back to crawling in the mud? Was it that I was condemned never to find forgetfulness because his cursed fame would always find ways to remind me? Was it that I had been fooled for a second time or ... the thought – as it had just dawned on me – that I would no longer be able to write? He was my inspiration. Where would I find the strength to make him my hero once again after all this?

'I am you,' he had told me once – when was that? – in my dreams.

The reasons for my misery were many. I decided to go into the first bar I would find open, drink a bottle of wine, and then ... go back to the inn and slit my wrists open. It was the only way to take sweet revenge against this callous bastard. I wished I could actually become a vampire, return from the dead and horribly torture him. Only that thought gave me some relief.

'Here we go again,' Vicky would say if she saw what a mess I was. 'I'm afraid for you when you let yourself stew in this emotional juice.'

The historic city centre was a small pedestrian street,

surrounded by old houses with painted facades. Their ground floors housed shops, pubs and beer halls.

I entered the first beer hall I found; it was called the Mona Lisa. As soon as I stepped over the threshold, I thought that I was seeing things. I definitely knew who that plump girl with the plum-coloured hair, sitting with her back to me, was. It was her! But what was Melina doing there? She'd never told me that she had friends in Germany.

I approached her like one hypnotised, suddenly feeling very happy.

'Hey, Melina,' I approached her but... I would have felt really stupid if I hadn't already exhausted my stupidity allowance. Of course it wasn't her. I left, deeply disappointed.

I sat at a table and ordered red wine. A whole bottle.

Then I got the idea to give Melina a call. I would be charged a crazy amount of money since I was calling a Greek mobile number, but it was the last thing I cared about. She wasn't surprised to hear from me.

'You sound awful,' she said calmly. 'What happened, Vera?'

I told her everything, I rambled on for ten minutes without taking a single breath. In the end, I confided in her – with disarming honesty – about my decision to kill myself; I had nothing good to live for anymore. I felt such a failure, and so unlucky. He had ruined everything I had. When did I let him gain so much power over me? I was without any excuse.

'He stole my stories,' I whined. 'The stories I could write. How can I live without them?'

She listened to me without interrupting.

'Nobody took your stories away,' she finally said, somewhat severely. 'These stories are yours alone. Nobody can steal them from you. Not even him.'

'And yet,' I insisted, 'that's what happened. He gave them to me, and then he took them back. It was bound to happen this way.'

'Look,' she hesitated, reluctant to continue, 'normally, I don't like giving such straightforward advice. Everyone needs to find their own way. And I wouldn't normally tell you what I'm about to share with you. You must make your own discoveries when the time is right. But ... I will make an exception, because it seems to me that you really need it.'

Suddenly, my whole life was hanging from the words she was about say. Whatever they were, my self-preservation instinct, which was slowly dying, prayed that they were the right ones.

'It's just a game,' she said after a few seconds of silence. 'You shouldn't lose your cool over a game.'

'A game?'

'The game of the Great Hide and Seek: We call it that because we come into the world with our true potential hidden.'

I couldn't understand a thing of what she was saying.

'Let's say you're an actress,' she continued, 'and you take part in a play or a movie. Your part is to fall in love with your co-star and his character is supposed to abandon you. Would an actress ever kill herself because her part involves being betrayed? Of course not!'

'Of course not...'

'The most extreme thing you would do would be to have a discussion with your co-star, after the end of the shoot or the performance, about what – in your opinion – worked best so that you can repeat it, what didn't, and what you could do to improve it, isn't that so?'

'Yes! I guess so...'

'You're going through the same thing right now. You're part of a play; the difference is that you haven't realised it till now. But, deep down, you do know, we all know our parts, but we don't remember them. We sense where we came from, why we were born, and what the true part we were destined to fulfil is.'

'What is this play, Melina? What are you telling me?'

'The play of Creation. It's been performed non-stop since the very beginning.'

Geez, I didn't have the slightest wish to start dealing with Melina's metaphysical interests again.

'And what do I do now?' I literally felt lost.

'This plan, dear, has foreseen your spiritual and personal growth, progress and happiness. All signs point us in that direction, even when we're going through a narrow path; it doesn't lead to self-destruction and misery.'

'And if I choose to ignore this plan,' I said defiantly, 'if I keep wanting to die; what will happen then? Will someone punish me?'

'No, nobody is going to punish you. You will simply, and quite needlessly, hurt yourself. You will waste your useful-ness in this world. And, also, you will never know the end of the play. Let me put it this way: suicide is an irreversible, violent act, with no justification.'

I slowly took the way back, repeating Melina's words to myself. It was an unexpected escape from the despair I had sunk into, from tomorrow's pain that I thought I wouldn't be able to handle.

The more I walked, the more I found everything she had told me impossible and baseless, the more I believed in my initial reaction – and I did think she was a little crazy. But, I had calmed down a bit, and I didn't want to kill myself any longer. And what if she – there was a one in a million chance of that happening – was right?

'You're ruining everything,' she had told me. 'If you die, the same will happen to the performance. It will be indefinitely postponed. Is that what you really want, Vera?'

When I arrived at the ... haunted inn, it was around one in the morning. Strange silence enveloped the house whose windows were all dark. I climbed the three floors to my room, dragging my feet.

But ... as soon as I tried to unlock the door ... I realised that something was wrong. What the heck! I was sure I had locked the door before I left. I didn't have time to turn the lights on. A loving presence chased away the darkness. His hands pulled me out of the depths where I had sunk. His breath gave me the oxygen I needed to live for a few more years.

'Will you forgive me, baby, for the bullshit I say from time to time?'

Before I could say anything, I found myself sobbing in

his arms. Again, I lost my words and after I held him tightly in the twilight for a long time, and after I soaked his shirt with my tears and crumpled it by the way I was gripping him with my nails, I tried to tell him how much I needed him and how cold it was out there, but I couldn't get the words out. 'Yes,' I finally said, and it was the absolute affirmation of what I felt for him and couldn't name.

'How did you get in?' I asked him.

'You gave me the keys, did you forget?'

Indeed, I had forgotten that I had given him my keys, and that was a huge mistake. Because, as it turned out, there are doors that lead straight to hell.

That night, I decided to get a few keys back and lock some doors within me. Or at least try to.

I owed it to the memory of the little child hidden in my soul and who had had blind trust in him, in this man, against all reason. But this naive child was no longer alive! She had been murdered a few hours ago, and it was too late for apologies.

So, I decided that I couldn't trust Constantinos anymore. I had seen the cruel face love could sometimes have. I had been horrified to discover how easily it could become dangerous. Lethally dangerous.

Chapter 11

Milk Caramel on His Teeth

There are moments when the futility of this world, the aroma of mocha coffee and a rare day of sunshine in the forest of Boulogne become tightly connected, creating a bittersweet nostalgic scent. But, this only happened in spring. And, once in a while, even joy can become painful.

At other times, a spoonful of vanilla-flavoured mastic sweet, or black cherry conserve, remind you of a scratched knee. The number of times you fall flat on your face depends on how raw you are when you come out of the oven. If you come out of there before your time, you will fall for someone many times. If you come out overcooked, you will fall in love just once – but it will be strong – so as to break the stone wall of your isolation.

He chattered on for some time, talking about random things, and I listened to him, and waited. Then, once again, he changed the subject.

'There's a knife at the edge of every fierce passion,' he said. 'Lust is sharp if there is no love to round its edges.'

I thought at first that he was talking just like me when

I was writing, but I soon changed my mind. Constantinos usually had a more bombastic way of expressing himself. He could say the simplest thing in the world in a melodramatic way. His profession was probably to blame.

So, I wasn't surprised when he continued talking about the reality of other people and his reality. He had been beaten within an inch of his life, he told me, to combine these two, but to no avail.

'Now that I think about it, I no longer blame the people who used to see me as a problem child, of course. I've always been different from others; I was conscious of it and it was painful. Not belonging anywhere, in any group or category. I imagine that my parents' reaction and that of the rest of our family and friends was due to their surprise. They had no idea how to deal with me and this upset them.'

He was whispering, without any major changes in his inflection. He told me that he had suffered a lot in his life in order to get to where he was in the present.

I was struggling to hide the fact that I didn't feel sorry for him, for the misery he claimed that he had experienced. *After all*, I wanted to shout out, *you have everything. Everything, everything, everything! There is nothing in this world that fate has denied you. And that's very unfair, dammit!*

The truth is that I was jealous and this feeling contained a hint of resentment, which I refused to acknowledge. I envied him because he had succeeded. With his audacity, his stubbornness, his talent, his masculinity, his charm, using any means he possessed.

The night was whispering reverently outside the

windowpanes. For a moment, I thought that he had also charmed her with the strange darkness that his eyes projected and she was leaning against our window to hear what he was saying.

Once again, I had that inexplicable feeling that someone was standing right there, but I didn't bother getting up. There was no doubt it was just my imagination.

I leaned on my elbow and looked at him lying next to me in the twilight. It was two in the morning. A velvety silence had spread.

The night shook off her myriads of stars and sent them off to illuminate far away galaxies. In this small town, under the shadow of the slumbering mountains, a melancholy north wind was blowing that night.

He began to describe an abandoned two-storey house that used to be across the street from his family home in the district of Nea Krini, Thessaloniki. That unfinished skeleton of brick and cement was destined to house his ambitious plans for a while. He would gather all his best friends there every afternoon and they would perform plays – in a completely amateur way, of course.

It was just what the other guys wanted, the neighbours found it amusing, and their mothers took it upon themselves to sew costumes from old unwanted clothes. They even sold tickets, ten cents each, which was a large sum back then. Many times, during their rehearsal breaks or even during the performance, they would start fights and beat each other up for no reason at all.

'They said I was very bossy and a downright brat.'

He talked about it with pride, as if he had been knighted. Constantinos had been bossy and a brat as a child! Who would have thought?

Once, when they were performing a romantic play with knights and ladies of questionable character, all hell broke loose. His father, who was disgusted by his son's antics, suddenly jumped onto the stage and started smashing everything up.

His father had been a harsh, difficult man; things became tense every time he came home and everyone would stand at attention before him.

His father beat him black and blue in front of his mates, who had long ago accepted him as their leader, and he had worked hard to accomplish this.

Anyway, he felt so much anger and bitterness because of this humiliation that he felt the urge to grab a discarded brick that lay somewhere nearby and dash his father's brains out with it right then and there, in the middle of the debris of his ruined play.

'I imagine that the deep anger that stuck to me like a second skin stems from those years and perhaps even further back.'

When he started making some money from acting jobs, he felt a wild satisfaction, a mad joy, which could only be likened to drunkenness.

'I felt so great and invincible, as if I had the whole world at my feet.'

That's how he began to show me the 'snapshots' of an eventful life, and the more we 'looked' at them, the more clearly I saw how blurry and shaky they were, how wrongly focused, like the work of a clumsy photographer.

'My family says I'm the one who drove him to an early grave. The stroke he suffered was caused by the shame he felt for the career path his son had followed. Asimakis Aravantinos, the respectable merchant and family man, had a good-for-nothing actor for a son. That's what being an actor meant to him! How could he face his social circle with such a worthless son?

'"You killed him!" my aunts accused me to my face at his funeral.

'I felt such relief that the tyrant had finally died, just as I had wished. I was ecstatic, and I'm not ashamed to admit it.'

A sour taste in my mouth warned me that I was becoming too affected by this man. I shouldn't let myself get so actively involved in his 'drama', which I was now sure, he greatly exaggerated about. It was the only way Constantinos could really enjoy his dramatic monologues.

'When it dawned on me that these lights that shone on me were nothing but darkness in disguise, the darkness that lived in my soul, I got scared. I was afraid that everything was pure, dumb luck. Someone wanted to mess with me and they were offering me the stars, while the huge maw of the abyss was opening beneath my feet. Deep down, I also felt terrified that my sin wouldn't go unpunished. I was the one responsible for my father's death; I had wished it with my entire being. It was as if I had committed this premeditated, but unintentional, murder.'

When he had panic attacks, he told me, he just had to try the various drugs and alcohol cocktails at the endless parties he was invited to in order to deal with them. They had the power to calm him down, or even make him laugh, but it was just another show he was putting on, just a small reprieve from the pain.

'I kept wearing this fear even when my actual clothes turned into rags and I had to throw them away.'

I vaguely remembered that troubled period of his life when he was always stoned and starting fights for stupid reasons.

'In a moment of inspiration, I thought that the solution wasn't in hiding behind my clothes; I needed something more drastic. I had to change my skin.'

So he began looking for darker parts, for cursed characters who had a connection with the supernatural. Safe in the knowledge that he was in front of the camera, he could fearlessly go against every demonic element. This became a kind of psychoanalysis because he started getting better. He knew it was just another show, it wasn't his real life, but for a long time he refused to differentiate between the two.

'In this respect, I was lucky that I became an actor; otherwise, I would have gone mad. But you never get something without paying the price for it. In each of my parts, I left a piece of myself behind. In the end, I was in danger of losing my soul altogether – if we assume that I had one.'

I wanted to tell him that he hadn't lost these pieces for good. I had salvaged them and brought them back to him. Nothing is wasted, after all, nothing of what you give.

I got up, feeling upset. He had managed to leave me shaken even though I pretended to be unaffected. I poured a few inches of Martini into a glass. Of course, there was no ice; I would have to go down three floors and get some from the kitchen.

'I need a drink,' he said.

'There's only Martini here.'

'It'll do just fine.'

I didn't escape the journey to the kitchen. I put on my robe and slippers.

I started going down the stairs. Absolute silence reigned over the inn. My footsteps were silenced on the carpeted floor. The wind was whistling, and, occasionally, strong gusts of rain made the skylights rattle. These sounds became deafeningly loud in the stillness. I quickly made it to the second floor, trying to be as quiet as possible and that's when I stopped in my tracks, petrified. I firmly held on to the railing and blinked several times to make sure that my eyes weren't deceiving me. Fear allowed me to do nothing else.

A dark figure was standing at the end of the corridor. It was nightmarishly still, with a dead body's rigidity. It was standing near one of the room doors. It was trying to listen in on what was happening inside the room. It might have even been attempting to get in, I don't know. I couldn't make out who it was. Once the shadow sensed my presence, it hastily turned the corner the corridor formed and disappeared from sight.

With bated breath, I approached No 23; it was Eleana's room. With my heart in my mouth, I reached the corner of the corridor, more than ready to scream. But, there was no one there. Only absolute, almost unreal, stillness. I wondered whether I had dreamt this whole scene. My teeth rattled from fear.

Why do I feel that this silly girl will cause us big trouble? was my next thought.

I wondered who the occupants of the rooms round the corner of the corridor were. Alexander, Avgoustakos and Marianna. There was also a WC at the back, and a small storage room I had seen the Scarecrow going in and out of quite often. Of course, anyone could hide in there. After I thought about it for a while, I found it perfectly reasonable. But I didn't have the courage to wake everyone up at this late hour, just to look for something that I wasn't sure I had seen. When you're in the dark, there's always the possibility of misunderstandings and flights of fancy.

I went down the rest of the stairs on trembling legs. I got the ice and hurried up the stairs and back into the room. I took a few sips from my drink in order to recover and sat on the bed. He didn't seem to have taken any notice of my agitation since he was lost in his thoughts.

'For years, I wandered around in a misty landscape. Shadows would appear from behind trees and when I tried to touch them, to discover the face behind the mask, they – the women in my life – would fade away like smoke.'

He has a way with words, I thought. *Such a performance could get him many awards.* I was instantly ashamed of my cheap thoughts.

'Then I met Nadia and I immediately believed she was different. She was the most beautiful creature I had ever seen, fragile and sensitive. For a while, I thought that I had found my other half, and it was a fantastic feeling. Nadia was sensitive, but in a neurotic, crazy way that drove her to constantly looking for validation and attention from the first man who appeared before her. She clutched on to me with despair, but it seems that my support alone wasn't enough for her. And so, although we had already set a date for our wedding, she changed her mind at the very last minute and decided to take up with Symeonidis, a producer, who, she claimed, offered her more confidence and security. I was too unreliable to be able to help her.

'"We may be alike in character," she had told me, "but that doesn't mean that we are made for each other."

'I felt like the stupidest and most worthless man in the world, a loser. I struggled for months to accept our break-up, and I realised that it was impossible. So, I decided, by process of elimination, that the only solution was to kill her. I couldn't get her back, I couldn't forget about her, so what was left? If I wanted to stop suffering, if I wanted to put an end to all this, then her death was the only way I could free myself. So, I started planning my next steps with cold rationality.'

I had really begun to feel troubled. His talent had already dashed any objections I might have had about him. But, who was this person sleeping by my side? Who was I actually dealing with? With the Constantinos that everyone knew or with a would-be murderer?

'But, it seems that I'm lucky; perhaps because, deep down, I'm a good man, as I've been told. Things turned out quite differently.'

I knew what happened next. All the newspapers had buzzed about it back then and the channels had turned the news into a circus. They began to dust off every unknown aspect of Nadia's life, the actress having been killed when her car overturned in one of the many winding roads of Sounio. The autopsy revealed that she had been dead drunk. Then, all the details of her relationship with Constantinos came to light.

'Don't you see? For the second time in my life, I had wished with all my soul for someone's death, and it had actually happened. After that, I didn't know if I was really lucky or cursed.'

'It might have been pure coincidence,' I said, but he didn't seem to hear me.

Shortly after that, he left for France. He had been meaning to go; there was nothing holding him back. Greece had very few opportunities to offer him and he had big dreams for himself. There, he met Virginie and settled down.

'My wife was very good to me; she grounded me and supported me a lot. I owe her a great deal of gratitude for this,' he said with a deep sigh. He leaned wearily on his side.

'Why are you telling me all this?' I finally asked him.

'Why? ... Because sometimes, the darkness inside me

stirs, and I realise that it has never really left me, and that's what I've been afraid of these past few days...'

'Don't be,' I whispered to him. 'I don't intend to let anything bad happen to you.'

'But I might hurt you. I've done some bad things in my life, Vera.'

'I know.'

'I won't even pretend that I regret them.'

'I'm aware of that too. And I also know why you did them.'

'Why?'

'You had to. It was your way, your path. There was no alternative option.'

'There are a lot of things you don't know about me.'

'There's nothing I don't know about you.'

****

At 8.30 in the morning, my eyes shot open. My alarm clock was raising a racket. He wasn't next to me. I assumed he and the crew had already left. I threw the duvet aside and got up.

When I went downstairs for breakfast, absolute peace and quiet reigned in the dining room, which smelled deliciously of freshly baked cake and freshly brewed coffee.

'The others left a while ago,' Frau Matilde announced, her rosy cheeks stretched into a smile. Her eyelids fluttered like mischievous sparrows.

I must remember to ask her sometime why she's always so

happy, I thought listlessly and started to nibble on the piping hot traditional *stollen*.

At two in the afternoon, a small van, which had the words Zoo *Hellabrunn* printed on one side and *Munchen* on the other, entered the castle courtyard.

The tall skinny man moving with feline grace that came out of the van must have been around fifty and he had an extremely toned body. A cold smile hung – probably by a thumbtack – on his thin face; you would think that if it was somehow dislodged and dropped on the ground then he would be left with no smile, and also without a mouth.

In a matter of seconds, he became the focus of attention of the actors and technicians that surrounded him with expressions of impatience.

When he opened the back door of the van, loud exclamations, mixed with fear and admiration, fluttered around the gathered crowd. Everyone took a step back. From the depths of the van, the head of a grey wolf emerged, looking haughty, but obviously wary.

The animal jumped out with a graceful move that made his glossy fur ripple. Then, he stood petrified under a dozen pair of wide-open eyes studying him with awe. The wolf in turn drew back before the crowd of onlookers.

'Don't be afraid, he's harmless,' the German animal trainer said coldly.

'Oh, he's so beautiful,' Evelina chirped, overly excited.

'Wild thing,' Eleana lisped while Avgoustakos couldn't stop taking pictures.

The wolf, as calm as a pet, came and lay down at the feet of his handler, who was in consultation with Venetis and Stamatis about the animal's treatment during shooting. The German handler would also be present to direct the wolf's reactions.

'Can you go find him and wake him up? We're starting any minute now.' Stamatis sat beside me and gave me a friendly nudge. His look was flooded with saucy innuendos.

'Who?' I asked absent-mindedly.

'Come on, Vera, I thought you were smarter than that! Constantinos, who else? He must have fallen asleep somewhere in the castle. Again. You're working him too hard,' he added in a sickly sweet voice. He would never lose the opportunity to make a dig about my relationship with our lead actor.

The truth is that the whole story had become something of a joke. Even if he could only steal five minutes from the shoot – fortunately, breaks lasted quite longer – Constantinos would disappear through the halls of the castle and fall asleep wherever he could find: on an 18th-century sofa, in a four-poster bed; the museum was, of course, full of traditional furniture from past centuries.

We had to 'comb' every corner of the castle in order to find him and wake him up every time. Usually, this was the duty of the museum guard, who shuddered at the terrible ease with which Constantinos jumped over the protective ropes and entered areas restricted to the public.

I climbed a small staircase with iron railings leading to

the upper floors and entered a long corridor. I passed by displays depicting scenes of everyday life in the 18th century with life-sized mannequins, heavy pine furniture and household utensils made from tin.

As I had suspected, I found him in the large bedroom with the wooden bed, where a few scenes had been scheduled to be shot. He was dead to the world, with his shoes on the blue cover. I almost shrieked, anxious about his mistreatment of the silk fabric. I gently shook him. In vain. So, I had to use more effective means.

'What is it? What happened?' He shot up, annoyed.

'Wake up. They're waiting for you downstairs.' I tried to hold my laughter back. A sleepy mumble was his reply.

'Constantinos, please, get up. You'll be late!'

'Let me get some more sleep,' he complained, 'five more minutes. I'm terribly sleepy. Go on ahead and I'll follow you in a minute.'

'Come on, just try.' I pulled him by the hand.

'Dammit! Can't anyone have a quiet moment to themselves?'

He jumped up, now utterly ticked off. He desperately tried to straighten his wrinkled clothing, looking dishevelled, and adorable. I burst out laughing.

'Why are you laughing? Do you see something funny?' He was still pissed off and it made him irresistible.

He walked to the window, opened it and breathed in the fresh air. He ran his fingers through his hair and stayed still for a while, gazing at the forest that stretched out on the foot of the hill.

Nature had turned that part of the landscape into something enchanting. The beech trees had intertwined their naked branches into strange formations and had created impenetrable vaults. There were also huge oaks with gnarled roots as sharp as the talons of wild birds, and elms, along with huge bushes and other unfamiliar plants.

'I had a dream,' he said. 'I saw myself entering a man's dream, and it was a very beautiful feeling.'

'Do you often do these tricks?'

'I suppose so. It's my job.'

'And ... how do you do it?'

'Oh, I can't tell you. It's a professional secret.'

The icy wind crept in from the open window, making me shiver.

'I feel a little bad about last night,' he began apologising awkwardly. 'I don't know what came over me and I told you all those things. I don't like burdening others with my problems.'

He must have felt uncomfortable after opening up to me, but I couldn't understand this contradiction. He always poured all this stuff out in his interviews. There was no great mystery surrounding his personal life. Why did he start feeling bad about his past right now?

'But ... the truth is that I felt a lot freer afterwards, as if the feelings of anxiety I had felt moved elsewhere. But let's leave it at that.' He ended our conversation with a vague gesture.

I couldn't think of anything to say that would be fitting for the occasion. That always happened when I was dealing with real people. I could sit in front of a piece of paper and come up with a dozen different philosophies, but when it came to actual discussions, I got tongue-tied.

At that moment, Stamatis appeared in the doorway.

'Here you are. Venetis wants you downstairs. We're starting any minute now.' Then, he saw me. 'Sorry for interrupting you...'

'No, it's ok. I'll be right there,' Constantinos said and disappeared down the stairs.

I put my jacket, hat and gloves back on, and went out into the bitter frost. The cold made me feel better – it somewhat cleared my head – though my chest still hurt from the worry I felt.

As soon as I stepped out, Katia's behaviour surprised me. Something was wrong with the picture I saw. The woman was sitting next to the wolf and she was stroking his head as though he was a puppy. She didn't seem to care that her long sheepskin skirt was touching the wet grass. The animal seemed to be enjoying her attention; you could see it from his half-closed eyes.

'Wolves are very intelligent creatures,' she said when I approached them, 'and sensitive,' she added sadly.

Wolves are sensitive creatures? I had never heard that before!

When I added a wolf in my story, I had completely different things in mind.

For me, the she-wolf was the embodiment of a nightmare. All the hidden traumas that lived in the dark areas of the mind and soul found the most appropriate manifestation in this animal. In the film, the she-wolf springs from the castle's labyrinthine catacombs and hunts the heroes down. She manages to injure the protagonist before falling dead from the bullets of the Jewish David Ezra. An angry, dangerous creature that had many similarities with a presence that had haunted my life. The presence of my mother. I froze when I realised the similarities.

'Not to mention that they're in danger of becoming extinct. It's obvious who the actual wild beast on this planet is,' Katia added wistfully.

Constantinos came to join us just in time. He seemed thrilled by the spectacle.

'It's really tame,' he frowned when he saw the wolf up close. 'Who knows what has been done to him!'

'Would you prefer him in his natural state?' I asked.

'I think it's a very misunderstood animal,' he said and tried to touch him. But the animal got spooked. The wolf crouched and let out an angry growl. Constantinos abruptly pulled back his hand and seemed unsure of what to do. The wolf showed his teeth for the first time and narrowed his eyes menacingly.

'I always say that wolves have an infallible instinct,' Katia said with deep satisfaction, 'and they can see through people at a glance,' she continued, throwing Constantinos a poisonous look.

It was remarkable how much these two 'liked' each other.

A mutated substance, something between sleet and hail, soon began to fall, decorating our clothes with icy pebbles.

The wind began to howl threateningly, and it was now time to wrap things up.

****

After returning to the hotel, a surprise wearing glasses and a cashmere sweater was waiting for us in the lounge.

Papanikolaou was sprawled on the couch in front of the fireplace, enjoying his whiskey and leafing through a book of engravings.

When he saw our group enter, shouting and teasing each other, he suddenly turned melancholic.

'Welcome, my lone rider,' Evelina squealed joyfully.

'It's like you said, sweetheart.' He kissed her on the cheek. 'Only lately, I've been feeling more and more lonely and less and less like a ... rider. That's my job: it's a one-man show. How I envy you all,' he said as he kissed us one by one. 'Teamwork and creativity are very important things.'

'What brings you here, Nick?' Venetis greeted him.

'I came to fish for hilarious, behind-the-scene happenings, my friend. Everybody has questions, they want to learn details. The media in Greece and France are salivating at the thought of news from your set and they sent me here on a mission to get all the hot material. So, I'm warning you. Don't hide anything from me! I travelled all the way here; don't I deserve a tiny exclusive?'

We all sat around the fire in an attempt to ease the tension. Frau Hilda was going back and forth carrying trays with coffee and pieces of freshly baked banana tart.

'Well, how do you feel, Constantinos?' Papanikolaou lost no time in asking.

'About what?'

'About coming back to your homeland, working in a Greek production,' he meekly explained.

'To tell you the truth,' Constantinos said after much thought, 'I don't feel like I have a home in any country. It may sound harsh, but it's how things are. In France, I still feel like a cultural refugee, and in Greece I don't fit in anywhere.'

'Yes, but it was your choice to leave. Nobody drove you away. In fact, I would say that the opposite is true.'

'You act as if you don't know how it is. Sometimes, you don't need anyone to tell you to leave. You can realise it by yourself when a person or a place is forcing you to. I think that there's a whole art of knowing when to do just that.' His tone showed that he was reluctant to continue this line of conversation.

'Which of my photos do you like more, darling?' Evelina's appearance lightened the atmosphere. She had come downstairs carrying some photos. She showed them to Papanikolaou so that he could choose.

'You're a goddess, my love, from the front and from the side...!' The eloquent look he threw on her sexy behind suggested that something else was on the tip of his tongue.

Avgoustakos, who never strayed too far from anything, had another tempting suggestion.

'Nick, we've discovered an amazing taverna with Greek

food nearby. Are you in?' His plump cheeks stretched into an eager smile.

At half past eight, when most of the group left, I announced that I couldn't join them. I needed to relax and unwind by taking a hot bath.

When I was left by myself, I revisited my earlier thoughts. Katia and the wolf. The wolf and my mother. Connecting element: the wild animal. The buried nightmares. Constantinos. My love for him. Katia's hatred. My mother. Katia, once again. What did the two of them have in common? I had all the pieces in my hands and I was trying to put them together but the resulting image didn't fit. I had to allow time to work its magic in order to unite all these motley elements.

And that old dream that had almost scared me out of my wits? The girl with the wedding dress and the severed hands in Katia's family home? Who was the dead girl that was struggling to tell me something? Didn't Katia have a daughter? Why does she never talk about her? All I know is that she's a History of Art — I think — student in Italy. The dream was a sign; there was no doubt about it.

****

Night fell like a menacing shadow that kept growing. It was midnight when I went to bed all weary, but sleep wouldn't come.

Frustrated, I kept wrestling with the covers: one minute

I was too hot, the next, too cold. I kept tossing and turning, full of tension, until I couldn't take it any longer. I got up and went out onto the balcony to smoke a cigarette. I was shivering by the time I stepped back into the room and slipped under the duvet.

Suddenly, I heard a knock on the door – I held my breath – was it actually the door or was it just what my heart wanted? I whispered a subtle 'yes'. His shadow came in first, and he followed. He came and sat next to me. I touched his cheek and it felt incredibly warm.

'Your hands are cold,' he said. 'Lie down,' he said after a while and I obeyed – a really strange thing for me to do, if anyone knew my habits.

The silence that surrounded us contained the unbearable nostalgia of a familiarity we had experienced in a time long forgotten. Even my breathing sounded loud enough to hurt that fragile silence.

I tried to stop breathing. I wanted to hear only the light crackling sound the sheets made as his hand crept over them. He explored my body. He did it so slowly, almost indifferently, that you might have said it was the last thing that interested him. For a while, I kept thinking that I was almost asleep, I had already begun to relax and nod off. Perhaps that was his purpose, to get me to go to sleep and then make love to me. But why would he do that?

'Stand up.'

The whisper sounded deafening to me. My body unconsciously did what he asked.

'What do you want me to do next?'

He didn't answer me immediately. He just stood opposite me for a few seconds that seemed endless.

'Take off your clothes,' he said quietly.

He was whispering in that husky, sensual voice that the actors who don't shout or scream in films are trained to use. Even if the world is falling apart around them, they won't lose their self-control and will remain calm.

This scene seemed a bit forced but it didn't stop me from obeying the voice that sounded like a magic flute to my ears. Even if he asked me to jump off the balcony naked, I would do it without any questions or objections. Fortunately, he didn't ask me to do anything like that, he just said, 'take off your clothes,' and this sounded quite normal.

'Won't you help me?'

He threw me a look that left no room for objections.

I slowly let my robe fall to the floor. Slightly trembling, I also slipped out of my nightgown.

'Take everything off!' he insisted.

I was left naked in front him, in the twilight. He looked at me without reacting at all, as though he had been hypnotized. He said that he thought I was beautiful and then I realised that I had been holding my breath for a long time.

Finally, he got up and came close to me. An enormous supernova was menacingly approaching planet Vera. Huge tidal waves were already sweeping across the planet's surface and, sooner or later, it would be swallowed by them; it was inevitable.

It was only a matter of time before he turned me into a tiny ball of matter in the palm of his hand and absorbed me.

He took a handkerchief out of his pocket and blindfolded me. I was shocked. I didn't even dream of reacting.

He led me to the bed and made me lie down. I could hear his breathing, quiet and even, tickling my ear. I felt his lips very gently touch my cheek. I still felt uncomfortable. A few more seconds passed before I figured out his plan. I started to suspect something when he lifted my head and pulled the pillow from underneath. I was overcome by indescribable impatience. He had obviously removed the pillowcase. He immobilised my hands by tying my wrists to the headboard.

'Scared?' he whispered.

'Should I be?'

'Perhaps...'

'Are you going to hurt me?'

'I could very easily do so if I wanted to...'

'Do you want something like that, baby?'

'You're under my control, you know...' I heard him laugh softly.

'Well, then, do as you like...'

For some time, he did absolutely nothing. I felt him sitting next to me, lurking in the dark. I heard him, I smelled him: he was like a vicious animal that lets his prey go mad from fright before devouring it.

Then his hand began a long journey over my body. He started from my neck and fought a bit with my ears, but he soon trailed downwards. He explored thousands of paths that I had never even imagined existed. I was sure that all these routes would forever remain etched on my skin. Then, I wouldn't wear skin any longer, but a fur coat in order to hide the marks on my skin, or to reveal what I was at that moment: an affectionate cat purring with delight at the hands of her master.

'Take the blindfold off, I want to see you!'

'Not yet!'

He continued 'torturing' me slowly and, to make the situation even more unbearable, he began kissing me everywhere, until I felt myself transforming yet again. I was no longer a cat; I became something else, something with an indefinable shape. I felt myself constantly melting and stretching until I finally realised what I was: a milk caramel toffee between his teeth, one of those soft candies wrapped in golden foil that used to melt in our mouths, when, as children, we ate them.

When he removed the blindfold from my eyes, at last, he was on top of me, naked, and he was mine. It was the loveliest sight after being in the dark for so long.

He continued his journey giving me 41, 51, 101 kisses and that was all I needed! I finally understood the magical part that numbers played in my life. At that moment, I felt it with my entire being that we had reached the Ultimate Oneness. Afterwards, peacefulness fell over us, a wonderful tranquillity that concentrated all the nectar and the ambrosia of my past life and that of the next in a single drop of time. And this extract of pleasure was mine, just mine, and it would remain so for all eternity. No one would ever be able to take it away from me.

'Tell me a story, Vera. I want to hear a new story,' he asked me early in the morning. I wasn't surprised, I had expected it. He would have said it sooner or later. And it was also time to seriously start thinking about my new book. And, once again, he was meant to be the one who would push me to make the start.

'I'll tell you one,' I finally said, 'but, will you tell me about the dreams? How did you know about Mr Leroi giving his greetings to me when we were in Paris?'

'Of course I'll tell you,' he murmured dully.

I started telling him a story about a prince of old times, handsome, but corrupted. The villagers of the area feared and hated him because ... on moonless nights, he would send his men to grab any village girl he lusted over, preferably a virgin...'

'And then? What happened after that?' Constantinos started laughing softly, 'And you expect me to play this guy?'

I didn't give him an answer.

'One day, a woman caught his eye, but she was married ... He abducted her ... But, she wasn't afraid of him ... And then he fell in love with her, with a passion that bordered on madness ... The woman fell pregnant ... The villagers were enraged by this shameless whore. So, one night, as the jackals howled, they beat her to death. Before she died, the woman cursed her beauty ... Her lover sensed the danger but he couldn't stop this evil from happening. They rushed to his tower to burn him ... He let his dogs loose on them ... After these events, terrible rumours left the crowd stupefied. The prince had completely lost his mind ... he was demanding toddlers, and babies in the crib, in return for his own murdered child. Who was the worst human beast in history?' I turned to ask him but I saw that he had fallen asleep.

I doubt if he had even heard half of the things I had narrated. I also didn't quite understand what I had been rambling on about all this time. Why was the spectre of death bound to float over every passionate erotic embrace?

How did this fairy tale end up being so cursed and bitter?

And how could he fall sleep without solving Mr Leroi's mystery for me, without saying a word about my own anxieties ... even though the filthy liar had promised?

Chapter 12

Revelations

'Can I give you a small piece of advice, sweetie?'

Evelina pulled me aside when I went downstairs for breakfast in the morning.

The others headed for the dining room.

Her look told me we were in cahoots with each other – I never figured out about what. The diva always treated me with polite condescension.

'I hope you don't take this the wrong way...' she started – though the tone of her voice clearly said: *You can take this the wrong way. I don't care. I'll say what I want* – 'but you were too loud last night! The whole place heard you!' she finally blurted out and looked at me with angelic sweetness, full of 'friendly' understanding.

The whole place? I had no idea that there were other people around us when we were making love. I thought it was just the two of us. On an island cut off from the rest of the world. Lost in deep space. That's what I thought. And then ... who had made all that noise? As far as I remember, I was holding my breath the whole time.

'Oh, really?' was all I could say and hurriedly walked ahead, feeling very awkward.

In the dining room, a new shock was waiting for me. Well, they do say, "a guilty conscience needs no accuser."

'Honestly, why are you writers so kinky?' Stamatis started chewing me out as soon as I set foot in the room.

He was holding a thick book in his hand and brandishing it like a bat. There was no doubt he was talking to me.

'What? What do you mean?' I was dumbfounded. That was definitely a catty remark. He was beating about the bush, not like Evelina, who had been pretty straightforward with me.

'For example,' he continued fiercely, with a passion he hadn't shown before, 'if, in one of your books, the protagonist is a woman, you think it necessary to tell us every detail of her first menstrual period and how she felt, what tools her gynaecologist used to examine her, when she lost her virginity, you give all the painful details. If she's unlucky enough to be giving birth, you give all the gruesome details.

'As for men, you have it in for them. The way he masturbated when he was younger, the shock he suffered when he caught his parents in bed, how his mother beat him, how he felt like a eunuch when he couldn't get it up with that babe. And there's dozens more I could mention! I don't understand why you enjoy degrading people. And the funny thing is that the more one humiliates their long-suffering heroes, the greater writer one is thought to be...'

'But, that's how life actually is.'

I could barely hold my laughter. I recognised the book: it was a famous American author's latest bestseller.

'Really, and you want me to believe you? That two or three insignificant moments can describe someone's whole life?'

'No, of course not, but it's those moments that define and highlight someone's character.'

'Why shouldn't a man's life be defined by – let's say – a nice wine?' Avgoustakos piped in, in the midst of devouring a slice of bread with jam.

'Or a good shag,' Stamatis interrupted him.

'Accompanied, of course, by the necessary hors d'oeuvres,' Avgoustakos explained, so as not be misunderstood. He had begun to drool.

'Don't give her any ideas!' Stamatis told him. 'An author can even describe, in great detail, the whole process that comes after digestion, if you get what I mean.'

'Stamatis! We're trying to have lunch here!' Hatzipetridis scolded him.

He apologised, though he didn't seem to be really sorry. I was doubled up in laughter.

'I think this conversation has fallen to very low levels,' I said, wiping the tears from my eyes. 'Anyway, I don't feel obliged to apologise in the name of all the authors around the world. Everyone does what they think best for the sake of realism in their story.'

An hour later, Constantinos and I were on our way to Munich.

The weather was quite nice and the one-day break we had from shooting was invaluable. I had come up with the idea for this trip. I insisted on showing him the city of my student years, where I had begun my post-graduate studies in the Theory of Literature. I never completed them because even more unfortunately, I got married.

Only very recently had I understood what they say about the pleasure of driving fast. So, even though we were on a country road where the speed limit was strictly predetermined, I found myself exceeding it many times.

'These Bavarian landscapes are so boring,' he sleepily grumbled. 'All the villages look identical; the houses have the same pointy roofs. Even the grass is standing at attention.'

I couldn't agree with him. I fleetingly pulled my attention away from the steering wheel in order to admire the scenery. It was beautiful, painted in the colours of autumn in the way that can only be found in these northern parts. The leaves were marked with dark red, wonderful splashes of colour. Small and larger fenced farms. Houses with pretty gardens and lawns. Calmly flowing rivers. A withered sun, as if it had just come out of a tin, was sparingly giving us some feeble sunlight. A weak rainstorm appeared, but it stopped just as quickly.

'You know what landscape left a lasting impression on me?' he continued absent-mindedly. 'In Spain, between Malaga and Granada, there are endless fields full of orange and lemon trees. We're talking about thousands of trees, and their fragrance is so strong that it can be overwhelming.'

That reminded him of a song whose lyrics were derived

from a Federico Garcia Lorca poem and he started singing it softly. It described the many thousands of lemons that can be found from Cadiz to Seville. It seems that he didn't remember the rest of the lyrics. He stopped and stared out the window.

Something stirred within me at the sound of this song.

'Have you ever heard of it?' he asked me.

I had, and I was very familiar with it! Only I hadn't heard it for nearly 25 years, perhaps even more.

Suddenly, time held no meaning. The years that had intervened were simply crossed out. People stopped getting older and time stood frozen. There was only me, wrapped in a pink blanket made of a soft mohair material, clutching a doll that I carried with me everywhere even though her eyes were missing.

My father would sing me several songs every night before he tucked me in. I remembered this particular song very clearly. It contained many unfamiliar words and it confused me as a child.

'What is Gibraltar?' I would ask my father.

'A place very far away, near the edge of the world.'

My father would lower his voice until it became the air that whistled through the leaves of the orange trees and would hold his eyes wide open. He liked spooking me with his fairy tales.

'Have you ever been there?'

'I haven't... but Odysseus has, a long time ago, and it's just as good. He met a beautiful woman there – she must have been a goddess. She was called Calypso. She loved him and did everything to keep him by her side. She would treat him to nectar in golden cups, and ambrosia, and made him stay with her by force for seven years.'

'And what happened then?'

'After Odysseus managed to escape, he went to ... Cadiz!'

'Where is that?'

'Well ... somewhere nearby,' Apostolis Kalogeras had told her, scratching his head in embarrassment.

'And what did he do there?'

'*Contrabando!*'

'What is *contrabando*?'

'Smuggling!'

That's how I came to believe that my father had the answers to all the questions of life, both true and false.

After that, of course, I asked what smuggling is and what smugglers do.

'They're very tall men, who only work in secret at night, and always get into trouble with the police.'

I came to the conclusion that they must be heroes to do such dangerous things.

'Where did Odysseus go next?'

'Afterwards, he went to ... Andalusia,' my father told me excitedly, though I'm pretty sure he had no clue where Andalusia was. 'There he rescued a beautiful girl from the clutches of a dragon called Franco. The dragon had driven his country to a terrible and bloody civil war – just as it happened here in Greece. Odysseus then rescued the girl from the clutches of the dragon that wanted to marry her by force.'

[277]

At this point, the story turned into a nightmare, but fairy tales should be a little scary, otherwise they sound boring and fake, as my father would say, and people who don't have anything important to fight for in their lives turn very weak.

So, Odysseus killed the dragon and married her, and the people of Andalusia made him their hero and cheered for him for days and nights without end. Because 'the people that are very wise, only bow down when the stars of love in the heavens rise.'

'But, wasn't his wife Penelope already waiting for him?' I sometimes woke him up from his 'delirium'.

'Yes... of course...' He always hummed and hawed with such questions that brought him abruptly back to reality. 'She was waiting for him, of course... but if someone has wanderlust in his blood, if it's his destiny to always wander, as they say in my village, then he'll never be happy sitting quietly in the same place.'

He always stayed silent beside me until I fell asleep, lost in his daydreams. Riding the wind, he saw, for the first time, exotic places with fragrant winds that treat you to spices, cinnamon, cumin and ginger just by the sound of their names.

Every night, he would blend together stories taken from Homer, fairy tales, folk songs, and his own imagination, and then he would serve them to me on a silver platter, to his princess, as he liked to call me.

And all these stories had the same refrain[8]: the one Constantinos had been singing to himself. It talked about a little girl gazing at the ships arriving in Malaga's port.

By that point, I was always half asleep and I couldn't ask him if Malaga was beautiful, and how it was possible for a man's bitterness to make a lemon tree wither. So, I was left with a few questions.

I turned to Constantinos to tell him the rest of the song and I saw that his head was resting on the side and that he had fallen asleep. A transparent peace spread like an invisible net that enveloped us. The whistle of the wind could be faintly heard from afar. Nothing seemed able to crack that delicate silence. As if all the elements of nature had conspired to hold their breath and let him sleep.

Time stopped once again. Constantinos was a little boy who was quietly sleeping. That deep wrinkle between his eyebrows, the one that appeared whenever – all the time – he wanted to tell the world, 'I demand you take me seriously; there's more to me than just another handsome face,' had disappeared.

And who was I? His mum or something like that? I was mature, there was no doubt there. He was immature and I had to protect him. Or was the opposite true, just as I had thought earlier?

How do the borders of time diffuse and melt like chocolate in a bain-marie? How do old shadows emerge stronger than ever when you thought you had banished them for good? Roles and identities get mixed up and, though you are a little girl, you find yourself a mum with obligations and the one you thought resembled your father is nothing but a man-child.

And all that because of a thread that escaped from the fabric of memory after it got snagged on a verse. I smiled and just gazed at him. *He's so handsome*, I thought once again. Even if I spent two thousand years just looking at him, I would never get bored at all.

More thoughts dropped by for a visit, and they were welcome, as I let my eyes travel on different parts of his face. For a few hundredths of a second more than I should have. But that short amount of time was enough for something bad to happen. There are many cases of instant karma in this world, even if they are caused by mere thoughts.

A furious car horn broke me out of my reverie. I heard the tyres squeal on the asphalt. Was it just me or did I really let out one long terrified scream? As if in a dream, I saw myself struggling to keep the car on the wet road but it was too out of control and it followed a drunken zigzag course. I had entered the left lane without checking to see who was driving behind me at a higher speed. The other driver beeped angrily at me for not letting him overtake me. I reacted spasmodically. Panic gripped me when I saw the highway disappear from my field of vision. The car left the road and, with an ugly jerk, fell into a field. During all this time, my leg was stuck on the brake and I was hysterically thinking: *Why won't the damned thing stop?* I wasn't thinking clearly enough to realise that the wheels had jammed. The car followed a crazy route in the field. I saw the thick trunk of an oak approaching, getting dangerously close, with the frightening wish to smash us with its trunk but...we stopped a few inches before we crashed into it. I don't know if it was a miracle, but the car stopped, and that's the important part.

I was sweating and trembling. My chest ached from the pressure of the seat belt. My mouth was dry. My heart beat deafeningly until I finally saw that nothing tragic had happened, apart from me getting the fright of my life...

'Are you okay?' I said, but I didn't have the chance to finish the phrase.

The co-driver's seat was empty. I jumped out of the car in the grip of panic. I saw him walking a couple of hundred yards away. *When did he find the time to walk that far?*

'Constantinos, are you all right?' I cried out hysterically, but my legs weren't being of great help and I couldn't run to him.

He mustn't have heard me because he continued trudging forward like a sleepwalker. He climbed up a small hill and leaned against a tree. Though I could only see his back, he appeared to be admiring the view as though he didn't have a care in the world. Stumbling along the way, I managed to reach him and touched him lightly on the shoulder. *He's just smoke and will dissolve*, I thought, *like a morning mirage*. He was very pale. *He was killed*, I continued thinking to myself. *I killed him, and this is his ghost*. Unbearable pain engulfed me at this thought. He turned towards me very slowly and I saw that he had an out-of-place smile.

'When did you find the time to rewrite the script, Vera?'

There was something unsettling in his eyes that made me freeze.

'You've brought everything upside down,' he continued

very quietly, his voice coming out like a slight breeze. 'This is the second time you perform your magic tricks. Of course, I won't say we didn't glimpse death. But a second shock is sometimes needed in order to recover from something else that's tormenting you. Isn't that what they say? We glimpsed death,' he echoed his earlier words. 'I have never heard a funnier phrase before.'

'What are you talking about?' I mumbled, terrified.

I wanted to shake him in order to make him come to his senses, but I didn't have the time to do so. His body began to shake with crazy laughter and he plopped himself down at the root of the tree, grasping his head. I just stood there, looking at him as though I had turned into stone. That laughter scared me more than the look in his eyes, even more than his words, because it didn't sound like the laugh of a normal person.

I stood still like this for several moments until I realised that something was bubbling up inside me. It was a tiny giggle that began to rise up like a stream from the bottom of my belly, then thickened and became a snigger, and my mouth turned into a huge question mark. My laughter quickly turned into a torrent that made me shake all over. I fell on the grass beside him, clutching at my stomach. I was drowning in liberating laughter that was trying at all costs to claim its freedom from the darkness of fear.

'And what does Death look like, if we caught a glimpse of him? And I might need to put him in one of my stories. Shouldn't I know what this guy looks like?'

I felt wrecked as I tried to wipe the tears that kept leaking from my eyes. I was very happy with the wonderful discovery I had just made. Up until then, I thought that the bloodletting of fear begins with love, but, quite unexpectedly, another weapon had been revealed to me.

It seems that fear wanted to have the last word. When we got back in the banged-up car – the bumper was slightly drooping and the right wing had deep scratches on it – it made a menacing reappearance.

'I ... I'm not sure I can drive,' I stammered.

My fingers were nervously tapping on the steering wheel, which suddenly looked like a guillotine to me.

'Let me try,' he said and I let him take the seat behind the wheel, despite knowing he hadn't driven in years. But you can't forget how to drive, it's just like riding a bike, isn't that what they say?

'What was that you said before ... For the second time ... What magic tricks do I perform, Constantinos?' I asked him a little later, on our way back to the village.

Neither of us had the courage to drive all the way to Munich.

'Not right now, I'm driving! Can't you see?' he said with pride.

He was truly very proud of himself for having managed this without two-three years of psychotherapy.

'You say very strange things at times,' I insisted. 'Do you think I don't notice? Will you tell me the truth, eventually?'

'No!'

He was looking straight ahead and didn't even care to spare me a glance.

'Why?'

'Because the truth is a bit strange, you know. Not to mention incredible.'

I was about to burst with curiosity.

'It's related to that accident you had back then ... isn't it?'

'Maybe.'

After this diplomatic answer, he didn't say another word. I didn't dare bring this topic up again, seeing how he had clammed up. *Let him be*, I told myself, *some extra time is needed until we can see the pearl.*

****

We had somewhat calmed down from the shock of the accident by the time we returned to the inn. We found most of the others gathered around the fireplace. They were drinking coffee and chatting with each other. Venetis was explaining his plans for the next day's shoot and his ideas about the post-production editing of shots of the wolf he had taken. He seemed excited.

I sat silently in a corner, lost in thought. I was unable to follow the conversation. Constantinos had gone upstairs to take a bath.

I was looking at the flickering fire, absent-mindedly sipping my coffee and munching on biscuits, so I didn't get wind of when the conversation changed. But, the topic was too saucy for me not to notice and it had been started by – who else? – Papanikolaou.

'Sex,' he explained in an erudite manner, 'is a libation to

eternity. We all owe our existence to an erotic spasm. Isn't it our duty to return this favour to the Eternal Soul that gave birth to us? By repeating, of course, as often as necessary, this bloodless and quite admittedly enjoyable act by way of sacrifice?'

'That's beautiful, Nick,' I said spontaneously. 'Is this the quote of someone famous? How come I never heard it before?'

'Yes! It's mine! Do you like it?'

I searched for the notepad I always carried with me for such moments.

'May I write it down?'

'And love? What role does love play in it?' Evelina purred.

'Love, my dear, is a terrible torture. Uninvited prejudices, guilt, and denial of all kinds invade love. Only a masochist would voluntarily agree to submit, repeatedly in fact, to this torture. No, no, I'd rather burn in hell. "Remove this cup from me," as Jesus said.'

He stroked his tousled grey hair with a calm movement, stretched back on the sofa and burst out laughing.

'And, without doubt, here lies the big difference between a man and a woman,' he continued, addressing Evelina. 'Women always get more pleasure during sex when it's coupled with romantic feelings, but with men the opposite is often true.'

'That sounds very cynical,' Evelina insisted.

'Why? Sex is much more sincere, more tangible, than the nebulous feeling called love. It isn't a bad check, or a stock market bubble. It's paid upon delivery. Just think, what could be more honest than telling a woman: "My fair lady, I want to make love to you."'? You women should appreciate this and not demand a whole lot of flirting and lies before sleeping with a guy. Long live sex,' he said, raising his glass of whiskey.

Naturally, he found a staunch supporter in Stamatis, who looked at the journalist with his mouth wide open in wonder. Amused laughter by everyone present followed.

'How about you, Vera? Do you think I'm right?'

I suddenly woke up from my daydreaming. For a moment, I thought to ask him to repeat the question so that I wouldn't say anything irrelevant.

'I ... I want to say that your words sound quite interesting and I must tell you that they don't surprise me at all. It was exactly what I expected to hear from you and you didn't disappoint me.'

And after having exhausted the diplomatic channels, I had to say something meaningful. At least, I felt I had this obligation by the way he looked at me, as if waiting to hear the absolute truth.

'But, you will allow me to see things from a different perspective,' I continued. 'Humans are disposable and ephemeral. The only eternal and indestructible thing is art; I think we all agree on that. And no one can deny that many masterpieces owe their existence, their inspiration, to love. I don't care if it's for a person, an idea, or for love itself. And that's the only reason why I think love is worth the hassle.'

'The truth is that artists need love – unhappy and

unfulfilled love, as a rule – you have to admit it – in order to be able to create.'

'It may be so!'

'But as for me, God took pity on me and I didn't become an artist. So I'm not obliged to submit my mortal flesh to this painful ordeal.'

I didn't get what this ordeal he was talking about was exactly – that of love or that of artistic creation? – but I preferred not to ask him.

Stamatis came and sat beside me.

'Hey, Vera, what's the deal with the kid?'

'Alexander?' Jeez, I had completely forgotten about him in my daze. 'What happened?'

'How should I know? He's been locked up in his room since this morning and hasn't come out at all. That boy's really weird.'

His words made me feel worried about Alexander. I don't know why I felt responsible for him. I thought I could do something for him, but I kept postponing it.

Climbing the stairs to my room, I came upon two forbidden lovers in the middle of a loving, not to say suspicious, tryst. They were sitting on the steps leading to the second floor. The beautiful Eleana, Alexander's cause of misery, sat on the landing, with Avgoustakos by her side. He was looking at her as if she was the juiciest appetizer he had ever seen. His hand was between her legs, hidden under her usual mini skirt, irreversibly high, at a spot that left no doubt about his intentions. It was as clear as rain.

Her eyes were lowered and so she didn't immediately realise I was there. She had that innocent look on her face that said: *It isn't my fault I'm so beautiful*, which, combined with her audacity, made her completely infuriating. At that moment, I truly hated her. I couldn't understand what kind of vulgar game she was playing. What did the plump, kind-hearted Avgoustakos have that a young man with a rare beauty like Alexander didn't?

When she saw me, Eleana grew flustered. She suddenly grabbed his hand and pulled it from between her legs. 'See here? It clearly says that you are a very lucky man. Within this year, you'll become very successful in your job,' she pretended to read his palm.

This scene looked like something out of a tragic comedy. Comic for the nervous reactions of both of them, and tragic at the same time, for the unexpected of her fate, her own fate that she had failed to predict and had caught her unprepared. I slipped past them and knocked on Alexander's door.

'Alexander, what's going on?'

He was half-lying in bed with his eyes closed. When he opened them, I realised that something was very wrong. When he began to speak, I was completely sure.

'What time is it?' His gaze was hazy, his eyes bloodshot, and his voice came out almost slurred.

'Five fifteen in the afternoon.'

'Is today Sunday or Monday?'

'It's Tuesday. What happened to you, Alex?'

He started laughing nervously, as if what I said sounded really funny.

Then I remembered something very important that had escaped my notice.

'Wasn't your last scene shot yesterday? Shouldn't you be gone by now? What about the premiere you have back in Athens?'

'I'll go,' he whispered, annoyed, clutching at his head as if all these questions had made him dizzy.

'When?'

'In a bit...'

'What do you mean?'

No reply. He remained icily indifferent. I stepped closer to him and gently shook him.

'Alexander, get a hold of yourself and talk to me please.'

'Don't tell anyone,' he flashed me a listless smile, 'I'm not in the mood for goodbyes.'

Suddenly, I realised what should have been obvious from the beginning.

'What did you take?'

'Nothing... just a little pot, I did nothing else, I swear. It usually feels good, but now I feel like there's something crushed in here...' he mumbled and pointed to his chest. Then he began to snicker and speak in gibberish.

I was in despair. I had no idea what they do in such cases. I helped him go to the sink so that he could throw some water on his face.

'I'm going down to fetch you something to eat. You haven't eaten all day, have you?'

'I don't want to eat. I want to die,' he said in a serious tone as he sat on the edge of his bed.

'Don't be ridiculous.'

I was getting very tired, almost exasperated, with all this melodrama.

I brought him a chocolate mousse and an apple juice I found in the kitchen and he devoured them with gusto.

'But, first I have something important to finish,' he continued the conversation we had left midway, with his eyes empty.

I closed the door quietly and left him fast asleep. I returned to my room, feeling somehow relieved. *Childish antics*, I told myself, *he'll eventually get over it.*

****

Night had fallen for good when I went to Constantinos' room. I found him lying in front of the fireplace. He was leafing through Jacques Lacarrière's *Dictionnaire amoureux de la Grèce* 'Listen to what he writes here! It's very interesting.'

He began to quote from the passage, translating on the spot:

'Words act like passages. To go where? And, most of all, to get out of where? Well, yes, to get out of this dead end, the dead-end of this finite and closed world, where deficiency, deprivation and failure seek to imprison you. Aporia (Question), aporos (pauper). They are two of the oldest Greek words. We come across the word 'aporos', 'pauper', in a passage of Heraclitus. It's the impossibility to move further ahead, to go on, to cross over, to free oneself. The being in a state of bewilderment

and adrift 'aporia', without the possibility of an outcome, or an aftermath, incarcerated in its own present time, like being in maze, an utterly empty place.'

That was why I had so many questions and was looking desperately for someone to answer them. But, at that moment, something inside me was telling me – in a very loud voice that I couldn't ignore – that I would soon get the answer to my greatest, my most agonizing question. Had he actually managed to get into my dreams back then? How did he know about Mr Leroi and the greetings he sent me in Paris?

He closed the book and left it on the side. We spent several minutes in absolute silence. Only the crackling of the fire could be heard.

He got up and trudged to the window. He opened it and the wind burst into the room, carrying a breath of freshness with it. Rain fell in a whining monotone. A very discreet kind of rain falls in these parts. It doesn't particularly disturb you and in the end you get used it and learn to ignore it.

I didn't understand what he was staring at for so long outside the window. But when he turned towards me, a small fire of determination was burning in his eyes. This flame also held mocking undertones, but it was certainly promising incredible confessions.

Before he could even say a word, he had stolen my breath away. I saw it in his eyes that he was in the mood for conversation. At last, I would hear the answer I had longed for for months and even years.

'I sometimes imagine, you know ... or it would be more fitting to say that I fantasize...'

'What?'

'I hope you won't think it funny that a man like me, I mean... an actor, could somehow be useful. In other words, I'm not just an entertainer...'

I was clueless about what he was getting at. I sat on a throw pillow that was on the floor and rested my elbows on his knees.

'Why not? What's strange about that?'

'As crazy and as unbelievable as this might sound, do you promise that you won't laugh?'

'Laugh? Tell me, please, this is no time for joking around!'

'It's just that I have never told anyone about this,' he said with some hesitation. 'I have no idea how it will sound.'

He glanced at me and looked startled. I must have been looking at him very strangely as I mentally begged him to make himself clearer.

'Back then, you said I had come in your dreams and made you wake up.'

'Not you per se; it was Mr Leroi.'

'Maybe I tried to make you hear me, but you were too sound asleep and all of the doors leading to you were closed. Maybe that's why I decided to send Mr Leroi, one of my personas, who knows how to deal with such circumstances. And because I knew he was a little bastard, I told him to be gentle with you. Well, he did the rest.'

'He woke me up by giving me kisses.'

'Many kisses.'

'Wasn't one enough?'

'It seems that it wasn't. One kiss isn't enough for modern princesses, they need more.'

'Ah, I see!'

'The time of the old fairy tales has passed and we must adapt to the new circumstances.'

'And then you broke the door down...'

'Not me. It was Mr Leroi.'

'And he asked me for some melomakarona. What did that mean?'

'How should I know? I like melomakarona and I guess I missed eating them while in Paris. Anyway, we're getting closer to what I want to tell you. There are times when I like to think that I have the ability to enter other people's minds, their subconscious. Wire fences and darkness can be found there. Infinite thoughts flutter around frightened, unable to find a way out. And yet there are a few exits, even though they can't see them at all. I like to think that I can show them a way out, even if this path cuts through the darkness.'

I couldn't help but admit that, yes, the way he spoke was truly prefect. The world should be grateful that he became an actor.

'Even if they feel utterly alone and helpless in the icy silence. At other times, when I'm in a good mood, I imagine that I can even enter their hearts. There, you find rising mountains, huge rock formations built from unacknowledged fear and pain. Unapproachable and terrifying. Then, I don't really know what to do.'

I wanted to tell him to stop, I couldn't bear listening to

him, I couldn't bear remembering everything that I went through during the time I was writing, but I didn't dare interrupt him.

'So, that's what you did to me too,' I finally got the courage to whisper.

'I suppose so. I never felt happier in my life than when you came and found me in Paris and told me that you had written a story about me. Deep down, I knew what had happened. I wanted to hear a story. A beautiful story. I needed a fairy tale. So, I found you and asked you to make one up for me. A fairy tale just for me, where I would be the main hero. And so it happened.'

He took a deep breath and stayed silent, with his eyes staring blankly ahead. The hands of the clock travelled through a great part of their trajectory before we were able to recapture the thread of our words.

I was leaning on his chest and listening to the powerful beat of his heart, the blood that flowed through his veins. His woollen jumper felt scratchy against my cheek. The fire in the grate had died out.

Twilight, full of shadows and a lovely melancholy, filled the room. He was holding me in his arms and his body was shouting that he was alive and couldn't be otherwise, that he would never become a stranger to me, and that I could never have another life separate from him.

'Did I scare you?' he asked.

'Yes!'

Little by little, the bugs of my rationality began moving their antennae. The magic scattered.

'But ... these things don't happen, Constantinos,' I finally said what I had been suppressing for so long, after getting excited by his words. 'How could they? What you said is really beautiful; it could make a wonderful script, but...'

He wrinkled his forehead and narrowed his eyes. His face betrayed his astonishment. How could I have dared to question what had been a sacred moment for him? I must have left him terribly disappointed.

'They do! Of course they do! I'm telling you myself!'

'Yes, but I don't understand. How can all this be explained?'

'They can't,' he said with a quiet smile. 'I didn't say anything of the sort. And that's the beauty of it!'

Chapter 13

Crimes Seen and Unseen

I often wonder if I was happy at the time. Normally, I should have been, but what I remember is that I would wake up every morning with a sense of anguish. It was the viewers' agony about what the scriptwriters have in store for their favourite series, but when I found out what was in store for me, I wished a thousand times that I had never learned any of it. But, it was too late for making wishes.

Meanwhile, I was very busy with the changes happening to me. They were rapid and unexpected, and caused me great discomfort. A strong wave of energy had me overwhelmed. The rigid cast that encased me was about to collapse into a million pieces. I was no longer made of stone and imprisoned. I was as carefree and awkward as an inexperienced girl who sets out in the world for the first time. A baby chick that has just come out of its shell. 'The bird fights its way out of the egg,' as Hermann Hesse wrote[9].

All my senses were sharpened to the fullest. Every colour seemed brighter before my eyes. Music sent me unprecedented vibrations; it penetrated and flowed so delightfully into my being. There were mornings when the beauty of my world seemed unbearable.

My hearing had also intensified. Sometimes the wind would bring words out of nowhere, beautiful words I had never heard before. I captured them and made up rhymes or short stories with them.

At the same time, I noticed that my intuitive abilities were in overdrive. But, neither my heightened senses nor my sharpened intuition nor my dreams succeeded in warning me about the tragic events that would follow. It was as though a knife violently tore the curtain of our time in that sad, rainy place to pieces. The order of our world was brutally disturbed and I have never been able to explain or accept what happened, no matter how much I struggle to believe that everything happens for a reason.

Now I know that, sooner or later, in everyone's life, the time comes when they are put to the test. That we all carry our very own demon that torments us and against whom we must fight. I didn't know it back then. But, now I do. Lesson learned, and I now think it's true that humans become more beautiful and stronger after a painful ordeal. If they manage to survive, of course. At least, we defeated our own demons. And we came out of this nightmare alive. Not completely unscathed, but we survived.

Below, I quote some extracts taken from my diary. During those dark days, I took up a habit I had left forgotten for years. It was fortunate I did because I would have lost the thread of the narration without it.

They found Eleana this morning. Frau Hilda was the one who discovered her. I only heard a deafening shriek at the break of dawn.

I jump up. Barefoot, I rush down the stairs to the second floor. The scene I'm greeted with is completely surreal. Venetis is standing outside Eleana's room. He is holding a mask in his hands and he's examining it, his face a ghastly pale, as though he has seen the Devil with his own eyes. It's a beautiful Venetian mask depicting a face with a serene and melancholic expression, a heavenly smile, and framed with rich curls made of papier-mâché. I don't understand why he's looking at it like that.

'You shouldn't have touched it,' Marianna muttered mechanically. 'It's evidence.' Evidence? For what?

I feel completely in the dark.

In a matter of seconds, everybody has gathered at the spot. They enter the frame with the jerky movements of the people you see in silent films. They hover outside the room's open door; no one dares enter. I finally understand. A flash of horror passes through my mind. I know what sight awaits me! I can imagine what the macabre spectacle looks like quite vividly.

Frau Hilda is babbling, between gasping breaths, that she saw the door standing ajar and she knocked in order to check on the girl. She received no answer. Then, she entered the room and saw her. Having said these words, her skin turns a waxy colour and she slumps to the floor. Nobody pays attention to her. The Scarecrow is also there. Gibberish comes out of her dribbling mouth and she is crossing herself non-stop.

Venetis is sweating profusely and is almost delirious. He looks very funny in his plaid pyjama bottoms and white vest. Avgoustakos is only wearing boxers; his flabby gut trembles with every breath he takes. He looks terribly groggy and confused.

'What happened, guys?' he asks the others repeatedly.

Nobody answers him. We are all caught off guard. I cower in a corner; I'm just a silent observer.

Vangelis looks more rigid than a mummy; he's smoking and the ashes are falling on the carpet. If Frau Hilda discovered this, she would faint in an even worse manner. I am struck by everyone's stillness. They look like lifeless dolls. And the silence. Such deafening silence always conceals a howl in its depths.

Nobody has any rational suggestions to make. No one is willing to be the first to spring into action. Constantinos exits Eleana's room. He's very pale, his eyes narrowed dangerously. He has seen quite a few fake corpses in some of his films but never the real deal, I guess. I try to catch his eye but he is looking down. He doesn't seem to notice I'm there.

At that moment, Katia appears. She looks flawless, as always, dressed in a long robe embroidered with red flowers. I'm blinded by their vivid red colour. They almost look like splashes of blood. 'I took a sleeping pill last night and I was fast sleep,' the woman says, and she is the only one who has risen to the occasion.

'What happened, you guys?' Stamatis arrives, full of excitement; he almost looks thrilled. Once he realises what's going on, he begins to stutter, blush and, eventually, leans against the wall like an empty sack.

Alexander? Where is Alexander? Without a second thought, I run to his room and find him still asleep, practically dead to the world. No matter how much I shake him, it's impossible to wake him up.

I go back to join the others. Evelina has stepped into the foreground. She looks so vulnerable and real without any make-up on. Her eyes widen and she lets out a hysterical shriek. She starts sobbing, and Marianna quickly follows suit. And it's as if their cries drew us out of our stupor. Everybody begins to make timid movements – like puppets manipulated by invisible strings.

'We should call the police,' someone says.

'Frau Hilda must have already called them,' another person answers.

And, indeed, heavy footsteps can be heard galloping up the wooden stairs.

'The cops are here,' Marianna says, wiping her eyes.

Everybody scatters like frightened woodcocks and makes way for the approaching police officers.

Then, for a single moment, I also become a witness to the macabre scene in the depths of the room. She is lying naked on the bed. She is beautiful. And also dead. The mask has been returned to the spot it was originally found, next to her. A bullet hole is barely visible below her chest, at the height of the diaphragm. It almost looks like a random scar at first sight. Then, I notice another horrible detail. Her hands are tied to the railings of the bed! With a pillowcase! And her eyes are covered by a blindfold. Everything grows hazy around me; darkness is falling over the scene.

If I faint right now, no one will tend to me, I think to myself, and it's the only thing keeping me upright.

The German police officers made their way through the crowd; they enter the room and push everyone out, closing the door with a bang.

I can't breathe; I feel I have run out of air. Almost on autopilot, I stand up, go down to the ground floor, and slip outside through the back door.

This is where the houseowners park their bicycles. They have neglected to place a guard here, though there is one at the front door; I saw him.

A sickly day is dawning with a yellow and grimy sky; it looks as if it has been spluttered with mud. As though it's getting dark before the day has even begun. The south wind sweeps the fallen leaves and swirls them around. There will be no dawn today; this night will come directly after the other.

I walk in the empty street, under the slight drizzle. A storm will break out any minute now. I don't feel the cold. A strong pain in my right big toe makes me realise that I'm walking barefoot, without even slippers on. I have stumbled on a stone. What am I doing out in the street like this? Like the girl in the street with the locked houses, the girl I had seen in my dream so many times. My favourite nightmarish dream. I don't care that I'm shoeless; nothing matters anymore.

I don't see which way I'm going; I'm not haunted by the memory of the bed or her naked body. It's her tied hands and blindfolded eyes. And the blood, a velvety spot on the white sheet.

Can someone explain this to me? I'm unsure if this was a silent scream to myself or if I said it out loud. A murder of crows flies off frantically over the beech trees.

I walk for a very long time. When I return to the inn, I'm soaking wet from the rain and my legs ache horribly. I must have been a sorry sight. A crazy woman wandering the streets in her nightgown, her hair a bad mess. The chief officer of the investigation barked in German: 'You have put yourself in a very precarious position by leaving the premises.'

'I returned on my own volition,' I said weakly.

Frau Hilda has overcome her shock and has already got back to doing her chores. She makes coffee. The kind-hearted Frau Matilde is lending a helping hand and doesn't leave her side, although it isn't her shift.

In the meanwhile, everything is over. They've already taken the body away in an ambulance. In a zippered plastic body bag, I imagine.

The place is full of cops. Most of them are at the crime scene dusting for fingerprints, taking photographs and searching for the murder weapon. The rest are permanently under our feet. They have forbidden us to leave the inn and do anything else until they finish with gathering evidence and the questioning.

Ravaged words and numb phrases crawl into my ears. I

can barely pay attention to anyone who might talk to me; there's a constant buzz in my ears.

Everybody's focus wasn't on the dead girl, but on the eerie mask that had been found next to her. What does this mean? Speculations are aflame. 'The killer has given us a hint of his identity by hiding it at the same time,' I heard someone say. 'He's messing with us,' another said. 'This man is pure evil,' a third man adds. 'He's mocking us,' the first one repeats his earlier thoughts. 'He's playing a cat-and-mouse game with us.'

I slump on a couch. I have to find him! He has to take me in his arms and calm me down, reassure me that the paranoid thoughts that are tearing my mind apart aren't true. I will believe him! Whatever he might say to me, even if it's the most absurd thing in the world, I'll believe it. Just to feel his arms around me.

That's when Alexander appears in the sitting room. He looks spectacularly calm, almost indifferent. Who knows what else he had taken to make him sleep so soundly.

'I didn't do it, Vera,' he says. 'I swear. I want you to believe me.'

'You were supposed to leave, Alexander. Why didn't you?'

No answer came from him.

I forced myself to swallow two sips of coffee and then I went upstairs for a quick bath. I put on some clean clothes and went down to Constantinos' room with bated breath. I think he's asleep by the way he's lying on the bed with his eyes closed. How can he sleep at a time like this?

'We need to talk, Constantinos!'

'I have nothing to say.' He didn't even bother to open his eyes.

'There must be something you can tell me!' *Why won't he look at me?*

'I'll talk when I want to, Vera!'

I have the urge to hit him! Holy Mother of God, I would gladly kill him right now.

Instead of doing just that, I slam the door shut and run away. I don't know where to go, so I keep going up and down the stairs without end, until I find out by one of the crew members that the Greek consul in Munich is here and wants to see all of us.

Mr Karydis is a nice little man, who's unfortunately going bald, with glasses, and a kind face. He speaks haltingly, trying to keep everyone calm. He tells us that due to the importance of this murder case, although it isn't required by law, a senior Greek police officer, specializing in matters of security and crime fighting, has been commissioned to work alongside the German police and is due to arrive tomorrow. The Germans were initially reluctant to accept such interference in their work, but the Greek officers fought hard until they managed to convince them. Even the Minister of Public Order intervened. Who made all this fuss? How far does Avramoglou's influence extend?

Mr Karydis kindly asks us to assist the German authorities in solving the murder and assures us of his support, which is basically moral support. There isn't much else he can do.

After our brief meeting with the Consul, we were all

immediately transported to the police station. They started the interrogation in the presence of the prosecutor that had been appointed to the case. Herr Dortmund has definitely singled me out because I am one of the first to be questioned. He is a tall, dull-looking man in his mid-forties, with short blond hair and fake tanned skin. His cheeks sport twin scars that look as if they've been made with a razor.

He asks me what I know about the case, if the victim was seeing anyone, what type of person she was, if she had any quarrels with anyone. If there are any rumours circulating among the crew.

I tell him about Eleana's promiscuity, her pathological weakness for the male sex, the relationships she had with various men, Alexander, and the tension that existed between them. He then asks me if I had noticed anything suspicious in the last couple of days. I describe the shadow I saw outside Eleana's door a few nights ago. Something I cannot name flashed behind his carefully blank look.

'I have to ask some intrusive questions, Ms Kalogera,' he tells me afterwards. 'Was there anyone else with you last night?'

'No,' I answer, 'I was alone and asleep. I have no alibi – just like most of the other members of our group – but I also don't have a motive.'

Late in the afternoon, after being questioned by the police, we return to the inn. There's a police car with two policemen parked near the front door, just in case.

Frau Matilde is wandering from room to room, looking sombre and quite lost. I don't know what she has seen until now, but it has made her jumpy. Tonight, I find it impossible to sleep. I knock on Katia's door and ask for a sleeping pill.

'Just take half of it, it's very strong,' she advises me as she gives me one. 'What do you think about all this,' she asks me before I leave.

'I can't think about anything right now, Katia. All I want is sleep. I'll think about this horrible situation another time. Tomorrow perhaps.'

11TH NOVEMBER

And so, we temporarily stopped shooting a film and we found ourselves starring in our very own stage drama. Because some of us have many things to hide. The problem is that I'm one of them. And because the others behave as if they also have skeletons in their closets, I seriously doubt that the police will be able to untangle this mess.

Avramoglou arrived early in the morning, looking thunderous. I have no idea how he managed to cover things up and keep everybody's tongues from wagging so that the horrible news didn't even reach the press. It would be a disaster for the film for people to find out that there is a murderer loose on set. But, I'm not so sure that we will manage to keep it hidden until the end.

At noon, there was a new arrival. Major Dialinas from Thessaloniki came just in time. We were all beginning to realise what a terrible situation we had found ourselves in – like a scene taken right out of a thriller. Trapped like rats in an inn of terror with a maniac in our midst.

It seems that some had recovered from the initial shock and were beginning to find the situation interesting, if not thrilling. Humans can't stand the very breath of death at the back of their neck for too long. There were several people who wanted to treat the whole thing as a joke. There were plenty of theories about the identity of the killer and scenarios ranging from corny to downright outlandish. *Soon we'll start putting bets on it.* I'm shocked with what calmness that thought crossed my mind.

Only Evelina is still randomly bursting into tears; she is inconsolable. Her mascara runs down her cheeks and smudges them. 'I always knew that something bad was going to happen,' she keeps muttering to herself, always on the verge of hysteria.

Dialinas was the first to come and see us. He is in his mid-fifties, of medium height, with blue eyes and grey hair. I would say he was a charming man in his youth. He wants to hear our testimonies about what happened first-hand in order to form his own opinion. Then, he will meet his German counterparts. At first, he seems ready to start slapping everyone around. His disdainful look clearly shows that he thinks he's dealing with a group of irresponsible children who are idly wasting their time and then call 'daddy' to come and clean up their mess when they bite off more than they can chew.

Only when he sees Constantinos does he lighten up. 'I have to remember to ask you to sign two autographs for me, Mr Aravantinos,' he says. 'For my daughters,' he explains in a softer voice. 'They practically demanded it.'

I feel the urge to start laughing. A man, who in the past had quite a few run-ins with the police, is now the only one who commands some respect. The good side of publicity. Soon, a new round of questioning starts all over again.

When I return to my room, it's already dark. Constantinos is there, sitting in the half-light, smoking. I don't even bother to ask him if he took up this filthy habit again. It's such a minor offence; everyone here is on the verge of using drugs.

'Thank you for not saying anything,' he tells me.

'There isn't a chance in hell that I'll talk to the police about us; it's a personal matter. Not just yours, but mine too. So, you don't have to thank me.'

'Yes, but we're dealing with a crime here. You've hidden information from the police, do you get that?' he whispers with a sinister laugh and hugs me.

Is that what he's been waiting for? To test my loyalty to him? To see if he can trust me?

'You've also kept things from them. Did you tell them that Eleana came to your room on the night of the murder?'

He abruptly lets me go.

'How do you know that?'

'I saw her. Coming out of your room with downcast eyes and trying to look like some kind of holy maiden, like she usually does. It must've been around 9.15pm.'

He seems to understand that this is no laughing matter.

'She came to bum a cigarette off me.'

'You'd recently quit smoking, if I'm not mistaken.'

'Not that kind of cigarette, the other kind...'

'I see!'

'I always carry some with me; they help me relax.'

I nod once more in understanding and then I become anxious all over again.

'Did you at least get rid of them now that the police are always in the way?'

'Yes. Do you believe me about Eleana?'

'I do.'

The truth is that I desperately want to believe him and that I'm teeter-tottering on a razor sharp edge. I promised myself to be cautious, not to give him my unconditional trust ever again, and now I can't even do that. I think I should stop trusting myself.

'So, you and Eleana didn't...'

He immediately explodes with anger, 'Is that what you believe? That I wait in line in front of the bed of every female nymphomaniac so that I can jump in when she's looking for a new partner? Do you think so little of me?'

'Don't you think, though, that it was a diabolical coincidence?' I start shyly after having calmed down a bit. 'Her hands were tied... What I'm saying is...'

'It wasn't a coincidence!' he interrupts me. 'Someone is copying me. And in a very morbid way!'

'Who can it be?'

'The killer, I imagine. Have you spoken to anyone?'

'Of course not! How about you? Did you perform these tricks on some other women in here?' I would have burst with curiosity if I hadn't asked him.

'No!'

'What then?'

'I have no idea!'

Here we are, then! Two beings in a state of bewilderment, trapped in a maze with no possibility of escape. That's why I sit and write. I have the hope that I will find the words to help me explain, to escape, to put the broken pieces in order. To complete the fragmented puzzle. But, it seems that I'm asking too much. So, I beg him to stay with me, to hold me in his arms. Perhaps this will be some kind of help.

'I can't, Vera. I'm sorry. I need to be alone.'

And he leaves. So heartlessly. I go downstairs to the living room. The police have gone. Avramoglou is furious.

'I'll find the asshole that set this all up and I'll kill him with my own hands. I'll be damned if I'm going to wait for the police to do something!'

'Should I assume that you know something that we don't?' Katia asks.

'No, but I will! That creep doesn't know who he's dealing with!'

I go to bed early. I need to sleep, to forget about everything, even for a little while. I'm just praying that the frightening dreams don't come back. Watching thrillers on TV is very different from actually living one.

12TH NOVEMBER

I wake up in the middle of the night feeling profound anger. He left. Just like that. He left me all by myself the one time I asked him to stay with me. And I covered for him! I hid things that could attract the attention of the police, such as the seemingly innocent visit Eleana paid him, and I didn't even mention it. I tried to protect him and, in return, he left me on my own in the grip of fear. I get up and pour myself a drink.

But, of course, what else should I have expected? I'm just an occasional lover. Only that. I'm not his wife. He has no obligation to care about me. I become ruthless with myself when I'm angry.

And what if by believing that I'm protecting my lover and myself, I'm actually helping a murderer? This suspicion brains me. What if the whole "hands tied to headboard" was just a trick? Such monstrous similarity and coincidence wouldn't have been believable. Also, he very well knows that he has a hold over me, and I have repeatedly given him reasons to depend on it. He is no fool. He knows very well that I would never be able to accuse him, and that's why he followed this tactic.

But why kill Eleana? I can't find a single decent reason. Unless... This second suspicion is even worse than the first. I have to make a phone call, first thing in the morning. Many things depend on this phone call.

I slowly relax. No, I don't believe that Constantinos committed this murder. But, I suspect that he will soon be the culprit of another murder. In a few days, when the shooting ends. Then he'll return home, to his life. To his wife. That will kill me, but no one will care, no one will blame him for that crime. People aren't tried for such offenses. I'm getting my just deserts!

I have a headache. So many erratic thoughts are unbearable in the middle of the night. And it's too late to knock on Katia's door and ask her for one more pill.

In the morning, when I go downstairs to the dining room, everybody is gathered there.

Venetis says that we will resume shooting.

'We have to wrap things up and leave this freaky place before other troubles find us.'

Avramoglou couldn't agree more.

'I can't act under such conditions,' Evelina complains, 'I can't stand this.' She is once again on the verge of tears.

'I've acted under worse circumstances,' Constantinos mocks her.

What kind of a man is he? I look at him surprised. I know what he would answer me if I asked him. 'A professional,' he would boast.

By the time I pour myself a cup of coffee, the topic has changed.

'I don't think that a man who kills someone with a gun suffers from paranoia or something similar,' I hear him say. 'Unless he isn't insane... Or if the killer is actually a woman.'

'Is that your investigative experience talking?' Avramoglou taunts him. 'What else could the nutcase who is responsible for this madness be?'

Constantinos doesn't even bother to give him an answer. He just lets himself hide behind the mist that his eyes already wander in. This way, Avramoglou's barbs miss their target. I always suspected that his whimsical look is by no means a sign of weakness. I would say the exact opposite is true.

'What did the girl ever do to anyone?' Avramoglou goes on. 'She was just a child!' he remarks with bitterness. For the first time, I see signs of humanity on his harsh face.

After breakfast, I go down to the basement where there's a phone booth. I don't want to make this phone call upstairs and have anyone eavesdropping. I call Vicky and ask her to give me the number of the neurosurgeon who operated on her father a few years back. What was he called again?

'Andreadakis. Why? What do you want him for?'

'Don't ask. I can't tell you right now.'

I try more or less to explain my inquiries to the distinguished professor. Can a man who has had a serious head injury become dangerous, or even act erratically? As soon as I blurt everything out, I realise how vague, if not downright silly, I sound.

'There isn't a simple answer,' the bemused doctor tells me. 'I would have to examine the patient, or review his medical files. Do you have them in your hands?'

I hang up, quite disappointed. Zero in the quotient. I should see this as a sign to immediately abandon my ambitions for a police career.

At eleven o' clock, Herr Dortmund appears, looking quite harried, along with Dialinas. They came to arrest Alexander. Of course, they don't call it that. They phrase it in a more elegant manner. They're just bringing him in for further questioning and the like. The truth is that I expected such a development and I was afraid it would happen.

Just before they leave, they remind us that no one is allowed to leave the city for any reason whatsoever.

I run to Alexander's side as he comes down the stairs. I tell him not to worry; I'll inform his parents and they'll hire him a good lawyer.

'No! They can't know anything! I didn't do it; they can't accuse me of anything!'

In the afternoon, two policemen came back to escort Avgoustakos back to the police station. Venetis, too! We were bowled over! What did Venetis have to do with this case?

The fingerprints found in the victim's room belong to these three men, Herr Dortmund claimed in his frosty manner. The evidence doesn't lie.

'I saw him!' Vangelis announced triumphantly. 'The night of the murder, he was in her room!'

I was dumbfounded. And so was everyone else.

'And how do you know?' Evelina attacked him shrieking.

'I had gone for a piss, if you must know. And the toilet is directly opposite the room. I saw Venetis going in while I was coming out, at around 2.35pm.'

His terrible joy could hardly be concealed behind his words. He had finally succeeded in bringing Pantelis down. He should have kept an eye on this snake. Now the only thing left for him to do is to take the director's place with everyone's blessings.

'Do you see now why he went and picked up the mask when he found it next to the dead girl? He wanted to muddle the waters. Because he knew they would find his fingerprints in the room!'

I'm sure that, once he's on his own, Vangelis will start jumping for joy as high as the ceiling.

After this, anything is possible. Everyone is a suspect and the laws of probability leave no one out.

I don't have anyone there for me. I feel suffocated, and I need to talk to someone. I knock on Katia's door. I haven't seen her for hours. She has shut herself up in her room and spends her time reading.

'This morbid atmosphere is very depressing to me,' she says.

We all are like unwound pawns running back and forth, without the slightest idea who's pulling the strings. That's the most frightening thought. In retrospect, when I revisit these memories, it's unbelievable how we managed to make it out of that maze.

'Forgive me for being blunt, but that's the stupidest thing I've ever heard!' she leaves me speechless when I express my meagre suspicion about Constantinos' possible guilt. 'You know very well that I don't like him. I have him capable of many things, but not murder.'

I'm glad to hear these words coming from her. I feel relieved, and also completely stupid.

'I'm rarely a bad judge of character, Vera. You have to trust me on this.' She gives me a loving – I would even say maternal – smile.

I ask her to give me another sedative and I return to my room.

It's the second night he hasn't come to my room. What kind of cruel game is he playing? How can he be so cold and aloof? How can he not understand how much I need him? And I can't even cry in order to vent my frustration. It's horrible not being able to cry.

I'm half-asleep when a bizarre idea hits me in the head. 'I know who the killer is,' I stammer. I know who's behind all this. My mother did it! She killed Eleana! So what if she isn't here? That's a minor detail! Her presence haunts the universe. She is omnipresent: she sees everything, she controls everything and she criticizes everything. She has the ability to make me feel like the most miserable creature in the world; she's the one who didn't hesitate to verbally abuse me for my choice of bridal gown on the eve of my wedding, would she let such a tiny detail stop her?

She did it to warn me that loose women get what they deserve in the end. That eventually, down the road, it will be my turn to pay. I jump up. 'Mum, I'm sorry,' I shout frantically. 'You call yourself a grown-up, and yet you're expecting your mother to come and save you?' I beat myself up and burst into tears.

I get up out of bed, quite shaken, my mind an enormous blur, and darkness threatens to engulf me. So I find myself running down the stairs, only in my nightgown and without any slippers on. I rush to his room.

'What is it?' he mutters groggily when he opens the door. 'What happened?'

He's wearing only a pair of boxers and he's rubbing his eyes, a bit confused. I want to tell him that every moment spent away from him feels like I'm dying, that I have experienced many such instant deaths and I can't stand them anymore, but I tell him something else instead.

'Give me a cigarette,' I tell him briskly.

'What?'

He doesn't seem at all happy to see me; he looks rather annoyed.

'What's the matter with you? It's the middle of the night.' I see it in his eyes that he thinks I'm being hysterical, if not something worse.

'I want a cigarette,' I repeat like an automaton. 'One of those ... "special" cigs you have. Give me something, anything you've got.'

'I don't have anything!'

'But, that isn't what you told me earlier! Don't lie to me!'

'Shut up,' he says, at a loss. 'I told you that I threw them away. Keep your voice down. I told you that I wanted to be on my own for a few days. Is that so hard to understand?'

I turn my back to him and run down the hallway. My eyes are blurred with tears; I don't watch where I'm going.

'Go to hell,' I growl as I bang the door of my room shut.

I can feel my mother's shadow once again. She's here with me. Why did I ever imagine that I could escape? '*I told you, Vera,*' she says sharply with an air of resignation. '*You shouldn't trust them. See what's happened to you now? Your father didn't hesitate to leave me even though we had two young children together. What do you expect from this actor? What are you doing with a married man? God will send fire from heaven and burn us, my child!*'

I sleep poorly that night. I wake up drowned in tears. There is no one beside me. It's very windy outside and it has started raining heavily once again. I don't feel very well.

My stomach is churning. I pray that I don't start having the panic attacks that used to plague me, and begin to vomit.

13TH NOVEMBER

It's our fourth day in the mousetrap. Everybody is on edge. A hollow roar is riding the coattails of the storm that is about to break out, and we're all in a daze.

There are five suspects so far, in my opinion:

The first suspect is Alexander. As much as I don't want to admit it, he had many reasons. He was in love with her and she constantly provoked him. She flirted shamelessly with every man on the set. And no one can predict how far an extremely sensitive man can go.

The second one is Avgoustakos. I don't know what reasons he would have to kill her, but it was proven that they had had a brief fling.

The third would have to be Venetis. I still haven't recovered from that surprising revelation, and I can't imagine why he would kill her, but he was in her room that night, and that, at least, needs further investigation.

And the fourth one, Constantinos. I will not spare him from my suspicions so easily. He is occasionally capable of losing his self-control and becomes violent. I saw him with my own eyes the night he made that horrible scene outside the taverna and made my blood curdle.

And the fifth? Evelina? Followed by a large question mark. What if there was a speck of truth in Constantinos' suggestion that the killer might not have been a man? What if Evelina suspected her lover's relationship with the girl? I hurriedly reject this scenario. It seems too far-fetched... Naturally, I don't intend to say anything to the police – about the last two persons, at least. The police know about the others.

The murder weapon hasn't been found anywhere. They said it was a nine-millimetre handgun, not very difficult to obtain. The killer must have used a silencer... since no one heard any gunshots.

Whoever did this had carefully planned everything. He must have brought the gun with him from Greece; where else could he have found it? That means that this person was determined to kill, and a risk-taker. But, then, how did he pass through airport security? It isn't my job to answer these questions, but they keep tormenting me.

But, of course! How didn't I think of it? Any member of the crew could have hidden a gun in the machinery, equipment or cargo that was transferred here by land, and then retrieved it. So, that's another dead end.

Today is worse than yesterday. The director of the project isn't present. And everything is going to rack and ruin in the absence of the guiding force behind everything. The day's shoot was haphazard and mismatched. Only now do I realise how much we miss the confidence and calm strength that Venetis exuded.

Stamatis has lost his eternal cheerfulness for good. His mobile phone is constantly glued to his ear. 'Yes, Xenia, yes, my love, I miss you.' Now that things have got difficult, he's hanging onto his wife for support, even from afar.

Avramoglou is the only one free to come and go as he pleases because there are no charges hanging against him, but he doesn't take advantage of this privilege. He insists on prowling among us with angry eyes and a terrible anger hanging from his whiskers. It must be one of the few times that he doesn't have complete control over a situation and this makes him see red.

Alexander came back in the afternoon. He seemed more solemn than ever. As if he had suddenly matured in a matter of hours. They don't have enough evidence against him that could lead to an official arrest.

Avgoustakos, along with Venetis, returned later in the evening, both looking very tired and unwilling to speak to anyone. Their further questioning didn't pay off for the police. I feel very sorry for Venetis. Now he will have to face not only Evelina's wrath, but that of his wife, too.

So we're back to where we started. To zero, that is.

'Tomorrow, we resume shooting,' Avramoglou announces, looking preoccupied with something. 'I handled all the negotiations myself. Of course, there will be discreet police presence on set.'

We breathe in relief. It's some kind of a solution. So that we don't just sit around and stew in our own juices. But that tomorrow will be very late in coming. But we don't know that yet.

14TH NOVEMBER

Everything is set in motion once again, slowly and numbly. The "machine" has rusted from non-use and needs oiling.

Venetis is struggling in vain to get it back in working order. His obvious hatred towards Vangelis, and the ice that has formed between Evelina and himself, torpedoes this effort.

The actress behaves like a lady whose honour has been besmirched. She walks around with a permanent sour expression on her face and her nose wrinkled in disgust.

Constantinos is distant and absent-minded. They still act their parts perfectly, but it's obvious to everyone that there's no chemistry between any of the actors today. The scenes are shot again and again, but with the same – in my humble opinion – poor results. We are such fine professionals. 'The scenes will flow smoothly together after they have been through the editing process,' Venetis mutters worriedly to himself.

I've seen this played out before, I'm bored of it. We had formed a close-knit group, loved doing our jobs, and treated each other with kindness and respect. Past tense. At some point, we got to know each other too well. Then, a rock was hurtled in the middle of the still waters, and all the muck hiding at the bottom rose to the surface. There's always dirt hidden at the bottom of people's souls and it doesn't take long to come up. A pebble is enough. Especially when it concerns a serious crime.

In the afternoon, when we return to the inn, George, Eleana's replacement, has arrived. He is wearing a skin-tight shirt and leather trousers. The male make-up artist is endowed with a toned body, though he is quite the chatterbox. And, it didn't take long for anyone to figure out his sexual preferences. He is very happy to meet us. He doesn't know what he's getting himself into. Ignorance is bliss.

I have just had a bath and am getting ready for bed when I hear the scream. The nightmare has returned. *Dammit, I hope they didn't discover another body!* That's the first thought that crosses my mind. From now on, these two things have become inextricably linked in my mind: Scream equals death.

The tragic scene takes place outside Alexander's room this time. Marianna – her face an ashen white – stammers that she came looking for him because she hadn't seen him since the night before. She leans against the wall and starts crying. Her blonde hair looks like straw to me. She must be in her late twenties but there seems to be an old woman standing in front of me now. She is that shaken from the shock she has suffered.

I refuse to believe that it's happening for the second time. It's just a bad dream, I keep repeating to myself, but the awakening part is slow in coming. My legs don't obey me, they become heavy like lead. The distance I have to cross – to the end of the corridor, where Alexander's room is located – seems impossibly long. I knew it! Death never knocks only once. Blood asks for more blood! I didn't want to admit it.

At last, I reach the end of the corridor and lean on the doorframe so as to keep myself from collapsing. His body is sitting behind the desk, his head between his hands, his face resting against the wooden surface. His fingers are rigid, just like those of a wax figure.

I can't see his face because it's hidden behind his hair. It looks damp, probably by the spilled liquid that had once been in the overturned glass next to him. A part of his cheek is visible, and it looks as if it's been made of pale wax. He's been dead for hours, but no one sought him out, since we were used to his long absences.

Frau Matilde must have been convinced that the inn is cursed. With admirable perseverance, she watches the efforts of a lifetime collapse. She pulls at her cheeks. She will have no reason to laugh from now on, probably for the rest of her life.

The police are summoned once again. Dialinas arrives, looking angry with us. What kind of twisted game did we think up this time in order to get him into more trouble? It seems that the cause of death is either poison or drugs. The autopsy will tell. A short note was discovered next to the body. It simply read: "I killed her. I'm sorry." That's what they told me. I didn't read it myself. I can't see anything in front of me. Why is the frame with the still life on the opposite wall shaking? There isn't an earthquake.

I try to steady myself against something. Someone manages to grab me before I collapse. I rest my head on his chest, I take in his scent. I know immediately who it is. 'Let's go upstairs,' he tells me as he drags me to the stairs. He has his hand wrapped around my waist to keep me from falling down. I must look a mess because he looks at me with pity.

We go to his room and he helps me sit somewhere. I sit and gaze at the fire in the grate like a lifeless puppet.

'What a nice fire! And the flames, look how they jump around like crazy. Ah, finally, some warmth within this coldness.' I try to get my mind off that horrible sight, even if I have to say nonsense. I struggle not to let my mind descend into the abyss. To not allow horror to enter my veins.

He gives me a drink, I gulp it down in one go; I couldn't even say what it was. He tells me something but I can't hear him. My ears are buzzing.

'Come to me!' That's the third time he repeats himself. He is no longer cold and aloof. He has pulled his mask off. Now he wants hugs and caresses, and he is very demanding. He seems lost and hopeless.

It's your fault, I want to tell him. *You never liked Alexander.*

It's my fault, I say afterwards to myself. *I took no notice of the distress signals the young man was emitting. I thought they were childish antics. I was too busy with my own problems.*

It's your fault, I silently repeat to myself. *You left me on my own! Where have you been all these days?*

My anger has the magical power of awakening my inner Sleeping Stupid.

'Leave me be! I want to be alone!'

Quite the dramatic statement. A huge question mark is projected in his eyes. He probably didn't expect this. Apparently, he thinks I'm his little toy. He can play with me as long as he wants and then throw me in some corner when he gets bored. I see myself heading towards the door.

'I can't play this game any longer, Constantinos. It has become too dangerous.' Absolute confusion reigns in his gaze. 'I can't stand you anymore, Constantinos! I want you to get out of my heart... I want you to leave my thoughts!'

I probably shouted because I see him getting upset.

I don't know how all this came to me. I didn't rehearse it; the words just came out completely spontaneously. The truth is that I have been scared for many days. Ever since he talked to me about that strange metaphysical experience – our possible meetings in dreams. If what he said is true, then it means he's in my mind. From there, he can control everything. He can make me do whatever he wants. Such a suspicion is unbearable. And when he leaves? What am I going to do then?

So, here I am, committing a heinous crime against myself. Because I know what I say will also hurt me tremendously. Of course I don't want him to leave. I want him to keep living inside me, even if I'm just leftover crumbs on his erotic table. I don't care, I have no ego left. But I'm afraid, so I have to kill my own self. But, that's how I always react. Instead of waiting for someone else to shoot me, I prefer to fall on the knife by myself.

'As you wish,' he says coldly, 'I'll go! But you'll hate it.' He hasn't learned how to lose, obviously.

He tosses me my room keys.

The truth is that I wanted to get them back, but not like this. I go out in the hallway. Why do I have the bitter feeling that many other things died along with Alexander?

My room is a mess. The cops have torn it apart, like all the other rooms. I anxiously look for my notepad. Many things are scattered haphazardly on my desk. Finally, I find what I was looking for. It's a small piece of paper where I wrote down all my thoughts a few days ago, when he had spoken to me, in front of the fireplace, about that fantastic "meeting", that magical and inexplicable happening that took place within our dreams. But, I had been able to "explain" it, and I was very happy about it. I wanted to read what I had written to him.

Let me tell you what I think "really" happened. One night, we were both walking through secret passages, dreams, and guided by words-passages, we found ourselves in a place untouched and unproven, where time is abolished. There is no safe passage for going there. It is the sanctuary. Not everyone can enter.

These are the words I had written back then. I rip the paper into pieces and I almost have the urge to swallow them. Then, perhaps, I would be able to wipe away all the traces of the romantic fool I had been.

There's a new round of questioning. We are once again called to the police station. The Dialinas-Dortmund duo once again pick our brains. Then, I finally understand why the Major appears to be at the end of his tether. We aren't the only ones to blame. He is mostly frustrated with his arrogant German colleague, who insists on pointedly ignoring him throughout the investigation.

I tell them that it's very possible Alexander committed suicide. He had expressed such a desire. Moreover, heartbreak is a powerful incentive for people with like sensitivity. But, I'm convinced that he was incapable of murdering someone. The more I think about it, the more absurd it seems.

It's past midnight when we disentangle ourselves from all of this.

Absolute darkness accompanies us when we return to the inn, silent and numb. There's not even an owl to break the eerie silence of the night.

I enter my room and lock the door. The shadows of the

tree branches battle against each other on an imaginary window stage. Nightmarish figures in a relentless shadow play.

15TH NOVEMBER

I have no idea what happened today. I spent the whole day deep in a redemptive slumber. It's a good thing that Katia provided me with the necessary sleeping pills. Coupled with a Martini, they make for an amazing cocktail. I strongly recommend it to those suffering from incurable dreaming.

16TH NOVEMBER

I thought that the worst was over. That we couldn't fall any lower. But it seems that the nightmare has several floors; we've taken the lift and we're racing to the bottom.

I wake up from my 24-hour aphasia to discover two things. The autopsy report for Alexander was completed. The official cause of death, according to the toxicological analysis, was suicide by poison. They still have some faint doubts as to his being guilty of the murder. From what I understand, because the note found next to him was very clumsily written, with illegible letters, the official graphologist was unable to reach a clear-cut conclusion.

They are in a hurry to close the case. To make everything return to normal. We all want that. Under these conditions, we turn a blind eye to many things.

Now I blame myself that I didn't insist on them continuing the investigation. Because I was the only one who knew

Alexander so well and had so many doubts about his guilt. The others don't care. You should never wait for the others to take the first step. Often, you are lost in an indifferent crowd and you must act like the solitary hero who fights against everything. I didn't do it. I didn't have the courage. I thought that cowardice was the most disgusting thing in the world. And, of course, I paid dearly for it; the price of cowardice is always very high, just like that of stupidity.

Dialinas stopped by to say goodbye, fortunately without telling us to 'go to hell'. He gets the autographs he wants and takes his leave.

The second thing I learned wasn't new. I knew it first-hand. I shouldn't have gone against his Majesty, Mr Aravantinos, because he has very effective means hidden up his sleeve in order to retaliate: such as becoming attached to Evelina, who also has strong reasons for wanting to get back at her lover. Lack of imagination, you might say. Honestly, I expected something more original from them, but it seems that the old proven methods are the best.

Between the breaks, they disappear in the woods or in the corridors of the castle together, and they are always the last ones to return. They have vacant, secretive smiles on their faces. They never miss the opportunity to look into each other's eyes, to touch each other.

I find these antics absolutely childish and cheap, but I find myself incensed, nonetheless. As for Venetis, I fear that he will suffer a stroke and then we would be doomed. I notice his anger is simmering like a huge pot and I wonder when he's going to explode and start leaving destruction in his wake. Or when my patience will run out and I'll jump on Constantinos and kill him in front of everyone. But, I don't want to give Herr Dortmund the opportunity to capture the most incompetent killer of his career.

But, for now, we sit in a civilized manner behind the monitor and calmly discuss shooting angles, panoramic shots and nearby eateries. We observe this painful farce unfolding before our eyes like random bystanders. The bad thing is that we are responsible for what is happening.

Venetis slept with Eleana and he has no one to blame but himself. And I had the audacity to turn my back on ... His Majesty. I certainly don't expect any leniency after such inexcusable misconduct.

In the afternoon, we see Avramoglou off. He is flying back to Greece on an evening flight from Munich Airport.

'My job here is done. I put my trust in you that all will go well.'

Something in his tone didn't sound very convincing...

'Yes,' Stamatis says, 'fortunately, everything has been solved.'

'Bullshit,' Avramoglou cuts in with his usual rudeness, 'nothing was made clear!'

'What do you mean?' Stamatis stutters. 'The killer was found.'

'I have serious doubts about that,' he says after much thought. 'That young man didn't look like a murderer to me.' He abruptly ended the conversation at this point.

For an instant, I'm happy to hear that someone else has

the same doubts as I do. But, the feelings of guilt come back and start haunting me. Should I go and talk to the police? And, tell them what? I don't have any significant proof in my hands. Or, do I? I feel confused, and completely helpless.

18th November

For some time now, I have been wondering what kind of person Constantinos truly is. After lengthy deliberations with myself, I have come to a conclusion. He is not normal. In fact, I believe that he is half man, a quarter angel and a quarter devil. But which of us is completely normal under the surface? Who can vouch for someone's normality? But perhaps the proportions keep changing. I can't make any sense of this.

For now, I can only see the last quarter, which is outrageous and provocative. I have no doubt, though, that he still hasn't shown me the worst side of himself, a much uglier version of his.

I look at him carefully while he's sitting at one of the corners of the table, next to Evelina. The smoke of his cigarette pervades the air around him like a gossamer piece of fabric. For an infinitesimal moment, I have the illusion that it's the fires of hell that surround him. Then he laughs, and his face lights up. His laughs are so rare. Then the smoke forms a transparent ring suspended quivering over his hair. He looks like an angel now, untouched by the sins of the world.

Tonight, for the first time after the tragic events, we decided to go out as a group once again. So, here we are – Where else? – at the Acropolis taverna. I didn't want to go out with them, I can't stand seeing him, but staying locked in my room would be even more unbearable.

So, we were once again gathered around the long, narrow table with retsina and wine flowing abundantly, and kind-faced Mr Aristides overjoyed to see us.

We are breathing in a sacrilegious atmosphere. Just a few days ago, two young people's lives were lost, and here we are ready to go on the spree again.

People forget quickly, struggling to overcome their painful experiences, and when they manage to do so, they never look back at these events ever again. "Man is soft, a sheaf of grass[10]", and these blades of grass are swept away by the wind of time and scattered right and left. And what recently whistled past our ears, what ruffled our hair, was a wind of death.

Tonight, though, everybody seems willing to enjoy themselves as if it was their last day on earth. It's evident by the way the cutlery clangs against each other; by the glasses that are filled and emptied with great frequency; by the eyes that flutter; the loud laughter that ends in a wild crescendo. This is the first time I see them dancing, and so erratically, with a lot of stumbling and drunken antics.

I, unfortunately, can't drink; my stomach roils unpleasantly at the thought. So, I have to content myself with watching them in their orgiastic fun, which seems so unnatural. With their Dionysian shouts rattling the windows. With dissonant notes springing from giddy throats.

But there's also another smell in the air, a simmering

tension, but I can't pinpoint where it's going to erupt. All my senses are tense just like the animal sniffing the storm before it even gets close.

My fears are sadly confirmed. Venetis is the one who finally explodes. Wine helps, of course, in overcoming the barriers of reason and dignity. At one point, he gets up, staggering, and grabs Evelina by the hair. He starts slapping her repeatedly in front of everyone.

Constantinos, who until that moment had been shamelessly flirting with her, makes no move. *What a gallant knight*, I think. Chivalry was just what we needed right now.

But Vangelis makes the wrong decision by attempting to defend her. It seems that apart from the director's chair, he also covets the director's mistress. But, he is too lean, too puny, to be able to fight Venetis off Evelina. With a shove, the director sends him flying on some of the dishes.

Stamatis is snickering shamelessly. The others are a moment away from clapping. Evelina is screaming like a banshee. The owner is pulling at his hair. A couple of chairs end up as nothing more than firewood. Eventually, two or three guys, technicians from the filming crew, get involved and manage to save her from Venetis' hands, though she is in a sorry state. But Venetis' wrath hasn't deflated.

'You're a big fag, Aravantinos!'

Constantinos channels his old evil self for a moment and gets ready to shoot his own insults back at Venetis.

'No, guys, stop it, for goodness' sake!' Mr Aristides flails about.

Who pays any attention to him?

I guess the two of them probably threw some punches at each other, but I didn't stay to see any more. The last thing I saw was the statue of a Caryatid being smashed, another example of this general prostration of our morals. I exit the taverna feeling the irrepressible urge to vomit but as soon as the frosty air hits me in the face, I begin to feel a bit better.

'Are you leaving, Vera?' I hear Katia's voice behind me.

'I can't stay in there. I'm disgusted by all this.'

'But you should have stayed.'

'If I stay, I'll just feel more disgust.'

'This is our world, Vera. This is who we are. You ought to know that.' I can't believe my ears. Is it Katia talking like that?

'Why should I specifically know that?'

'Because you're supposed to be the writer. How do you expect to become good at your job, if you don't experience these depravities at first hand? Humans carry a lot of filth in their souls, sweetheart, don't you close your eyes to it. Don't let yourself believe an illusion!'

I'm in no mood for such philosophical debates.

'I know that, Katia. I wasn't born yesterday.'

I get into the car and turn the engine on. I drive around aimlessly for a very long time. I don't even know where I'm going. The signs on the side of the road dance before my eyes. The darkness is pitch black, the road deserted, only a few trucks are on the road and they keep blinding me with their lights. Eventually, I realise that I have nearly driven all the way to Munich.

I am tempted to stop in a Bavarian pub and drink beer

until I get dead drunk. But, then, who would pick me up and drive me back? This fear keeps me in check.

I return to the inn at two o'clock in the morning. It isn't quiet; in fact, I would say the exact opposite. Muffled conversations, doors that open and close, and the lights on in some rooms create a sense of muffled unrest. There's also the wind that doesn't seem to die out.

On my way to the stairs, I bump into Evelina. Her hair still looks wild but she is calm. She's sitting on the first step with a bottle of vodka on her lap.

'My baby,' she whines, 'I miss my baby. I haven't seen my child in a month. What kind of shitty mother am I?'

She bursts into tears and keeps snuffling. Occasionally, she stops and takes a strong swig from the bottle. I begin to feel sorry for her, but, unfortunately, I can't give her answers to the questions she's asking herself.

Stamatis appears on the stairs.

'I'm going to buy flowers,' he mumbles drunkenly. 'My wife is coming. Tomorrow, she'll be here.'

'At this time of night?' I'm left speechless.

'Why, aren't there any overnight florists in Munich? And where is this fucking German efficiency everyone is talking about?'

He falls into a chair and begins to groan as he wipes his forehead. Everyone is going nuts, it's pretty obvious!

I feel the urgent need for some kind of alcoholic drink. I'm the only one sober in a world teetering dangerously close to the edge of a cliff. I head for the living room, perhaps a small fire is still burning in the grate. Perhaps, I'll find some peace and quiet over there.

'Don't go there! It's sizzling hot!' Evelina snickers behind me.

Once I open the door, I understand what she means. George, our new make-up artist slash hairdresser, was in a passionate embrace with another young man from the crew – I think his name is Thanasis – on one of the sofas. They don't even notice me when I walk in. I instantly turn around and leave. This isn't an inn, it has become a brothel. The two elderly German ladies won't be able to escape the heart attack. Nah, on second thought, I don't think so. They're difficult eggs to crack.

As I go up the stairs, I have the most devastating inspiration of the night. Why don't I go see how he's doing? I'm worried that he might have been hurt. These sudden sensitivities will be the death of me. But, I don't know what to tell him, I'll improvise. He looks crazily excited to see me.

'Come in, baby! I've been expecting you!' He grabs me and drags me into the room. He pulls me against him. He is so drunk you could smell the alcohol and cigarette stench from miles away. His eyes gleam dangerously in the twilight.

'Stop, Constantinos, I'm not playing this game. Stop it!'

'Why? I thought that you liked my games. Why should I stop?'

'Because I'm going to kill you!' I don't even know what I'm saying.

'That's the way I like you!' He attempts to embrace me. I try to escape, but he's stronger than me, even if he is stumbling. 'Come and I'll show you my latest game. It's called Only Sex. You'll see, you're going to like it!'

'You're completely vulgar!'

'That's who I am. You chose me. That's how you wanted the protagonist to be.' What he says is true, and it freaks me out even more.

'Why don't you admit it? You're just like me. That's why we're perfect for each other.'

A terrible fear grips me. The slope that goes downhill is fast approaching and it looks very slippery. A sudden dizziness, an irresistible desire to let myself fall, to give in to this raunchy laughter that springs from the depth of my cells, and the way that everything spins around me without me having even drunk a sip of wine, I still don't understand how I found the strength and stopped this carousel before I fell.

Too bad... because it's liberating to fall sometimes. Afterwards, you have no other choice but to get up again... I didn't even realise how I was able to peel him off of me. I push him away.

'What do you want, then? Why did you come?'

'To see if you're okay.'

'Oh, don't worry. It isn't the first time I've got into a fight. Nor will it be the last, I guess!'

Until this moment, I confess that I was terribly jealous of his wife. From now on, I would start feeling sorry for her.

He goes into the bathroom and puts his head under the tap. When he returns, he seems a little more sober.

'You said you didn't want any more dealings with me. I

guess I'm too unstable for your tastes. How come you're suddenly so concerned about me, Vera? And so late at night?'

'Because I love you!' Could I have just blurted out a love confession? That's impossible. I'm left speechless at my own actions. So is he. Yet, I did say it. It's a phrase too heavy not to leave any traces.

'I know,' he says, after endless moments of silence. 'The whole world loves me. Besides, I have so much money.'

He falls back onto the bed, laughing hysterically. Too bad I don't know any French. It's the ideal language for cussing politely, or so they say. But I have no intention of cursing him politely. *Horrible, selfish prick* is the tamest curse he heard. The rest cannot be repeated here.

'Stop it! That's a very ugly way to show your love, Vera!'

I instinctively look for the door. Do I have the time to run away? Things have got ugly. His eyes are glinting dangerously. He grips my shoulders and shakes me so roughly that it hurts.

'If you love me, as you say, don't ever again say you're leaving me. You aren't going to escape me, and you know that very well. I can make you suffer in ways you can't imagine. I can send you very bad dreams. And I will, I swear it. Is that what you want?'

'No!'

'Good! I'll tell you when to leave. You will do only as I say. Am I clear?'

'Yes.' What else could I say? I don't want to sound like a broken record.

'That's it! And now you can physically prove your love to me.' He pulls me towards the bed.

I turn to see his face, confident that I will see a reflection of myself: a monster. I was wrong! He's an angel. Only, this world is a very inhospitable place for angels, and that's why he's covered in so much mud. Just like the rest of us.

'Calm down, sweetie. No woman acts like that when I take them to my bed,' he says in a poisonous voice when I push him away once more.

'Go to hell,' I scream as I storm out of the room.

He starts laughing once again.

'I just came back from there. I won't bother going back, I'm sorry.'

I'm such an idiot. I confessed my love to him. I gave him the last, the strongest powerful ace to fight me with. As if he didn't already have enough aces in his hands.

'What's wrong, Vera?' Katia appears next to my still-open door. I must have forgotten to kick it shut after I furiously rushed in. Her burgundy velvet robe is slightly dragging on the floor, her fluffy slippers caress the carpet. She doesn't seem to have been suddenly awakened just now, but she looks upset, and she's right to be. It's around three in the morning.

'What did he do to you? You roused the whole place!'

I just realise that we must have become the laughing stock of the entire inn, but it's the last thing that concerns me.

'He's a brute!' I start bawling.

'Come now, don't act like a child. You act as if you don't know how men are.'

'He's a brute, I tell you!' I've run out of characterizations.

'But you owe him your gratitude.'

'What did you say?'

I only hear crack-brained things tonight. My patience is running thin.

'Constantinos has showed you many of his faces. Don't you think that all these aspects of himself he revealed to you are a good source of inspiration?'

She's right, it's undoubtedly so. I have to come to terms with it. One day, I may become a good author, but, as a woman, I will remain an utter failure, forever and ever.

'He hasn't showed me all of them, Katia. He didn't show me the person I expected to see. He's not in love with me; I'm just a fling for him and nothing else.'

'I think he isn't that person at all, and that's why he didn't live up to your expectations. This man is in love with himself above all else. And with his job, of course.'

This woman has the amazing ability to cheer me up.

Serves me right! Why did I get involved in this? Love is a very unsettling feeling. It slips in and dusts off the most remote corners of your soul. But some of your worst things are hidden there.

Those who sit quietly in their houses, nestled on their sofas, with their lives all tidied up, are very wise to do so. With the doors tightly shut against any disturbing emotions. As for myself, what did I gain by pursuing the very same emotions?

Some time must have passed since Katia left. I'm quite calmer now, but I can't go to sleep. The cuckoo clock on the ground floor sounds five times and it resonates on all floors.

A faint knock on the door makes me shoot up.

'Sorry if I woke you up. I can't seem to fall asleep.' He's standing on the threshold of my room looking quite lost. I can't believe my eyes. He looks sad and worse for wear. At just that moment, I notice that he has a bruise on his forehead and that his lips are a little swollen.

'I keep having nightmares these last couple of nights. I was thinking ... perhaps we could try to sleep in each other's arms? Please...'

I'm never, ever, ever falling in love again! That's a promise! Tomorrow I will write two affidavits, I will sign them with the blood of my heart and I will send them by registered mail: one to God and the other to the Devil. At present, however, since I fell for it, I'll let myself enjoy it.

'Yes, my love!'

'I like it when you call me that.'

He lies down next to me and I listen to his quiet breathing.

'Vera,' he says half asleep after a while, 'did you come to my room two nights ago?'

'I don't understand what you're saying.'

'The other night, I suddenly woke up. I had the impression that someone was there. Probably a woman. When I turned the light on, she was gone. I'm not sure if it was a dream or reality.'

'No, it wasn't me. Are you serious, don't you lock your door?'

'I guess not, I hadn't locked it. I was waiting for... Hoping, actually, that you'd come to me.'

I want to tell him that he doesn't need to make up such

stories in order to convince me to take him in my arms. Unfortunately, for myself, I'm easily persuaded with even a few arguments. But, I see that he has fallen asleep. I'm still awake. I dread the dreams that will come. The last couple of nights, I have the feeling that Alexander is prowling around their edges. If he appears and asks me why I abandoned him, what am I going to answer him?

It's getting lighter outside when I finally fall asleep. But the nightmare is still lurking. A voice emerges from the depths of the dream, made of fog and stardust, lost in the twilight of the centuries. It's so calm and deep that it has entranced me.

'You did well to kill Alexander,' it says calmly. 'Boundless sensitivity must be eliminated if you want to survive. And unbridled sexuality – yes, I mean Eleana – must also be harnessed. Otherwise, you're doomed.'

I don't even think of objecting to that wise voice. What it says sounds so normal; it speaks with such warmth and life. It seduces me.

'Now, you have to kill your mother, too,' the voice continues. 'The nightmares of the past, the demons, and the paranoia should go to hell, don't you agree?'

I find it very reasonable.

'And then...'

'No,' I scream, 'not Constantinos!'

'Of course not,' the voice says with a laugh that springs from the cavernous tunnels of the subconscious. 'That's how love is. You can't kill love. It's impossible. I meant that you would be free after that. You know the meaning of that word. Have you ever felt it? Unless you're a coward. Are you?'

I don't know. I don't understand what this voice is saying. I need to find someone to help me understand.

20TH NOVEMBER

I'm leaving! I can't stand being here any longer. I know it's cowardly to run away like this, but, fortunately, I'm not a man and that has some advantages in the end.

Today, it was confirmed once again that "Bad things come in threes". Especially, when evil has many faces. There was no shoot today. The weather is very bad. It's snowing and a devilish wind is howling. So, we're left with nothing to do. The rest have scattered: some have gone to the nearest town for coffee, a few preferred to drive to Munich for shopping, and others are locked in their rooms.

At eleven thirty in the morning, when I went down to the living room, a nasty surprise was waiting for me laid flat out on a small side table. "Many Kisses from Mr Aravantinos to His Screenwriter" was the banner headline of the yellow rag that called itself *Yellow Fever*, paraphrasing the title of our film *Many Kisses from Mr Strasse*. A giant-sized photo of the two of us in a tender embrace was printed under the headline.

This made my blood boil. Where the hell did they find this photo? Someone must have been following us the day we stole a few moments to ourselves and took a walk in the forest. That was the only time we were so affectionate towards each other in an open space. Someone must have set us up, just so they could get this picture.

I read the article's shocking details and I blush. Besides containing many inaccuracies, it is also very far-fetched. I'm pretty sure that tomorrow the other trash rags of this kind will all follow *Yellow Fever*'s example.

Through my haze, I think that I've already found the culprit. Without a second thought, I grab the newspaper and rush to Venetis' room.

'What's all this, Pantelis?'

He drives me crazy with the way he shams indifference while stroking his beard.

'Why are you asking me?'

'Doesn't your wife work for this rag?'

'So what?'

'Don't pretend you don't know!'

'Welcome to the celebrities' club, Vera,' he mocks me. 'From now on, your life will be in the public eye. People are dying for gossip, love.'

'Listen here! I don't like seeing my life become fodder for these sleazy tabloids, dammit!'

He becomes wild. His auburn moustache is ablaze. He abruptly dumps his smoking pipe – he had been thoroughly cleaning it out all this time – to the side.

'Watch your tongue, please.'

'Watch your cronies.'

'I don't have any cronies!'

'You've found a nice way to get publicity for your film, Mr Venetis. Congratulations!'

'I have nothing to do with it. How many times do I have to tell you?'

I don't believe him. I throw the newspaper on the floor and bang the door shut behind me as I leave. I'm practically vibrating with anger, I'm afraid that I will fall apart. My legs are shaking.

Katia says that I shouldn't get so upset. She claims I'm overreacting and that bad publicity is preferable to no publicity. That sounds very cynical to me.

'You're worried about him, aren't you?'

'Katia, he's married. I didn't want for this story to come out this way.'

'That's his problem. Why should you get involved?'

'I'm very much involved; I'm not an innocent bystander.'

'If you want my opinion, by the way, I don't believe it was Venetis' doing. Just think about it, who controls everything around here? Who has singled out Constantinos from the beginning and is quite obvious in his dislike?'

'You mean ...Avramoglou?'

'It's very likely. He has his own people in the crew, that's for sure. One of them must have been following you and found the perfect opportunity to take your picture.'

'Yes, but Venetis also has his reasons for wanting to expose Constantinos.'

'Only, he didn't have the time to set things up. The animosity between them is too recent.'

I find this to be a very logical explanation. Moreover, the picture must have been taken days ago, long before he got into that fight with Constantinos.

'Be careful not to go against Avramoglou,' she warns me in a cold voice. 'You'll be ruined! He can make you disappear from show biz in a single night.'

I had no such intention. A second face off with the big boss would be going too far.

I had never felt so humiliated in my entire life. What I feel for him has nothing to do with that sensational story published in that yellow rag.

Eventually, I realise that my legs won't hold me for much longer. I feel like I'm coming apart at the seams. None of my body parts seem to obey me. If you add the terrible sleepiness I feel, and my frayed nerves due to recent events, I feel like a wreck.

I almost crawl up the stairs to the communal bathroom and spend a long time under the showerhead. Under the refreshing, purifying water. I wish it could wash all this shame away. I hope that there's a speck of truth in the ancient beliefs about water's redemptive qualities.

After my shower, I hastily start packing. My job is finished, anyway. There's no reason for me to stay another day.

He asks me where I intend to go when I say goodbye to him.

Honestly, I have no idea. My claustrophobic flat in Lycabettus doesn't sound very inviting. But, I had time to think about it. I just want to leave, the sooner the better.

'You can go to my summer home in Evia if you like. You'll find peace there. It's very secluded and quiet; at this time of year, there's hardly a soul around.'

He grabs a bunch of keys from a drawer and gives me

two of them. *There's hidden symbolism in this gesture*, I momentarily think.

'What? Are you going to leave like that? No farewell kiss?' He laughs very slyly.

I can't help but burst out laughing.

'You're unbelievable!'

'What am I?'

'You're my heart.'

'And what else?'

'You're everything to me, Constantinos.'

He looks very happy with my show of affection.

I know I have shared too many things with him. So far, I only speak and he merely listens, accepts and demands. I do not believe that there can be a relationship where one just 'gives' and the other just 'takes.' These two go together. Besides, he has already given me so much. The mere fact that he exists makes this world I live in a bit more beautiful.

It gives me terrible pain to be separated from him in such a way, without knowing whether I'm going to see him again, or when. At the same time, however, a secret voice tells me that we are never separated from the people we love. We carry them within ourselves. I don't know, maybe this too is a way to make the separation more bearable.

I hastily say goodbye to everyone I come across. I leave a short letter for Venetis and get in the car. Night has already fallen and the wind has started blowing. The roads are snowy and deserted. The trees bear their snowy burden without complaint. Clouds are lurking low in the sky. This crazy north wind that leaves nothing standing in its path has also scattered my life to every corner of the world.

At the far end of the street, I turn and, for the last time, I take in this strange city with the sad sky, where the most shocking events of my life took place. I didn't get to know it as much as I should have. But certainly, I will never forget it.

Chapter 14

The Aesthetic of Terror

It was late afternoon by the time I arrived in the settlement of Skala in Oropos. After I left the airport, I went home to get some clothes, got into my jeep and left right away. I boarded the ferry to Eretria and in less than ten minutes and after following his instructions, I was standing outside his house.

That was it, I couldn't be wrong. He was very detailed in his description. It was a sleek maisonette of modern architectural design with clear influences from tradition, a successful coexistence of stone and whitewashed walls and gigantic windows with a panoramic view of the Evian Gulf. At the far end of the garden, I spotted the covered swimming pool; a paved path was leading there.

I took a look around. I couldn't see a single soul for miles. The nearest house was about half a mile away and it seemed uninhabited.

The scenery was idyllic. I only found the presence of ivy on the west side of the house very strange. It seemed like a sneaky, evil creature, which threatened to strangle the house with its tentacles.

Meanwhile, dark clouds were gathering on the horizon. The sea roared in the background. The soil smelled of the storm that would soon arrive.

In the garden, I was welcomed by Mr Thanasis, who was holding a pickaxe in his hand and his baggy trousers were covered in dirt. Apparently, he was the man who took care of everything, as Constantinos had told me. The man said that his wife had tidied up the house, the kitchen was well stocked with food and there was enough firewood to last for days. Just as Mr Aravantinos had requested.

The furniture inside the house was minimal and carefully selected. A casual and carefree style, suited to the rural character of the house.

Just in time, Mrs Angeliki rang the doorbell. She brought me a bag of early oranges, a freshly baked cheese pie and a loaf of farmhouse bread. She lit the fire and left discreetly.

I was in his home! He had given me the keys and allowed entry to his own place, and this was the greatest happiness of all.

I took off my shoes and I carefully counted the rough Karystos stones that covered the floor underneath the soft carpet. I sank into the leather couch and let my fingers caress its chocolate smoothness, the pillows made of fur and suede and the light honey-coloured table. Two suede bean-bags, a walnut trunk and a plain lamp also made up the living room.

I became rather nosy when I went into the bedroom and started rummaging through the wardrobe there. Finally, I found what I was looking for: a flannel shirt. I put it on and it felt wonderful against my skin. As if I felt his touch on my skin.

I lay on the couch and covered myself with the woollen throw. I could hear the rain approaching. I instantly fell asleep next to the fireplace without even stirring at the wind raging outside, without any painful thoughts or nightmares. A sweet warmth wrapped itself around me. Somewhere far away, fishbone-shaped lightning shattered the sky.

Early the next morning, I woke up with my mind made up about what I wanted to do. I made coffee, congratulated myself for lighting the fireplace without any help, and lay on a large throw pillow in front of the fire with a notebook balanced on my knees.

Did We Have the Same Dream? That would be the title of my new book. It would be about the many faces of love and how we simply choose to see the one that suits us. About people who appear on our path and have something important to tell us. If we don't listen to them, we will keep meeting them along the way. About the dreams that deserve our absolute acceptance since that's where the more genuine half of ourselves lives. About the life that seeks no answers, probably because it has found the answer within itself.

I will write about all those magical things that took me too long to discover and how, even if I eventually learned to find them, I owed everything to him. This way, I would always be sure that I had him imprisoned in my fingertips.

****

During the next two days, it was raining heavily. The rain rattled on the roof of the house, on the thick tarpaulin that covered the pool and on top of the barbecue shed in the garden. A devilish southern wind that was very strong thrashed the trees surrounding the house. The rose bushes lost all their petals. I didn't dare slip out of the house. In the kitchen, there were enough supplies to last me for ten days and there was continually a fire burning in the fireplace. I wrote incessantly, like the time when I had him as a companion and a guide in my dreams.

Constantinos called me two or three times in order to make sure that everything was okay, and he shared news and other details from the shooting with me. He was on marginally better terms with Venetis, shooting was scheduled to wrap up in about a week and everyone was optimistic about the outcome and so on and so forth.

I listened to him chatter on and on, lost in my thoughts. I caught myself feeling anxious, looking for some hidden promise in his words that we would meet again, a hint that he missed me, but in vain.

Of course, I could never have imagined how quickly I would be seeing him again and under what dramatic conditions. It seems that this man attracted not only people's looks and success, but turmoil and destruction, as well. And since I had got so close to him, I too was affected.

I had spent five quiet days in Evia eating, taking long walks and writing nonstop when I received an unexpected phone call.

It was afternoon. Faint sunshine was reflected on the floor. At noon, Mrs Angeliki brought me some fish that her husband had caught. After lunch, I went out and walked aimlessly by the sea for a long time. I collected pebbles in strange colours and seashells that had been washed up by the storm.

Without realising how it happened, because the sky had been almost clear, it started raining again. A beautiful storm was raging around me. I saw the rain droplets exploding before my eyes with the power and grace of the first buds of spring. I had never seen such rain drops; as large as hail, but as transparent and bright as dewdrops. And, strangely enough, they fell in slow motion – they seemed in no hurry to reach the ground – and I could touch and enjoy their crystal transparency.

Everything was so clean and clear, even the storm. Nothing foretold the nightmare that would follow. I now think of an Oscar Wilde quote: 'Fate does not send messengers; it's too wise, or too cruel, to do that,' and I still don't know if I agree or not. At that time, however, no messengers were sent to me. I would have figured it out. I got back to the house soaked to the bone. I ran to the bathroom to take off my wet clothes and take a hot shower. As I got out of the shower, the phone rang. I was pleased to hear Katia's voice. It was a pleasant surprise that broke the monotony.

'How are you, Vera? Are you by yourself, sweetheart?'

I wasn't used to Katia being so sweet towards me.

'Yes, just myself to keep me company. Where are you?'

'I'm back in Greece. I've been in Athens for a few days. I came to see my doctor.'

'Is anything wrong? Are you sick?'

'Nothing serious, I hope. Anyway, it'd be better if we talked in person. Where exactly are you? I was thinking, if you don't mind, of dropping by for a visit. Constantinos explained what had happened more or less, but, to tell you the truth, I didn't quite understand him.'

I should have been surprised by her initiative to invite herself. Katia was too discreet to make such a faux pas. But, I didn't notice this detail. I hadn't seen a single human being for days, why should I be so unfriendly? I gave her detailed directions on how to find the house and she promised to arrive around six in the evening.

From this point onwards, things unfolded rapidly. Both for me and for Constantinos. Everything I describe on his behalf, he narrated to me himself afterwards when it was all over. It was a tragic end, of course, but everything was over.

Shortly before Katia arrived, I went out into the garden to wait for her in case she got lost. It was already dusk and it had gotten chilly. I wrapped myself in my coat and walked around impatiently. The soil produced a sweet aroma. I smelled the air that brought the rain with it. The clouds had not dissolved. From time to time, the signs of a new storm appeared and the horizon was marked with consecutive lightning as if the foundations of the world were shaking. I felt lucky that I would have company during such an awful night. I was, without any doubt, planning to invite her to stay. I wouldn't let her drive back in such weather.

At last, I saw her appear at the end of the dirt road. I

was very surprised to see that she wasn't driving her car, but was on foot instead. She was around a third of a mile away and all I could make out was that she was talking on her mobile phone. I could neither see the expression on her face – she was still too far away and darkness had already fallen – nor could I hear what she was saying. But I heard her laughter – it was pretty loud and hoarse – and was bewildered once again. It was so unlike Katia to have such a shameless laugh.

Around that time, Constantinos' mobile phone rang. He had forgotten it in the living room of the inn. Marianna had to yell out to him repeatedly until he finally came downstairs to pick it up.

'Well done, darling!' An unearthly chill was what he heard and not a human voice.

'Who is this?'

He closed his other ear with his free hand in order to tune out the other people in the group and be able to hear the mysterious caller more clearly.

'You put her head in the lion's mouth,' the voice continued, 'and now she's completely alone and helpless! How can a woman protect herself in the wilderness? There are many jackals, and quite a few venomous snakes, lurking around that summer home with the red railings and the ivy.'

'Who are you?' he screamed.

A deranged laughter was the only answer he received and the stranger hung up. He searched his call log for the caller's

ID. Nothing, the phone number had been withheld. What kind
of morbid joke was that?

He immediately called my cell phone: 'Your call is being
forwarded.' He then called the landline... One, two, three,
five, ten rings ... nobody was picking up.

It's to be expected, since I'm in the garden and waiting for
Katia. I stand still and watch her getting closer and closer
in her usual arrogant way of walking, like a woman who
has an appointment with fate. That confident stride and
the way she sways her hips remind me of someone but I
can't recall who that is and am forced to abandon that train
of thought. For a moment, I get the feeling that I see my
mother approaching, but what business would Theophano
have here?

I once again see that picture before me, illuminated with
the knowledge of what happened next.

I am the one who is once again waiting, but not in the
present. I am only six years old, the clouds on the horizon are dripping blood and I'm standing all alone in the
street with the locked houses. Even worse, the street without
homes. Night has fallen, it's pitch black. My mother comes
from afar, it's her I'm waiting for, I expect her to come flying to my face and start yelling that I'm a filthy girl, that I
don't deserve her love and the many sacrifices she's made
for me, that I'm nothing but an ungrateful, selfish being.
And, instead of getting up to leave, I stupidly just sit and
wait for her. Because if I leave, I know she will get awfully

angry, she will lock me out of the house, and I dread her bouts of anger.

He clutched at his head in despair. And what if it wasn't a prank?

After a few minutes of contemplation, he decided to call the police in Halkida, which was the nearest city to his summer home. He lost some precious time, though, until he was able to get the phone number from the operator.

'Of course, sir, we'll immediately make a house call,' the officer assured him in a sleepy voice, which was in direct contrast to his words.

Did everyone really speak and move so slowly, or was it just his imagination?

'Please, sir, can you give me more details about the exact location of the house?'

Damn, he had already explained everything twice...

'Okay, sir, we will contact you as soon as we have more information.'

He called the airport as soon as the police officer hung up. He was informed that the next flight from Munich to Athens would depart in two hours and that, fortunately, seats were still available.

'I need to go. Something very urgent has come up.' That was the only information he could give Venetis before he dashed off to the airport, leaving the director high and dry.

****

I was so glad to see her. I gave her a warm hug and she returned it very cautiously. Her face looked incredibly tired. New wrinkles had appeared on her face and I noticed that she had neglected to dye her hair. I felt worried. Something serious must have happened to Katia to make her neglect her appearance.

But when I noticed her clothes, I was relieved. She looked impeccable in her charcoal-coloured turtleneck, black leather jacket, woollen scarf around the neck, baggy checked trousers, and a black quilted, crocodile-skin bag. Once again, I felt awkward before the aura of the 'ultimate' woman and the poise she exuded. This aura certainly belonged to women who have a lot to teach you about style – if that elusive victory was something that could be taught. Once again, I felt like an immature little girl compared to Katia.

I closed the heavy garden gate and we headed for the house. Now that I think about it, this should have been a warning sign. The gate! It creaked in a mournful and creepy way, just like doors usually do in horror movies. But, I was too happy to pay attention to such details.

She crossed the threshold with slow steps. I expected her to inspect everything, to comment on the décor, to say something – anything! – that would reveal her approval or disapproval. But she completely overlooked the furniture, the walls, even me; I had the impression she didn't see me. Katia looked everywhere and nowhere in particular, with a lifeless, indifferent look in her eyes.

'You got some rest, I imagine,' she asked me, just like

an acquaintance would typically ask. 'This is a very idyllic place, exactly what is needed in your case.'

She took off her scarf and jacket and sat on the edge of an armchair. She had the look of someone who had just dropped by for a short visit and didn't intend to stay for long.

She did cross her legs with elegance and smoothed her perfect eyebrows with a light touch. At that moment, I noticed that she had no luggage with her. Wouldn't she be spending the night? I was disappointed.

'It depends,' she said thoughtfully when I asked her.

She took her cigarette holder out of her bag and lit a cigarette. She seemed tired but calm. As if she had reached the end of a road that had made her suffer many pitfalls and from then onwards the path she had to follow was irreversible.

'Shall I fix you a drink?'

'Bourbon, please, on the rocks.'

She took a deep drag from her smoke and exhaled only in a way a femme fatale could, with unparalleled grace, but also with huge relief, as if a heavy weight had been lifted off her shoulders. Katia, the femme fatale of my life, and of some other people's lives. From that day on, I began hating such women and the legends created around them.

'What happened that made you leave so hastily? I didn't quite understand.'

'It seems I was exhausted. I could barely walk. It's the first time something like this has happened. And it isn't like I'm not used to working hard.'

I realised I was chattering like a fool in an attempt to break the ice, and so I stopped.

'And you also had to work overtime,' she remarked almost casually, 'in Mr Aravantinos' bed. How could anyone stand all that? You're right.' She smiled with incredible sweetness, just like a loving mother.

For a moment, I couldn't believe my ears and couldn't get a word out. Only the loud crack of the ice cubes as they clinked against each other could be heard. The ice did actually break, but only the one in her glass.

'What are you implying, Katia? And in such a vulgar way! I didn't expect that from you.'

'Oh, I'm not implying anything, darling; I'm saying it quite clearly. Why? Am I wrong?'

She exhaled another cotton-like tuft of smoke, with her eyes half closed. Something frosty and scaly briefly flashed in their depths. I thought she was feverish; the small flames flickering in her eyes were that bright. For a second, I felt alarmed.

'Anyway, I won't allow you to...'

At that moment, the phone started ringing off the hook. It seemed to be bouncing in place and I rushed to pick it up.

'It's pointless to answer, Vera. In fact, it would be completely useless.'

Her voice was quiet and eerie. Katia wasn't making demands; she spoke meekly, as if she was stating an inevitable conclusion. I turned to look at her puzzled, ready to ask for an explanation for this bizarre behaviour. Then, I noticed a third eye, other than her own, which was burning with a dark fire. It was pitch black and steely; it looked like a big, gaping mouth that could catch fire at any moment. I gasped. The glass slipped from my hands, I saw it falling, falling and falling in slow motion, which lasted for an entire breath until – obeying the law of gravity – it reached its destination on the floor and stained the carpet.

The phone continued its desperate ringing – two, three, five, ten, fifteen times. I stood as motionless as a tin soldier. My feet were planted on the floor. The phone was struggling to warn me about something, but that something was already before my eyes in all its nightmarish immediacy, and it was too late for any warnings.

'He's looking for you,' she smiled coolly, 'but he's very far away. What can he do from wherever he is?'

I tried to appear furious, but I found it hard to do so.

'Is this some kind of a joke, Katia? Because I find it really sick.'

'What a coincidence! That's exactly what Eleana said when she saw the gun. What lack of intelligence. Frankly, I expected a more original reaction from you, darling.'

Half of her face was wrapped in darkness, due to the seat she had chosen. Only the other half was illuminated by the light of the room. For a moment, the part hidden in the shadows seemed repulsive and vulgar to me, though I couldn't say for sure which of the two halves was the most obnoxious.

'You.... You killed her?' I began to stammer, I let the cigarette slip from my fingers. The damage done to the expensive carpet was now irreparable.

Her look showed offended pride, *who else could have planned everything so perfectly, with so much intelligence and precision?* How could I possibly not have noticed?

'Why? Why did you do it?'

'The reasons were of a purely aesthetic nature, I want you to believe me.' She was silent for a moment, allowing my anxiety to climb even higher. 'I've always been in love with the tango,' she said with a hint of nostalgia, 'I always loved to tango. That was the problem. It isn't a respectable dance. It was the favourite of the women of the night and corruption, of the Argentinian whores when they were delivered to their pimps.'

I didn't understand a single word. But, I was starting to realise what kind of doctor she needed to see.

'It was an indecent dance for a girl of my class, but I was in love with it. So, I had to forget about it and, since then, I have only danced the waltz. It is such a delicate dance, it doesn't cause your heart to beat any louder, it's très chic, très jolie. But I had to get rid of the whores, throw them out of the dance – they had no finesse at all. Away from the dance, that's their place. What is your favourite dance, Vera? The dance of the Immovable Roses? Isn't that it? Did I get it right?' She let out that shameless laughter I had heard earlier, in the garden. That couldn't be Katia who was laughing so creepily.

'Well, some whores like Eleana should get out of the way...' she spoke in whispers as if she had grown weary of her own delirium. 'Whores have such bad taste; they always look so cheap.'

She sighed deeply and slid another cigarette in her

cigarette holder. A heavy silence, heavier than lead, followed. Eavesdropping heaven was preparing to launch its thunderbolts and I felt so helpless that I decided not to resist, not to fight for anything. My life seemed so flimsy and cheap.

I knew she would find me. No matter where I ran to hide, my mother would always find me. To punish me for being so vile, so corrupt. Now that I see it written, I know it sounds completely crazy, but at that moment, it seemed to me the most logical thought in the world. My mother had done all the killings, and she was now preparing to get rid of me, too. But, because she didn't have the heart to kill her own daughter, she had armed Katia's hand.

The storm that broke out made the sky darken and dangerously reduced visibility. So, his flight from Munich was delayed in landing.

He was about to explode from nervous tension. 'She must've had a reason to call me. It can't be; if she wanted to hurt Vera, then she wouldn't have let me know. She called me, so it means she wants me to get there.' That was the line of thought he desperately tried to hold on to, so as not to go mad from worry. As soon as the plane landed, his cell phone rang.

'We just arrived at the house you described to us,' the officer said. He must have found the mystery really fascinating because he sounded a lot more awake. 'We didn't find anything here. No one's home, Mr Aravantinos. Something strange is going on, though, because the lights are all on and the doors have been left wide open.'

He ran to the counter of a car rental company.

'Give me what's available, I need a car right away,' he insisted.

One hour later, he was parking the red Alfa Romeo in the backyard with the engine growling... The storm had temporarily stopped, but not before destroying the rose bushes and flooding the place with mud.

He found the police in great confusion. After the formalities and the official report drawn up by a senior officer, they entered their patrol cars and departed.

Tired and frustrated, he plonked down on the stairs. What was he supposed to do? His last hope seemed to flicker precariously.

****

The fire in the small gas stove was in its death throes for some time, but we weren't particularly concerned about it.

'Why did you bring me here?' I asked numbly after we had left the jeep and walked into the deserted fishing hut.

'Because the house will be swarming with police, you silly creature,' she told me in a severe tone.

The wooden hut contained only the barest essentials a fisherman would need in case of an emergency. Two camp beds, thick blankets, a makeshift kitchen with basic foodstuffs, a gas stove, and a worm-eaten table full of empty bottles. And one embalmed fish that made my blood freeze. The lamp gave off a stingy light in the shade of melted butter that made the place look like a grimy bucket.

A wave of disgust sprang from my guts and I felt my

stomach heaving. I feared that at any moment THAT, my old illness, would make an unexpected appearance.

'And why don't you kill me to get it over with?'

Where did I find the courage to talk so boldly? I was struggling to resist the fear, to not let it paralyse me because then everything would be over.

'Oh, there's no rush, darling,' she laughed sarcastically. Her face hardened, deep wrinkles appeared that made her look at least ten years older. 'But we're waiting for your lover, of course. He'll be here in two to three hours. And then I'll have caught myself two birds with one stone.'

'I find that expression too commonplace for your refined tastes,' I said.

'I see that you've regained your sense of humour. But you will lose it once and for all and then you'll understand.'

She gave me another one of her proud smiles, in which I detected traces of revenge and gloating. That must be the expression of fate when it plays its outrageously awful tricks on us, when it has us cornered, or when it drags us around like mindless pawns.

'What will I understand, Katia? What is all this? Why are you doing this?'

'Slow down. One question at a time. Why am I doing this? But, I explained it to you. Because it would be better if the world was rid of some whores. Take Eleana, for example. A very tacky and vulgar female. Cute, I admit, but with horrible taste. She slept with any man she came across. I wasn't bothered that she didn't keep any pretexts and that she didn't have any qualms. But, I did mind her complete

lack of style and manners. Once upon a time, darling, wom-
en had, you know, grace and elegance. The women of my
class were refined and tasteful. They didn't spread their legs
for every male that happened to be passing by. I remember
our brilliant ballrooms with the priceless chandeliers and the
marble floors, where wonderful evening parties were held.'

Her eyes gazed at nothing; she became removed from the
passage of time and sank into a foggy haze. For a moment,
I was tempted to attack her and grab the gun, but I lacked
the courage to attempt anything so risky. Such things were
only successful in films.

'It's a purely aesthetic matter, darling, as I said before.
Back then, women wore tight corsets that gave them grace,
long petticoats, and romantic dresses. They put up their hair
and left only small curls to frame their temples. Their movements, their laughter and their words exuded respect and
nobility. They lowered their eyes and blushed when men
looked at them.'

'Excuse me, what era are we talking about?' I brutally
interrupted her reverie.

'Is historical accuracy the issue here? I'm speaking, of
course, about the old days, about the women of my own
class.' Her smile was dripping honey and sugar, but insanity
had finally infected her gaze.

'Do you mean to tell me that you killed Eleana because
she had no style?'

Terror had begun penetrating my cells. Till that time, it had
been hovering by the door like a dog impatient to come in.

'Because she was a whore with no style. Because she

was a severe insult to my aesthetic sensibilities. That's why I killed her!'

'And how did you manage to do that, Katia?'

If I could figure it out, if I could explain the unexplainable, then, perhaps, I would find a way to save myself.

'Oh, but it was very easy!' she crowed happily. 'Of course, I had planned everything in every detail long before we even left Greece. I left nothing to chance, as you can imagine. I didn't hate her, nothing of the sort ever happened, I want you to believe me, I simply found her not fitting with the pieces of the world that I see around me. Everything was motivated by a deep sense of appreciation I have for the female sex. That was all. Of course, in the beginning, I didn't have bad intentions. I only intended to find a way of knocking some sense into her, or even giving her a fright, if necessary. She left me with no other choice, though, but to kill her. She dragged the circumstances to the point of no return. That evening, I tiptoed outside her door. I wanted to see if she was alone; of course, she wasn't. All too familiar sounds were coming from the room... if you know what I mean? It would be in bad taste for me to be more descriptive.'

She stopped for a moment to take a breath. She lit another cigarette and carefully stroked her eyebrows with a finger. She had a faraway look in her eyes, the look of someone who stumbles upon an invisible barrier, rebounds from it, and returns to where she was before.

My breathing had become very shallow from the agony I was in. My whole body had begun to complain about the lack of oxygen.

'I waited patiently for some time, hidden in the small storeroom at the end of the hall until. At some point, Venetis snuck out of her room. I suffered the same shock all of you had when the police took him away for questioning. I hadn't been expecting that. But, this incident decided her death sentence. That girl had no morals, stopped at nothing. She would get us all infected by her promiscuous habits! At that time, I hadn't really intended to kill her, but, from the moment I saw Venetis, I knew I couldn't turn back. This nymphomaniac, insatiable female had to disappear from the face of the earth.

'Lust, you know, is a highly contagious disease, much more despicable, and infinitely more dangerous than AIDS. It can be transmitted with a single look, with a random touch. And she infected us all. The same thing that Constantinos is doing! You certainly know now what I mean, I don't need to get into extensive details. This man is the devil himself,' she completed her reasoning.

My anxiety had skyrocketed. And then ... and then? The words writhed on the edges of my lips and I must have looked at her with huge anticipation. Imagination had become entangled with horror in her troubled mind; the fairy tale had been derailed on a rough and rugged road.

'I would have never thought you would be so over-religious, Katia.' These words escaped me almost involuntarily.

'It has nothing to do with religion,' she answered calmly. 'It's just a matter of good taste and bad taste, I already explained that to you. I wanted to remain anonymous in case she struggled in an effort to save herself. That's why I wore the mask before entering her room. It was a smiling mask, a beautiful authentic Venetian mask, with an expression of heavenly peace. I regret that I wasted it on her. But that flighty female, instead of cringing in fear, instead of begging and showing signs of remorse, she began to snicker and shamelessly mock me. But, her behaviour drastically changed when she saw the gun. I will never forget the questioning look that took over her face. In the beginning, she was annoyed that I had disturbed her rest after her tryst, but when she realised what was going on, she acted as if I was Jack the Ripper himself. But, she should have expected it. Didn't she know that whores always come to a bad end? I killed her very gently, I want you to believe me, she didn't suffer at all, she just fell gently back on the pillows without any groans, or moans, just like a cloth doll.

'I tore her clothes off – which is ironic, since it's my job to dress people up – to highlight her inner nakedness, and staged the scene in a way that matched the degenerate nature of the room's occupant. I tied her hands to the railing of the bed with the pillowcase. I'd looked into your room from outside the window when you were playing a similar game with Constantinos and I thought of playing a small prank on you. Those windows with no shutters are a downright temptation, don't you agree?'

She threw her head back and burst into a horrible laugh that made the tin roof squeak.

Then she spent some time in silence. The satisfaction she felt for the successful conclusion of her murderous instincts was clearly imprinted on her face. All that was missing from this absurd scene was a theatre curtain, which would gently fall on the stage with velvet folds, and then gracefully be lifted up, with the audience applauding entranced, so as to make the situation completely ridiculous.

My stomach was tied into knots. I had the impression that if I tried to say anything, my throat would get scratchy. Everything sounded so simple – all these wild events had such simple explanations that it was almost absurd. And I had foolishly believed that...

'And you were stupid enough to suspect that he had committed the crime. You must trust him so much.'

Her last words hurt me even more than a bullet would have. I hid my face in my hands as the macabre narration continued.

'I regret, I truly regret, having to kill Alexander too. But he was also hopelessly infected by her illness, it was impossible for him to escape. Moreover, I needed a culprit. Someone had to take responsibility for the murder in order for the case to be closed, and he was the easiest target. That night, I went to his room. He was completely distracted and utterly drunk. He had probably smoked pot, or who knows what else, because he couldn't even see straight. I poured the poison in his drink, before his very eyes. He didn't understand a thing of what was going on. When he began to lose consciousness, I grabbed his hand and "helped" him write that note where he confessed his guilt.'

She spoke so calmly and sanely, it was as if she was narrating a science fiction story to a wide-eyed child.

'I never imagined that it would be so easy and simple to

kill. And imagine that it was my first time. But I had waited so long, you don't know how much I had been waiting for this moment.'

Katia was telling me a fairy tale at that moment, a hideous and awful one. The time had come for the fairy tale to become a nightmare, as my father would have said, and it caught me completely unprepared.

'What do you want from me, Katia?'

'To bring him here! I want him here! I want to see his expression when I scar you for life! I want to see how easily he betrays you and runs to save his own skin. Then you will understand how cowardly and selfish, how big a hypocrite he is. How he's not worth a single dime, and how he wouldn't even give one for you. You will soon be able to enjoy your prince and his self-sacrifice. Wait and see. It'll be worth it.'

She once again let out a shrill laugh that pierced my ears like fiery pins. I crumpled into a corner, folding my knees to my chest.

'Of course I'm kidding,' she said shortly afterwards. 'My plan isn't so disorganized. It's him I want. Bastards like Aravantinos don't deserve to live. After I get rid of him, they will very easily believe that you killed him and then committed suicide. They all heard your bad fight that night. There are witnesses that heard you screaming that you would kill him, Vera. And erotic passion is a prime motive for murder, no one will even think of doubting it. One night, I tried to do it in his room, but he wasn't very cooperative. He suddenly woke up and I didn't dare go on with my plan. It certainly grieves me that the seventh art will lose such a star, but what can you do, you can't have everything.'

'Why do you hate him so much, Katia? What did he ever do to you?'

Her style changed abruptly. She was overcome by melancholic reverie. Her eyelashes were wet; a thin film of transparent moisture covered her eyes. A smile so faint, so elusive that it was almost invisible, sweetened her face for an instance.

'He is torturing my little girl,' she said slowly.

'Who is your little girl, Katia?'

I shouldn't have asked her that question. I wasn't prepared for what I would hear in reply.

'He has you on a string, Vera. He blinded you with his cheap love tricks. When he grows bored of you and discards you, it will make you suffer. How can you possibly not understand?'

It was my turn to burst out laughing, but it was a very bitter laugh, because I watched as all of my suspicions were confirmed. All this time, it was as though I had been listening to my mother's ramblings. Only she could turn so bitter and cynical.

'I don't like people playing with the feelings of others. I don't like it one bit.'

'You're sick,' I could only mumble, but these words made my throat feel numb and I lost my voice.

'And, yet, you owe me your gratitude, Vera. Thanks to me, you will see his real face. When people face death, they don't have the time to resort to lies and hypocritical tricks.'

He hung about for some time, wandering like crazy in and out of the house, the silent house that scoffed at him with its wide open doors and its excruciatingly bright lights that didn't have any essential clues to give him, and around the damp garden that wrapped around him and squeezed him almost to the point of suffocation.

His head was about to break in two from the pain, but he didn't stop examining the slushy soil, the mushy piles of leaves, the soaked stairs, inch by inch, begging them to reveal some of their secrets to him. Everything looks so much easier in detective films, he thought. A loose thread always appears out of nowhere, sooner or later, and the hero grabs it by the edge and then the plot moves headlong towards the final solution.

He knelt on the ground, staining his trousers with mud. The rain continued falling and soaked him to the bone. A deadly cold pierced him.

And then he saw something. At the edge of the narrow path, he noticed the deep tire marks left in the wet earth by the wheels of a jeep. They were heading in the direction opposite the one taken by the police cars earlier. Suddenly, a faint light came to life within him.

'And now what role should I play?' he wondered. 'Who would fit better in this situation? The dreamer, the inspector, who despite his fear, proved himself to be a brave man, or that bastard Leroi, who vanished into thin air when everything went to the dogs?'

But, all of these parts had already rolled off him and had fallen on the ground, no longer useful to him. He felt naked and exposed. Nobody could help him any longer. All his clothes were tattered beyond repair. He had known that this day would come, he had always known, and he had waited for it with trepidation.

As if an invisible hand had persecuted him and was now crushing him in its powerful fist. Now, that it had found him in a vulnerable position, it would turn him into pulp with wild pleasure. And, along with him, all of his characters. Because they were all one and the same. They had penetrated deep into his skin long ago, just like Hercules' poisoned cloak had stuck on his skin, and he had been unable to tear it off him, unless he was willing to lose large pieces of his own skin... But, at least, he was dressed... He had some kind of protection. But now all these characters were lying dead on the muddy soil. He didn't know if he felt free or nightmarishly naked.

But, time was running out. Every lost minute was precious.

It kept raining heavily and lightning fell, when he finally decided to venture out into the cold. He found the only clothes he had left. It was a jacket made of fine leather, very soft to the touch, and he felt joy when he saw it fit him like a glove. He put it on and slipped out into the dark night. He knew what to do. He didn't need to study any scripts, he didn't need any film heroes.

And the strange thing was that he didn't feel the cold or any fear.

Perhaps because he had suddenly discovered what love was: An expensive jacket made of soft leather, which you wear over your heart when all lies are over and you feel neither cold nor fear.

He got into the car and turned on the engine. The house sent him one last mournful goodbye. 'Forever,' it was shouting *to him, 'The place where you're going is forever.' But, he didn't hear anything, only his uncontrolled heartbeat and the lightning that tore through the sky.*

****

The only sound that tore through the veil of silence for a while was the annoying ticking of an ancient-looking clock on the table. It stood there, rudely marking the passing of every minute, of every second, to remind us that we were nothing more than disposable creatures moving towards a definite end.

I looked at the embalmed fish. Its mouth was hanging open with an expression of stupidity and its frozen eyes had an empty look and the yellowness of a stale embalmed animal. If Picasso had put it into one of his paintings, its two eyes, fins and scales would be placed on one side, the visible one. People would show all of their features in the light, nothing of theirs would be hidden in the dark. Their vices, virtues and base instincts would all be in plain sight if they were in one of Picasso's paintings.

The fire eventually died out, the gas that had been fuelling it was almost gone by the time we entered and hissed to a stop, leaving a pungent smell behind. Cold and panic were now wandering around the house in each other's company.

'And how will he find us here?' I dared ask her.

'He'll find us, don't worry, I left traces behind us. He just has to be smart enough to find them.'

'Why would he come, Katia? Don't you think that he

might not come at all? That everything you planned might have been pointless? If, as you say, he doesn't give a damn about me, why do you think he'll come?'

'Oh, but he will be unable to refuse this part – that of the knight, of the lover, who fights to save his beloved. It's very enticing. Don't worry, he won't miss the performance. And, somehow like this, he'll lose his life.'

She rubbed her eyebrow with her finger. This movement had turned into a nervous habit, the only clue that betrayed she was dealing with an underlying frustration.

The clock kept ticking and tocking, ticking and tocking, ticking and tocking until the banging sound of a gunshot smashed the relentless march of time into pieces. The clock spewed forth its minutes and hours, its hands sprang away from its face and it was left bare, with a gaping hole in the middle, like a mouth whose life had been stolen away.

'I have an idea,' Katia finally said, 'so that we could pass the time in a more productive way. I think it's a bit frustrating to keep waiting like this. I'll ask you questions and you'll answer, all right? Try to be honest with me and don't try to fool me with lies. I'm not so stupid as to believe in fairy tales.'

She spoke so reassuringly that for a moment I wondered whether everything was a nightmare, or just some kind of a misunderstanding.

'And what happens if I answer correctly?'
'Then, I will kill you quickly and painlessly, otherwise ...'
'Oh, you're too kind.'
'Shut up!'

She got angry for the first time and that won me a slap – not a strong one, luckily enough. But, I thought that I had achieved a small victory. If I managed to throw her off her game, perhaps there would be a way for me to escape, perhaps not all was lost if I made her lose her legendary composure.

A small flame of hope inside me was struggling to shake me awake and sweep away the lethargy that threatened to swallow me. I felt drained of every question, of all feelings of anticipation.

'Do you love Constantinos, Vera?' she began the first round of questions.

'I won't answer you, Katia!'

'That's the right answer, darling. But, this way, you aren't even using the cheap excuse that would at least justify why you're sleeping with a married man. Do you believe in God?' she continued unfazed.

'I don't know.'

'You aren't exactly helping your situation. I would have been surprised, however, if you had answered "yes". Do you love your mother?'

'No.'

'That's the right answer. And why not?'

'Because she's a lunatic, just like you!'

'Do you see, now, what your problem is? You don't believe in anything, you don't love anyone.'

'It's not the right time to psychoanalyse me, I think.'

'And yet...' She was a hair's breadth away from me. '... I love you. I'm doing everything for your own good.' She stretched out her hand and gently stroked my cheek, then my lips. 'I want to open your eyes, Vera, and make you clearly see who you're dealing with.'

She spoke tenderly, just like a good old friend, or something even more, like an older sister. Or maybe that touch wasn't friendly or sisterly at all? I jumped as her fingers slid down my neck, towards my shoulders, and then my chest. I pulled back and glued my back to the wall, alarmed by this unexpected turn of events.

'Now, if that hurts, it's not my fault. The truth always hurts, darling, sometimes, it even kills.'

The river of time was once again flowing among us. Torrential rain whipped the roof and the window frames, threatening to pull them apart. Lightning and thunder were waging their own battle in the sky, but what took your breath away was the roar of the sea. With a concealed longing, I was expecting a giant wave to rush inside the cabin at any moment, and put an end to this torment of waiting that was driving me crazy.

'She doesn't intend to kill her,' he thought relieved. He stood with his back glued against the log cabin and he occasionally stole glances through the windowpanes. He had found us by following our trail on the ground. He had seen the jeep parked outside the small cabin and had figured everything out. 'Otherwise, she would have done it already. It's me she wants, that's why she called me out here.'

He pulled out his cell phone to call the police, only to discover that the stupidest thing in the world had happened to him. His battery was dead and what he now had in his hand was a useless contraption. With muffled curses, he threw it in the mud.

The rain was still falling furiously, making his despair even greater. He had run out of ideas. He was almost tempted to plop down in a puddle of rainwater and start crying.

'Don't move or you're dead!'

The voice that roared against the wind was strangely familiar. He couldn't believe his ears. A familiar, obnoxious, body shape slipped out of the shadows of the night behind the trees and headed toward him with long strides.

'You want to hear a final truth?' I finally broke the silence. A small flame of resistance had got stronger inside me and it was growing bigger and bigger. Besides, I had nothing to lose; it was all or nothing.

'I don't care about the grudge you bear against Constantinos. I don't care if he loves me or not, if he gives a damn about me or if he's simply using me. I love him, Katia. I realised it just now when you said that ... you might kill him. Don't kill him, please! It's not his fault, I caused everything that has happened, he didn't make any mistakes, I am the one responsible, it would be really unfair if he died, so unfair, you wouldn't want to be unfair, isn't that so, Katia? Don't kill him, please!'

I finished my feverish delirium and burst into irrepressible sobs.

'Shut up!' she shrieked. 'Stop bothering me with your vulgar boyfriend.'

Her face twisted into a mask of hatred. Her fingers that tightened stubbornly around the gun appeared to be shaking slightly. The skin around her nails had whitened from the tension. With trembling anticipation, I could see that she was beginning to lose her self-control.

'The truth is that I didn't expect these words from you, I thought you were a bit more of an opportunist. Thumbs up and well done for your self-sacrificing spirit and talent. You will become a great author ... if you manage to survive, of course. But, forgive me, darling, you have terrible taste in men. You're standing over there and begging for whom? For a sorry excuse of a man.'

'I don't care what he is. I love him, do you hear me?' I insisted with childish stubbornness, sniffling all the while.

'Really? How many times have you fallen in love, Vera? I imagine quite a few. And where are all those men you say you loved? That you believed, even for a moment, that they loved you back? Why have they all left you all by yourself?'

Pure poison dripped from her words.

'When are you going to open your eyes, darling? When will you see that all men are worthless dogs? All they know is how to chase after you and then abandon their toys wherever they find; they run away like little scared bunny rabbits. A large inflated balloon, that's what man is. He's nothing in front of the greatness hidden inside a woman.'

A bright light lit up in my head and made me instantly see another truth, the last and more poisonous one.

'You don't like men,' I stammered astounded.

'Of course not! Why would I like them? I see no decent reason why. I hate them!'

She had kept her prim appearance intact all this time. Not a single hair was out of place on her head. She stood there: icy, elegant, and unbending. Her former confidence had been fully restored and I couldn't help but admire her for that. I felt like a scarecrow with faded jeans, a sweat-shirt and muddy shoes. My hair kept falling in my eyes like wilted lettuce leaves.

'Look, Katia,' my eyes must have looked as crazy as hers when I told her this: 'I'm leaving. I'm sick of being cooped up in here. I'm going to get some fresh air because I feel as if I'm suffocating.'

I got up like an automaton and headed towards the door. When you plummet down the final steps of despair, then you are capable of doing the wackiest things. All I could see was the door, that plain door that had the audacity to keep me away from freedom and the fresh air.

'Where do you think you're going?'

For the first time, a touch of panic appeared in her voice. I wouldn't give her the satisfaction of turning around and facing her but I was sure that I had her cornered for good and I prematurely congratulated myself.

'Out! I need to get some air.'

'Don't take another step, Vera, or I'll be forced to shoot you!'

She screamed, beside herself, – I still had my back turned to her – her voice rivalling the cries of tragic heroines in a melodrama.

I was consumed by this strange feeling that we were

performing in a play here, a parody without apparent purpose and meaning. But, it would be of some worth if someone researched the topic and found out why the parts had been distributed so unfairly, who the director was, who had written this macabre scenario, who had dressed the heroes and classified them in time and space, and how to get to the damn door without getting a bullet or more in my back.

At that very moment, when the night and the storm were holding their breaths and an unnatural silence fell under the sickly yellow light of the lamp, with that dead fish gazing so shamelessly at me, both apathetic and mocking in its non-existence, with the storm at a lull, a strange idea came and wedged itself in my mind.

'I'm sorry, Katia, but I will have to spoil your brilliant plan. You'll have to shoot me in the back. And then who will believe that I committed suicide? Someone who commits suicide can't shoot themselves in the back, of course!'

I wasn't sure which of the two of us was crazier, but I really felt very calm when I said these words.

Then, time started moving very quickly, as if it had gone numb after sitting still for so long and thought to kick its engines into overdrive. Everything unfolded at a dizzying speed that could hardly be captured by the human eye. Only a recording camera could accomplish something like that.

The door burst open after someone violently kicked it from the outside.

A wave of cold air hit me in the face.

I was startled and took a step back. With an instinctive movement, I protectively placed my hands over my belly.

'Put the gun down, Katia! The police are here,' Constantinos said. He must have been pressing his lips together when he spoke because his voice came out hoarse and drawling.

'Come in, Mr Aravantinos. Don't just stand there,' Katia growled in excitement.

Constantinos appeared in the doorway, his long coat dripping wet, his hair stuck to his forehead, his eyes filled with rage. He was surrounded by thick darkness. I had never seen him so angry before.

'Get out of the way, Vera,' Katia screamed as my body hid him from her eyes.

Get out, Constantinos! I tried to convince him with subtle gestures.

'Go away this instant!'

I heard
the fatal click
the iron mouth that spat out fire
felt
his hands throwing me forcefully out of the way.
I saw
Katia's face, purple with hate,
Constantinos jerking backwards as if he had gotten kicked in the stomach,
Katia preparing to fire another shot,
Avramoglou's enormous silhouette at the open door
Katia dropping dead by his bullets.
I didn't understand how he got into my arms,
I saw

my hands become stained with blood, hot blood, his blood,

I felt

the horror of losing him as his life slipped from my hands, an unbearable pain where my heart was.

'That bitch, she thought that she could fool me!'

These last words came from Avramoglou.

Then, the police pounced in.

Then someone turned off all the lights and all I heard was a muffled thud as I slumped to the floor. All I remember was that I kept clutching at my belly. And I had the taste of blood on my lips. A metallic taste, somewhat salty, as if I had been licking a piece of iron.

So many things had happened within mere seconds.

Able to crush even the bravest of souls.

Especially mine.

Chapter 15

A Kiss of Life and a Box of Melomakarona

So, that was it! I killed my mother. Without actually having to kill her. Everything happened because of me. Only, instead of my mother, it was Katia who paid the price. For a moment, I had so clearly identified her with Theophano in my mind that it was like coming face to face with the same woman. It was not only that they resembled each other. They both came from aristocratic, but effete, families. They had failed in their personal lives and viewed the male sex with endless distrust, which turned into hatred, caused by psychological wounds.

Both of them represented the same kind of woman who fought tooth and nail to cause me deadly injury at my Achilles' heel: my desperate need to believe, to give, to love unconditionally. And I caused that unhappy woman's death. She died because of me.

Everything happened just as the Voice had said in my dream, 'Now is the time to kill your mother, too,' it had told me, 'and then you'll be free.'

But, perhaps, I oversimplify things, I don't know.

But I was no longer trapped in the nightmares of the past. I felt so free, floating high up there in the Land of Clouds, with a white scarf made from a fluffy cloud, wrapped around my neck. I was floating for some time, while all around me clouds with their funny aprons waved at me and little stray stars buzzed around my head.

'She is wallowing in guilt,' said the first star.

'A lot of guilt.'

'And she's reckless.'

'Very reckless.'

'With suicidal tendencies,' added the fifth.

Oh my God, if stars started criticizing me, too, I was lost.

Later, they told me I had suffered a major shock, that's why it took me so long to regain consciousness. When Constantinos opened his eyes, he saw me wasting my time and 'scolded' me.

'What are you doing up there, Vera? Get back on earth! I need you urgently.'

At some point, I woke up in a blinding white place. At first, I remembered nothing. Neither who I was nor what I was doing there. I saw that my clothes were stained with blood and my heart jumped. The memories hit me suddenly and I hurriedly jumped out of bed. But a strong wave of dizziness kept me put.

'Where is he?' I grabbed the sleeve of the nurse that came to check on me.

'Please, calm down! You have to keep calm.' She forced me to sit back on my bed.

'He just came out of surgery,' she told me condescending-ly, and a bit sharply. 'The doctor said he is out of danger.'

When my dizzy spell ended, I rushed out into the hall-way and followed the first doctor I found in front of me. 'This way,' he said. We climbed up some stairs, then we went down some other stairs.

'You shouldn't distress him, he's exhausted. He's lost a lot of blood.'

I tiptoed into his room and sat beside him. He had his eyes closed and was breathing quietly. He looked so weak, abandoned to his fate – which didn't seem to like him very much – and ashen-faced, whiter than a sheet, but he was alive.

Baby, I'm crazy about you. If you die, I'm lost.

I avoided making such dramatic statements, of course. I kept it to myself. Then, to my great surprise, I spoke to an old acquaintance that I had cut ties with years ago: *Oh, dear God, let him live! I will never ask for anything else in my life, I swear! Just let him live!*

He finally opened his eyes.

'Hi, Vera.'

'How do you feel? Are you in a lot of pain?'

'I've been better,' he sighed with great difficulty.

'Why did you do that, Constantinos? Why did you step in the way?'

'Jesus, do you even have to ask? Because she was going to kill you, I saw it in her eyes.'

He was whispering, barely able to move his lips. I leaned over him in order not to lose a single word he uttered. He explained that he had arrived a short time earlier, soaked by the rain, because the car had got stuck in the mud and he had had to go on foot for the final part of the way.

He saw the jeep parked outside the small hut. He approached the hut and peeked in through the window. He figured out everything that was going on. He couldn't enter defenceless and unarmed. He decided to wait. Katia had no intention of using her gun on me, she was saving her bullets for him, Constantinos was sure of that. I was some kind of hostage in her hands. Then, Avramoglou appeared like a deus ex machina. They alerted the police and waited for them to arrive.

'Then you got up and did the unthinkable. I saw that Katia wasn't playing around. She panicked, and panic makes you unstable... especially when you're already mentally unstable. I didn't know what else to do... I almost lost it, too.'

'Oh, my God, so, once again, it was my fault. I had been wrong,' I broke down. 'Why am I so impulsive, so foolish?'

'It was just wrong timing, baby.' He attempted a smile, but it ended up turning into a grimace of pain. 'Don't blame yourself.'

'I just wanted to get out, I knew you were close, I could smell it in the air. My senses at the time were so heightened that I could hear ants walking. I wanted to run, to shout out a warning that it was you she wanted to kill. I didn't care about myself. I didn't think I was in danger, not for a moment.'

'Ok baby, don't cry now. Everything's over.'

The minutes rolled under the iron wheels of the bed, then

to the crack under the door, and poured into the hallway, skating on the shiny floor. I stood silent, gazing at him while holding his hand. I could sit in the same place for centuries, without any other desires or concerns, without eating or drinking anything, without needing any sleep; I just needed to look into his eyes and hold his hand.

But, I had to leave. A young policeman who was on guard duty reminded me, when he entered the room, that I had to go to the police station of the city and give my testimony.

I bent over Constantinos.

'Do you need anything?'

'Yes, I do...'

'What is that, darling?'

'You see, I would love to eat some melomakarona.'

I didn't know whether to shout out or laugh.

'I'll get some for you, my love.' I was laughing and crying at the same time.

'Vera ... I would also like a kiss, please.'

I lowered my head and gently touched his lips with mine. The officer discreetly left the room. Oh, if only I had the magical power to transform my life into a bottle of water which he drank from, drop by drop, and then, empty and useless, they could throw me away.

'Do you love me, even a little?'

'I have never loved anything or anyone more than you.'

He closed his eyes and smiled, fully satisfied.

'Take my coat,' he said as I prepared to leave, 'don't go out like that, it's too cold.'

I recalled that his coat had a bullet hole on the left shoulder and it was covered in blood.

Once I reached the exit of the hospital, I called Vicky.

'I need a big favour,' I begged. 'Go and buy a big box of melomakarona. Have them dropped of immediately by courier.' I gave her the hospital address. 'I'll explain everything to you when I get back,' was my answer to my friend's frantic questions.

I saw the reporters in the courtyard as soon as I left the hospital. They were rubbing their hands together to keep them warm while waiting for the medical report. I decided to exit through a side door to avoid them.

A glamorous figure appeared as I was heading for the police car. Wearing a light green car coat, a fuchsia jumper and towering stiletto heels, Virginie emerged from the taxi followed by her two daughters, the children from her first marriage. Her gait was ethereal, as if she wasn't a human creature, as if she was a gazelle crossing the savannah, followed by her calves.

I stood stone still as she passed by me, the scent of her expensive perfume floating behind her. I felt even sillier, even more of an outsider, and uglier than ever. *This is a woman that would have left even Katia fascinated*, my hair stood on end at the thought.

The reporters surrounded her like a swarm of bees and she faced them with a calm smile of superiority. After she managed to escape them, she went down several corridors, twittering like a bird of paradise, dazzling doctors, patients and nurses, until she entered her husband's room.

'Constantinos, you gave me such a fright! I was really worried, darling!'

I thought I 'heard' her voice berating him with coyness. But, perhaps I was just being mean. She may not have been that frivolous and superficial, she may not have all the evils of the world I was keen to ascribe to her.

****

Anyone walking even remotely near the vicinity of the police station in Halkida on that cold November morning would understand from the first moment that something extraordinary was happening. A tension-filled excitement, the excitement over the momentous event was obvious on the faces of the police officers. They walked back and forth with hasty, but rigid, movements, with mouths stubbornly clenched and their heads held high. In their eyes, one could detect the pride that something unique had happened within their territory. Not only was the arrest for murder like something taken out of a film, but there were also celebrities involved in the case, which made them feel great for the first – and probably last – time in their career.

When I arrived at the police station, the first thing I saw was Avramoglou's wide face. He was pacing back and forth, silent and impassive, biting on his ever-present cigar with savage pleasure. He was still wearing the long trench coat he had on the last time I saw him. His hair was uncombed and plastered on his cheeks, and he seemed more unkempt than ever. His shoes were covered in mud and his shirt was half-hanging out of his trousers. He didn't seem to give a damn about his appearance.

I begged the police to let us have a short private conversation, but they refused. So, under guard, in the presence of his lawyer, and while waiting for the prosecutor, Avramoglou was very talkative, illuminating every last detail of this dark story.

'I kept watch over you,' he admitted calmly.

When he returned to Greece after the murders, he hired a private investigator to find out everything about the past of the four people he suspected. He avoided mentioning who the other suspects were.

'Sarafidis did a good job. I knew him from a long time ago; he has worked for me in the past. He is very capable, devious, and has a way of opening doors that seem impenetrable. I wanted to confirm a suspicion that had persistently been twirling in my mind. The killer had most likely showed signs of a disturbed personality in the past. It is impossible for someone to simply lose it and start offing people.'

He stopped for a while, long enough to create the right atmosphere and heighten the suspense.

'And I was right. Fortunately! When he reported back that Katia had been hospitalized years ago in a psychiatric ward with severe depression, something clicked in my mind. Of course, it was just a single clue, but I had nothing more substantial in my hands. So I focused our investigation on her. Then, Sarafidis uncovered the family drama that marked this woman's life. Katia had an only daughter, Anita, who was studying History of Art in Florence. She must have been a very pampered child, and that's probably why she killed herself when her Italian good-for-nothing boyfriend, a self-styled musician, dumped her for the eyes of another girl, one of his compatriots.'

My mind raised the alarm at the sound of these words.

'She slit her wrists!' I abruptly interrupted him.

'Yes, how did you know? Katia didn't talk to anyone about it. She pretended that her daughter was still living and studying in Italy. That's what she needed to keep believing.'

'My God! The girl with the wedding dress!' I blurted out shrilly, not caring to hide my surprise. Everything slowly started to make sense. The pieces slid into place one after the other. 'The bride with the slit wrists in the cursed home ... The girl in the wedding gown at the home with the heavy curtains. She tried to warn me. Oh, my God!'

I continued to mumble to myself as if I was mental. A frozen river had flooded my guts, I shivered from head to toe, and I was furiously biting my nails.

Avramoglou looked at me, surprised at first, then with obvious contempt.

'I always said you were missing a few marbles. So, let me continue ... It seems that, from that point on, Katia's life went downhill. The sudden, violent death of her daughter had an immeasurable impact on her life. She became depressed and had to be hospitalized in clinics abroad. Her marriage collapsed. Her husband filed for divorce two years later, and it was revealed that he had been having an affair with his secretary for many years.'

He made a longer pause after this, allowing me more time to recover from the shock of the revelations.

'So, I became alarmed when I heard that after your own departure, she also returned to Greece. Sarafidis had become her shadow. Two days ago, he followed her to Evia, where she loitered in the wilderness around Constantinos' summer home as if she was looking for something specific. He saw her enter the fisherman's hut and sniff around. When he mentioned all this to me, I was almost certain. Overall, I could picture her plan in my mind. And last night, when I heard that she was coming to join you, I went and hid outside the hut. I wanted to catch her in the act. You know the rest.'

He was out of breath by the time he finished his account. He was explaining many things at the same time, and that clashed with his temperament. Suddenly, I remembered that somewhere around this point, he would find it necessary to become furious.

'Of course, you almost screwed everything up, Ms Kalogera! You foolishly made her shoot you and he thought it would be heroic to start kicking doors open. What was I supposed to do first? I didn't have the time to deal with all the crap you started!'

Then, he stopped talking altogether and I was left to watch him as he became submerged in his thoughts. His forehead was sweaty. His chair could barely support his massive frame. The clicking sound of his worry beads set the rhythm to the empty time as he threaded them with his fingers.

'You might ask ... did the police do any better? No, but let's forget about that!'

He mumbled softly, but he was only talking to himself. Our surroundings, the police officers swaggering in and out of different offices, the famous lawyer who was present and anxious to learn about the developments, and even I, had been excluded from his field of vision.

I wonder when people's lives are irreparably destroyed. When they leave the battle by themselves or when others take that decision for them? I wasn't sure that I could give a definitive answer to this question. Just like I couldn't decide who the most tragic figure in this story ultimately was.

****

That same day, after the questioning of the witnesses was completed – they also took Constantinos' statement when he came to – the trial date was set (the most likely sentence will be three to four months, with a possibility of parole, the famous lawyer promised with relief as he loosened his tie). I took the first available flight with Aegean Airlines, and rushed back to Munich.

I arrived at the village in the evening. Nothing seemed to have changed in the landscape, though it was still suffering from the constant bouts of rain and snow. There's the same grey sky, the never-ending rain, the clouds that hang heavy over my head, the trees bent in two, defeated by the wind.

When I walked into the inn, Venetis was sitting in the living room with Stamatis, and the former was cleaning out his pipe with the utmost diligence. When he saw me, he acted as if Euripides' deus ex machina had landed in front of him.

'Vera! I didn't expect that you'd return. And especially so quickly!'

He hugged me warmly and kissed me on the cheek. 'I was very sorry to hear what had happened. It must have been terrible. Nobody could have imagined what Katia was capable of. It must have been a terrible shock.'

'You can't imagine how awful it was!'

'But, you needn't have come back; we're almost finished,' he added after a short pause, looking at me questioningly.

I didn't reply. What could I say? Since I myself didn't know what had brought me back to this strange silent village, to this place that had become the setting for a colossal plot twist in our lives. *Perhaps I wanted to see this place once more*, is the explanation I later give. I wanted to let everything that had happened – and had been so traumatic and liberating, at the same time – sink in.

'Yes, indeed,' I said thoughtfully, 'but there's still work to be done in Athens, right?'

'Ain't that the truth? We urgently need to find a solution. Are you sure you're up for this, Vera? I have no idea how we're going to fill the void Constantinos created when he got injured.'

'I don't know what I'm supposed to do. But we'll think of something, won't we?'

'And to think that we only had the last scenes left to shoot. I can't let this film fail now. I'd never forgive myself.'

'Let's see,' Stamatis interrupted him, 'we have no lead actor, no stylist...'

'Don't mention the latter ever again, because you won't know what hit you,' Venetis growled.

'... Fortunately we have our script-writer back,' Stamatis concluded as if he had solved a difficult mathematical equation. He gave me one of his trademark sly looks, filled with innuendoes.

Then, I saw his eyes becoming as wide as saucers.

'What's wrong? Not feeling well? You've turned white.'

'It's nothing, it'll pass.'

I barely had time to run to the bathroom. I felt my head spinning, like someone was unscrewing the top with a screwdriver, and I had the strong urge to vomit.

Later that same night, I shut myself in my room and started writing. So, let's start:

We are now in the final minutes of the film. Jimmy and Jenny have been through hell and high water at the hands of the kidnappers in the castle and have been in danger many times. Jimmy has been wounded on the shoulder from the rabid she-wolf, and has been healed thanks to the nostrums of the gypsies who found them in the forest and gave them shelter. It was now time for the happy ending. The wedding ceremony. The unrepentant bachelor finally agrees to get married and Jenny is delighted. The wedding had been cancelled once before, prior to the abduction and their being dragged to Germany, because of a small ... disagreement with the client resulting in Jimmy being hit over the head and left unconscious. Then, Jenny was left out in the cold at the altar, which made her furious.

Now the script had to take a different turn. It was impossible to have a happy ending because the protagonist-groom was injured and bedridden.

I kept writing and tearing up pages. The next morning I showed Venetis the fruit of my labours in order to discuss how we were going to proceed.

SCENE 150 / INT /DAY- JIMMY'S OFFICE

Jenny is standing opposite Demosthenes, Jimmy's new assistant. She is gesturing wildly and pacing nervously back and forth. Demosthenes watches her with a wry smile.

JENNY
It's impossible. You're lying!
DEMOSTHENES
Come on, no need to get upset.
JENNY
Do you have an idea what that means?
It's outrageous!
DEMOSTHENES
Yes, it's bad luck
alright!
JENNY
What's this bad luck you're talking about?
He did it on purpose, I'd bet my money on it!

So that he wouldn't have to
marry me!
(She continues her furious pacing.)
DEMOSTHENES
Just admit
you're overreacting.
JENNY
Well, we can blame
Dimopoulos for the last time.
They beat the shit out of each other,
he was knocked out, or at least that's what he said,
while I was waiting for him like a moron at the stupid
church.
I'm fine with that.
And what does he do? He goes and crashes his motor-
bike.
Three days before our wedding.
It's mind-boggling!
DEMOSTHENES
The man was hurt.
He didn't run away like a thief.
JENNY
I won't let this go.
No, I won't give him the satisfaction.
She storms out of the office.
Demosthenes smiles meaningfully.

SCENE 151 / INT / DAY- HOSPITAL

Jimmy is lying in bed. He is pale. His left arm has been placed in a cast.

The door opens slowly. Jenny walks in. She is wearing a white dress and white shoes.

JENNY

(with sweet coyness)

And how does my darling man feel?

JIM

Like shit. Why do you ask? Can't you see?

JENNY

And why am I here?

To take care of my baby.

I arranged everything so that

your last wish could come true, my love.

JIMMY

What last wish?

I'm not about to die or anything.

JENNY

You are, my love, you are.

You shouldn't lie in front of a Man of God.

(A priest enters the room. Demosthenes follows behind, looking serious, wearing a suit (he is the best man) and holding the box with the marriage crowns.

Jimmy looks astounded. He feels trapped.)

JENNY

(with a huge smile that says 'I got you.')

Because if you don't marry me right now,

I'll kill you myself, darling.
She opens a box containing a pair of wedding rings.

'Good,' Venetis said after carefully studying my script changes and making some observations. 'Once he's somewhat recovered, we'll go to the studio and film the last scenes.'

'You should go,' I nodded. 'I won't be joining you. My part here is done.'

That's how Constantinos' initial wish for a final plot twist in the plot came true.

****

By late January, in any case, after superhuman efforts and endless late nights dedicated to the final stages of post-production and editing, the film was ready to be released in cinemas.

From all the reviews published in newspapers and magazines, which I collected diligently in a scrapbook, I was particularly impressed with one, probably because I agreed with the views of the Cinepolis magazine's film critic.

'It is fortunate that Aravantinos managed to overcome his innate narcissism and act his part with genuine humour and sensitivity.

Besides, the element that gives a uniqueness and a distinctive character to his interpretations is obvious if one pays attention to his films. His acting is subtle. Without melodramatic flares and intense explosions, with modesty, but also a certain clarity, he demonstrates, hidden behind his acting persona, a deeper compassion for his characters, no matter if they are good or evil, and a limitless compassion for human suffering, precisely because they are human.

He leaves an indelible mark of his identity on the character he embodies. To such a degree that it is inconceivable to believe that someone else could ever play this role except him.

This is grasped intuitively by the viewers and prevents them from forgetting his films so quickly, let alone him from going unnoticed.'

Was all this buzz around the film really only due to the successful outcome of our work or did the tragic events that marked the shooting contribute in any way? And to what extent?

I think that my question will remain forever unanswered.

Chapter 16

The Tramps of the Sky

There were days when I would obsessively do all the things I hated.

I spent endless hours stuck in front of the TV screen with a bowl of crisps by my side, religiously watching every series I could find, with unnatural dedication. I tried to keep my mind empty of thoughts, to keep it away from everything that would put me into panic mode.

That's how things could have been. For the stories that had been written, are being written, and will be written in the years to come, there couldn't have been a better ending. It doesn't mean that everything that scriptwriters come up with will eventually come true.

The phone rang once in a while, but I avoided picking up. I was afraid of the things that could be said. Constantinos left messages for me, but I would become so upset at the sound of his voice that I would stand up and leave the house, or I would turn the music up, so that I wouldn't hear its sound. Until I smashed the answering machine to pieces and regained my peace.

I didn't want to speak to him. I had nothing to say to Mr Aravantinos. I was afraid of his reaction, whatever that might be, though I imagined it would be explosive.

He had given me everything I ever wanted in my life, everything I had imagined in my wildest dreams, and there was nothing else I wished to have anymore.

I felt every day being recorded on an invisible file that left its mark on my genes so that the strength of the love I felt for him would be passed on from generation to generation.

I even daydreamed that my child would inherit its mother's ability to love so purely and so intensely, and I felt the greatest happiness in the world.

And I would immediately burst into tears and feel sorry for myself because I had been left all alone, and no one cared about me at this turning point of my life.

Those days, my dreams were utterly crazy. More often than not, my baby was starring in them. Sometimes, it talked to me with gentle words of wisdom, just like a grown-up, it admonished and guided me, which seemed very strange to me; at other times, I saw it transforming into something unnatural within me, which filled me with panic. I would shoot up from my sleep, soaked in sweat, and I would get out of bed in the middle of the night to fix myself some mushroom soup and drink some calming tea.

My doctor assured me that my body would slowly put this hormonal storm to rights and I shouldn't be worried. But, on nights when rain fell mournfully, I would feel a bit blue and lonelier than ever, which seemed unbearable to me.

The very next morning I would wake up brimming with

happiness and preen in front of the mirror, admiring my radiant skin and shining hair. I was grateful to my guardian angel who had wisely placed so many gift-wrapped presents in my path. I was terribly eager to hold this tiny creature in my arms and swear my eternal devotion to it. Then, I would feel guilty for burdening it with my insecurities and my moodiness, and I would silently ask for its forgiveness.

The happiest and strangest period of my life flowed somewhat like this, until I entered my second trimester, and I grew more relaxed.

In order to keep the panic attacks at bay, I resorted to every modern woman's stress relief: shopping. I was looking for a green outfit; I didn't care if it was a dress, or a feminine-cut suit.

My feet were killing me by the time I found it, but it was worth the trouble. The silk A-line dress with the lace embellishments and the fur-trimmed sleeves perfectly brought out the colour of my eyes, as the sales assistant pointed out, and its elegant cut hid the few extra pounds I had gained. When I discovered my grandmother's locket, an old family heirloom, that had been lying forgotten in a drawer, and I saw that it went very well with my dress, I felt an indescribable completeness.

For the first time ever, I was desperate to look beautiful. It was a matter of life and death to look calm, a bit aloof – if possible – and elegant – of course – for the press night that would follow the film's premiere.

****

When the long-awaited night finally arrived, the remnants of my self-confidence had evaporated. It wasn't just because of how nervous I felt at the thought of seeing him again. I also had to deal with the discontent I felt towards the changes my body was going through daily, presenting me with new, stress-inducing experiences.

'Trust yourself to the One who knows you best.' I remembered Melina's favourite quote. 'It's sure to bring you only the best of things.'

The Intercontinental Hotel's reception hall was packed with people when I walked in. Camera flashes blinded me from every corner and made me feel disoriented for a moment. Evelina was the first person I spotted; she was impossible to miss. The lead actress was wearing a deep red, silk evening gown with a velvet collar, a slightly puffy A-line skirt, and it was cut in such a way that it left her washboard abs bare to everyone's gaze. She was literally glowing. She was talking to three reporters at the same time with amazing ease, taking advantage of all the charm she possessed. I was too far to be able to hear what she was saying, but I could see they were entranced by her. They were hanging from her lips. Thankfully, Papanikolaou finally noticed me and came over to greet me.

'You look gorgeous.' He kissed me on the cheek. 'Come, I'll introduce you to some very useful people.'

He started introducing me to various important people,

and I was desperately trying to memorise their names and faces.

'Mr Politis, president and CEO of the Brother and Co. Advertising Agency. Mrs Venezi, TV Producer and shareholder of Delta Television.'

I was pretending so hard to look happy while being introduced to all these people that I nearly reached breaking point.

My eyes vainly tried to catch a glimpse of him in the surrounding crowd. He must be somewhere nearby; my crazily beating heart could feel it.

Fortunately, at this very crucial point, Papanikolaou introduced me to the right person.

'You must have heard of Mr Danielidis before.'

How could I not know the extremely likeable grey-haired theatre director? He was one of the few people in this profession that I particularly admired. Born in a family of left-wing supporters, he had consistently served avant-garde theatre for 30 years, gaining many accolades. Recently, in fact, I had spotted his book, a hefty novel with a socio-historically based plot, in various bookshops.

I was pleased to see that he was the sweetest man. He was quite tall and thin, with an angular face and piercing eyes.

'Will you allow me to share my opinion with you, though I've never been tempted to become a critic?' he said after he congratulated me on "this psychographic allegory" – that's what he called my book. Obviously, he thought of me as the youngest member of the group and he felt the obligation to admonish me.

'You write very well,' he said, – the more interesting our conversation became, the warmer his voice got — 'but I'm convinced – and I say this from experience – that you can write better. How else can I put it? I don't think you've reached your full potential.'

'Everyone does the best they can, Mr Danielidis.'

'Look now,' he suddenly said, 'what do you think writers are? Lovers of detail, that's what they are. Some people chase birds, others money... and a naïve few, love. Well, writers chase details. They take a grain of sand, grind it into dust and place a speck under the microscope. They will scrutinize a mosquito. At the same time, they keep an eye on the whole beach, from one end to the other. Or in other words, it's like looking at a stereoscopic image. The initial picture is different from what you discover in its depths. But, in order to see it, you need to cross your eyes. That's my favourite theory. A writer is a person that spends most of the time cross-eyed and likes collecting grains. Humble and insignificant grains of the sand of destiny.'

'Will you allow me to write it down?' I pulled out my notebook. 'I also know a thing or two,' I laughed out loud. 'But, this way, tears start running unbidden from your eyes, not to mention that you might end up with a permanent tick.'

'Do you think it's possible to cure yourself? If you dive into the depths of the stereoscopic image, you can't return to the surface ever again. You're doomed to wander in the deep, like a damned soul. Lars von Trier said that talent is a neurological flaw of the brain, a malfunction that allows some people to see things which the rest ignore.'

'So, not only do they squint, but they're also malfunctioning. I can believe something like that. According to your words, people who call themselves authors must not be particularly happy.'

He didn't have the time to answer because Constantinos descended upon us like a tornado.

'Excuse me, Mr Danielidis, but a journalist friend of mine wants to ask us a few questions.'

He grabbed me by the arm. *Instead of looking for me, you just sit and idly chat with other people,* his eyes seemed to be telling me and I was sure that I had made him angry even before I could utter a word.

'Since when are you so eager to speak to journalists?' I protested as he dragged me behind him through the crowd of guests. 'They should be chasing after you.'

'You look very beautiful,' was his answer. 'Oh, he's an old friend, one of my own people, and the questions are pre-arranged.'

'What do you mean?' Once again, I felt silly, as if I was playing a game that others had set up for me.

The low hum of people conversing filled the hall, which was decked in its festive best. Satin, velvet and silk rippled and swayed in every corner. People wandered around with measured movements and always within the permissible limits. The smiles were also very well polished. The foam of the champagne quickly fizzled out in the crystal glasses. The white gold, amethysts and diamonds worn by the guests were well on their way to the road of excess.

'Are you satisfied with the result, Ms Kalogera?'

The journalist – Constantinos' friend – stuck the microphone in front of my mouth and the camera started taping.

'Of course, I'm very satisfied,' I also pressed "play" on the imaginary CD containing my TV personality voice, 'I think that everyone did an excellent job. I have to thank the whole team – they became a very close-knit group – who showed real dedication to their work. I would also like to express my gratitude to Pantelis Venetis, who perfectly directed the film; to our producer, Mr Avramoglou, who generously sponsored us; to all the actors, and, of course, to Mr Aravantinos, who so touchingly accepted our offer and gave me the great happiness of seeing him portray my lead character.'

'Everyone is talking about the excellent working relationship between the two of you. How would you describe it?'

'It was a fortunate turn of events. Mr Aravantinos is a wonderful actor – and he has proven it once again – but he's also an excellent colleague.'

'In the past, there were rumours that he's a particularly difficult and demanding person. Is there any truth in this?'

'A difficult person? Well... No... I wouldn't say that. He's better described as being a perfectionist and very demanding in his work.'

'Is it true that you will work together once again on the script of his next film?'

'Who said that?'

'Sure,' Constantinos, who hadn't said a word the whole time, unexpectedly intervened, 'if she allows me, I'll just keep her all to myself.'

He threw his arm around my shoulders and the cameras started flashing once again.

'Yes, I mean, what I want to say is that I'd like that a lot. Besides, no matter what I might write in the future, he will always be my inspiration for the main hero. It'll be written for him. '

'And why is that?'

The sly expression on the journalist's face was quite eloquent. *Oops, now he has me cornered*, was my fearful thought. But I decided not to give him the satisfaction.

'This actor is an endless source of inspiration for me. I can take a single phrase he says, a movement or a grimace, and write quite a few pages using them as my base material. He's so different and utterly unique.'

'What would you say about the tragic events that overshadowed the shooting of the film?'

'I'm afraid that it's a very big issue, and quite unpleasant for such a pleasant evening. I hope we have the opportunity to talk about it another time.'

The journalist and the cameraman thanked me and started gathering their cables and the rest of their equipment.

'Don't worry, they've already interviewed me and I said only the nicest things about you,' Constantinos assured me in a jubilant tone and then he suddenly disappeared from my side.

I lost him in the crowd. I spotted him a bit later in the company of Virginie, who had been sitting alone in a corner earlier. She seemed nervous, absent-mindedly playing with the pearls of her necklace. I thought about going over there to greet her, but I couldn't find the courage.

I was pointlessly wandering around among the guests. All the attention was focused on the lead actors. Who cares about an unknown screenwriter, especially when networking isn't her strong point?

Once again, I tried to find Danielidis so that we could continue our conversation but I saw that he was busy, surrounded by a large group.

So, I took a glass of white wine, just so I wouldn't be empty-handed, and I went out onto the terrace to get some air. It was a sweet, cloudless night and not quite as cold. From up there, I could hear Athens' endless murmur of a thousand noises mixed together, and I could see millions of bright lights.

'Good evening, chérie.'

The female voice coming from behind me reached my ears like a cool breeze.

Oh, my God, this tops the cake! I turned around, pretending to be in a cheerful mood.

'Virginie, how are you?'

She spoke in broken Greek, but with so much grace, despite making several mistakes. It made me uncomfortable, because I didn't sound at all like her when I spoke in Greek, even though it is my mother tongue.

'You're a little fatter than the last time I saw you, but you look well,' the French woman gave me a faint smile.

Her eyes carefully 'scanned' me from top to bottom.

'You look impeccable, as always.'

Unfortunately, I had to continue using these empty pleas-antries.

'I want you to know that I wanted for long to talk to you, but never found the good opportunity,' she began, gently resting her elbows on the railing.

Her silhouette appeared like a flexible and fragile curve in the moonlight. She was wearing a Mary Quant dress made of ivory silk, with a clear 60s influence, and had her hair tied back.

'I know about you two,' she bluntly got to the point, 'I mean about you and Constantinos. He told me.'

I felt as if I had been punched in the stomach. *I better watch my tongue, rather than say something foolish*, I thought.

'It isn't the first time that this happens,' she continued unabashed, 'but now I feel, I think – How should I put it? – that sometimes it's not so simple. Or is it wrong to think this?' she asked me shyly, almost in a child-like, yet civilized, manner.

'What exactly do you want me to say, Virginie? I don't understand.'

I could hardly look her in the eye. Her look betrayed all the pain and fear hidden behind her dispassionate attitude.

'I want you to tell the truth. Are you capable? Can you tell me? Es-tu amoureuse de lui? Do you love Constantinos?'

I instinctively rested my hands on my belly, and then touched my head, which was once again bothering me. I returned my focus on the conversation only after great effort. She wasn't stupid; I panicked that she may suspect some-thing, and that would be a real disaster.

'I wouldn't say so,' I finally said, picking up whatever debris was left of my courage. 'If you really want the truth: what happened between us was meaningless, and now it's over.'

That was all the courage I had left. The next lie I would have to utter would make me faint.

'I hope you get what you deserve,' were her final words to me.

Her face was crumpled with misery, but she had a hateful look in her eyes.

'I'm sorry, Virginie, I didn't mean to hurt anyone, that wasn't my intention.'

But, she had already turned her back to me, and then I noticed her pumps; they were the epitome of femininity with Swarovski studded stiletto heels.

'As for how faithful he is, you will discover that on your own,' she threw a last stab at me, tougher than the crystals on her heels, before she disappeared in the throng.

Unfortunately, the night was far from over. The press conference should have started long ago. Where the hell was Venetis and why couldn't I find him anywhere? All the other participants were already in place.

He is definitely doing it to impress the crowds. He will be the one to arrive fashionably late and looking all arrogant, I thought, boiling in anger.

I desperately wanted this whole carnival to end so I could once again retreat into the solitude of my house, where I could cry in peace over my unlucky love life, which had become my favourite pastime lately.

As if to confirm my thoughts, Pantelis made his spectacular appearance at that very moment, accompanied by his assistants, and giving kisses, smiles and handshakes right and
left, a genuine star. The journalists gathered around him.

'You know, when there is a creative ambience, when the
whole team works together just like a family, despite all the
differences, the result will be impressive. It doesn't really
matter who thought of a close-up, or a panoramic, or a specific angle. An atmosphere of familiarity and cooperation is
what counts.'

He responded to the journalists' questions like a loving
father figure, rubbing his hands together. He had an expression that clearly said, 'You're giving me a headache, but I
like it.'

'My memory is quite selective. I only keep what I want
to remember,' I heard him diplomatically evading the persistent questions about the shocking events that had happened
during filming.

For quite some time, I had been struggling to resist my
impulses, but I finally gave in. I headed towards the buffet
as though I was spellbound and filled a plate with pastries
and fruit tarts.

'Why did you disappear on me, Vera?'

My heart was undecided on what to do. There was no
need for me to turn my head in order to see who that stern
voice – the one that unlocked all of my soul's hidden doors
with incredible ease – belonged to.

'I called you a few times but I always got the answering
machine.'

'Did you want me for something in particular, Constantinos?'

'I will always want you for something in particular, sweetheart,' he said with an angry look.

He invaded my personal space and I realised that he was nearly drunk.

'Please, we will become a laughing stock.'

'That's why you'd better come with me with no objections.'

He dragged me through the crowd of evening gowns that gently swished and the smoke of expensive cigars that bothered my nostrils.

We left the reception hall, away from indiscreet glances, and ended up in an empty room next to the hall. That's where the interrogation began.

'What's the matter with you, Vera?'

I was struck with a host of complaints and reproaches: I left him all alone in hospital during the most difficult time of his life; I stole away like a thief, not giving a damn about him, I didn't even show a smidgen of interest, and he had believed that ... and so on and so on. He even accused me of being a calculating cold fish!

'You're wrong. I was shaking at the thought that you might die! You can't imagine how worried I was!'

'Is that why you sent two or three get-well cards and some flowers? You're a saint, I can't find the words to thank you,' he sarcastically threw at me.

'What did you expect me to do? What else could I do? Your wife was there, did you forget about that? What would my part have been? By the way... your wife knows every-thing, doesn't she?'

'Yes, I told her. I always tell her everything; there are no secrets between us.'

Perfect! He said it as though it was the most natural thing in the world.

'And what about her? I mean, how did she take it?'

'Oh, we're a modern couple, sweetheart. She also tells me about her flings. Virginie and I are two very good friends.'

'She loves you Constantinos, I could see it in her eyes. She loves you and she's afraid of losing you, there's nothing friendly in her feelings for you.'

'And I love her,' he said in an indifferent tone.

I had the urge to scream, to spit in his face, to slap him, and such other things women usually do in similar cases. I was afraid that I would throw up; my stomach was churning.

'What do you want from me, then?' I leaned against the wall for extra support.

'I can't live without you, baby. I want to be able to see you... I need to feel you beside me. I need you.'

I was sure he was putting his action skills to full use. He wrinkled his forehead – one of his favourite habits – and he looked as if he was about to cry.

'You keep wanting things, Constantinos, and you just take them, but you never ask others what they need. Could you try and be less selfish, please?'

I wondered to myself how I hadn't killed him yet, how I couldn't find the courage to tell him off, at least, and blow off some steam, but I had let him roam free within me, so much so that my knees shook and my heart throbbed painfully with every word he said.

He took a soft ball out of his pocket and began throwing it in the air, catching it as it fell, and furiously squeezing it in his palm, as though he wanted to completely squash it. His face looked as if he was experiencing the most painful surprise of his life.

'I didn't expect these words from you. You accuse me of being selfish and self-centred. I'm angry, above all with myself, because I fell in love with an ungrateful bitch like you! Do you really think I didn't give you anything, Vera? Do you have the nerve to claim something like that? There are no words to describe the anger I feel. I at least expected an apology for your disappearance and this is what I get instead? Fine, then, you can shop for dreams during sales. I'm leaving!'

The situation was beginning to look black and stormy. My courage abandoned me.

'Anyway, we should go back next door. We'll be late and they'll be looking for us. I have no desire to hear their comments again.'

'I'm not coming!'

'Why?'

'Because I'm leaving! I can't stand being here any longer. I can't deal with all this noise. I feel like I'm suffocating!'

'You have to be here, Constantinos! You can't leave. They're here to see you. You're the star of the evening.'

'You can't stop me! I've told you before that I hate being

forced to do things. I could never stand being pressured into things.'

I didn't dare to tell him anything else. I only caught myself looking at him with incredible longing when I discovered how dapper he appeared in that grey jacket and black shirt, how handsome, even if he was a bit thinner than usual, how sophisticated his glasses were, how adorable even his shoes looked.

I had to admit that I missed him and I felt unbelievably foolish for wanting him so much, for loving him to such a painful degree, for being crazy about this spoiled, rude bastard.

When I walked back into the reception hall feeling embarrassed, all eyes were on me. I walked up to the spot where the panel for the film had been set up.

The technicians were checking the microphones and the reporters had taken their seats. Venetis, Stamatis, Avramoglou and Evelina were already sitting behind the long table.

'Vera, you're finally here! We're starting any minute now,' Venetis called out. 'Where is Constantinos?'

'You know, Pantelis... he left.'

'What did you say?' Venetis and Avramoglou roared in sync.

Shortly before the press conference, I was given the difficult task of informing the journalists that 'Mr Aravantinos was unfortunately forced to leave early due to a sudden indisposition' and whoever believed that excuse, good for them. I'd never boasted about my acting skills.

****

My baby is restless tonight. I'm not saying it's deliberately trying to bother me – it's too early to feel any of its reactions – but some faint fluttering in my belly warns me that it's very cranky. I keep changing positions to make it feel more comfortable.

The truth is that the meeting I had with Constantinos earlier in the evening was very distressing; so much so that I don't even dare admit it to myself. Only my baby understands me. Perhaps it sensed that it met its father and that's why it's so confused. It knows. This tiny little bean knows everything.

What I do know about my tiny little creature is that it currently weighs around 100-120 grams, is 10cm tall and loves being mischievous in utero. Its organs have all been created and are continuing to evolve as it splashes around in the ocean of the amniotic sac. I crave those kinds of details. In the ultrasound, my baby's tiny nose, lips and eyelids – closed and without eyelashes – could clearly be seen. Its heart beats 110-180 times a minute. It's a perfectly shaped tiny tot with skin so transparent that the arteries are visible. It already has vocal cords that it will use to let out a magnificent cry upon its arrival in the world. It tightens its fists, sucks its thumbs and moves its head around. I know many things, but I'm always eager to learn as much as possible.

The only one who doesn't know what's going on is Constantinos, but I'm not going to be the one to tell him. I have promised myself not to let him find out, for as long as possible at least.

I will never forget the doctor's condescending tone as he stoically answered my questions.

'A baby? I'm expecting? You mean I'm pregnant? This means I'm not sick! This means that ... Are you sure?'

I must have looked very silly as I repeated the same question for the fifth time.

'I am,' the doctor gave me a patronizing smile. 'Twenty years of experience are enough to let me know without a doubt when a woman is pregnant.'

'No I didn't mean anything by that,' I murmured ashamed. 'I mean, I thought that I couldn't have children. Do you understand? This is a huge surprise for me. I didn't expect that, you understand?'

I must have fallen asleep for a while and I woke up after some time with the feeling that someone had cleaned the condensation that clouded my eyes. The world opened spotlessly before me, freshened by the morning rain, like a dewdrop on an orange peel.

'I understand,' I whispered, 'what I should have realised long ago.'

Avramoglou – the stingy, brutish businessman – had acted just like the Jewish David Ezra, the character from my book. He stalked Constantinos and me, exposed us to the always-hungry-for-gossip tabloids, but then he saved us from the jaws of the rabid she-wolf, meaning Katia, only to demand his reward, the lost treasure of the Nazis the

Jewish people were trying to reclaim: the film's earnings, in Avramoglou's case.

Alexander, who had been lost in a stony moment of inaction. Alexander, who couldn't understand what he had to do in the Dance of the Immovable Roses. What was it that he couldn't understand? That sensitive people, and the dreamers, die every day trapped in a macabre dance, part of a ruthless world. This is where the Voice in my dream comes in and justifies my having 'killed' Alexander and Eleana. I did kill, but only in my book, not in reality. What was reality and what fiction? Where did the dream end and where did the truth begin? Where were their limits? They had become entangled with each other and caused many tragedies.

The veils that covered the essence of things had started to be pushed back by an invisible wind.

Oh, my God, what did I write? How is this possible?

'The gypsy! I have to find a witch,' I said frantically and shot up from my bed. But, then, I sat back down again, blinded by the lightning of recent revelations. 'Probably not. She will come and find me. I have to wait for her.'

To lead me to the spring from where I will get the water – where is the water? To get it to Jimmy, meaning Constantinos. Yes, but this means that my heroine, myself, has a long way ahead of her, a difficult path, strewn with thorns and sharp rocks, as she's searching for the pure water of life. And all the while without any shoes on because she would have to carry the water that would heal her lover's wound in them.

By writing this book, by making this film, by loving this

man, I had tried to heal myself from the trauma of a life full of twisted guilt and unconfessed fears.

I sometimes think that the world of waking is the greatest illusion. You don't have any control over the entire image because you are part of it, and of the delusion that refuses to admit that it's asleep while being awake, and awake while being asleep.

Yes, I understand! I begin to suspect many of the hidden mysteries now, but that's no great help. I still feel pain, I still have questions, and I still feel tormented. I'm still human at all times. I still feel worried.

I guess it's like the worry of the people who were able to see another order of things behind the thin veneer of plausibility. Of those who seek to escape in dreams. Of those that open otherworldly doors and daydream, and have one foot in an outer dimension and the other on earth. Sometimes, they might come across a soul mate wandering around and burrow in her dreams, even by force. Then, something magical happens. They find an ally, someone to take care of them and give them hugs. Of course, all this only happens in dreams. Reality is a wild desert for these heavenly tramps.

****

The next day, I had an important business meeting early in the morning. Only when I climbed up to the third floor of the PROTO Channel offices and sank in the leather chair opposite the desk of Mrs Diavati did I somewhat relax. I had stopped drinking coffee, but, that day, I made an exception; I absolutely needed it.

The channel's executive producer – in her mid-forties, blonde and quite plump – offers a summary of her current project: A new series based on an important historical fiction novel, a representation of the interwar era, and they want to collaborate with me.

I told her that I would be very interested in working with them and with great pleasure, but... I doubted if I could do it within the time frame she required.

'Don't worry. You won't be the only one working on this,' Mrs Diavati replied with a smile.

When Pelia walked into the office looking regal in an ethereal honey-coloured dress, smiling, and with such warmth in her green eyes, I breathed a sigh of relief.

'How are you, honey? Long time, no see!' she fondly drawled the 'r', as if she was grinding bitter almonds into a sweet paste.

'The truth is that I have been reading many curious things in the newspapers in the last few months, but I would also like to hear your side of the story.'

Before we left, Mrs Diavati didn't fail to state that she would be expecting ten script outlines for as many episodes of the proposed TV series as soon as possible.

We sat in the bar downstairs. It was almost empty at the time; only two or three journalists were there, drinking coffee and chatting quietly. Pelia chain-smoked, as usual, and was already on her third coffee of the day. I just got myself some fresh juice.

'I don't know where to start. So many things have happened lately.'

'Is it true... what I've read about your relationship with Aravantinos?' she said thoughtfully as she stirred more sugar substitute into her coffee.

'If you remove all the spicy details, yes.'

'Are you in love with him?'

She asked me in such a simple manner that I replied just as naturally.

'Yes.'

I couldn't hide it from her; anyway, I didn't even want to.

'And what do you intend to do about it?'

She drank some of her coffee and pinned me with her deep green eyes. They emitted comforting warmth – I could look at them for hours and draw courage from her.

'I don't know. There's nothing I could do.'

'Don't you think he at least deserves to know?'

She looked meaningfully at my baby bump that had started to show.

'Perhaps I should,' I stuttered, 'I don't know...'

Pelia fell deep in thought for a while. She smoked and gazed absent-mindedly out the window that separated us from the outside world, and at the yard with the trellis attached to the building.

'So, I don't have any magic recipes to offer you, but I always believed there's a magical spring hidden somewhere for everyone. They need to find it by themselves, even if the road leading there is steep and harsh. Life isn't easy, Vera, for those who love in this world. You must have learned that by now.'

Were my ears deceiving me? Once again, I had the impression I was dreaming while still awake. Pelia was talking just like the witch in my book. And when the dream finds its way into reality, the situation becomes surreal.

'I already know that. I know many things now, but I'm not in the position to say if they are useful or not. I'm afraid that I've lost control over my life, that I'm wasting it. I don't take any decisions for myself, someone else moves the threads and guides me wherever he likes.'

'It's not so bad to devote your life to making your dreams come true, to use it and witness its slow but beautiful decay. And what about those people who jealously keep it locked in their wardrobe, carefully preserved in mothballs, what do you think they gain?'

Her voice came out in warm waves with a touch of hoarseness that gave it a unique sound. I felt that wayward 'something' that made strongholds within me slowly collapse.

'As if people have a powerful time-pesticide that combats the woodworm of misery. They act as if they are eternal and indestructible. They invest the joys they encounter so that they can redeem them with interest in their old age – these foolish people – when they'll only be able to eat soup. Instead of spending them on the spot and enjoying them. What can I say, chérie?' she concluded as she coquettishly picked up her stole and put on her coat. 'Follow your heart. It knows best. That's also how you grow into a person with a beautiful soul. To ripen without rotting.'

She bid me goodbye and walked away, majestic and care-free, until only the sound of her heels on the tiles resounded in my ears, as it faded in the distance. A song of eternal femininity, lust for life, sweetness of life, and the ripe fruit that you slowly savour, without a hint of sourness left behind on your tongue.

Chapter 17

Did We Have the Same Dream?

He dreamt of a moonlit night in July. Drops of honey – honey? – dripped from the branches of the acacia tree outside his window. The bright moon was rising in what truly was a very strange sky.

This dark cloth spread over the City of Light, which glimmered with thousands of stars, had a totally unexpected, festive appearance. It didn't look like the sky anymore, but rather like a cinema screen.

'I tawt I taw a puddy tat,' Tweety said his catch phrase and the party began. All the crazy cartoons he had ever seen rushed onto the sky-screen: Donald, Goofy, Mickey Mouse, Uncle Scrooge and Huey, Louie, Dewey; Bolek and Lolek; Asterix, Obelix, Getafix, the old Druid, and the other Gauls had set up a magnificent feast; suddenly, Witch Hazel, Georgie the Giant, a whistling Popeye, a broom-carrying Olive Oyl, and the eternally munching J. Wellington Wimpy burst onto the scene. All the characters started performing every crack-brained antic they came up with while Tweety,

Sylvester, Bugs Bunny and Porky Pig, sang *La Marseillaise* in each other's arms.

Constantinos was howling with laughter in his sleep; he had never laughed so much, nor had he ever felt that someone was gifting him with a piece of the heavens.

Afterwards, the cinema screen faded away, the cartoon characters trudged off to bed but the show wasn't over. Paper planes started falling like rain from the darkness of the celestial dome.

He didn't know how but he was sure that they had made a long journey before flying through the open window and landing on his sheets.

He got out of bed and went out in the street, as if he was spellbound, and followed the way the paper planes came from. He found himself going down Boulevard Saint-Michel towards the Luxembourg Gardens. He passed through the iron gates and took the path lined with chestnut trees.

He didn't even wonder why the Gardens were open at night, he just kept walking, and there, to his great joy, next to the Medici Fountain, where orange and yellow goldfish swim, he saw Vera.

She had just got off a paper plane and was fixing her hair that had been mussed by the wind. He looked at her reproachfully.

'Why are you doing such crazy things, Vera? Don't you know you aren't allowed to put yourself in danger when you're in a delicate condition?' he scolded her, very sweetly, though.

Immediately, he realised what he had blurted out and

almost made himself wake up. But, he stopped himself in time because he didn't want to miss how the dream would unfold.

'In your condition? Why did I just say that?' he stammered, looking at her belly.

'How did this happen, Vera?'

He could sense he was talking nonsense but he found nothing better to say.

She just kept gazing at him with a faint smile on her lips. *She must have copied this enigmatic smile from somewhere,* he thought. *Perhaps some experienced lady at the Louvre taught her.*

She passed him a few of the paper planes, asked him to unfold them and read them. They all said the same thing. That she loved him immensely, so much so that she was embarrassed to say it out loud – she could only write it down – and that her whole life was nothing but a dedication in a book written just for him.

He sat transfixed on the grass and felt more frightened and powerless than ever. Not even all those demons, ghosts and fairies that were after him in his films had managed to put him in such a state.

'Why did you do that, Vera?' he asked her, for a second time.

'I didn't get pregnant by myself, you know,' she said, a Mona Lisa smile still painted on her lips.

'I mean, why didn't you tell me? Why did I have to chase you in dream after dream before I found out that you were pregnant?'

'You aren't the one doing the chasing, Constantinos. I am. Because I have something very important to tell you.'

'Another important thing? I can't deal with this! I'm definitely going to wake up now!'

But she took him in her arms and made him forget everything. He slipped back into the dream, locked in her vanilla-scented embrace. She tried to find words worthy of the occasion, the words that would accurately describe what she felt for him, the man who had turned her flimsy life into something substantial, but she couldn't think of anything decent and so she stuck to the tried-and-true.

'I love you so much, Constantinos. Please don't abandon my dreams, they're worthless without you. I want to be close to you in any way possible, whenever you need me, for as long as you need me. I want to live for you, write for you and always have you as my hero. What do you think?'

'I think I deserve such an offering. I worked so hard to be worthy of you. I even took a bullet for your sake,' he said after a brief hesitation. 'But what are you going to do with a selfish bastard like me, have you thought about that? Are you sure that you can handle me?' And those were the most honest words he said that night.

'Of course! And I don't think you're a bastard. You're a magical creature, Constantinos. You had changed my life before I even met you. I love you,' she said once again, near tears.

'And I love you, baby.'

It was the first time he had confessed something like this; never before had he found the courage to tell her.

'You're the only one who can save me from dying a little inside every day. But, I fear that I'm accepting a very difficult task. And in addition to that, I have to look after you. Between you and me, sometimes, you act unbelievably foolishly.'

'Do you want to pick a fight with me right now?'

'No, I want us to meet once more in the other half of our lives. Because you might belong to me in dreams, but I need to be part of your waking life. So, I think that every time we come together something magical happens...'

'No need to get graphic!'

'Why not? Is there anything more beautiful than making and having children?'

They stayed there for a while, sitting on the velvet grass – the sensual sculpture of the nymph Galatea entwined with her shepherd lover playfully winked at them in the background – until darkness drew its curtains shut and sent the moon off to sleep. The hours had rolled by so quickly that the sun almost had a panic attack, because nobody had warned him that, due to exceptional circumstances, he would have to delay his rising for a short while.

'I'm afraid we have to wake up,' she said in a wistful voice. 'Dawn is breaking.'

'Do you mind if we stay here a while longer?'

He kept her in his arms and kept counting the kisses he placed on her neck and back. He still had a few dozen left until he reached 42.

'No, not at all,' she said between giggles. Suddenly, she

remembered the question that had been tormenting her from the very beginning.

'Constantinos, why 41 and a half kisses?'

'I don't know. Perhaps because that was my age when I met you.'

'And you came to me in my sleep to tell me how old you were?'

'No, I came to give you all of my years – my life, that is – so that you could turn them into a script. The script of our story.'

****

'Now, is this a happy ending?' the little orange fish in the nearby pond wondered.

'What is a happy ending?' the big canary-yellow fish fumed. 'This isn't an American movie, you know! Of all the crazy things that we saw in this film, is that the only question you have? Anyway,' it pensively purred, 'love rarely has a happy ending. If it brains you, it sends you diving in deep waters without any breathing equipment, and not all of the Labours of Hercules are enough to help rescue you. But, how can I explain this to you? You're too young to understand.'

'I do know!' the stubborn little orange fish insisted. 'Inspiration is the same thing. It turns up uninvited when you're ready to fall asleep and if you don't let it burst out of you like bubbles, you'll suffocate.'

And it went on swimming, proud of having said something so profound.

The fish do know a thing or two, if not everything – they also have no worries – even though some might say they're stupid. People are stupid. Probably.

'As for me, I don't like that ending,' the little fish pouted. 'I want something more realistic. They have been driving me crazy with their fantasies.'

He didn't have the time to finish his words because a great storm broke out in the garden. A vicious flash of lightning sliced the horizon in two and fat drops started falling from the clear sky.

'Oh, I think that the baby is coming,' Vera said, clutching at her belly.

'What?' His eyes almost bugged out of his head. 'Not here, wait ... not now! I can't deal with this.' He started running up and down the lawn in a panic-stricken daze.

'I can't wait, you know. It isn't up to me.'

She began taking deep breaths, already soaked in sweat. The pain was coming at regular intervals.

Then he realised that she was slipping away from his arms. Vera was becoming smaller and smaller, and was starting to fade in the horizon, just like those falling stars that disappear before you have time to make a wish.

'You didn't tell me, is it a boy or a girl?' was the only thing he managed to shout out.

'A boy,' he thought he heard her say as she vanished before his eyes.

Chapter 18

Nocturnal Worries

'Could you two quit traipsing all over these fantasies and finally return to the real world? I want to eat! I'm as hungry as a wolf!'

I could have sworn that those were the words spoken by His Majesty; it wasn't just my imagination. But when I opened my eyes, after the anaesthetic wore off, and found myself holding a bruised small creature crying like a puppy in my arms, I was mystified by my baby's ability to 'talk' to me. For a moment, he seemed to me like an alien. I have the urge to scream and return it to the nurse, who is looking at me with a doting smile.

'Congratulations,' she told me and started giving me advice on breastfeeding and changing nappies.

He has quite a personality. I looked at him with a sleepy smile. But of course... who else would he look like? The tiny miracle, which Constantinos and I had helped create, seemed to be smiling back at me, but I was wrong.

'How are you feeling, honey?' Vicky bent over me after

the nurse took the baby – with his belly full, and calm – back to the baby ward.

'Like I've been struck by a street sweeper.'

I sat up and rested against the pillows with great effort.

'Come on, you're being extreme.' She was rather amused by my melodramatic tone. 'As if you were the first woman on Earth ever to have gone through labour.'

'I may not be the first, but it's definitely the last time I'm doing this. Too much hassle, it was almost the death of me.'

She brought the water cup that was resting next to me close to my lips so that I could have a sip. An IV drip was still connected to my right arm and I couldn't move it at all. My whole body hurt.

Only a while later, after the first anxious days passed, would I have the chance to come to terms with what had happened to me in all its glory. As if a happiness capsule had popped open inside me and flooded me with incredible sweetness. Each and every one of my cells was swimming in this newfound sense. That's how happiness is: strange and unfamiliar, it takes time and courage to endure, even more than misery, which is, after all, a situation more familiar to most people.

'As if millions of other women have never said that before.'

I get ticked off when my words aren't taken seriously, and Vicky has the annoying habit of doing just that, but I didn't say anything. I looked around me. The room was full of flowers and potted plants. The bright July sunlight streamed through the window, but thankfully, the air conditioning was working at full speed.

I begged her to take all the flowers away. If my allergy flared up, then I would start sneezing nonstop.

Vicky grabbed two or three pots and made her way to the door, but there I saw her suddenly stop in her tracks.

'Hi,' she just said, 'welcome,' and hurriedly disappeared out the door.

'What are you doing here?' I said, also quite stunned.

'I came to see my son! If you allow me to, of course.'

His biting sarcasm was a slap in the face. He looked quite stern as he stood at the opening of the door, with his hands in the pockets of his baggy trousers.

'Who told you?' I dared ask him, and then I cowered against the pillows, dreading the storm that would follow.

The look in his eyes told me quite clearly that he was in no joking mood.

'You did! Fortunately, you're quite chatty in your dreams.'

I continued looking at him as if I had seen a ghost, biting my lips and waiting for the worst. He sat at the edge of the hospital bed and began to fiddle with the edge of his shirt, keeping his mouth stubbornly shut.

For a few minutes, I was even afraid to take a breath from the agony I felt. My mouth had gotten dry, but it didn't register, just like everything else I had been through in the last few hours; I even forgot about the burning pain that pierced various parts of my body, and my hand that was immobile and bruised.

I was so happy to see him; all I wanted was to touch him. Even if it was with the tips of my fingers, to make sure that he was real and not part of a dream. No matter what he said, or what he did, I was ready to burst out in tears from happiness.

'Seriously, are you completely insane?' he erupted in anger. 'This life-changing event happened and I get no word from you? What bullshit is this, Vera? Didn't I have the right to know, dammit? What am I to you, anyway? You did what you wanted, you used me to get pregnant, and then you got rid of me just like that? How could you ever think that I would go along with this? You really need some sense knocked into you, and if you weren't in this condition, I would have gladly done it myself.'

I could stand it no longer, I was seconds away from bursting into giggles, and then he would be furiously mad. How times have changed! Men are now complaining that we use them as mere objects. Instead of laughing, I decided that it was imperative I act with a tried and true female technique: I burst into tears.

'Please, don't shout. You can't imagine what I've been through. I didn't want to cause you any trouble, Constantinos, that's all. I didn't want to use the baby against you, why can't you understand?'

'Baby, you're damn selfish, do you know that? And then you say I'm self-centred!' His voice had softened a little and he just stood there looking at me with a touch of compassion in his eyes.

My mother turned up just as I was describing to him, with an enormous smile on my face, how wonderful our baby was, though a bit wrinkled – but that's how all babies are, at first, since we come in this world a bit squashed – and how much I would like it if our son got his father's nose.

'I think, Constantinos, that you have the most beautiful nose I have ever seen.'

I was struggling not to laugh or to cry because the effects of the anaesthetic had worn off and even the tiniest move caused me pain.

'I'm finally meeting you, Mr Aravantinos,' Theophano said icily as the besotted grandmotherly look in her eyes, and her smile, were wiped off her face the moment she saw Constantinos.

'Contrary to what is customarily said in such circumstances, my daughter hasn't told me a word about you. And I rarely, if ever, go to the cinema. So, I only know you by name.'

She smoothed her hair with an old-fashioned – and strangely touching – coquettish gesture, and gracefully extended her hand. He hurried to get up, and kissed her hand with exaggerated flourish, but it had a direct impact on her attitude towards him.

'Of course, now that I can take a look at you, I have no doubt what Vera saw in you, and fell in love. We might rarely talk to each other, but she is my child, I understand how she feels.'

She sat in a chair and crossed her ankles before straightening the pleats of her skirt with great care. My mother never crossed her legs; she considered it to be an indecent posture. She sat still for a while, looking at the floor without speaking. But, soon, she returned to her good old self and started scolding us, as if she had two naughty students standing in front of her.

'I should, however, point out that both of you behaved in quite an unacceptable manner.'

She started fanning herself. Her nerves were flaring up again.

'Mum!' I made a timid attempt to restrain her.

'This is not the way I raised my children, sir! I gave them a Christian upbringing. I never expected such shameless shenanigans from them. You are married and, in addition to that, you also live in a foreign country. What type of connection would you be able to keep with my daughter? Why are you taking such serious matters so lightly? I know my daughter, she was always gullible and too trusting, and men always managed to trick her. And behold the results. She became a single mother! Who would have thought that my own child would end up this way? Dear Heavens, what a shame! What a disgrace!'

'Muuum!' I hissed once again, and I tried to give my voice some harshness, but to no avail. I just silently wished that she wouldn't begin expressing her various disapproving views on the character and morals of these 'mummers', as she contemptuously called actors.

'You should tell us about your intentions, Mr Aravantinos! In my days, that is how a true gentleman would act,' she concluded with as much restraint she had left.

'Mum! We no longer live in the past, you have to realise that at some point!'

'Be silent!' she told me scornfully. 'A woman who doesn't

have a man by her side will always be alone. And that doesn't change in any era.'

I wish I could scream at them to leave me alone. I would be able to take care of myself and my baby just fine. But, such strenuous activities were forbidden in my condition so I limited myself to a grimace of dissatisfaction.

'Let your mother be, Vera. We have to admit she's right!'

A faint smile of vindication formed on my mother's lips.

That cheeky bastard! In the end, he might even bring my mother round, I thought to myself, smiling.

'Anyway,' he stood up, putting an end to my mother's scolding, 'I'm sorry that I didn't have the time to bring you any gifts, Vera, but do not think that I completely forgot about it. I'm not that rude. I just need some time to edit a script that I have in mind.'

My mother hastily bid us goodbye. She gathered up her bag, fan and scarf before she discreetly took her leave, which was quite unlike her. She left behind her a light aroma of lemon-scented perfume; was that *4711* that she had been using since time immemorial?

'What kind of script?'

'I want to be by your side,' he said earnestly. 'I want you to live for me, to write only for me, and I will be your only hero. What do you say?'

He looked certain that he had said something very original.

I wanted to start squealing and clapping, I wasn't a new mother anymore, I was a ten-year-old girl, watching the tightrope walker complete his act without falling to his death, feeling ecstatic.

But, when I opened my mouth, my maternal side stepped in.

'It sounds good. It only needs some revising. It is one thing to have a passionate love affair, and totally another to deal with the reality of raising a child. I don't mean to frighten you, but this is the most difficult and challenging script we'll find ourselves working on.'

'I can imagine. Besides, I'm used to having a hard time with the scripts you write.'

****

During the three days I stayed at the clinic, he came and sat beside me, he kept me company and he talked about co-workers I had never heard of before, and about other matters, some more important than others. Although I was burning to ask him what he intended to do with Virginie and if he had talked to her, he didn't utter a word about this matter.

He brought me flowers, ice cream and clothes, and loads of baby accessories, useless and expensive. He also gave me a Byzantine-style necklace: a carved pendant made of pure silver with a precious stone as red as blood.

'Thank you for not asking that despicable question,' I told him one day, teasingly, 'if the baby is yours.'

'Of course he's mine!' He looked at the baby boy and scowled. 'He's the spitting image of me. Either way, I could never believe that there could be another man in your life after me...' It was an interesting point he made. '... At least not so soon,' he added, just in case.

I never felt more in love with him than the moment I saw him holding our baby so clumsily, as if our son was a toy that his father feared he would break.

It's really wonderful to observe the twists and turns life can take. No matter how much of your innocence you lose along the way, life returns it wrapped in a blue baby vest.

'You know what I think?' he said after a while. 'That if we had met in a past life, we would have definitely been kindred spirits. You know... those who say they can communicate with the power of thought and read each other's minds from a distance.'

I looked at him as he chattered light-heartedly, taking such serious matters so lightly, and I didn't argue with him. I thought it would be pointless to explain that if we had met in a past life, and if all these phenomena contain even a grain of truth, then I would definitely have been his mistress. I fervently wished to play the same part in my present life too. To be his mistress. I considered it to be the most important thing in the world. I wanted to have children with him, many children, as many as I could handle. *You must have many children*, I wanted to tell him, *who are as handsome as you. There is so much need for beauty in our world.*

'For how can you explain the fact that you understand what I want to say before I have even said it?' he continued his monologue. 'How can anyone explain that the words you make me say are exactly what I would have made myself say?'

'What actually happened back then, Constantinos? When I had those dreams. What happened?'

'I have no idea,' he replied, puzzled. 'Are you still wondering about that?'

'You called out to me.'

'No, *you* did. I hadn't even met you yet.'

'Alright, *I* did. Don't you agree, though, that the whole thing needs an explanation?'

'No! I don't need to know anything else; I've already told you. It just happened, and it was lovely. Why should we dwell on it now?'

'Because I think that...'

'I don't want to re-open this discussion. The more we discuss it and rationalise it, the more magic is lost, and that's something I hate.'

When I was discharged from hospital, he left immediately for Paris, and, for a while, I lost his tracks. Then, he began calling again, and quite often, stressfully confiding in me about the various bureaucratic procedures that were acting as roadblocks in the divorce case.

Four months later, the divorce was almost finalised. When I wasn't taking care of my baby, I was working on my second book. Constantinos was getting ready to leave in a few days for the shooting of his new film in Malta.

We had moved into a beautiful house with huge balconies, a garden and a pool in Agia Paraskevi. Neither too far from nor too close to downtown. We wanted to be close to all the happenings of the city, and the airport, as he would have to make frequent trips.

Everything seemed to be settling down and peace was slowly returning to our lives. Peace? Only if one excludes a few – not wholly unexpected – nocturnal worries that had just begun.

****

'Shit! This has turned into a nightmare.'

He fell back on the bed sheets and let out an angry sigh. It was the tenth consecutive night that the same thing had taken place.

I jumped out of bed all flustered, hastily put on my dressing gown, and ran to calm the baby down. Naturally, I always left Constantinos in the lurch. My son would claim my hugs for half an hour and then all I wanted would be to get some sleep.

We could never have imagined that a tiny little human would be such a handful. At first, we tried to outsmart him by changing the time of when we made love. But, he didn't let such tricks hold him back. It was as if he could sense when daddy planned to do naughty things with mummy, and he would immediately demand my attention in the most deafening manner. I was afraid that he was a baby with developed intuition. Of course, how hadn't I thought of it before? He got that from his parents.

As I sang my baby son back to sleep, I kept thinking that, ever since I met Constantinos, and probably even before that, ever since he came to me in dreams and thrilled me with his stories, I could hardly sleep, each time for different reasons.

But, strangely enough, none of these reasons was unpleasant. In fact, Constantinos had awakened me for good.

I went out on the balcony with the baby – my little one was gurgling contentedly – cuddled against me. I saw him standing in the dark, smoking a cigarette.

It was a mild October night. The full moon was sailing in the sky, the city was turning its lights off, enjoying the truce that the night had declared between two days full of stress and fatigue.

A few shadows were still wandering under the street lights; perhaps they were a few night owls, or couples. Our leafy road was very quiet. I couldn't help but wonder at how much my life had changed within a year.

He told me the same quite often. How differently he regarded himself and the world nowadays. He had no doubts that he was different, so unlike ordinary people. He was just what he was, and he found it wonderful. That strange, dark sadness – a vicious circle with no purpose – plagued him no more. He had the fantastic feeling that he was the link of a chain that remained unbroken through an endless renewal. He felt that he had found a tangible and feasible purpose. There were times when he dared to say that he was almost happy.

A small seed had planted itself in our lives, and it kept growing, until it reached incredible heights. It was if we were witnessing a new life, full of undiscovered opportunities, a second chance to see the wonders of the world from a new, crystal-clear perspective: through the eyes of a child.

He nudged the door slightly open and stood at the threshold of the baby's room, watching us with a grim look in his eyes. I was patting my son's back – while yawning – to lull him back to sleep. *He's going to start again*, I thought.

During such moments, the annoying bug of insecurity stirred within Constantinos and pestered his mind. He was afraid that he had lost his greatness, that the time of his monarchical reign had definitely come to an end.

He saw himself being exiled slowly but surely to the role of a mere bystander in the family home. He would sit idly in an armchair and resent my excessive – as he called it – devotion to the baby. He would tell me, with a touch of sarcasm, that our son's whimpers sounded like a divine melody to my ears, that his fussiness showed how much he needed my cuddles and that, during breastfeeding, I had an angelic smile on my face. He was right; I was madly in love with my son.

'His skin is velvety soft,' I would say adoringly and spent hours with my nose buried in his rosy neck. I was addicted to his infant scent. I felt deprived when I had to stay away from my son for a few hours.

Then, he never failed to remind me that, once upon a time, it was his arms that felt like velvet or silk when he wrapped them around me, and, at night, I would sleep with my nose buried in his neck, so that I could breathe in his scent.

'I don't believe you're jealous of your own child,' I joked about it.

'Only a completely irrational and immature man would

feel this way, and you know that's not who I am,' he would tell me to "reassure" me.

After a while, though, he would start grumbling again – it was cute, I won't deny it, but I did find it a tad exhausting. He complained that he couldn't see it in my face anymore when we made love – whenever Baby, His Majesty, gave us permission to be together – that look of abandonment and worship I used to have. My senses were constantly on alert in case I heard our son crying. Not to mention my new book, in which – once again – I had used him as inspiration for the protagonist. I hadn't worked on it for weeks.

'This is a horrible situation,' he claimed, and that it couldn't go on any longer, something had to be done right away ... and I would laugh at the tragicomic tone of his protests.

And what took the cake was when, one day, he cut out an article from a popular science magazine, had it framed, and gave it to me as a present.

'Feelings of love' the article said, 'lead to a suppression of activity in the parts of the brain controlling critical thought. A research study conducted by British scientists showed that romantic love and maternal love have the same effects on brain function. They repress the activity of the nerves associated with critical evaluation of other individuals and reduce negative emotions. Both couples and young mothers who participated in the study showed decreased activity in the areas of the brain responsible for critical thinking.'

At other times, though, he would silently approach the baby's crib and lightly caress one of his chubby cheeks.

Feelings of enormous gratitude would fill him that a tiny human allowed his father to touch him, kiss him and help him discover that softness and innocence are sometimes contagious. This way, his negative thoughts left him in peace for a while.

But, no matter how you look at it, he was used to playing the lead; he was unaccustomed to being limited to supporting roles. I didn't know when the time would come – but it would be very soon now – when he would put his foot down and demand his rights once again.

After a while, when I returned to the bedroom, walking on tiptoes, I found him half-asleep, muttering something unintelligible. I bent over him.

'I want a double burger,' I heard him whisper.

'What are you talking about?' I laughed as I caressed him. 'Where do you think you are?'

I shouldn't have woken him up because he was in the mood for a chat while I could barely keep my eyes open.

'I mean that I want a double helping,' he clarified.

'Of what?'

'Of love. Will you give it to me?'

'Of course I will! Now, go back to sleep.'

'Vera,' he said after a while, 'tell me something. Am I your baby?'

'No, Constantinos, you're too old to be my baby. Will you ever stop acting like a child?'

'Be honest with me, do you think that I'm being childish?'

He leaned on his elbow and gave me a searching look.

'No darling, you're the most adorable man I've ever met.'

'And what else?'

There was only one way to put his mind at ease, so that we could finally get some sleep. I took him in my arms and made him rest his head on my chest.

'You're my bright star. When I'm with you, I could tread even on the darkest paths.'

'And what else?'

'Go to sleep, my love, please. I'm beat!'

THE END

Zurich, 2004

ENDNOTES

1. From Homer's *Odyssey*

2. Seferis, G.: Collected poems: 1924-1955, *Reflections On a Foreign Line of* Verse, Princeton University Press, 1981

3. Kundera, M. *The Art of the Novel*, Harper Perennial Modern Classics, *2003*

4. Kundera, M. *The Art of the Novel*, Harper Perennial Modern Classics, 2003

5. Besant. A: *Thought Power*. 1st ed. Chennai, India: The Theosophical Publishing Society, 1901

6. Shakespeare, *Much Ado About Nothing*, Act IV, Scene I

7. Shakespeare, *Much Ado About Nothing*, Act IV, Scene I

8. The lyrics of a song from Federico Garcia Lorca set to the music of the composer Christos Leontis.

9. Hesse, H. *Demian: The Story of Emil Sinclair's Youth*, BN Publishing, 2009

10. Seferis, G.: Collected poems: 1924-1955, *The Last Station*, Princeton University Press, 1981

ABOUT THE AUTHOR

Hara Nikola (Nikolakopoulou) lives in Greece. She studied Greek Literature in the University of Athens and holds an MA in Creative Writing from the University of Western Macedonia.

Between the years 1992 and 1999, she worked as a copywriter for multinational advertising agencies.

She presently lives in Kalamata, where she founded her own school of creative writing in 2013.

Her short stories and fairy tales have won awards in national competitions and have been published in literary magazines and anthologies.

This is her first novel.

Her other published works include:

- I Dimiourgiki Graphi sto Gymnasio [Creative Writing in Secondary Education], (Athens: Ekdoseis Sideri, 2014)

- Mellisses Iereies, Dio Nouvelles [The Bee Priestesses: Two Novellas] (Athens: Ekdoseis Gavrielidis, 2015)

Contact: nikolako333@gmail.com

www.ingramcontent.com/pod-product-compliance
Lightning Source LLC
Chambersburg PA
CBHW030537260626
47157CB00006B/2077